For my good friend Katherine Hale

All the best!

Carla Salvo

Just Say the Word...

Carla Salvo

Just Say the Word...

Just Say the Word / Carla Salvo
ISBN: 978-0-615-34105-7

Piccolina Publishing
4320 - 196th St. SW, Suite B519
Lynnwood, WA 98036

www.piccolinapublishing.com
www.carlasalvo.com

Book design by Jessica W. Chandler

Printed in the United States of America

3 5 7 9 10 8 6 4 2

Library of Congress cataloging-in-publication data to come:
Salvo, Carla

$\mathcal{A}$ special thank you to all my friends who lended encouragement and support throughout the process of writing this book. Thank you to my talented and thorough designer, Jesse Wray, to my driven and beautiful daughter, to the sweetest Mom on the planet, to Bill, and most especially to my personal cheerleader Adrian, who would not allow me to utter the words Can't or Fail!

A portion of the proceeds from the sale of this book benefits one of Carla Salvo's favorite causes, People Helping Horses. If you would like more information on making a direct donation, please contact PHH at info@peoplehorses.org

For my beloved grandmother,
Pitrina.

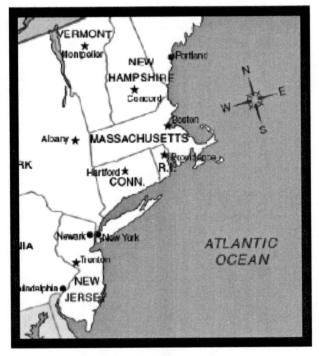

Chapter 1

*I*t was a dark and stormy night!" Franco muttered under his breath as he scaled the low steps of the downtown Seattle Police Department building. He tugged hard at the collar of his raincoat to position it up snug against his long neck, attempting to keep the biting November rain away. It was late, well after eleven p.m., and he was a little pissed off at being roused from his warm bed. His lovely newlywed wife Carolyn had awakened him by pushing his shoulders hard: "Wake up, Franco! Wake up!" *It couldn't be morning*, he grumbled to himself. Within a couple of minutes, he realized it clearly wasn't. *What the…?* Franco hissed to himself.

Franco was tall and fair, his blond hair fell in near ringlets around his ears. His ethnic background distinctively Arian, his eyes were stark blue. A powerful gust of wind and

rain stung like pellets against his lean frame as he reached
for the front door of the glass-enclosed lobby of the Seattle
Police Department. His mouth felt dry and he swallowed hard,
feeling his Adam's apple move in the process.

"Rita needs us; she's in some kind of trouble. Come
on, come on, hurry up, Franco!" Carolyn had said while
spinning her robe around her shoulders, and disappeared into
the bathroom. Within ten minutes they were in their car,
Carolyn at the wheel. Once more conscious, Franco asked:
"What kinda trouble could Rita get into? She's so nice."

"Damned if I know," Carolyn responded abruptly. "It
was noisy in the background, but she said it was serious and
she needed an attorney. She would never call this late if it
wasn't important."

Carolyn pulled up to the curb in front of the building
on Fourth Avenue; Franco exited, while his wife drove off
to park the car. Franco strode through the lobby toward
the main reception desk. He knew this building well, but it
looked so different to him late at night. He smiled to himself
thinking that he must be dreaming or watching a very old
Film Noire movie. There were a few scattered individuals
sitting in comfy-looking lobby chairs. Others were standing
on the perimeters of the immense foyer, speaking in hushed
tones. Everything looked grey to him but it could also look
like that on any rainy Seattle day or night. *What could be
so wrong? Had there been an accident?* As he approached
the desk sergeant on duty, Franco groped for a serious reason
why he was not in his bed on this ugly evening. "I'm Franco
Janszyck," handing the officer his business card. "We're
looking for Rita Napapolus."

The officer looked over his reading glasses and asked,

"Who's that?"

"Rita Napapolus, a family friend. She called my wife and said she needed an attorney." *This cop is beyond retirement age*, Franco thought to himself.

The desk sergeant then grumbled, "What's she here for?"

"Not sure. We got a call about thirty minutes ago. Just said she was here and needed an attorney." Sergeant Mahoney picked up his phone and punched in some numbers. "Yeah, some kid lawyer to see a Ms. Napapolus lady. Where's she at? Huh? You're kidding!"

Looking a little confused, the officer turned back in his chair toward Franco, whose trench coat was now dripping small puddles at his feet. "What?" Franco asked. "What is it? Is she okay?" At that moment, Carolyn came through the huge glass doors behind him and Franco turned to see her shaking her arms and umbrella. A smile crept across his lips as he thought how darling and beautiful Carolyn looked, even drenched by the cold rain. Carolyn was born on Guam and she boasted perfect skin and teeth, thick black chin-length hair and dark twinkling eyes. Rita and Carolyn met almost ten years earlier when Carolyn had been a student temp at the stockbrokerage firm where Rita worked.

Franco watched for a moment as she shook her shoulders and then her legs, bemused that she did so like Molly, their Chihuahua, who he was sure was peacefully sleeping on their bed. He turned his attention back to the sergeant to see that the man had one eyebrow cocked, his eyes peering over precariously perched eyeglasses, his finger tips together, stretched wide.

"Your Ms. Napapolus has been visiting with our

homicide detectives this evening, young man."

"Homicide? Did she witness a homicide?" Breathless, Carolyn had now wiggled into position in front of Franco, facing the weary cop.

"Don't know. You'll need to talk to Detective Parker. He's on his way down right now. Both of you type your names into the computer log, please."

Carolyn and Franco exchanged worried glances, but without speaking, both were nonetheless sure that Rita had perhaps been near the scene of a murder, or saw a vehicle that may have been involved, something along those lines. But why the phone call to them? Why was she there so late at night? They hurriedly keyed their names into the computer log. To the right of the desk, an elevator "dinged," and Carolyn and Franco instinctively pivoted on their heels to see a man possibly in his early thirties, alight into the expansive room. His boyishly handsome face and dark features shown through his fatigue, yet he smiled a warm and genuine smile: "Hello, I'm Brent Parker. Carolyn and Franco Janszyck?

"Well, I'm Franco Janszyck and this is my wife Carolyn Echon," offered Franco.

Carolyn and Franco simultaneously bombarded Detective Parker with the whos, whats and whys of Rita's presence there at such an ungodly hour. Brent Parker peacefully raised his hand and said, "Come on. I'll take you upstairs so you can talk to her yourself. You're her attorney, right? She opted not to answer some questions and said she wanted her attorney. She's fine, really. She hasn't been charged with anything, *yet*. She is, however, a prime suspect." Aghast, the couples' jaws dropped simultaneously as they hypnotically followed the detective into the elevator.

The Downtown Precinct building was just a few years old. It was modern and pristine, even in the questioning and holding cell areas. "This is a nightmare; it's some kind of mistake, Franco. Rita wouldn't hurt a fly," labored Carolyn as they stepped off of the elevator and proceeded down a long corridor. She was near tears as they followed Detective Parker through a gated entry and down another hall to an open alcove. There were no other people, other than an officer that either of them could see in the subdued lighting. The female officer sat near the doorway of the room, lightly thumbing through a magazine. She stood as the trio approached and asked Carolyn and Franco to step through a metal detector. Detective Parker stopped short and turned -- Franco thought for a moment that he was going to click his heels together, but could see that the young officer was just as weary as he and Carolyn were.

Extending his open palm, the young detective glibly said, "We call this our guest quarters. It has a pleasant area for informal talks and questioning. There are only two cells and a sitting area, and they're just a short walk from the Homicide Division. We question the lowest risks here. This guest is considered a mixed bag, however. Your Ms. Napapolus has no priors to speak of. One speeding ticket, one for technically running a red light. No complaints ever filed against her. Good work record. Nice little house. Raised her kid by herself. Everything but one thing…"

"What *thing*?" asked Carolyn.

"It's a pretty important thing," the young detective said, "but we'll get to that in a minute." They turned toward the area where Rita was waiting in a wide alcove, between a pair of cells that faced each other. The alcove looked like a small waiting area, but was devoid of any tables or lamps. A ceiling can light glowed softly.

She looks smaller than usual, thought Franco, as his eyes rested on the small dark-haired lady, *like a little bird in a cage*. Rita was snoozing peacefully, embraced by an oversized chair, shoes off, her legs bent and folded. Her medium-length hair, usually perfectly coifed, was fan-spread on the back of the chair. Her cheeks looked rosy, even though the skin tone was olive. She was not a classic beauty, but pretty, nonetheless. Rita looked like she was taking a little catnap, and her eyelids fluttered when the three approached. She jumped, suddenly alert, opening her eyes to reveal the Oreo Cookie eyes that the young couple knew so well.

"Hi, kids! Ooooh, you two are *the best*. I'm so sorry but I had no one else to call. Don't know any other attorneys, you know!" She sounded almost chipper.

Shaken, Carolyn ran to Rita, and sat on the arm of her chair. An exhausted looking Rita reassured Carolyn with a smile. "It's okay, Honey. It's a mistake. The police will figure it out. I'm fine." Rita looked so tired, Carolyn thought. Rita was in her late forties, but petite and fit and looked like late thirties instead. "My Greek genes," she would tell Carolyn and Franco. There she sat, looking like a little girl, a very tired little girl. "So, she hasn't been charged?" asked Franco.

"No, sir," the detective responded wearily.

Rita heaved a huge sigh from her small body. "Silly, isn't it?" she chirped, with a slight tone of disgust thrown in for good measure. "Unbelievable that they might think I would dirty my hands for the likes of Brandon Perry." *Piss and vinegar*, Franco thought, amused. *So like Rita, even late at night*. "This is bullshit," continued Rita, gesturing her hands upward. "I was pretty sure they were going to arrest me, so

I called you. The *other* detective," Rita snapped her fingers a couple of times, "Detective Chadwick? He was pretty rude and insisted I was lying, so I was bracing myself for an arrest. They don't stop until they get their confession. You know, like on TV."

Brent Parker intervened, "That would be the lead detective on this case, Bob Chandler."

"Yes! That's the guy. Chandler. Quite pushy, just like in the movies," Rita scoffed sarcastically.

Franco turned to the young detective, who stood looking dejectedly downward at the floor, hands thrust into his pockets. "Can we step outside to talk?" asked Franco. He turned to his wife and asked, "Honey, will you stay with Rita while I talk to Detective Parker?"

"Of course, Franco."

"Is that alright, Detective?"

"Sure, we can talk in my office," replied the detective. After leaving the guest quarters, Franco and Brent navigated through a fairly noisy and busy office suite alive with bodies on the phone, staring at computers, and typing on keyboards. Phones rang at ten different desks at once. It seemed more like a pressroom rather than a homicide unit to Franco. They entered a small office with a view to the west that was blissfully quiet when Brent Parker closed the door behind them. From the window and through the rain, Franco could see the Bremerton ferry moving through the darkness like a brightly lit aircraft hovering in space.

"Have a seat there, Mr. Janszyck," Detective Parker offered with a slight of hand. He plopped into a comfy-looking black leather chair. Behind him were what Franco thought to be the predictable photographs that a young detective might have in his office: Brent, a smiling, sparkling groom with a gorgeous dark-haired bride; a photo of a dog; one of a handsome-looking woman who Franco guessed must be Brent's mother. Franco realized it could be his own cramped office.

"Hope you don't mind my saying so," said Franco, "but you have a lovely wife. Carolyn and I are newlyweds, too."

Brent Parker's eyes shifted uncomfortably. He looked uneasy before quietly responding, "Julie was killed by a drunk driver just a few months after we married. She was crossing a city street on her lunch break." He smiled. "She was a delight."

Franco felt himself shrink inward. *Idiot! See where small talk gets ya?* "So sorry for your loss, Detective."

"Almost three years already," murmured the young detective, shrugging his shoulders while avoiding Franco's gaze. A deafening silence followed, but Franco drew a long breath and finally spoke.

"With all due respect, what is going on here, Detective?" asked Franco.

"I'm not the lead investigator in this case, but was present when she was questioned. We *asked* your friend to come in to speak with us in regard to the murder of Brandon Perry, sir. We called her at work and invited her here, so to speak. She agreed and said she wanted to have dinner first. She showed as promised, at the time she said she would. Ms. Napapolus was very cooperative up to a point. Once we started asking about her past, she stonewalled us. Technically she could have walked out, she's not under arrest. She insists she was at home at the time that Mr. Perry was killed. As you may have read in the papers, this man was shot with his own .45mm at fairly close range. Theoretically speaking, it could have been a hired hit. She may not have been at the scene, but her prints were everywhere in the victim's house. This leads us to believe that she definitely knew where the victim had a handgun and either confronted him at his place or paid someone else to do it. The holster was slung on the right-hand bedpost. Perry was a lefty."

"Her prints at the scene mean nothing," said Franco. "She dated the guy for a while. I saw the news report on TV. This is ludicrous and a tad dramatic, don't you think, Detective?" challenged Franco. "Rita is outspoken, but she wouldn't... she *couldn't* kill anyone!" Franco felt a little nauseous, thoughts careening through his head. He and Carolyn *knew* Rita. She couldn't do something like this. Murder: NEVER! Guilty of a tart tongue sometimes, but not murder. "I'm here to help her as a friend. She is not my client *yet*. She hasn't been charged." After what seemed like five minutes, Franco asked: "Now what, Detective?"

"Well, she called you because she thought she'd be arrested and charged. Sorry to say, but like she expected it. I've seen killer grandmas, so nothing surprises me. I'm not here to judge. Maybe you can figure it out. There are a couple more things you should know, Mr. Janszyck. I can share a certain amount of our findings about Rita, but not everything. I'm referring to information she did not volunteer; it's stuff we discovered while we were investigating her background and her relationship to the murder victim."

"You can call me Franco if I may call you Brent."

"Okay then, Franco. Thanks. Anyway, the FBI and local police had been investigating Brandon Perry for over a year. Apparently, he was a very charming con-man who juggled multiple scams. His specialty was ripping off women and the elderly: those most likely to run away with their tails between their legs. Some reported the rip-offs, but most wouldn't press charges."

"Why didn't they press charges?"

"For a couple of reasons. Mr. Perry brought many to the depths of bankruptcy. They could not pursue the matters legally with no money. Perry was also adept at covering his tracks and not leaving a paper trail. Most were cash transactions, but he wasn't shy about weaseling his way into people's lives and actually stealing valuables, often right under their noses."

"So, how does this tie my friend into the picture? I'm not following you here, Brent."

"It's like this: because Rita Napapolus dated the scumbag, even for a short time, the feds looked into her activities as well, to see if she was involved in Perry's illegal activities."

"That's absurd! Rita would never rip anyone off!" protested Franco.

Brent Parker raised his palm. "Okay, okay. Your friend probably didn't steal from anyone as far as the police or FBI can tell, but it appears that she may have been one of Mr. Perry's victims."

Franco touched his fingertips to his temples like it was too much to take in. That could be considered motive for murder, if indeed what Brent was saying proved to be true.

"The FBI discovered some of Rita's mail at Perry's place. We suspect he may have lifted some from her home during the course of a 'sleep-over,' and discovered some of those wonderful quick-cash checks enclosed. We don't think she brought the mail there because Perry's prints were all over the contents of the mail, but *not* Rita's. He ran amuck for the next several days writing checks to himself, but not to Brandon Perry."

"Say what?" Franco pondered Brent's last remark for a moment before asking: "Are you saying this Perry person had other associates in these scams?"

"No, Sir. He had several identities instead. That's another reason the victims didn't press charges: the aliases were all dead ends. No one knows for sure what his real name was. Perry is no doubt just one of many names. When we ran the aliases through the databases, we couldn't come up with any photos to identify. He must have authored new names for each new scam. All but one name: he primarily used Brandon Perry in the Seattle area. That name was tied to his employment history and he rented a house in Covington using it. Checks from two of Rita's credit card accounts were written to several different males to the tune of over fifty grand in a relatively short period of time, roughly two or three days. American Express contacted Rita to alert her and to ask if she authorized these transactions. She may have been at a loss if she hadn't recognized the names of any of his aliases. She said she hadn't looked at her statement because she didn't owe balances on those two cards. She had no clue this happened until American Express called her. Federal agents know it was Perry *now*, but didn't at the time it was happening, as they were just beginning to look into Rita's background."

"So that would put motive to rest, Brent. If Rita didn't recognize any of the check recipients, she probably didn't connect the theft to Perry. And, she wasn't liable for the full amount of the checks, either."

"But she may have suspected it was Perry," Brent surmised, crossing his arms and leaning against the wall of his tiny office. "And sorry to drop another bomb on you, but there's more to this."

"Huh, more?" asked Franco. "How could there be more?"

"No easy way to say this, but your Ms. Napapolus' history stops short about twenty years ago. Before that, it appears she didn't exist. Rita Napapolus appeared about nineteen some-odd years ago when she arrived in Seattle with her toddler, Hannah. So far, the feds have hit a dead end. They didn't find any birth records or missing person's reports to match either your friend or her daughter. I think it's fair to say that, as her attorney, you might prepare yourself for her eventual arrest. Unless, of course, we come up with other suspects. Unfortunately, we found little to connect anyone else to this murder," Brent explained, shrugging his shoulders. "Mr. Perry kept a small arsenal of handguns in his home. Ms. Napapolus' prints were on several of them. To work at the brokerage firm, she was required to be fingerprinted, so they are on file. Rita explained to me that Perry liked to show them off and insisted that she hold some of them to feel the weight in her hands. She said she was humoring him."

"She's innocent until proven guilty."

"I'm not passing judgment, Franco. Yes, she's presumed innocent at this point."

Franco's steps were hard and deliberate as he walked back to the holding area. The fluorescent lights blurred as he floated through the busy office, around the corner and down the hall. Carolyn and Rita stood waiting beyond the gated entrance, Carolyn's arm around Rita's shoulder. Their roles looked reversed to Franco. Carolyn was a Mom, Rita a child.

"Can you give me a lift home?" Rita asked demurely.

"I think you need to call in sick tomorrow, Rita," snapped Franco. "You're coming home with us."

"No way! I have two feline daughters waiting for me. I can get a cab. I'm quite exhausted. Aren't you?" Rita daintily side-stepped Franco. She was now standing next to Brent Parker. Turning to the young detective she cooed, "Young man, would you kindly direct me to my personal effects and check me out of this hotel? I'm going home."

Franco was astounded at how calm Rita seemed. Working to keep his voice down, Franco bent close to Rita's ear and hissed, "Wait! Wait one minute! What the hell is going on here, Rita? Want to fill us in on what's going on?"

Rita drew her lips inward in a moment of total frustration. Snarling like a dog through her teeth, Rita was careful not to raise her voice. "I don't have a clue, Darlin'. Really don't want to stand here for a brainstorming session, either; I just want to fucking go home. When I figure it out, I'll let ya know. Make a deal with you, though. You drive me home, and even though I haven't called in sick for three years, I will tomorrow. I'll work Friday, so we can meet on Saturday or Sunday, deal?" Rita asked with upturned palms.

A little ashamed that he had nearly lost his composure, Franco shrunk back. The evening's discoveries were not at all what he expected. He actually expected little or nothing of this at all.

"Is Hannah home?" Carolyn asked, referring to Rita's twenty-six-year-old daughter.

"Nope. Northeastern Europe this time. Wanted to do

some more exploring before going to prison!" Carolyn and
Franco knew that this meant that Hannah would be returning
to the United States soon and wouldn't have the opportunity or
means to travel again for some time. Hannah had landed her
first real job as a field reporter at King-5 TV in Seattle. She
had given up her apartment when its lease expired, so that she
could be free to travel for a while. Hannah had been staying
with Rita for the time being, and they had planned to look for
an apartment for Hannah a little closer to town.

The next ten minutes were spent processing Rita's
departure from the Seattle Police Department. Everyone was
very quiet until the trio exited. In the car Rita asked Franco
what he discussed with "the nice, young detective." All Franco
divulged was that Brent Parker was not the lead investigator
and that she would be filled in when they met on Sunday to
talk. "Rita, we'll start fresh on the weekend. Okay?"

"Kay, Franco Darling."

Franco drove north in the driving rain to Rita's house.
Graciously, Rita invited them inside, but all three of them
understood it was a polite but vacant gesture. She kissed
them both with a smile and they waited in the driveway of her
meticulous rambler until she unlocked the door and entered.
Once inside, she leaned her back on the door, while the streaky
shadows of the car's headlights drifted across her living room
walls. Her heart was beating fast. *What the f---? What is
going on? Who killed Brandon? The cops must already know
who I'm* **not**....

Chapter 2

The next morning Rita awoke to the sound of meowing and purring, her cat Bella sitting squarely on her chest. Fully grown and nine human-years old, Bella was very petite, just like her "mom:" a silver-tabby mutt with the occasional copper spot on her coat. The cat often nipped Rita's hand to get her attention, whenever she stopped stroking the feline's tiny head. Sydney snoozed nearby on the floor. An overweight British tortoiseshell mix, she almost always appeared at one's feet the moment the refrigerator door opened.

When the reality of the previous evening finally set in, Rita felt as though she was levitating above her bed. *Did that really happen?* In a heartbeat, she dropped into the center of her bed and covered her face with her hands. *I can't run away again*, she thought to herself. *I have a life here, a real life!*

Rita rolled over to check her alarm clock: three-fifty. The alarm would go off in about thirty minutes, so she reached out and turned it off. She then grabbed the phone to call work and left a message that she would not be there today. After slipping the phone back onto its cradle, Rita swung her legs off the edge of the bed and wiggled her chilly feet into her cozy slippers. She plodded down the hall to the kitchen, adjusting the thermostat on the wall outside of her bedroom. In the darkness of the early morning, she gazed out at the torrents of rain beating against the kitchen window of her little rambler. For once, she felt good about using a sick day. She felt as dark and beaten as the Pacific Northwest November, so staying home that day brought comfort. Transfixed on the rain streaming down the large kitchen window, Rita stood at the counter brewing coffee. Adding a touch of cinnamon to the brew reminded her of her grandma's kitchen, and for a moment her glowing Nonna stood before her on the hardwood floor. Shaking herself conscious again, she sipped the sweet, hot coffee while walking back down the hall and climbed into her warm bed. She drifted into the soft light of a dream that led her up the walk on the side of a house where her grandmother stood waiting on the back porch. "Figlia bella, vené," her grandmother beckoned smilingly. The old woman extended her arm outward toward Rita, and Rita could see her own arm reaching out for her grandmother's hand. Rita consciously thought to herself: *Nonna, stay with me please; I need you.*

She was jolted hard when she heard what she thought was the alarm clock, not recalling that she had already turned it off. It was the phone. She brushed her hand against it, sending it plummeting to the floor. Groggy, she glanced at her clock. Ten twenty-three! She groped the floor with her extended arm and widespread fingers, much like a blind person.

"Hull-o, good morning."

It was Carolyn. "How are you feeling, Rita?"

Rita felt herself make a twisted face. With a grin she replied, "Like shit, of course. How are you?"

"Worried sick. Aren't you?"

"No."

"What? Why not?"

"Cuz. What do I need to worry about?" Scratching her head and taking a deep breath, she moved her legs to the side of the bed and onto the floor. "I *didn't* murder anyone. If it goes to trial, I *can't* be found guilty. I'm innocent and justice will be served."

There was a silence on the other end. Rita thought Carolyn's cell phone call dropped. "Carolyn?"

"Yes, I'm here, Rita. I'm sure that's true, but it's not that easy. If you are arrested and charged, well… it's complicated. Franco and I need you to come over on Sunday to discuss this. We need to be ready to firm up your alibi, just in case."

"Alibi. Hmmm," thought Rita aloud. "I was home the night Brandon was murdered."

"Anyone at all that can confirm that?"

"Sure! Sydney and Bella were here. I'm sure they'll vouch for me."

"Rita! This isn't funny!"

Rita was scared, but had hoped her humor would lighten the mood. "Okay, okay. I don't have an alibi, but I didn't kill that jerk, either!" lamented Rita. "I don't know what to think, Baby. Not sure why they're looking at me."

"Franco spoke with the detective last night so he'll

be able to tell you more when you get to our place, okay? So, you'll drive down, right? Come down early Sunday by ten-thirty or so, and we'll start working on this right away. I'll make the shrimp scampi that you like for brunch!"

"Yum! Sure, Doll. I'll be there by ten-thirty, easy. I'll see you then. Love you. Tell Franco hi, and thank him again for me."

Chapter 3

*O*n Friday morning, Rita robotically readied herself for work, but then again, that was pretty much the way the entire day would go. Emotionally exhausted, she practiced a Mona Lisa smile at the mirror before flicking off her bathroom light. Her mind wandered back to the evening before last: the event was surreal, dreamlike. Friday was business casual day, so that took some pressure off Rita. As expected in the fall and winter months, it was misting lightly as Rita drove to the transit center to catch her bus. It was the same routine most workdays, but she enjoyed visiting with the other commuters. It also gave her time to read a book, listen to music or just relax. She purposely faced the right-hand side of the bus during the commute, so that she could enjoy the view of Lake Union for all of thirty seconds as the bus crossed the

Ship Canal Bridge. She entertained herself by contemplating whether or not the bus driver really believed no one noticed that he was slyly picking his nose. A polite bunch, some commuters read while a few spoke in low murmurs on their cell phones.

After stepping off the bus, Rita enjoyed a peaceful walk through Pike Place Market. In the early morning hours, few people were there, mostly vendors and delivery folks. The rumbling of the trains by the water summoned memories of a childhood place far away. She welcomed the sound but was also saddened by it.

Shortly after arriving at the office, a young woman named Katie paused as they passed in the hallway. "Reet, you look a little tired. That's right, you were out yesterday. Are you okay?"

"Thanks, Babe. I'm fine," Rita responded. "When you get to be my age, the tired-thing is pretty common! But yes -- I didn't sleep much the last couple of nights. I'm just a little off-kilter," Rita said, leaning toward Katie with an earnest smile. "How about you, Honey? How are those wedding plans coming along?"

Katie gushed: "Oh, just fine. All the usual snags and set-backs, but pretty darn okay."

"Good girl," said Rita, picking up Katie's hand in a maternal way. Smart, pretty, and hard-working, Rita always liked Katie. Rita and Katie said their "see you laters" and headed back to their desks. Glancing over her shoulder, Katie said: "Oh, by the way, Rita: you *always* look great, even if you are a little tired."

"You're my favorite liar!" They laughed like Wilma Flintstone and Betty Rubble, cupping their hands over their mouths as not to disturb others around them.

Time advanced slowly that morning. Rita looked forward to a lunchtime walk to rev up her metabolism. Opting to eat smaller meals throughout the morning, she rarely ate an actual lunch. She felt it was counter-productive to stay indoors for the entire day, too. After what seemed like an eternity, she looked at the lower right-hand corner of her computer screen to discover that it was almost one-fifteen. Relieved, she hurriedly put on cotton socks and walking shoes and grabbed her little red raincoat from behind her door. Crossing the hallway of the busy brokerage firm, she tiptoed around the corner of Katie's cubicle and looked in to be sure she was not disturbing her. Katie looked focused as she worked on a computer document. Strewn about were various pieces of paper, but what always warmed Rita's heart were the photographs Katie displayed of herself and her fiancé, various nieces and nephews, dogs, parents: all the most important loved ones in her life. Other than Hannah, Rita really didn't have a family and she envied those who did, but in a loving and curious sort of way. "If anyone looks for me, Honey, I'm going for my walk."

"Okay, Reet. Have a good one."

The fog and drizzle had long lifted, and the day was now unusually crisp and clear for a Seattle November. When she reached the street, Rita turned side-to-side trying to decide which way to walk. She drew a long breath. She was so tired that simple decisions were a bit difficult, but she was grateful that it was Friday and that she would have a break again tomorrow. Then, reality slapped her hard. Much of this weekend would be spent with Carolyn and Franco. She always looked forward to the time spent with them. *Oh, yeah, Rita. Remember? The police and FBI are ready to pounce!* This

Sunday would be different. Back to reality, she could feel the pavement smack hard against the rubber soles of her Converse tennies that her daughter Hannah often made fun of. She walked down the hill to the west toward the waterfront.

People and traffic were muffled blurs as she walked First Avenue. Nearing the Pike Place Market, Rita crossed the brick street toward the its shops and bakeries. It was quiet in the autumn months, but she loved this walk any time of year. There was a short line as she neared a pirosky shop, so Rita ducked in to buy a couple of the smoked salmon variety that Hannah liked so much. She paused as she remembered that Hannah was still traveling in Europe with her closest friend, Heidi. "I'll have the rosemary chicken today," she said to the teenaged boy behind the counter. She planned to eat the savory concoction for dinner. With Hannah away, she didn't cook much.

"How's the book you're writing, Ma'am?" the kid chirped.

Rita laughed out loud. She had once told the boy that she was writing a novel about a woman who moves far away from her hometown to start her life over in the Pacific Northwest. The novel's main character frequents a pirosky shop at the Market. She told the young clerk that she wrote in the delightful teenaged boy who always took her order. He flashed a big Cheshire Cat smile as he handed back her change. "It's coming along, slow but sure," Rita replied. In truth, such a story had been in Rita's head for years and she only occasionally pulled out her laptop to work on it. With little leisure time, it was difficult to feel inspired or muster the energy to do so very often. Each time the young man at the pirosky shop asked, it sparked her to write and it was a welcome distraction from everyday life.

Energized but calmer, she did not hurry back to the office. Crossing the street toward the Market's north edge, she was reminded of how lucky she was to live in such a beautiful, green place. The Olympic Mountains on the peninsula, Puget Sound, the Cascades to the East, rivers, lakes, and forests. On a clear day, Mt. Rainier was clearly visible from her office window. She never tired of the beauty of her surroundings and enjoyed a good quality life in Seattle. *Oh, but the traffic*, she thought. Reality, again.

On the walk back to her office, Rita needed to scale three steep blocks. Distracted by her thoughts, she did not notice the KOMO News van until she was practically on top of it. Suddenly, there were microphones in her face and a camera lens staring her down. Rita was surrounded by a news crew.

"Ms. Napapolus. Are you Rita Napapolus?" Startled, Rita squirmed her petite frame through the unwelcome swarm and whirred through the revolving doors of her building, racing to the elevator bays. It seemed an eternity for an elevator to return to the lobby. She could hear the news crew being stopped by the building's security guards, giving her enough time to escape into the elevator. A man and woman stepped forward, the gentleman extending his arm to keep the door from closing before the woman could join him. *Come on, come on, get in,* Rita thought.

The parted doors finally closed and the elevator rose. The couple looked nervously at Rita, who was out of breath and had beads of perspiration on her forehead. Rita flashed a nervous smile, and the couple hastily exited when the elevator reached the tenth floor. Reaching the thirty-first floor, Rita rushed to her tiny office, and was startled again to find her young boss, Scott Stein, whirling around in her desk chair. "Quick, Rita. Close the door." Still breathless, Rita closed the door behind her and leaned back on it. "When were you going to tell me, Dear?"

"Tell you what, Scott?"

"Ree: we're friends. You've worked for me and Dad for over ten years. What's the deal? I asked the reporters outside what was going on. They were stopping people and asking if they knew who *you* were. Pretty desperate, I would say. Didn't you see the paper this morning? The news?" Scott was not a judgmental person. His face showed a great deal of concern for her, almost fear. His piercing blue eyes locked Rita's. He was a beautiful "child" in Rita's eyes: pale-skinned, dark hair, full lips, which were now parted waiting for Rita's response.

"No, but I'm sure you're going to tell me all about it." Rita replied sarcastically.

"Person of interest, prime suspect? Murder, Ree? Wanna tell me what's going on? You don't have to, but my dad and I can help. Do you have an attorney yet?"

"Yes," Rita whispered. "I do."

"Grab your coat. We'll go down the service elevator to the parking garage, and I'll get you outta here. You are officially on a paid leave now, but we can't have the media tearing in here. I've called the police, and they're going to keep any busy-bodies out of here and I'll tell everyone you're not here."

"No, Scott, *please*. Can't I stay right here?"

"Hun. Not good for you. Not good for the firm. You can do some work from home if you'd like. We'll get this straightened out, but right now we have to get you out of the building."

"Okay, Scott." Rita's eyes were filled with tears. She swallowed hard and snatched a Kleenex from a box behind her desk. Scott stood and put his arm around her, and together they looked at Mt. Rainier, which seemed deliriously translucent. Its peak, crisp with snow, seemed to float eerily above the surrounding mist. *Thanks for making an appearance for me today*, Rita thought as she looked at the giant mountain. *This might be the last time I see you from this window, friend.*

Scott turned and softly said, "Let's go, Lady."

"Wait, Scott. Give me a minute to pack up my photos of Hannah and put an out-of-office reply on my email."

"Five minutes, tops, Rita. I'll get my jacket and be back."

"Yes, Boss," smiled Rita. Looking over his shoulder, Scott quietly closed the door behind him, leaving Rita to complete the tasks. She hurriedly put the framed photos in her carry bag, along with her dress shoes, setting the paper bag containing the pirosky ceremoniously on the top. Her heart sank as she gazed at the mountain; reality was setting in. *What is going to happen? When I wake up will this all be over?*

There was a tap on the door, and it opened. "Reet? Are you ready?" asked Scott.

"I'll never be ready," groaned Rita. He spirited her through the hallway and toward the service elevator. Jittery, Rita thought of Katie and spurted, "If you could let Katie know that I needed to attend to family business, or something. Would you?"

Scott held her close as the elevator descended down to the parking garage. Rita often thought that if she had ever had a son, he would be like Scott. Scott and Franco, she loved both of them.

Scott hustled Rita toward his BMW 540i. Rita melted, because she lusted for a car sportier than her old Volvo. Scott chivalrously carried Rita's bag for her, dropped it behind the driver's seat, and zipped the Beemer toward an exit. He waved an electronic key across the parking kiosk and a gate ascended. "We made it!" Rita laughed. "Scott, put the top down, would you?"

"Are you crazy? It's freezing out!"

"No, it's not, and it's not raining. It'll be a while before I get to ride with the top down."

"Anything for you, Dear," sighed Scott, and down came the top. They exchanged sideways glances and laughed.

"Let me drive?"

"Well, *almost* anything, Rita!"

After jettisoning onto the freeway and shifting into overdrive, Scott took Rita's hand in his. She looked down for a long time at their entwined fingers and squeezed hard. "We'll right this, Rita. It'll be okay."

"Yes, Scott." The Beemer tore up I-5, and in no time arrived at the transit center where Rita left her 940.

"I'll follow you to your place."

"No, I'm okay. I have to stop at the store, anyway."

"Ree, don't stop anywhere today. Just go home. I will go to the store if you need me to. Otherwise, I'm followin. I'm followin you anyway, cuz I know you're lyin about the store."

"Alright, alright!" Rita shouted, but it was not in anger. She was stubborn. Scott smiled and brushed her cheek with his knuckles. Rita grabbed his hand and kissed the top of it. For a few seconds Rita smiled, but Scott sensed her fear. She jumped out of the car and Scott watched while she unlocked her grey Volvo, which she affectionately called the "Grey Ghost." Scott followed Rita's car closely as she drove the back streets to her little house, and he watched as she backed into her garage. Putting his BMW in Park, Scott stepped into the garage to say goodbye to Rita. They embraced in the shadows, and stepped back, gazing fondly at each other.

"Okay, Son," said Rita. "Go home to that nice wife and kids, and drive carefully. Thanks for putting the top down for an old lady."

"No problem, Rita. Call me if you need anything. Maybe you should get out of here for a while."

"I'm going away, day after tomorrow."

"No, I mean *away, away*."

"Police told me not to go anywhere right now. If anyone comes here to annoy me, I'll just call 911."

Scott kissed her on the forehead, and Rita watched him back down her short driveway. Forcing a smile, she waved goodbye to Scott. When the garage door hit the floor, she ran her hands through her hair and sat in a lawn chair in the garage next to a little café table. Hands shaking even more, she grabbed her pack of cigs, lit a smoke, and tried to relax. Too distracted, she crushed out the cigarette and walked toward the door that led into her home. So many times, she had wished to be home early on a Friday afternoon, but today she wanted to be at work. She walked through her house checking the windows and doors, and took a hot shower to help calm herself. After watching some mindless TV, she hunkered down for the night praying she could wake up in a different place.

Chapter 4

*U*nusually late for her, Rita slept in that next day until seven a.m. She shuffled through her boring routine, but her mood lightened as the sun began to make an appearance. It helped to make her feel mildly optimistic that the events of the preceding days would be a thing of the past in short order. No laughing matter, she knew she needed to concentrate on why Brandon had been murdered and how she fit into the scheme of things. Brainstorming with Carolyn and Franco might be the ticket. These two bright young people could help her figure this mess out, she was sure. Within the week, the police will have moved on. She made an effort to feel positive that her life would resume its course.

Due to the fact that she was now "on vacation," she did not rush in her accustomed manner. The laundry and

the chores *could* wait; no need to rush to complete them by
Sunday night. Nonetheless, she felt uneasy, so she vacuumed
quickly and threw a load into the washing machine. Taking a
quick inventory of her pantry and refrigerator, she decided to
run to the grocery store. The entire next day was reserved to
discuss her unfortunate situation with Franco and Carolyn, so
she might not have the time this weekend. The meeting was
consistently on her mind, and she worried that she might need
to reveal some personal information that she would rather keep
private. *You gotta do what you gotta do, Lady,* she resolved.
It's outta your control right now.

     The day was crisp and clear, and it was only a
five-minute drive to the grocery store. Having lived in her
neighborhood for nine years now, Rita knew the store clerks
by name. Of course, they wore name tags, but they knew Rita
well, too. She gathered the items from her short list quickly,
but stood in the check-out line much longer than it took to
choose her purchases. Glancing at magazines and tabloids
covers, her mind was questioning why police thought she
might be involved in Brandon's death. What did they know
about *her*? Would this go away fast enough to spare Hannah
the details?

     In spite of everything, Rita felt well-rested that
morning. She decided she would go out later in the day to do
other errands, and headed home to put away the perishable
groceries. Turning right into the expanse of the half-circle
cul-de-sac on which it stood, she applied the brakes firmly.
There, at the curb sat two cars: a county sheriff's and a Seattle
police cruiser. Two male officers stood rigid in her driveway,
while a female officer stood close by on the sidewalk. Rita
proceeded slowly, lowering her car window. Her mind racing,

she nonetheless held her composure when she spoke. "Good morning, officers," she quietly spoke. Everyone looked incredibly tense. She continued, "I believe I know why you are here, and I'd like to turn my car around to back it into the garage. You see, I have groceries in the trunk that I need to remove. The lady is welcome to sit in my car while I do so, if you'd like."

"Ma'am, I'm afraid not," said the officer. "You'll need to put your car in Park and step out of the vehicle. Now, please. Please put your hands where I can see them."

Fucking attitude, Rita thought to herself. *Like I have a gun with me! I couldn't fire if I wanted to*. Her hands were shaking uncontrollably. She was sure that the neighbors were in their windows, wondering what was going on. The deputy sheriff stepped forward quickly. He motioned to the female officer and said, "Well, I think we can accommodate Ms. Napapolus for five minutes. Officer Freeman, would you sit in the car while the lady backs it in? We can talk to Rita inside." The woman looked at her clearly pissed-off partner, who nodded a grudging approval. Officer Freeman entered the car and politely said, "Okay, Ms. Napapolus. You can back your car in now."

Rita was shaking visibly. "Just a few seconds? My hands don't seem to be working very well right now!"

Officer Freeman offered a sympathetic smile. "Of course. Take a deep breath, but make your turn slowly as not to upset the other officers." Rita took Officer Freeman's advice, and slowly was the only way she was going to back that car into her garage. The men followed the car's progress closely until they stood beside the driver's side of the car. As she backed in, Rita could see her two friends and neighbors,

Gail and Robert Brown clutching each other on their deck
above, worried expressions on their faces.

She sat for a moment, and stepped out slowly when the
sheriff opened the car door. The male police officer stepped
forward, and quietly began, "Rita Jean Napapolus. We have
a warrant for your arrest. You have the right to remain silent.
Anything you say can and will be used against you in a court
of law. You have the right to speak to an attorney, and to have
an attorney present during any questioning. If you cannot
afford a lawyer, one will be provided for you at government
expense." Rita felt nauseous for a moment. The words echoed
in her head, dreamily suspended in mid-air. She steadied
herself as she waited for the young man to finish reciting the
Miranda Warning.

Rita looked at all three of the officers and meekly
asked, "May I put my groceries away? I'd like to call my
attorney from here, and a friend that will come and care for my
cats." The three officers looked stunned at this response, but
once again it was the sheriff who broke the silence. "I think
that would be okay, don't you, officers? Officer O'Brien?"
The Seattle police officers nodded reluctantly; this was not a
typical arrest for any of them. Here stood a small, pleasant
woman, barely more than one hundred pounds. They were
careful to hide what, if any, personal judgments they might be
harboring. Their job was to arrest a murder suspect, and take
her into custody.

"All right, then. It's just two bags; I'll take them out
now." Rita was thoughtful and moved slowly. Her optimism
shattered, she opened the trunk with the three faceless figures
hovering very close. To Rita's total amazement, Officer
O'Brien extended his arms into the trunk and said, "I have

this one, Ma'am," taking the second paper bag from the trunk. They passed through the door and into the kitchen, Office Freeman leading the way. It took just a few minutes to put things away and make two phone calls, one to Franco and Carolyn, one to Gail Brown, who had a key to Rita's house for emergencies. "No, Gail. Everything's fine. Don't worry. I'll explain later. Yes, Hannah is fine, too! I'll call you later." Her tone soothing, Rita was not so sure she would be making that call to Gail anytime soon.

"May I brush my teeth and pee?" Rita asked. "Also, may we forego handcuffs? My neighbors, well…" The three officers looked weary, too. Rita felt almost sorry for them. "Please? I am not resisting arrest."

This time it was Officer O'Brien who spoke first. "Yes, you are in no way resisting," he sighed. "Officer Freeman, check the bathroom before Ms. Napapolus uses it, please."

"I assure you. I have no handguns, but please check out the bathroom, Officer Freeman. I'm rather proud of the way I remodeled it!" Rita said with a smile. After using the bathroom, Rita set out some fresh food for her cats and within a few minutes, the four exited via the front door.

As she walked to the police cruiser Rita looked up to see Gail's outline behind the deck's sliding door, obscured by the reflection of light. "May I wave to my neighbor?" The three officers nodded, and Rita waved her hand quickly, smiling in Gail's direction. Again, the officers looked amusingly befuddled. Rita sensed this and said out loud. "I don't want her to worry. She's not just my neighbor, she's a good friend." Officer O'Brien tried not to let his guard down. Waving a reassuring smile to a neighbor was not typical of a murderer, but during his short but full career he had witnessed many suffering from varying degrees of psychosis and schizophrenia. *Things are often not what they seem*, he reminded himself.

In the car, Rita quietly commented about the clearness of the day and Seattle's sunshine of late. She also felt grateful that the ride would be a short one. The officers were not rude, but they were not obligated to respond at all, and Rita knew this. She was very careful not to say anything about the immediate reality of the moment. She limited her one-sided conversation to her weather observation, concentrating on the beauty of the day outside the car window. The police car came to rest at a side entrance of the downtown precinct. Her demeanor appeared calm to the law enforcement trio, but inside Rita was screaming, *Jesus fucking Christ! Someone* **help me***!*

The sheriff's car pulled in directly behind them. Rita hoped he would reinforce the fact that she had totally cooperated with the officers during the arrest process. She now wondered if her requests to pee and put away the groceries looked bad. Like a wet dog wicking away water, she shook the thought away. *Paranoia, Girl. Deep breath. You haven't done or said anything stupid.*

Officer O'Brien opened the door and put his palm out to motion to Rita to stay seated. "I'm sorry Ms. Napapolus, but I'll have to put cuffs on you now. We'll put your hands in front, though. You'll only have to wear them for a few minutes until you're fingerprinted, photographed and taken upstairs. Do you understand?"

"Of course I understand, young man. I appreciate your letting me leave my house without them."

So polite, thought the young officer. *Schizophrenic, maybe -- maybe not.* "Okay, step out and extend your hands out for me."

Where am I? Rita thought sarcastically. *When will I wake up? Glad I put on makeup this morning; mug shots are not my thing.*

It took almost an hour for Rita to make her way to the questioning area where Franco and Carolyn were waiting. Nervous, she was careful not to speak anything other than polite yes and no responses when addressed. Officer Freeman remained with her the entire time. This time, Rita was taken to a pristine but drab questioning room, rather than the comfortable "guest quarters" she enjoyed earlier that week. "The kids" were waiting inside. As soon as she stepped through the threshold, Rita shook her head at the sight of a large mirror at the room's far end and cameras mounted into two ceiling corners. *No windows.* Rita hated rooms without windows. Officer Freeman removed the handcuffs from Rita's wrists. The three group-hugged, clenched in the uncertainty of the moment.

"Rita, I'm not qualified to defend you at a trial," Franco said. "I'm just a general practice attorney, you know that. We're going to need to find someone else to defend you. Bail will be high, so you need to be prepared for the worst."

"I know that, Sweetie, but I need an attorney today, right now."

"Yes, yes you do, and we're happy that we can be here with you," Carolyn said, holding Rita's hand. Carolyn had been allowed to bring bottled water with her and offered one to Rita.

The blurred silhouettes of two men were present

outside the frosted-glass door panel. Their voices hushed,
Rita could not make out what they were saying. When the
door swung open, it revealed the bright face of Brent Parker,
the young detective the three had already met. Since this was
just mid-day, this time he looked refreshed and rested. An
older man meandered through the door behind Brent. His face
weathered and serious, the man appeared to be in his late fifties
or early sixties, and wore a battered trench coat and fedora.
Is this guy serious? Rita thought. *He looks like a detective in
an old movie!* Somewhat fair, he had some brown spots on
his face and hands. He seemed average looking to Rita, but
she tried to always think the best of people, even when her
gut screamed not to. Today her gut screamed that she would
not like this man. When Brent Parker opened his mouth to
introduce him, he was cut off. The older man dove right in.
His tone was flat and dry, perhaps desensitized by years of
dealing with the criminal element. "Ms. Napapolus, now you
know why you're here. Shall we discuss it?" *Condescending,
too*, thought Rita. "You killed Brandon Perry, and we have the
proof, so why don't you just tell us how it happened?" Rita
knew that this man's ultimate goal was to get a confession
from her.

Rita began to speak, but Franco interrupted
immediately. "It's okay, Franco. I can answer this gentleman's
question." She extended a decisively ignored hand. "I'm Rita
Napapolus and *you* are?"

"Detective Bob Chandler, Ma'am. I'm gonna ask you
a series of questions."

And so it began: pretty much the same questions over
and over again. Rita was glad to have gotten a good night's
sleep, as it was clear to her that this man was trying to trip her

up by asking the same questions, but by presenting them to her differently phrased or with a slight change of information. *How transparent is this?* "Detective Chandler, you asked that question before. Don't you remember? You asked it differently, but you asked," she replied coyly. "I did not kill Brandon Perry, and will not admit to a murder that I did not commit. I readily agreed to give hair and blood samples. I have nothing to hide and am presumed innocent until proven guilty. Isn't that the way it goes?"

Franco cleared his throat nervously to signal to Rita to stop her antics. She understood the importance of being respectful but she almost expected Detective Chandler to whip out a bright light to shine in her face, in an attempt to weaken her resolve. The craggy detective paced the floor behind her, occasionally bringing his face down close to her shoulder to ask a question. As scared as she was, Rita laughed inside, *He's trying so hard to intimidate me by putting that ugly mug close to my face! Not working, dude.* Considering the circumstances, she remained calm. She was dying for a cigarette, but most certainly was not going to verbalize that request. Although Brent Parker sat across the table from her, he did not ask her any questions. "How are you, young man?" Rita ventured. Franco shot Rita a sharp look. "Just askin the kid how he is, Franco!" Carolyn feared Rita might be tiring, but her friend resumed a placid expression and put her clasped hands on the table.

The verbal volleyball was served into the third hour, then the fourth and fifth. Rita answered truthfully at every turn. She was reminded of the physical evidence several times: *Your prints on the gun, your DNA everywhere at his place, the murder victim had ripped you off, he had your hair in his*

clenched hand. Yadda, yadda, yadda. Until today, she was
unaware that it was actually Brandon Perry that ripped her off
with her credit card checks. In turn, she began to ask Detective
Chandler questions. "What are you talking about, Detective?
Even if that were true, I had no way of knowing that the names
on the credit card checks were Mr. Perry's aliases!" Rita's
voice was sparked with contempt upon learning this fact and
in the next moment, being accused of having known Brandon
Perry had been the perpetrator. She knew the physical
evidence pointed to her, along with a possible motive for
murder. The burden of proof was on her shoulders; it would
be her defense attorney's job to persuade a jury that she had no
knowledge of her forged credit card funds.

There was a rap on the windowed door. It opened
narrowly and a bailiff's head poked through the opening. "Uh,
Detective Parker? Can I see you for a minute?"

Again, Franco interrupted Rita when she said, "There's
no point in continuing. I've told you everything I know. I
didn't kill Brandon and I don't know who did. I'd be willing
to take a lie-detector test if that will help prove that I didn't."

"Reet," interrupted Franco, "don't make any
statements you might regret later on! Now keep quiet!"
Broodingly, Rita crossed her arms and tried to relax in the
uncomfortable chair. Brent Parker returned to the room and
sat down again. His face showed that he was the bearer of bad
news: bail had been set at one million dollars bond.

Obnoxious as ever, Detective Chandler sighed, "I
guess you'll be staying with us for a while, so we'll take a
break until you decide to tell the truth. I'll leave you alone
with your friends to talk things over. See you soon, Ms.
Napapolus."

Feeling defeated and exhausted, Rita, Franco and Carolyn reflected that at least a bond is set, however unreachable. Ten percent was required up front in order for a release, along with the stipulation of being under house arrest. "Ten percent is still $100,000, so it looks as though I'll have to stay, at least until the arraignment," moaned Rita. Her head was spinning, she thought of her daughter's return from Europe. There was no way she could hide this from Hannah, even if/when she was proven innocent. Following a few minutes of a brisk discussion about where to look for a good attorney, another rap sounded on the door. Brent Parker stood inside the questioning room and spoke to the person outside. Stiffly turning around, he astonishingly proclaimed, "Someone has posted bail." Stunned, their reaction of ebullience was delayed, and they burst with relieved laughter at the nature of this unexpected announcement. This was followed by the obvious question: "*Who* posted bond?"

"Some hot-shot defense attorney from San Francisco," was the young detective's response. "The bailiff brought the attorney's card, and said you should call him, Franco."

"Huh? Did he say me?"

"Yes, the bailiff must have told him that you were in here with Rita. He said Tuesday would work best for him."

Franco looked at the perfectly printed business card. John Sciandra, Attorney at Law. *An Italian name,* thought Franco.

Officer Freeman appeared through the door again, looking bewildered. "Rita can be released, but only with a tracking device on her ankle. We can fit it right now." After sitting stiffly for so many hours, they rose from their chairs and stretched a bit.

"I'll accompany you, as well," chimed Brent Parker, as he and Officer Freeman led the three to an elevator. As they walked, Brent explained that travel within a small radius was permissible, and only by advance request. Beyond a certain point would require a police escort. If Rita's movement and distance exceeded the outlined limits, a unit would be dispatched to pinpoint her whereabouts. He also explained the boundaries in which she wouldn't have to report: a walk to the mailbox was the only exception. Rita immediately advised she had plans go to Carolyn and Franco's the very next day, of which Brent quickly recorded on a small note pad he pulled from his jacket pocket. Point blank he explained, "You will be under surveillance, but mostly for your own protection from media hounds and the curious public. On Sunday, you'll be followed to Carolyn and Franco's and you must call in when you leave their home. You'll be followed home as well. You may stop at a store if needed, but decide and report before leaving Carolyn and Franco's. This will most likely be the only time you will travel on your own between now and a trial date. Do you understand? Any questions, Ms. Napapolus?"

"No questions. I understand," nodded Rita.

Feeling deep pangs of humiliation, Rita was fitted with an electronic tracking device on her ankle. Holding hands, she and Carolyn exchanged glances. "Sure wish I was at Nordstrom trying on shoes," quipped Rita.

"I wish you were, too, Rita," murmured Carolyn. Rita, Carolyn and Franco were escorted to a side exit near a parking lot. Anxious to leave, Rita burst into tears as soon as she was outdoors. "My daughter is going to kill me!"

Franco was confused. "Rita! That's all you can say about this? Your daughter is going to kill you? What is going

on? Can you tell us, please? You don't seem terribly surprised
that someone just posted a million dollar bond for you! Come
on, you must know."

Rita was *almost* as confused as everyone else
around her. "I need time to think about this, Franco. I'm
not entirely sure what's going on, either. *Please*, just take
me home." Exhausted by a full day of questioning and
red-tape procedures, the three spoke little during the ride
to Rita's house. Thinking it would lighten the mood, Rita
said, "Did you see that Chandler character bark his questions
from behind? Each time he came close, I wanted to hold my
nose, he smelled so bad!" Franco could see Rita's face in
the rearview mirror. He thought Rita looked scared and not
amused, however, she made a vain attempt to mask it with
humor. Upon their arrival at Rita's place, they turned on the
TV and ordered out for pizza. Much to their dismay, the story
of her arrest was the top story on the six o'clock news, but
the reporter stated she was remanded to the custody of her
attorney. A few cars circled through the cul-de-sac, but no
one came close to the house, probably deterred by the fact
that a police car had been stationed directly across the street.
Carolyn and Franco stayed at Rita's home until almost ten p.m.
The three friends confirmed the meeting time for the following
day and the young couple headed for home.

Rita stood cloaked by the blinds on her living room
window and watched as the couple's car slowly pulled away.
Emotionally drained, she wondered to herself: *How did this
happen? Could **he** have posted bail? But, how would **HE**
know I'm in trouble?*

Chapter 5

She drifted in and out of sleep throughout that long night, so at one point Rita decided to get up to watch TV for a while. Passing the outer perimeter of her small living room, she caught a reflection in the darkness outside. Doing a 180, she walked the hall to the room at the farthest end of the house. Under cover of darkness, she tiptoed to the window, standing off to one side. There in the street, enveloped in the fog, was a patrol car. She wondered if they were there to protect her privacy, or were dispatched to be sure she wouldn't go "on the lamb." Either way, she felt a wave of comfort for at least having a cop close by in the event she needed one. Shrugging her shoulders, she walked down the hall again to the kitchen, removing her coffee maker from a cabinet. She stumbled about the kitchen and looked at the microwave clock that read

two-thirteen. Rita's motions were one of a person on auto-
pilot: she fed the cats, changed their water bowl, washed a few
dishes that were in the sink, and folded some clean towels that
she had carried in from the garage. This was a familiar routine
for Rita most mornings, listening to the weather forecast on
TV while in her robe and slippers. After an hour or so of this
habitual activity, Rita was hit with a wave of exhaustion and
plodded back down the hall, glancing over her shoulder to be
sure the police car was still there. Reassured, she crawled into
bed, where she almost instantly fell into a deep sleep.

Around seven, Rita awoke again, but lingered and
snoozed on and off for almost another hour. She finally
brushed the bed sheets aside, extending her right leg toward
the ceiling to surmise her new anklet. She turned to Bella,
who was still peacefully snoozing on the edge of the bed. "I
love anklets, but never thought I'd be wearing one of these!"
It seemed odd that she slept so hard in the midst of what she
knew was a waking nightmare. She crept down the hall, just
stopping short at the edge of the living room, peering her eyes
around the corner of the wall, and toward her living room
window. No cop car. She shuddered a bit, and wondered
if they really were absent, or watching her nonetheless. *I'd
really prefer them to be out there somewhere,* she thought.

Jumping through her morning hoops, she brewed
coffee and smoked a cigarette in the garage. Rita did so
discreetly and few people knew she smoked at all. She had
been raised that it was unsavory to see a woman publicly
smoking, even though her dad smoked freely, anywhere, at
any time. While despising the double-standard, *not* smoking
in public was perfectly acceptable in Rita's mind; the old-
fashioned mental barrier helped her to keep the smoking to a

minimum. After showering, Rita thoughtfully chose jeans and a nice black three-quarter length sleeved cashmere sweater and took the time to do her hair and make-up nicely. In reality, she was feeling panicked inside, but taking her time and distracting herself helped whenever she was stressed out. By then, it was almost nine-forty-five. She would have to leave soon to make it to Carolyn and Franco's by ten-thirty. She hastily called the phone number Brent Parker had given her to report her departures.

Surprisingly, the sky was blue-grey and almost totally free of clouds, and the air was bitingly cool. Seattle was enjoying a relatively dry November. Rita cracked the car windows to circulate the air, while taking advantage of the car's heated seats to stay warm. If this had been any other day, she wouldn't have a care in the world. She was on her way to enjoy the company of Carolyn and Franco, and to share the pleasure of Carolyn's shrimp scampi. *But this wasn't just any day*, Rita thought. How could she explain something that totally escaped logic? How could she prove her innocence? No one could confirm her alibi that she was likely watching a DVD on her laptop in bed about the time Brandon Perry was murdered. *How glam, Lady!* Rita smiled to herself -- she spent a lot of time home alone, with "her girls." It occurred to her that the only prayer she had was that Brandon's body wasn't discovered for approximately a day and a half, making the time of death slightly difficult to pinpoint, but then again, speculation could also lean toward a wider window of time in which to murder the victim.

Rita exited at the U-District exit and headed west toward the Janszyck home in the Wallingford neighborhood. It was a "new" home for the newlyweds. An older bungalow,

Carolyn and Franco restored it to its former glory and added modern touches. Rita loved the wood floors and the large windows that bathed the house in heavenly light during the spring, summer and fall months. It had wonderful pillared doorways in the living and dining areas, and a kitchen with large, panel windows on two sides of the room. Rita loved old architecture, having grown up on the East Coast. The couple's home was an architectural feast for the eyes in Rita's mind. This type of home reminded her of the old homes in New England and she appreciated architecture as most might view art. Before she could even lock her car doors, she saw Carolyn's beautiful face appear in the relight window at the front door. As it opened, Carolyn's open arms extended as wide as the craftsman-style door. Carolyn's smiled looked forced, but Rita knew her friend just wanted to put her at ease. Carolyn took Rita's jacket and hung it in the foyer's closet. "Come on, Mom." She took Rita by the arm and drew her across an open dining area and toward the kitchen. Rita paused to look at a framed photo of Carolyn and Franco taken several years prior. In the photo, Carolyn sported gloriously long hair that cascaded past her knees. Before entering law school, she donated the thick trophy to Locks of Love, an organization that collects human hair for wig production. Their primary recipients were children with cancer and other devastating illnesses. Rita was very proud to have Carolyn in her life for so many reasons, and Carolyn's modesty, compassion and generosity were some of those reasons. Carolyn was a very busy law student at Seattle U while still working part-time for a law firm, so Rita rarely called on her favorite newlyweds for anything. One more semester and a bar exam, and Carolyn would be a practicing attorney, as well.

No doubt about it: she was brilliant *and* beautiful.

Stepping into the kitchen, the women found Franco sitting in a cozy breakfast nook sipping coffee from a mug. Although Carolyn was dressed and groomed, Franco was in a robe and pajamas, his fair hair comically disheveled and spiked. "Sweet Reet," he chirped, and Carolyn giggled.

"Okay, okay" Rita responded. "Enough."

Arching his eyebrows comically, Franco said. "Today, you have some splainin to do Loo-cee!"

"I know, I know," replied Rita, "but...."

"But, nothing," said Carolyn, "Take a seat." Carolyn shot a look at Franco to get moving. Franco, ever the good sport, rose to kiss his little wife on the forehead, and shuffled away with his newspaper tucked under his arm.

"Okay. Well..." Carolyn seemed more animated than usual. Normally, she was very laid-back and soft-spoken. She began bustling around the kitchen, and said: "...we can visit while Franco showers."

"Sure, Honey." Rita watched as Carolyn removed a coffee cup from a kitchen cabinet and poured. "Can I help with something?"

"Absolutely not. You sit and read the paper, or whatever you'd like to do. I'll cook; you relax." Carolyn carefully prepared the coffee just the way Rita liked it: light, warm and sweetened with raw sugar. She presented it in a gorgeous porcelain cup with matching saucer.

"Pretty cups, Daughter."

"My aunt sent them from Guam. You know, for a wedding gift."

"Lovely, yes. Very lovely," replied Rita, inspecting the cup in the light. "The glaze looks a little like Noritake."

"Yes, it does." Carolyn was as preoccupied in thought as Rita. Then there was a long silence, while Carolyn gathered her wok and cooking ingredients. "So, talk to me while I'm cooking brunch, okay?"

"Sure, Baby. What would you like to talk about?" Rita asked. She leaned back into the straight back of the breakfast nook's padded bench, crossed her arms across her chest and smiled fondly at Carolyn.

"Come on, Rita. I know you could not actually kill someone, but how can we explain what is going on? Why was this man found with a fistful of your hair in his hand? Your prints on the gun? This doesn't look good."

"It's been a long week, Hon. Let's just wait for Franco to get cleaned up and we'll talk about it. For now, I just want to hear about that honeymoon in Italy. I've never been there and want to, sooo much. Please tell me all about it. How you felt, how the food tasted, the art, the architecture. Start with Venice, please!"

"You're impossible sometimes, Rita!" laughed Carolyn. "Sure, I'll tell you all about it," she grinned. Rita propped her face on her hand, her elbow on the table to show Carolyn that she had her undivided attention. Carolyn relaxed as she gracefully moved about the room. Rita tried to focus on the specifics of Carolyn's adventure, but her mind wandered in and out of several places, one of which was Europe, where her daughter Hannah was. She missed her daughter and rehearsed scenarios in her head of how she was going to explain this mess. Her daughter would not be pleased.

While Carolyn reminisced about her honeymoon, she merrily sautéed chopped vegetables in a wok while rice noodles gently boiled in a saucepan next to it. No means

Italian in origin, she called the recipe shrimp scampi anyway. It was rather a Vietnamese version: with a Vietnamese black bean glaze. Rita loved it, so Carolyn cooked it whenever Rita visited. Franco appeared in the doorway of the kitchen; his hair still in a state of disarray, but now wet and spiky.

Rita turned to Franco as he retrieved plates from a cabinet and asked him several questions about what he liked most about their trip to Italy, and he went from one region to another in conversation. There was no one favorite place, he said. Each was wonderful in different ways.

The three of them chatted happily while they ate, taking their time to savor Carolyn's splendid culinary achievement. It was just past noon when they finished up. Franco rinsed the dishes and pots, then carefully loaded the dishwasher while Carolyn and Rita lingered at the table. Carolyn looked over her shoulder and then shot Rita a wink. Franco was pretty good about doing his share of the domestic chores, as Carolyn worked and went to school in the evenings, too. Thanksgiving week was coming up, and Carolyn looked forward to breathing a bit by taking a short break from her studies.

"Shall we retire to the living room?" said Carolyn.

"Honey, I'll never be able to retire, you know that!" laughed Rita. "The way things are looking, I might be taking retirement in the pen."

"Come on, Rita," remarked Franco, "we'll untangle all of this. But you need to be straight with us about everything, okay?"

"Sure," Rita sullenly replied.

Carolyn and Franco exchanged worried glances. Rita seemed far away and detached. Carolyn brought a pitcher of water brimming with ice and lemon slices, then retrieved three glasses.

"Look at you; aren't you sweet!" Rita beamed. When Franco placed a tape recorder on the coffee table, it was obvious that Rita seemed suddenly nervous and distracted. "Come on, babies! Is this really necessary?" her tone now injected with a false sense of humor.

"Ree," Franco said gently, "we need to record everything so that I can review it for any details that will help your case."

"Hmmm. My case. Yes." Rita blankly echoed. "Okay, then."

Carolyn smacked her hands together softly and with arched eyebrows turned to Rita and asked: "So, where would you like to begin?"

"Oh, I don't know. What are you looking to find out there, Franco?"

Franco looked slightly cross. His hands were up near his face, his index fingers at his lips, tapping the tips together. Seated to Rita's left, he stretched his long arm over the coffee table and snapped the recorder off. "How do you expect us to help you, Rita, if you are going to spar with us? This is not funny; you're in some pretty deep shit right now. We want to help you, and we're not going to tell anyone what's discussed in this room. If you did not kill Mr. Perry, you need to tell us exactly where you were and what you think happened. Both Carolyn and I learned that the police and FBI were watching Mr. Perry's activities. Because you were involved with him, however brief, they checked you out, too. But they were able to only go back into the history of Rita Napapolus, oh, about twenty years or so. Why *is* that? Huh? We need some information if we are going to help you." Franco stood. He placed his hands on his hips when he spoke, sarcastically moving his head from side to side. "Level with us, Dear! Did you not digest that Brandon Perry stole the checks from your place and wrote them to several aliases? To *himself*?"

"That fucking ass-wipe! Fucking Brandon!" seethed Rita. She turned to her two young friends. "Babies, I wasn't sure if it was the truth or if Detective Chandler was trying to trip me up! When it was happening, it occurred to me that it might have been Brandon, but none of the pieces fit, none of the names on the checks rang any bells!" Rita rocked backward into the plush, comfy couch, her bare feet side-saddled next to her, eyes cast down. Looking up, her expression was that of a pouting child. Her eyes were welled with tears, but she didn't necessarily look sad. "If...." she choked: "*when*, I tell you: you may never speak to me again."

Carolyn and Franco exchanged nervous glances again. The three of them just sat there for several seconds, looking from one to another and then back. Carolyn broke the silence by quietly asking, "Did you kill him, Rita?"

"God, no," blurted Rita, almost laughing. "A little bit of me wanted to! I wasn't worried about telling you that. I was referring to not being able to trace me back more than nineteen years. I simply changed my name, that's all. The police are not particularly bright because they're cops!" She laughed a nervous laugh, but Carolyn and Franco did not see the humor.

"Rita," replied Franco, "the FBI can trace just about anybody, though. How can you explain their failure to know that you just changed your name?"

Again, it felt as though a full five minutes had passed

but in reality, it was only about thirty seconds or so. "Don't know." Rita replied dryly, turning her glance away.

"You do know, you *do* know, Rita!" shouted Carolyn, jumping to her feet. No one was more surprised than Rita to hear Carolyn raise her voice, and Carolyn suddenly looked surprised, too. She put her hand to her chest and eased herself down into her chair. "Please, Rita. Don't be frightened. Tell us what you think happened."

"I'm not frightened, Sweetness. Embarrassed, maybe, but not frightened. Well, where do I begin?"

Franco sat beside Rita on the couch. He turned a softened gaze to Rita and said, "Begin at the beginning."

"There's so much, Franco. *Too much.* I had put it out of my mind all of these years."

"It's okay, it's okay," Franco reassured her. "Maybe you should start by telling us what your name was and why you changed it."

Rita swallowed hard. Her face flushed as she innocently asked, "The two of you will still love me, huh?" The three of them laughed lightly. "I *had* to. I had to change my name to start over. I really pretty much changed my identity, too. I changed Hannah's name, too. She had a different birth name."

Carolyn and Franco looked at each other in awe. Rita's words came slowly and deliberately. "My birth name was, uh, is Gina: Gina Bianco. I was born in Connecticut and not outside of New York City like I told you. I'm Italian and not Greek. Sicilian, actually." She paused for several moments before sighing "Whew! That felt good! I loved being raised an Italian; I *love* Italians." She laughed again, relieved to have said it out loud after so many years. "I had parents, grandparents and an older brother who I adored!"

"Wow! That's fantastic! So, they know where you are, right? Do you think someone in your family posted bail?" Franco asked.

Rita's lower lip moved mechanically, dropping from what looked like a hinged jaw. "Hell, no. They're all dead. *All* of them. I guess they know about it now, though!"

The sound of the pendulum clock in the kitchen could be heard, the silence was so pure. Carolyn moved from her chair to the couch and put her arm around Gina, who reached up and held her hand for a moment.

"These things happen. They were already gone by the time I moved away. *Ran away*, really. I got messed up and needed to escape so that Hannah could have a decent life. Ha! We've lived most of these years lean, but at least we were free. Or, at least I thought so until now."

Carolyn and Franco were already confused by these vacant ramblings, but Franco had managed to start the recorder a few moments earlier without Rita noticing.

"My gosh, it's been a long time since I've really thought about what my life there was like, my childhood. My grandparents: they were fab! *So* in love, even when they were very old. Hmmph! Oh, my." Tears were streaming down Rita's cheeks, but she was smiling from the sheer pleasure of being able to share the memory with someone.

"Continue, please, Rita," whispered Franco.

Peacefully, she looked up at Franco with a broad smile and said: "Alright. Man, it feels weird saying my real name out loud after all these years! I always liked my first name. Dad used to call me Miss Lollabridgida. You know, like the Italian movie star! Grandma called me Gia. And Joey, well

Joey called me...." Her voice trailed off and she put her hands
over her face and wept while Carolyn and Franco looked on
helplessly. "Oh, Joey. I miss you, Joey. Joey...." Carolyn
extended her arm, napkin in hand. Smiling as she raised her
head, Rita softly said, "Joey called me everything wonderful.
Hey, Beautiful. Hey, Gorgeous. How's my best girl?" It was
as though Rita was alone for a few minutes in a time-warp
while Carolyn and Franco watched. Suddenly self-conscious,
she said: "Well, kinda got lost there, didn't I?" Rita looked at
each of them, and drew a long breath. "I'm ready if you are.
My name is Gina and my parents were Sal and Elaine. I had
an older brother, Joey and he was *the best*. Anything Gina
wanted, Joey would try to get for her. All I had to do was just
say the word...." Rita eased back into the soft upholstery of
the couch and began to relax. "We lived in the foothills of the
Berkshire Mountains...."

Chapter 6

*T*he doors of the old stone school flew open and out
spilled waves of squealing children, like jellybeans
bursting onto the floor from a dropped jar. Although not
as vibrant as jellybeans in their mundane Catholic school
uniforms, collectively they formed sweeping mosaics of
color: blonds, redheads and brunettes in bright hand-knit caps,
mufflers and mittens to help guard against the biting New
England chill of early winter. Eight-year-old Gina stopped
short at the base of the mountainous carved-stone stairs to look
for her brother. The children split in every direction around
her like the waters of a stream around a big rock. "Joe-weee,"
she squeaked as fifteen-year-old Joey's angelic face appeared
through the swarm, his deep blue eyes and shock of black hair
a beacon in a crowd of blurred faces. He smacked his palms

together and opened his arms to catch Gina's embrace. Today Joey was dispatched to meet his sister after school and she looked forward to it all day, like a teenaged girl waiting for her date. Their parents needed to go into Hartford to see a doctor; Dad had a bad back and needed a specialist's advice. Joey high-tailed it across town in a half hour to be sure he would get to Gina's school from his high school in time. Gina loves spending time with Joey. *He is so fun*, she thinks, and he treats her like his buddy, not like a pesky little sis. Joey was almost exactly seven years older than Gina, and they were both Cancers. Joey reminded her about their common astrological sign whenever their birthdays neared, but it was years before Gina would understand what that meant. A few years prior to having Gina, Elaine had carried another girl, but miscarried at about five months.

Usually, Joey meeting her after school meant a walk downtown before heading home. They often snuck down the hill from school to share an orange soda at Tony's Lunch. An extra treat was visiting with their easy-going Uncle Jake who worked an extra part-time job there as a short-order cook. Joey's friends often joined them as they walked the long Main Street together, while they talked, joked and shoved one another. At a mere fifteen years of age, the boys seemed like towering skyscrapers, and they treated Gina the same way as Joey treated her: she was their *pal*. Today, there they all stood, with broad smiles, hands in their pockets. "Gia, Gino, Gee," they all greeted Gina in their usual, big brotherly ways, tapping Gina on her shoulders, tugging her thick braided pigtails, or lightly smacking her hands with theirs. Most of Joey's friends had younger siblings that either were in Gina's class or were close to her age. Today, there was Neil: tall and friendly, with generous lips and wavy brown hair. Another Joe, who lived right down the street, often had his two boxers in tow. He was much more serious looking than her Joey, with a pouty mouth, crew-cut hair and warm, brown eyes. Gina would look dreamily at Joe's face and then to the mugs of his dogs. It was like looking at a father and his children, their expressions seemed so much alike. Occasionally, he would surrender the two dog leashes to Gina, who pretended she was an Egyptian princess walking down Main Street with her two wolfhounds. It was always debatable who was walking who, however. Joe Flaherty's mom was Italian and his dad, Irish.

And then there was Francesco. Frankie. Gina idolized Frankie almost as much as she did Joey. Frankie and Joey were into weight lifting, and they mail-ordered magazines to learn how. Many of the books they ordered were advertised on the backs of comic books. The magazines featured Charles Atlas and his weight lifting techniques. Frankie had dark brown hair, the sides of which were slicked close with pomade, but curly on the top. He had the same olive skin as Joey and Gina, and his smile seemed brilliant and perfect to Gina. Gina knew that if she could marry someone like Joey someday that it *had* to be Frankie. He stepped forward and picked Gina up at the waist and kissed her squarely on the nose. This prompted Gina to dramatically swoon as she always did when Frankie kissed her, and well practiced, Joey caught Gina as she fell limp backwards into his arms. They all laughed at this game that they played time and time again. Secretly for Gina, it was no game. She was crazy about Frankie!

Today, Joey and Gina had to go straight home, set the table and get stuff ready for dinner. Elaine had the dinner prepared and all Joey had to do was put it in the oven and keep an eye on it. It was pretty cold out, so the walk up Main Street would have to wait for a warmer day.

"Gee, instead of walkin all the way around the block, let's take the shortcut through the woods," Joey whispered in Gina's ear, carefully balancing on a bent knee.

Gina pursed her lips out far. "No, Joey. Dad says that if he finds out we walk through the woods, he'll kick our asses!" She slapped her cupped hand to her mouth and, wide-eyed, looked around her to be sure there were no nuns within earshot. Joey and Gina giggled, their cold, red noses almost touching. They waved their goodbyes over their shoulders to Joey's friends, and Joey held Gina's hand as they walked Oak Street toward home. They ran along the side of the convent close to the school, and entered the edge of the small wooded area that populated the middle of the block separating their street from that of the school's. With winter's grey sky looming, the woods could be dark and ominous in the fall. But it was only three o'clock, so it was plenty light out.

Joey asked Gina about her day. Even at eight, she marveled at why he would give a rat's ass about her third-grade day. But she told him anyway because he seemed so interested. Today, she let her classmate, Kevin read her essay before the class began to give oral presentations. Kevin had begged Gina to let him take a look as he had forgotten about the assignment, or so he said. The teacher was out of the room and the moment before Kevin tried to hand the essay back, the nun re-entered. Instead of putting it aside, Kevin rose and read Gina's essay as his own, to the high praise of the teacher. Gina squinted her eyes at Kevin when he returned to his seat, and now she was in the uncomfortable position of making something up when it was her turn. She had a few minutes and hurriedly looked through her notebook for some notes that she had written on another topic before changing her mind and writing the finer essay that now sat on Kevin's desk. Gina stumbled through a mediocre and short essay, ad-libbing most of it. To her dismay, her teacher said: "Not bad, Gina, but you've written better." Gina mumbled, "yes, Ma'am," and took her seat, burning inside from shame and anger. She had worked hard on the essay that Kevin would get credit for. At recess, Kevin apologetically told Gina he was afraid of what the nun might do to them and said he thought he might as well read the essay when it was his turn. Gina's anger never lasted, and she always thought Kevin was a good soul who frequently needed help with English and Math. She told Joey all of what happened and how she felt about it.

"Geen, should I kick Kevin's ass for ya?" asked Joey.

"Naw, Joe. He didn't mean it. Kevin's okay."

The ground was rocky and they gingerly maneuvered through the thick carpet of colorful, fallen leaves so they wouldn't lose their footing. When they reached a familiar incline, Joey said: "You first, Gina. Hold one of your hands up, so's I can catch ya if you slip."

"Sure, Joey." Joey said the exact thing every time they reached that rocky incline. On the crest of that hill was a large rock that looked like the Rock of Gibraltar, with a concave plateau behind its peak. Gina and Joey sometimes hid there when playing hide-and-seek with other neighborhood kids, and they all called it "Tower Rock." Even though the terrain was very familiar, Gina was very careful. When she gently set one foot down, the ground seemed uncharacteristically soft and shaky. It rolled away from under her foot. Gina tumbled a few feet forward, scraping her hands slightly as she skidded to a halt. She bellowed when she realized that she had just stepped on a filthy, yawning hobo, who had been asleep in the leaves. He still had a bottle of cheap booze in one hand as he tried to sit up to see what all the commotion was about. Joey took one giant leap through the air, like he was playing Giant Steps. He scooped Gina up at the waist and ran through the woods with her under his arm, like a star quarterback with a football. Back in the woods, the drunk passed out again before he even knew what had transpired. Within ten seconds, Joey and Gina reached the edge of the woods directly across the street of their very own house. Joey set Gina down and looked at her hands, and wiped them with a hanky he pulled from his back pocket. "They're just dirty, Joe! That's all!" Breathless, they suddenly burst out laughing. Holding hands, Gina began jumping up and down. "That was fun, Joey!"

"That's my girl!" boasted Joey, and after looking both ways across the street, they high-tailed it up the steep stone stairs and onto the front porch of their house. After watching Jeopardy! hosted by Art Fleming, they obediently did as Sal and Elaine had instructed: put the meal into the oven, took a quick bath, changed into pajamas and did homework at the kitchen table. When Gina was finished, she and Joey looked at a book about horses that he had gifted her with last Christmas. Like so many little girls, Gina loved horses.

Soon, the familiar sound of Sal's Dodge rumbled up the driveway. Sal and Elaine entered through their back door, their smiling faces ruddy from the cold of the early evening. They were chattering happily and Gina could see that they carried three brown paper bags sporting the G. Fox & Co. logo, the largest department store in Hartford. That meant surprises for both of the kids. In one hand, Sal balanced a flat box that wafted the aroma of Franklin Avenue Pizza. It was like Christmas again for a few minutes while Gina tore into a smaller bag that Elaine had handed off to her. Squealing with complete delight, she pulled out a white leather Carnaby Street cap with a small, white rabbit fur ball at the top. Gina posed for Joey by putting her fisted hands under her chin. "Look, Joe, look!"

"I see ya, Sugar!" Joey said, smiling his biggest smile.

"Here, Charles Ass-less!" exclaimed Elaine as she handed Joey his bag. "You're so hard ta buy for, so I gotcha another pair of the blue jeans you like so much. There's some new t-shirts and winter socks in there, too, Honey."

"Thanks, Ma!"

To Gina, Elaine was like an angel. Dark haired, but pale and porcelain-skinned, she was short, robust and bosomy. Her eyes were fawn-brown, and her eyebrows light. Gina used to look at her in awe and wonder if she would ever sprout such breasts as Elaine had, but Gina clearly did not want them. A chip off the old man's block, Gina would inherit Sal's frame, which was slim and somewhat muscular.

After slinging his worn, wool jacket over a kitchen chair, Sal veered it into the adjoining pantry to swig a snort of whiskey for a quick warm-up. His black hair was wavy and sprinkled with a bit of grey. Sal had eyes like black olives, and he had a classic Italian schnoz and full lips. "Ya do your homework, Gia?" he inquired with raised eyebrows. "I see dat horse book out again!" he grumbled sarcastically.

"Sure, Pop!"

"Gee did all her homework, and she did it right, Dad," Joey defended.

"There's more, Lady Geen!" continued Elaine.

Gina dove into the large bag like a pup digging for a bone, as half her body was immersed in the G. Fox bag. "Oh, my God, oh, my God!" Screaming, she pulled out a short pair of white leather boots with zippers up the back, and pointed toes. "Joe! Joe! *Look!* Go-go boots!" Jumping up and down, she threw her arms around Elaine's waist and they all laughed in unison.

"You can wear them to church with the hat and your nice tweed coat with the fur collar. How 'bout that?"

"Yes, yes, yes, yes, yes, Ma. Oh, thank you!" Gina beamed. Pulling them on, she bent backwards to zip them up.

"Hows abouts your Pop?"

Gina leapt into Sal's lap, and he tickled her until she almost wet her pants. Spastically kicking her legs, she was a sight in pink floral flannel pajamas, go-go boots and a newsboy cap with a fur ball on top. Life was not always ideal, money was *always* tight, and sometimes Dad drank a bit too much, but all in all, the Biancos were a happy bunch.

"But Joey. He was the center of my universe," whispered Rita to Carolyn and Franco. "Even when he had girlfriends, he included me in lots of things. He called me Audrey sometimes. Said I looked liked a mini-Audrey Hepburn. He was my life at that time, always there when I needed him."

Chapter 7

Months and years swirled like leaves in a whirlpool. Gina and Joey remained closely bonded. As the holidays neared, Joey carefully scrutinized the TV Guide to be sure they wouldn't miss their favorite old holiday movie: *It's a Wonderful Life*, with Jimmy Stewart and Donna Reed. The Bianco family would sit and watch the movie together, as if it was the first time. The Biancos did not miss doing this one family activity together for nearly ten years straight. Throughout the previous week, they reminded each other of the movie's date. When the evening finally arrived, they sat like four ducks in a row on the sofa and all talked at the same time like the animated Sicilian-Americans that they were. On Thanksgiving morning, they watched Macy's parade on TV, and at Christmastime, they loved the holiday movies.

Joey always sat next to Gina with his arm around her shoulder. As the movie flickered on their teeny black and white television, she sometimes rested her head in Joey's lap. One of Gina's favorite scenes was when the characters George Bailey and Mary admire the moon during a leisurely walk home from a dance. Like clockwork, Joey would turn to Gina and mimic George Bailey's question: "Would you like the moon, Gina? Just say the word, and I'll lasso it for you!"

He tickled his giggling sister who breathlessly replied, "No, Joey. Lasso me a horse, pulll-leaze!" Life just couldn't be better than when she was with Joey.

Joey was a hard worker who saved almost every penny in anticipation for the day he would turn sixteen, so that he could get his driver's license and buy a car. While waiting to be of age to get a real job, he baby-sat neighbors' kids when he could, but mostly earned his booty by doing odd jobs. In the winter months, Joey shoveled a lot of snow. During the spring and summer, he mowed lawns and painted houses. When Gina was on summer vacation, she was usually in tow. Shortly after his sixteenth birthday, Joey earned his driver's license. The following week he drove up the Bianco driveway in a 1960 Chevy Impala. On that very day, something stirred in Gina and her love affair with vintage cars began. The Impala's skin was burgundy metallic, and it glittered much the way Gina's eyes did that very first moment she saw it. The upholstery was done in a burgundy and cream houndstooth fabric, with wide burgundy leather trim. The floor and doors were covered with burgundy carpet. Beholding the Impala was like love at first sight for both Gina and Joey. Immediately after showing his new wheels off to his folks, Joey pulled Gina into the car and off they glided to the Dairy Queen, near the town green.

If Joey's jobs were too physical or lengthy, Gina sometimes spent the day with her maternal grandparents, the Francovillas. Gina adored Sophia and Federico. Her grandparents lived literally on the "other side of the tracks," one block parallel and above the railroad tracks. The pleasant and modest neighborhood street was a dead-end. Gina had spent many spring and summer hours sitting on the guard-rails across the street to watch the trains below them come and go. When she slept over, she dozed off to the slow rumblings of the trains.

In Gina's eyes, her grandparents were the perfect married couple, even though their years together had been marred by hardship. Sophia and Federico bore their cloaks well, and weathered storms as a team. Even though they loved each other, Sal and Elaine seemed flawed in comparison. Gina's parents argued too much in her view. Her dad was sometimes harsh to her mother in the presence of others, which made Gina burn inside. At other times, she would catch glimpses of Sal grabbing Elaine's ass as her mother washed dinner dishes. Sal and Elaine would collectively order Gina to pay attention to her homework, while the couple continued giggling at the kitchen sink.

Of course, her grandparents were older, quieter, and in reality they simply did not have the energies of their younger counterparts. They seemed ageless and Gina never tired of the story of how they met and married, and their years growing up on Sicily. Grandma was still girlishly petite, wore her short hair crimped, and her skin seemed consistently radiant. Gina knew she had been a very handsome-looking woman in her youth from pictures that Elaine had at home. In Gina's mind, her nonna had drop-dead, movie star high cheekbones.

Sophia often smelled of Estée Lauder Youth Dew perfume and spearmint gum.

A sharp contrast to Sophia, Grandpa was quite tall. He shared a similar bone structure and also had high cheekbones, and hands that looked gigantic to Gina. For an Italian born around 1895, he was considered tall. Federico had been a coal miner in Pennsylvania after first arriving in America with his bride. Life dealt him many blows along the way, including injuries, black lung disease, and two strokes by the age of forty-nine. Now, her grandparents were both missing a couple of teeth here and there, but they still managed to keep a face on around Gina, even if their day was difficult. The Francovillas were amused by Gina's undying interest in their youth. Sophia indulged her with stories of her great-grandfather's olive orchard, and told Gina that he was a major exporter of olive oil to the southern mainland for many years. In those days, goods could only be transported from Sicily by boat, so it was an expensive venture. The Esparenzzas lived comfortably. Young Sophia was tutored by her older stepsister, who had studied in Brindissi. Few Sicilian girls were educated early in the twentieth century, but Gina's maternal grandmother was well-read, remaining so throughout her lifetime.

"My grandmother served a rather bland white cake that she designed especially for my grandfather. He couldn't eat certain foods due to the circulation problems from his strokes and such. She drizzled a little bit of liquid frosting on it, to sweeten it up. He was a semi-invalid. His left arm didn't function well. He walked with a limp and had to drag one of his legs, also his left side, I think." She paused thoughtfully and continued, "Ya know, I loved that cake. I loved just being there, cuz I was with *them*! Nothing else mattered." Rita glowed and smiled broadly. "Then, my Nonna Sophia would sit down facing me at their kitchen table and begin *the* story. Grandpa sat at the far end of the table slowly rocking in a rocking chair, with sleepy eyes. I would eat my cake, drink a glass of milk and listen...."

"Your grandpa wassa my brother Alessandro's besta friend. Grandpa cumma to the orchard to work when he was twelve, ter-teen. I, I-uh, eighta, nine-uh."

"She looked like she had a camera filter over her face. It was soft and glowing. Like in the movies, know what I mean?"

"Every day, every day, he atta our house. He eat-uh breakfast and dinner. Every day. My brother and him treata me sometimes like a bother-uh. Cap-eesh? But I sit across the tabla, and we look, and we look." Sophia gestured her hands, palms open, finger spread wide. *"Ma-róna! You grandpa become a very handsumma man one day. Always take-uh the hat off when I come outside. Smile-uh nice. I thinka, whattsa matter for him?"*

"We all laughed out loud at that part, every time."

*"He poor, mia papa petty rich. Papa invite boysa for
me to have dinner at home, go for walk, with papa behind.
He always telluh me 'if you no like-uh, okay, you justa tell
me, they come no more.' I no like. No like no-body." Sophia
winked to a riveted Gina. "My girlafriends in the vill-aug,
very jealouso! Sometimes, they marry who the papa e mama
say. Some happy, some sad, some fall in love-uh with the
husband, some not. Me, me I was looky. I choos-uh if I like.
But I no like-uh nobody. I like-uh Grandpa. Now we sit across
the table again, and we look." The old woman put her pointed
index finger against her lips. "See-ka-ret. Your grandpa save
his money for a lonnng time. Well, maybe one more yeara -
- seem like a very long time. He go to my father-uh, show the
money and say, mio e Sophia in love-uh. He say at the dinner
table, ev-er-ee buddy there-uh."*

"She sometimes took both my hands in hers. She
would look so solemn then. What an actress!"

*"Then, my papa, so seri-o-so, say 'whatta take-uh you
so longa?!' Oh boy-uh, we all laugh! Two weeks, we marry.
In my vill-auga, everybody come-uh. Beautiful. Beautiful."
Sophia cocked her head smartly, proudly. As is in mock prayer,
Sophia extended her clasped hands out in front of her, and
giddily exclaimed, "Thank you, the God! So beeee-autiful!"*

"Each and every time she told that story, my grandfather would slowly open his eyes when she was finished. He'd have this shit-ass grin on his face, and slowly turn that lit-up face toward my grandmother and their eyes would lock. I saw them just the way they looked in the old photos at home: young, hardy, smiling and with teeth, even!" Her eyes moist, Rita chuckled. Talking about these two people put Rita back in time with her grandparents for a few moments. "They were my buds. I sure miss them. I knew from the time I was very small that they shared the love like a man and a woman *could* share. You know, the whole package: friendship, commitment, respect. All they had to do was be each other's most treasured friend. That's something that has eluded me my entire life." Rita shrugged her shoulders, and cast her gaze downward, laughing. "Oh well. Thought I had love like that in my hands once, maybe twice, but it slipped through my fingers." Shaking her head she continued, "My grandparents deserved a much easier life than what they got dealt, but they held onto their friendship."

The sweetness of this story prompted Carolyn and Franco to exchange glances lovingly. Rita turned toward the window and the beautiful fall day beyond it. Wistfully, she sighed, "Never got tired of Grandma's story, *or* that cake. Never."

Chapter 8

*E*ven though Joey always had lots of girlfriends, when I was thirteen and Joey was twenty, there was a really special one for him. He loved Yvonne totally. It was obvious to everyone. Mom and Dad loved her, too."

During the summer months and especially on the weekends when Joey wasn't working, he and Yvonne often took Gina along on outings with them. In Gina's mind, she was still Joey's girl. Gina liked Yvonne a lot; she was smart, pretty and fun to be with, like Joey. In typical 1970's fashion, Yvonne wore her shoulder-length chestnut hair parted down the middle. She had a strong jaw and deep green eyes that twinkled when she smiled or laughed. *They twinkle a lot*, Gina

would think. She was the big sister that Gina would never
have, and she loved Yvonne almost as much as she loved Joey.
The three of them spent quite a lot of time at the lake close by,
where Grandma Bianco owned a small ramshackle seasonal
cottage.

In the spring the cottage smelled especially musty,
so Grandma Bianco aired it out and rolled up her sleeves.
Grandma would do a lot of housecleaning, and brought along
her cat, Booty, to do the "mouse cleaning." When asked why
the cat's name was Booty, Nonna Bianco would laugh and
say: "He keepa my foota warm at night, like a nice-uh baby
booty! Capisce?" True to feline tradition, Booty frequently
presented flattened versions of field mice to his mistress, who
laughed uproariously when she discovered her small trophies.
The grey/black Persian mix was clearly in mouse-hunting
heaven in the springtime! Nonna would simply bend down
with dustpan and brush in hand to gleefully whisk away the
prizes and dispose of them in the trash. Praising the cat in half
Italian, half English, she would open up a can of moist cat food
for Booty's reward.

"Pavlov had nothing on Grandma Bianco," winked
Rita. "She had the theory of positive reinforcement perfected
long before he arrived on the scene!"

Unlike Grandma Francovilla, Grandma Bianco was
brash and loud, but in a fun way. She was also short, but had
a round bottom and big breasts. She liked to attract attention,
and paid little or no attention to what others thought of her

frequent show-offy behavior. A stark contrast to Nonna Sophia, Concetta grew up dirt-poor and came to America to eventually make a small fortune with her husband by opening the first liquor store in their small town, attractively located centrally on Main Street. Her husband, Gina's Grandpa Sebastian, had been killed in a tragic car wreck just a few months before Gina's birth. Two years after his death, a flood swept the liquor store and several houses now owned solely by Grandma Bianco away from the riverfront where they stood. However unfortunate, this sequence of events left the widow in a financially comfortable position, and she wanted for nothing. Her days were spent performing personal pleasantries like gardening the front yard of the Bianco home, or sharing coffee and biscotti with her cronies. Gina loved her loud laughter and cocky attitude and used to think of her two grandmothers as "the angel grandma, and the devil grandma." Though she would always be closer to Sophia, Gina loved the two women equally. Nonna Concetta had an apartment in the Bianco home, which she co-owned with Sal, but not with Elaine. This had been a thorn in Elaine's side, but she saw it for what it was, a control game. She basically looked the other way, but the topic had been a source of heated debate between Sal and Elaine over the years. Elaine, always the good sport, curbed her tongue overall, as not to burden Gina and Joey with adult stresses.

Gina did not go everywhere with Joey and Yvonne. She was relegated to staying at home on most Saturday nights with Elaine and Sal, which she did anyway before Joey met Yvonne. When Joey was out with Yvonne, Gina felt pangs of jealously followed by guilt. Deep inside her heart, Gina knew that Yvonne loved Joey like she did, and it all suddenly

felt right again. Almost thirteen, Gina daydreamed of the day
that Joey and Yvonne would marry. One particular weekend
in February, Joey and Yvonne were on a road trip to Daytona
Beach, Florida, and bound for the Daytona 500. That very
same weekend, Mom and Dad went out to eat at a restaurant,
with two other couples -- a treat that was rare for Sal and
Elaine. When they did, Gina was free to watch any TV
program that *she* wanted. This time, she was feeling jealous
and sorry for herself, and was glad to be by herself.

Elaine had twisted Sal's arm hard enough to go out to
see a movie, after the dinner. She grated on her husband all
week, saying that everyone in town was talking about the film.
The film was adapted from a currently popular book, authored
by an Italian. "Come on, Sal. Pull-leaze, I want to see it! "
Sal told Elaine to go with a girl friend, but they had all seen the
movie, some with their husbands. Finally, her dad agreed.

Leisurely, Gina did some schoolwork while watching
TV. Concetta crossed the hall to invite her reluctant
granddaughter to watch The Lawrence Welk Show at her place.
As a child, Gina and Joey watched TV with their grandmother
on a regular basis, but the old woman didn't seem to notice
that the children now had their own interests. This didn't deter
Concetta, who asked Gina to dance with her like she did as a
little girl. Gina thought this hilarious, but dancing with her
grandmother was still fun and it made her grandmother happy.

After the program ended, Gina kissed her nonna
goodnight, and excused herself to resume her schoolwork. Her
heart definitely not into the task, she dozed lightly on the living
room sofa with the TV on. She woke up craving a sandwich
and a glass of milk, and so headed for the kitchen just in time
to hear the slamming of car doors beyond the back door. Mom

and Dad were home from the movie. Gina was carefully pouring milk into a glass, when the couple entered the kitchen, and she immediately sensed their tenseness. She smirked to herself: *They're at it again. The Honeymooners. Always arguing and making up!* As she stepped through the doorway, Elaine's head rotated toward Gina, a deer-in-the-headlights look on her angelic face. Sal followed close behind, looking as red-faced as a cartoon character Gina had seen on TV many times. The cartoon version of Sal's face would turn red like a rising thermometer, and when the mercury reached its peak, the character's eyes bulged straight out of his face, steam burst out of his ears and the sound akin to a train's whistle could be heard. Gina kept a straight face, but inside she humorously braced herself for whatever comical drama Elaine and Sal were about to reveal.

"Geen, dis guy lit a smoke in the theater tonight! Durin the movie! Can ya believe it?"

"Ya used to be able ta smoke at the movies!" barked Sal.

"Pop, they stopped letting people do that in the movies about ten years ago. Too dangerous!"

Sarcastically chiming in, Elaine said, "Well, that would be about the last time your father took me to a show!" Elaine rolled her eyes. Sal grumbled something in Italian, *probably a swear*, Gina thought.

Gina pretended to be focusing on putting together her sandwich. After dabbing mayonnaise on it, she carefully dragged the knife across her tongue.

Elaine screamed, "Don't be puttin' the knife in your mouth like that, Gina! Just like your bru-tha!"

I hope so. Hope I'm just like Joey, Gina thought

bemused.

Suddenly, Sal blurted, "I *had* to have a cig! Shit! I can't believe that actresses bare their breasts in the movies now."

Wow! thought Gina. *He forgot I was here!*

"And, the way they played Sicilians! We're not *all* murdering crooks!" Sal stomped away toward the pantry for his "medicine."

Pop is so easily offended. He really needs to get out more.

Even more sarcastically this time, Elaine retorted: "Huh! Men have been showin their boobs for years. What's all the fuss?"

Gina managed to keep her expressions in check through most of the insult exchange. Secretly, she and friend Maria begged a movie usher to let them in an exit door. The rating was PG-17, and it was necessary to be accompanied to the movie by an adult. The usher was Kevin, who long ago borrowed an essay from Gina. She had reminded him of that and other kindnesses she had shown him. Kevin relented, but Gina and Maria were confined to the closed-off balcony and had to stay there for the duration of the movie. Gina left the theater wondering why she didn't know about this secret Sicilian life, the Mafia.

Elaine and Gina exchanged half-smiles and sideways glances, Elaine shrugging her shoulders on her way to her bedroom. Soon after, they all prepared for bed, Sal methodically checked the locks on the doors, and turned off all of the lights.

"Thought I was dreaming at first. The phone ringing in the middle of the night seemed so loud. I couldn't understand what was going on at first...."

Gina toddled to the door of her bedroom, and cracked it open. In the subdued light, she could see her parents huddling near the wall phone in the kitchen. Her father looked totally pissed off! Elaine, who was actually on the phone, looked oddly serene next to Sal, his face bright red with anger. Gina then realized Elaine was speaking to Joey! "Okay, Honey, I understand. Yes, your dad is right here. He says that as long as the two of you are sure." Sal tried to grab the phone from Elaine and they struggled with the receiver momentarily like two small children fighting for a toy. Elaine smacked Sal's arm hard and he looked even angrier. Next, Gina heard her own name, followed by Elaine saying, "Honey, she's asleep in her bed." Elaine turned slowly toward the door of Gina's bedroom to discover her daughter's sleepy face suspended there. Her mom held the receiver out to Gina, who burst out forward. She sensed something serious and exciting was going on. Gina looked at the receiver in her hand and slowly drew the cradle to her ear.

"Joey? You okay there, Joe? Yvonne okay, Joey?" she was a bit frightened and breathless. Her fear melted with the sound of Joey's easygoing laugh.

"Baby, Joey is just fine. Yvonne is fine, too. When we come home in a few days, we'll have a big surprise for you, Gee! You'll see!"

"Did you buy me a horse, Joey? What is it?"

"Geez. No horse! But you'll like the surprise, I

promise." Gina could hear Yvonne close to the receiver and giggling giddily. In her mind's eye she could see Yvonne's eyes twinkling. Gina felt relieved. What could the surprise be?

"Come on, Joe! Tell. Tell me the surprise."

"No, Doll. Mom and Dad are not going to tell, either. You'll have to wait to hear it from me, okay, Gina?"

"Oh-kay," Gina yawned into the phone, feigning great disappointment.

"Gee?"

"Yeah, Joey?"

"You're still my girl, too. You know that, right? Even if I have a daughter one day, you and Yvonne will always be my girls. Right?"

"Sure, Joey," Gina nodded sheepishly. But in her mind she was thinking: *but I was here first!* "Night, Joey. I love you."

"Night, Audrey. Love you, too."

Gina plodded back to her room and flopped down on her bed. She could feel her heart beating excitedly in her chest, and could not fall back to sleep. Tomorrow was Sunday. She only had to deal with church and homework, so if she was a little tired, at least she wasn't at school.

The days following passed slowly for Gina. She tapped her fingers impatiently on her desk each day at school, to the chagrin of the nun who gently put her hand on Gina's fingers. Sister Frances Teresa smiled into Gina's face. "Something the matter, Miss Bianco?"

"Oh no, Sister. Well, yes, Sister." Gina stuttered. "Just waiting for my brother to get back from Florida with a surprise for me."

"Oh," cooed the sister, her face beaming with understanding. The nun knew Joey and had been his eighth grade teacher as well. "While you're waiting for Joseph Bianco to return, I'd like you to keep the fingers still. Can you do that?"

"Yes, Ma'am." Self-consciously, Gina folded her hands on her desk.

Each day, when the dismissal bell rang, Gina skyrocketed out of the school's doors until she reached the sidewalk. It was the first week of March and snow swirled around her as she panned the curb and streets. Each day, Joey was a no-show. *Well, Joey must have gone back to work today. He'll be at the house later.*

But Joey didn't appear in the evening, either. Gina ate quietly while her parents bickered during dinner for the next several days. Generally, they made light conversation, but the air was thick while everyone waited for Joey to make an entrance. Elaine's face looked worn yet glowing at the same time. Gina was entirely baffled. Sal looked angry; Mom looked like an angel. What *is* this daunting surprise? *Joey said that they wouldn't tell, so they already knew the secret surprise.*

Sal would say to Elaine: "Ahm gonna kill dat kid," and Elaine would snap: "No you're not gonna do nuttin, Sal. Cap-eesh? They love each other. Joey's so smart and already has a good job. They'll be just fine." Elaine would smile and say: "Think about what's comin, ya know? It's part of life, it'll be good." This would calm Sal for a while, but didn't lessen Gina's confusion. Her parents sometimes spoke distastefully about Yvonne's family and this confused Gina further. Whenever they saw Yvonne's family at church, everyone was

all smiles, but today it was more like: "The dad is a pretty good
Joe, but the mu-tha. She thinks her shit don't stink because
they have money. And that long hair and those big picture
hats; she thinks she's Veronica Lake, or somethin." Elaine
never spoke ill of anyone, this type of comment shocked Gina.
"She's too old to wear her hair long, like that."

But they adored Yvonne, and for Gina: that's all that
counted.

The sound of Joey's Impala coming up the driveway
on the side of the house crisply sliced the thickness of the air.
Everyone jumped like they were electrically shocked, leaping
to their feet, bumping into each other. The Biancos looked like
The Three Stooges trying to get out of each other's way. They
stood at the back door, three heads arranged at the left of the
doorjamb. All were nervously smiling, but their faces dropped
when Joey's solemn face appeared in the screen door of the
porch. For a split second, Gina thought Joey looked like a
black-haired James Dean. Without stepping into the house, her
brother stood on the back porch. Joey and Gina's eyes locked.
Joey looks sad, Gina thought. *I thought this surprise was
going to be a good surprise, that I'd like it.*

"Sorry, Gee. I got nuttin for ya. It was a mistake.
Please don't be mad at Joey, okay?" He flashed that sweet
smile that calmed Gina.

Gina jumped forward into Joey's arms. "It's okay,
Joey. Just want to see you. I don't care 'bout no surprise."
She wrapped her arms tight around his neck. Relaxing his
grasp, Joey let Gina slip to the floor and looked down into her
face.

"That's my girl. Go inside, Honey. Joey has to talk to
Mom and Dad."

"No, Joey! Ahm stayin right here. I'm part of this family, too," protested Gina, returning to Elaine's side.

"Go in the house like your brother says!" bellowed Sal, and Elaine and Gina bent backwards slightly like tall reeds caught in a sudden windstorm.

"No, boys. Gina is right. She's not a baby, anymore." Elaine's voice was soothing. She put her arm around Gina and held her close to her side. "Shoot, Joseph. What happened?"

Looking numb, Joey quietly said, "Her mom talked her out of it. She's going to college in New York, as planned."

Elaine gasped and jerked with surprise. *What the hell is going on?* "But what about the...?" Sal was now holding a furious Elaine back for a change! *What the hell?* Gina's brain felt as though it was taking a spin in the Waring Blender that sat on the kitchen counter.

No one moved an inch. Joey looked as though he might cry and Gina had *never* seen Joey cry, not once. Joey finally said: "Her mom convinced her to give it up." He slowly turned and left, driving off just as slowly as he had arrived. Her parents silently collapsed into porch chairs, holding hands. The screen door slammed hard behind Gina as she burst through it. She ran behind the Impala, but Joey's car turned the corner of the house and disappeared down the driveway.

Poor Joey. Poor Yvonne. Gina's insides began to boil. *That long-haired bitch with the big hats! Damn her. I will never go to ten-thirty Mass again, or I might have to hit her,* Gina thought.

Sadness pummeled the Bianco family again late that summer, as Grandma Concetta died suddenly after suffering a severe stroke and heart attack. Even at such a young age,

Gina could see how her grandmother's death greatly saddened her father. For the first time in her young life, she understood grief. She missed her grandmother and she missed Yvonne, too. She felt sure Yvonne would show up at their door one day with an infant. But as autumn turned into winter again, there was no word from Yvonne, either.

"I saw Yvonne only once again, just for a few seconds, in church," Rita stammered. "She wrote to me a couple of times from school in New York City after she took a year off to travel in Europe. She wasn't in fucking Europe," Rita said, sputtering sarcastically. "The following year, she sent me a freshman year photo, very seventies preppy. Private girls' college. Her hair was pulled back into a low ponytail and she was smiling. She had such nice teeth. But the twinkle in her eyes was gone. She had given the twinkle away. My brother did not smile again for a very long time, not like he used to. Even though he was always good to me and Mom, he seemed to hate women for a while. He partied a lot, drank, too. He changed girlfriends frequently. It hurt my parents to see him like that. Joey was tough, but was wounded and trying to hide it. Word had gotten back to us that the baby was a boy...."

Rita's eyes cast up and down, left to right, trying to avoid Carolyn's gaze, concentrating hard not to cry again. "I had my eighth grade graduation shortly after and turned fourteen. Joey started dropping by after work more often after that, and said he was thinking about enlisting. Mom and Dad went crazy and argued with Joey each time he brought it up. I don't know, maybe he thought he'd see Yvonne again, but her parents made sure that she stayed in New York and away from town."

"Enlist and join which branch of the service?" asked Franco.

"Army. Like Pop," Rita quietly replied. "The Vietnam 'Conflict,'" she spit forth distastefully. "When his number didn't come up in the draft, he enlisted. Was at Fort Dix, New Jersey for basic training. He called every week. Some of his unit went to Mannheim, but Joey went to 'Nam. We found out later that he lied to us about that, and volunteered for a tour of duty there. We thought he was just following orders. He came home for a couple of weeks before being deployed...."

The two weeks were filled with lots of activity at home. Elaine cooked for several days before Joey traveled up from New Jersey. He looked so handsome in uniform, but he quickly hung his clothes in the closet in favor of his civilian uniform of jeans and t-shirts. Lots of people came by to visit and the house was filled with the smell of coffee and baked goods. Frankie and the other boys were over a lot and it felt like a reunion of sorts for Gina, too. Still tomboyish, she was blossoming into a pretty, young woman. Elaine always was nearby when the boys were around, and tickling and sitting on the boys' laps was somehow no longer permitted. This perplexed Gina, but orders from Elaine were never challenged. She asked why after one visit, and all Elaine would say was "Never you mind, Girlie. You listen to me." Obediently, Gina would always reply, "Sure, Ma."

The two weeks flew by and Joey was busy, but still tried to spend time with Gina. On his very last day, they drove to the lake where he, Yvonne and Gina spent a lot of

time together, not even two years earlier. Even though the
water was cold, they swam anyway. On the other side of the
bay from Grandma Bianco's cottage, was a gargantuan oak
tree with a thick, knotted rope hanging from it. It loomed
precariously on a rocky slope and over a deep inlet of water.
On orders from Sal, it was taboo for his kids to swim there
when they were younger. Joey somehow managed to sneak
Gina to the tree without the elder Bianco's knowledge. Joey
and Gina spent over an hour taking turns swinging from the
tree Tarzan-style and then plummeting into the water. Joey
would go first and watch his little sister navigate her course,
prompting her to let go of the rope at the right moment. Gina's
lips were turning blue after that long hour, so Joey guided his
sister up the rocky embankment. "Okay, Babe. That's enough
for today, we gotta go. You know Ma's cooking a big dinner
and she'll be mad if we're late!"

"We're gonna catch hell anyway for going swimming,
Joe!"

"No, we're not. That's why we're getting out of the
water early and we'll sit in the sun for a while to dry your hair,
okay?" Anything Joey said was okay with Gina. Anything.
"Joey will stand by the car while you dress and we'll put our
clothes back on to warm up. You and I are going to have our
first serious talk, too! You're almost an adult, Gee." Joey
was smiling broadly, which put Gina's fears to rest, but
she wondered what the topic might be. Sex? *Oh, please.
Someone talk to me about it.* Elaine would never discuss it,
even when Gina asked her. Elaine's response was always
really a question, and not an answer: "Why do you want to
know that? Who you been talkin to?"

"Sure, Joe." Gina scrunched her wiry body down in

Joey's car to exchange her frigid swimsuit for some jeans and a long-sleeved t-shirt. Joey quickly took his turn to dress, while Gina leaned on the car facing away from Joey and toward the picture pretty lake that she loved so much. "Joe, what you gonna talk to me about? Come on, Joey," Gina called over her shoulder to Joey, as he zipped up his jeans.

"Important stuff, Sis. When I come back, you and I are going to have a mission of our own. You and me, it'll be our secret."

That was all Gina had to hear to become totally excited and animated. She clapped her hands together. *Joey is always so fun.* Impatient, she jumped up and down as if on a pogo-stick. "Hurr-reee up, Joey! Come on. I want to know what the mission is!"

"Okay, okay, okay. Keep your shirt on, will ya?" Gina giggled at that remark as she had heard Joey and his buddies repeat it many times over the years. Joey slammed the car door behind him while pulling on his shirt. "Let's sit over there on that bench." Crossing his legs, Joey sat and spread his arms across the back of the park bench. Gina sat off to his side and stared hard toward Joey's profile. He was pretending that she was not there. Gina suddenly smacked Joey's shoulder.

"What? Why'd ya do that, Gee?"

"Joey! Shit or get off the pot!" They broke into hysterical laughter. Joey was holding one of Gina's skinny hands. "What's the mission? Huh, Joey?!" Gina expected an imaginary mission from Joey, like a fun excursion.

With a whimsical Mona Lisa expression, Joey looked into Gina's face. "Come mere, gimme the towel!" Joey draped the towel around Gina's small head and gently toweled dried her hair. The smile seriously softened. "Baby, did you understand what was going on after I came back from Florida?"

"Come on, Joe. Course I do." *Oh, no! This might really turn out to be a sex talk. Oh, God! I thought we were going to talk about something fun!*

"When I come back, you and Joey are going to find that boy."

Gina flung the towel away from her face with one hand. "Oh my God, oh my God, oh my God, Joey!" Clapping her hands again, she leapt off the bench and jumped up and down. "Yes, yes, yes!"

"Now, most guys would back off when something like this happens. But Joey didn't sign no adoption papers. I checked: my name is on the birth certificate, a matter of public record. Do you know what that means?"

"Kinda, Joey."

"Well, it means that anyone can see a paper record, like a birth certificate. The public, er, a citizen can see a document like that. Understand better? Not sure why, but Yvonne put my name on it. Maybe her ma wasn't lookin over her shoulder." Joey's eyes panned the lake waters as he spoke. Gina resumed looking at his profile again, but this time she did not goad him.

"I'll help you, Joey. How can I help?"

"I need you to be my cheerleader, and keep my secret. When I come back, Joey will talk to a lawyer. Don't tell Ma and Pop, though. This will be *our* mission, right?"

"Oh, Joey," Gina erupted with ecstasy. "I can't wait!"

"Good! After I'm back, I'm going to take my favorite girl into the city for Macy's parade when Thanksgiving comes. How bout it?"

"Yes, please." Gina kissed Joey's cheek hard and snuggled close as he wrapped his arm around her. *This time, I'll share a secret with Joey that Ma and Pop don't know about!* The siblings sat for several minutes in silence, looking out at the lake in the afternoon sunlight. Soon, it was time to head back to their house. Gina loved riding in the Impala with Joey; they laughed and sang along with the radio. That evening was filled with good food and more laughter. Friends dropped by to visit late into the evening, and Sal and Elaine allowed Gina to stay up. She wasn't a baby anymore, after all. She went to bed to the sound of hushed conversation and laughter, and happily drifted off. Elaine woke her at about five the next morning, just a few hours after she went to bed. Joey and Frankie had talked well into the night, but Gina knew it didn't matter for Joey. He would sleep on the train back to Fort Dix. Elaine guided her sleepy daughter out of her bedroom and into the dimly lit kitchen. Gina was cloaked in foggy inertness. Joey and Dad were drinking coffee and talking a mile a minute to each other, but in a jovial manner. Joey was so handsome in uniform. Gina trudged forth to fall into his waiting embrace. "Don't go, Joey!"

"Come on, now. You're a big girl now, Gina. Practically a woman. You *know* I gotta go." Joey pulled back slightly, his mouth at Gina's ear. "Remember, Gee. *The mission*. When I get back." He looked deep into her eyes and smiling, kissed her on the forehead. Without looking back, Joey headed for the back door kissing Elaine's wet cheek as he passed. He was followed by Sal, who did the same.

"I'll remember, Joey," Gina whispered, as she watched Joey disappear into the darkness.

Chapter 9

*I*t was a day that remained forever suspended in time for Gina. A Saturday in which the sunlight progressively rose to Gina's bedroom window, warming her face and waking her. She rolled onto her side to look at her alarm clock. Eighten. Smiling, her eyes moved upward along the contour of her bedroom wall to the calendar hanging there. September twenty-ninth was framed in red circles and smiley faces that Gina had authored there. Most of the calendar's day squares were crossed with X's marking days passed. Gina checked off the days leading to Joey's departure from Vietnam. That date would be followed by another week to be discharged from the Army. Twenty, twenty-two days from today, tops, and Joey would be home, before October's end.

Gina rolled back onto her pillow and stretched her

arms to her sides, basking in the glow of the early morning
Indian-summer sun. Even through her bedroom window, late
September in the Berkshire's foothills was a joy to behold.
The hillsides looked like raging forest fires, glowing orange
and red. The smell of brewing coffee drifted up the stairs and
Gina knew Sal was up and enjoying some. Yup! There was
the familiar hack of the smoker's cough. Smoking a cigarette
and sipping a cup of hot java, her father was no doubt reading
the morning paper. It was a welcome comfort to Gina, even
if her father was smoking in the house. Elaine loathed it, and
he rarely kept his promise to smoke on the porch. Gina could
hear Sal whistling quietly. Everyone was a little more relaxed,
they were now on home stretch until Joey could come home.

"Every day that passed was one more beautiful than
the day before, because it meant Joey's homecoming was
one day closer. It was torture waiting. Every night, the three
of us watched and listened while Walter Cronkite reported
the number of days of the war, then the number dead. We
shuddered and sometimes Mom and I cried. We was, er, *were*
scared all the time. That Saturday morning, I bathed and got
ready to cheer at the football game. Oh, my God, that was fun!
That day was our homecoming game. You know, a king and
queen, the whole nine... should I say, hundred yards?" Rita
giggled just thinking about the high school memory. "The
entire week we were busy at school making stuff for the big
game, and I daydreamed about the things I was going to make
to decorate the house for Joey's homecoming!"

The fun and festivities were a complete distraction for Gina. She walked to the high school, and the early afternoon air was still fragrant with the smell of wood stoves cooling after a brisk night. The day raced by. Before long, the half-time celebration portion came and went, and proved to be a smashing success. At the beginning of the fourth quarter, Gina noticed that a police car pulled up to the field's far end. She immediately recognized her dad's pal, police chief John Bartaloma when he stepped out from a police cruiser. Gina sometimes called him "Uncle John" whenever the Biancos and Bartalomas socialized.

It was not unusual for the local police to stop by the high school to watch football games. The weather was great and it was an opportunity to keep an eye on the pulse of the small community at every level. From the field bleacher where her cheering squad stood, Gina could see Chief Bartaloma's concerned look. Uncle John usually flashed a big grin when he was out and about, always approachable and warm. Today, he acknowledged no one as he strode steadily along the sidelines. Even more surprising to Gina was that he seemed riveted on her. Flashing an unacknowledged smile, she lost her concentration when the cop stopped about twenty yards from where she stood. The frenzied fanfare whirred around her: whistles blowing, the crowd cheering, the opposing team's quarterback scoring a touchdown.

Suddenly, the moment became eerily silent to only her. When John removed his sunglasses, Gina thought it looked as though he had been crying, but she shrugged it off in an instant. Then she realized: *He **has** been crying. Oh, no! Mom and Dad!* was the first thought in her mind. In the distance, Gina saw her father alight from the police cruiser,

his face red, his breath sputtering. He was dabbing his eyes
with a hankie when Elaine materialized from behind him,
burying her reddened face in the side of Sal's chest without
looking up at Gina. Gina thought she might faint as she felt
the blue and gold pom-poms fall away from her limp hands,
and took backward steps away rather than toward them. John
Bartaloma moved faster toward her now, but Gina turned
and ran, sprinting down the hill from the school. Crossing
streets, ignoring the traffic lights, she pressed forward:
running, running, running. She ran across the railroad tracks
behind the A&P market and up the steep embankment to her
grandparents' street. Panting heavily, she literally fell through
the back kitchen door of her grandparents' house. Once
inside, there was no denying what had happened. There her
grandparents sat, side by side, all four hands woven together
tightly. Both were sobbing loudly and openly. Already on
her knees, Gina screamed: "No, no! This can't be happening!
NO! Please, *please* God, no." Blindly, she groped for her
grandmother's hand. Shakily, the three huddled together, and
Gina sobbed into her grandmother's lap.

Later that afternoon, Uncle John Bartaloma retrieved
Gina from her grandparents' to take her back to the Bianco
home. An Army lieutenant arrived and played taps at the
bottom of the stairs of the front porch, the same stairs where
Joey and Gina waited countless times for the ice cream man
over the years. "Your mom and dad need you, Gina. You must
be strong for them," Uncle John had told her. But Gina didn't
feel strong. Wherever Joey was, Gina wanted to be, even if it
meant dead.

"Almost two weeks passed before the body was returned to us. Even if it had been returned quickly, Joey had been blown to bits. We couldn't say a real goodbye." Rita paused and tilted her head thoughtfully. "Later on in life, I realized I must have been in mild shock. My mother's girlfriends came daily to be sure all of us ate something, and they got Mom cleaned up and dressed. Elaine was literally like a zombie. Our doctor was a family friend, so when someone told him about Joey, he quickly arrived with sedatives. He didn't write a prescription, he went and got them himself. Thank God, he came over quickly. Mom had been like a banshee before he arrived. Dad sat at the kitchen table with a shot glass and a bottle of whiskey and drank and stared off into space, like, for most of the day, every day for weeks. People's voices were distant. They moved past me like faceless shadows on a conveyor belt." Rita paused again and quietly laughed. "In college, when I drank or got high, I remembered how I felt that week. Only it wasn't a fun high." Looking at Carolyn and Franco's face, Rita smiled, "I actually was young and stupid once and sampled just about everything! Not heroin, though. Saw a couple of misfired needles and what it did to people. Needles were never my thing."

The long days and nights brought the family to another lost day, one in which Gina saw everything in varying degrees of grey. The mountainous hills still blazed rich and fiery hues, but she was color-blind to it all. Gina left the window shade down that morning, and sat with her skinny legs dangling off the side of her bed. At age fifteen, she was still as thin as a rail, as her dad Sal said. The bedroom door

creaked slowly; a sharp sliver of light creased the room and
Gina felt momentarily blinded. Her hands limp in her lap, she
looked down as her mother shakily groped her way towards
her. Elaine was wearing black, and her doe eyes were red and
swollen from crying. Grandma had brought Gina a navy blue
dress with a white collar the day before: a pretty little thing.
Gina knew she would never look at that dress ever again after
today. When Elaine entered the room, the dress's front sported
a wet spot where Gina's silent tears had fallen.

"Come on, Gee. We have to leave now." Elaine spoke
in a raspy whisper. "It's time to go."

"I can't do this, Ma. Please don't make me."

"You're Joey's girl, Honey. He wants you there. He
needs you there today."

"No. No, he doesn't."

"Yes, he *does*. Plus your fa-tha will be pissed if you
don't get movin, Lady." She sounded more like Mom when
she spoke "the wrath of Sal."

Gina turned and looked Elaine squarely in the face.
They collapsed into each other's arms, trembling. Elaine wept
softly while Gina stroked her hair.

"Okay, Ma. Okay. Don't cry. Huh? I'm comin wit
ya. It's just a bad dream, isn't it? Please tell me it's a bad
dream."

"It is a *very* bad dream. One from which we'll never
wake, Baby Girl. We'll just have to live with it for the rest of
our lives until we can see our Joey again. But we *will* see him
again. Don't worry, Gee."

"I'm not worried, Ma. Let's go. Okay? Joey is
waiting," said Gina, managing a weak smile for her mother's
benefit.

"Your hair looks nice, Honey."

"Thanks, Ma. Joey likes my hair this way. Loose, like this."

"Yes, yes he does." Holding Elaine's hand tight, Gina led her mother out of the bedroom, past the calendar that was now on the floor, ripped to shreds.

The remainder of that day was a sea of sad faces, distant voices and muffled sounds. The slow limo ride from the funeral home passed Gina's Catholic school. The children lined the street with their hands over their hearts. Joey was some kind of hero to everyone in town, but for Gina, he had always been and would always be a hero. The family would later learn that Joey had thrown himself on a grenade tossed close to several children, while his platoon had passed through a village. Unbeknownst to anyone, his last thought was of his sis. Joey was passing a skinny little girl with black braided hair, feeding chickens. Thinking of Gina, a smile waxed Joey's weary face. In a split second, a grenade appeared.

A closed coffin draped with the American flag, Mass at church, the reading of the Twenty-Third Psalm and a twenty-one gun salute was what Gina would remember of that day. Frankie and the other boys wept audibly, and trembled as they carried Joey's casket in and out of the church. To add to the horror of the bad dream, Gina spotted Yvonne kneeling in the farthest corner pew, engulfed in shadowy darkness, sobbing. Rage overtook her, but it was a welcome substitute for the grief that consumed her. *I hate you, Yvonne.* **You** *killed Joey. The Lord is* **not** *my Shepherd, and I want Joey back!* **Now!** Gina shuddered inside because cursing Yvonne, even in the house of God, felt satisfying. The sound of Elaine wailing filled that evening, and her mother's closest friend Mary called for the doctor again.

Visions of Joey's smiling face haunted Gina for months after that. She often awoke in a cold sweat hoping to find that Joey was sitting on her bed as he sometimes had, watching her sleep. But Joey was not there. She felt lost and alone. That fact that he was smiling in her dreams comforted her, and Gina convinced herself it was a sign that Joey was peacefully happy somewhere. She struggled in school in the months following, but managed to keep fairly good grades. *Joey wants it that way*, she would say to herself. She visited her grandparents more often, discovering her grandmother hiding sniffles behind a forced smile and a handkerchief. Sophia and Federico looked very, very old to Gina now. Both Elaine and Grandma wore black clothing for a long time after Joey came home, and Gina hated it. The world was as dark as that day that Joey was forever taken from her. No one would ever be the same again. Elaine and Sal rarely smiled again, either of them.

On the outside, it appeared to most people around her that Gina was coping with the grief of losing her brother. On the inside, her soul blackened quickly. She left for church on Sundays as instructed, but went for long walks instead, not wanting to be inside the church where Joey had been an altar boy. She was totally alone now, her parents so paralyzed with grief that they sent her to Mass by herself. She fantasized about blackening Yvonne's mom's eyes, should she bump into her leaving church. On those Sunday mornings, she often walked to the cemetery. Knowing Joey wasn't really there, she still found comfort in talking to him, wherever he might be. To help dull her pain, she started smoking pot and dropping acid with friends when they could get it, romanticizing to herself an artist's existence. She viewed sexual experiences as coldly as science experiments, wondering to herself what the fuss was all about. Her friends tried to lift her spirits, so she smiled and laughed solely for them.

"I was wildly jealous of my friends during this time. They had such normal lives compared to mine. At the same time, I loved them for trying to cheer me."

Gina continued to cheer at football and basketball games, and went to school dances just to avoid being home. Inside, she was as numb as her parents had become, having lost all hope and faith. *Hah! Faith.* That was Yvonne's mother's name. How could she have faith in the god that took her best friend away? That was destroying her family?

In the winter months that followed, Gina watched while Joey's Impala, parked in the back yard under a blue tarp, disappeared under a blanket of snow.

Looking rigid and stunned, Carolyn and Franco sat while Rita shared long-buried secrets. "It was as though my heart and soul had been lobotomized, so I experimented with acid and peyote buttons. Ahhh, the 70s! Never had a bad trip. I *needed* to be lifted, as far away as possible. If I wanted to, I could dance a Peter Max ballet and have Joey join me." Rita smiled as she extended her arms out to either side and rested them on the top of the sofa. Leaning her head back and looking to the ceiling, she exhaled fully. The smile melted from her face. "I didn't realize then, but for the next ten years, the Twenty-Third Psalm became both my scorn *and* my comfort."

Chapter 10

*T*he days and months that followed Joey's death showed the not-so-slow decline of the Bianco family. Sal drank steadily, losing himself in a bottle daily. He often stumbled about the house mumbling about his grandchild, the only piece of Joey left that they would never see. The French woman had killed his son, he repeatedly hissed. Ignoring Elaine and Gina completely, these drunken stupors were maddening for the Bianco girls. Elaine stood by helplessly, watching her beloved husband fall to the wayside, physically and emotionally. Elaine begged Sal to stop drinking: "I need you, Sally," she would cry. "I can't lose you, too." Gina would come home at four in the afternoon to find that Elaine hadn't gone to work and was forlornly sitting in the kitchen in her robe and slippers. Gina hid the family misery from others best she could, and progressively assumed most of the household duties. Grandma Sophia walked across town once or twice a week to cook and help Gina tidy the house. Gina was in awe of her grandmother's strength and resolve. Sophia cheered and praised her granddaughter frequently. After her grandmother's visits, Gina felt renewed and validated.

As Gina entered her senior in high school, she had become the sole parent in the household. All of the light and music had left the Bianco home. Sal began to falter at work and it was obvious that his health was declining. Elaine's physical and mental health digressed even further. Her dad's employers were fond of the Biancos and tried to convince Sal to seek medical help. His skin seemed yellowish to Gina and she grew increasingly stressed about Sal's poor state of mind.

As she did each Saturday morning, Gina fixed coffee and breakfast. The house was eerily quiet and she felt uneasy. Tiptoeing to her parents' bedroom door, she slowly pushed it open with her fingertips. Peering inside, Gina saw Elaine sleeping peacefully. Reassured, she stepped forward to draw the bedcovers up around Elaine's shoulders. Sal's back was to Gina, the covers off of his shoulders as well. Gina very carefully pulled the blankets up and let them gently drop close to her dad's neck and head. Easing back on her heels, she stood savoring the peace of the moment. She loved the two of them so, and wished to take the pain away, a wish she knew would never come true. Her eyes raked over Sal's head, his hair now almost totally white. *He had been such a handsome man*, she thought. At that moment, she realized that he was very, very pale, almost blue. Gina tip-toed around to her father's side of the bed. Sal's eyes and mouth were both slightly open. Drawing her hand to her mouth, she slowly backed out of the room.

Gina mechanically walked to the wall phone, and dialed. "Uncle John? I *need* you to come right away, please," she spoke. Sensing Gina's agitation, John Bartaloma pressed Gina to explain, but she firmly repeated, "I need you to come now, *please*. Mom's asleep, so please pull up quietly." Uncle John did as Gina instructed. They gently woke and shepherded an unquestioning Elaine to the living room. Gina called her Uncle Jake and asked him to drive to their house. John Bartaloma immediately called the Bianco family doctor hoping to intercept Elaine's anticipated shock or hysteria. Next, he called the coroner. Before the coroner arrived, Gina slipped back into her parents' bedroom, and stroked her father's cool head. Leaning close, she kissed his forehead softly. Trembling, she whispered, "Pop, I'm so sorry this happened. I love you; you were a great dad. I've missed you for a long time already, though. Rest now, Daddy. Rest. Tell Joey and Nonna Bianco how much I love and miss them. Would ya, please?"

Gina stood rigid again, hearing Elaine in the living room calling to Sal. "Sal! Sal! Get up! John is here for a visit. Come on! Gina made coffee." Gina entered the living room to see Elaine seated on the couch, wrapped in a blanket, rocking back and forth. Elaine's eyes shot upward to Gina's face. "Get your pop outta bed, Honey. Pull-leaze. Get him up. Get him up. Get him up...." Elaine tugged at Gina's bathrobe. Gina sat next to her and rocked, her arm tight around Elaine, who was staring straight ahead, still mumbling, "Wake him up, get him up, Gina."

"She never cried, just whimpered throughout the entire process: removing his body, the wake, the funeral. I could see my grandparents breaking under the strain of watching their only daughter go mad. My mother's deterioration accelerated out of control. Her son, her husband, both dead within three years. I didn't exist in her mind or memory." Rita bit her lower lip, the sadness apparent in the tone of her voice.

"My uncle and grandparents arranged for me to spend the summer on Martha's Vineyard after I mentioned that some friends were going there to work at a hotel. They scraped up some money to send me on my way; they wanted me be a kid for a change. It was just what I needed; I met lots of young people from all over the world that came to work the tourist season. My grandparents and uncle kept my morale up. They took turns having Mom at their houses while I was away."

"When I returned my grandfather said, 'Come in, bella. Vené and bring the world to me!' He would ask me all kinds of questions, like: 'What were the people like? What was the food like there?' He used to ask me that kinda stuff when I was a kid, too, even if I went on a school field-trip, or shopping in Hartford. When I returned from the island he asked, 'What did the air smell like?' I thought it rather odd, and asked him why he asked. He pointed a crooked finger to his head, and told me to think about everywhere I went. I was clueless! Then, I realized: well, I was on an island and the air smelled of the sea, of salt water. When I told my grandfather this, he nodded. 'Si. Commé e Sicilia!' His little quizzes made me concentrate on the smells and tastes everywhere I went in my lifetime. I became his reporter, so I paid close attention to all of it! He was MY teacher sometimes. He taught me to marvel in the senses and encouraged my artwork, from as far back as I can remember," Rita chuckled. "Poor guy. Couldn't really go anywhere and was thirsty for anything outside his back door. In the summer, he would put his rocking chair under the arc of a huge lilac bush, and close his eyes, taking in the fragrance. I would just sit on the back porch and watch him sometimes." Rita closed her eyes and inhaled deeply. Carolyn knew by the smile on Rita's face that her friend had momentarily been whisked backward through time and was now seeing her grandfather under that lilac bush.

"I'm sure he had many bad days, but never pitied himself in front of me. I was young and selfish, and spending time with him made me realize that I had everything to live for. He sometimes smoked a pipe, with cherry scented tobacco. The doctor made him give it up eventually, though. He grumbled about that. He didn't smoke much, but with his bad health and injuries...."

Rita was clearly off on a trip down memory lane, but Carolyn and Franco were totally captivated by Gina Bianco's story, as if she was someone other than Rita. They were relieved to see Rita smiling more as she continued.

"When I returned that summer, my grandfather asked me all of his questions and more. I was shocked when he asked if I had fallen in love. I told him I *was* in love, but the man was married. He shot daggers at me and I stared him down. When I began grinning and laughing, he realized that I meant *him*. He laughed his toothless laugh! Boy, I loved that man!"

"I started my freshman year at the community college right in our hometown. We hired a nurse's aide to come just for the hours that I was in class. Every once in a while Mom spoke like she was herself again, but it lasted only a

few minutes at a time. First, it was about once a month, then
every other month, every six months... she was all I had left.
Funny, she looked beautiful, though. She was like in a state of
suspended animation. Insanity seemed to just stop everything.
Well, almost everything. I didn't color her hair, but it was still
thick and pretty!" Rita chuckled. "I stayed in town so I could
take care of Ma, but I couldn't do it after a while. It just got
too hard, going to school and working part-time. Eventually,
Uncle Jake helped me to clean up the house to sell and I
moved into his place with him and his wife. They were good
to me, and worked second shift jobs while I worked and went
to school during the day. I guess that's one reason we all got
along so well -- we didn't see a lot of each other, and we were
all still grieving, quietly. Living with them had been intended
to be a temporary situation, anyway. Everything is temporary.
Mom and I had Dad's Social Security and life insurance, but it
wasn't going to last forever, especially if I was going to finish
school. We had to sell the house to afford a care-facility for
Mom. I convinced myself that if I could graduate and land
a job, I could take care of her, and that she would get better.
But she got skinnier and weaker. I'd sit in her room and talk
endlessly, even telling her about the college in Fairfield County
where I planned to go. I became friendly with all the nurses
there; they always seemed interested in my school plans. We'd
talk about it in front of Mom, but she just sat there, staring
straight ahead."

"It's sad, but I would play a little game sometimes,
turn the TV on in her room and watch to see if she blinked
and how long it took. On nicer days, I wheeled her around in
a wheelchair, or curled her hair, painted her fingernails. She
looked comfortable, and amazingly serene. Before I knew

it, almost two years went by and I earned my Associates. When I hesitated about going away to school, my uncle and grandparents insisted that I go and not worry, to have a life. *A life!* I felt as though I didn't deserve one after what happened to my family. Three weeks before school started, she actually spoke when I was getting ready to leave her room. It was bizarre."

"Why was it bizarre, Rita?" Carolyn asked.

Rita's eyes welled, but she did not cry. "She said, 'Bye, Babe. I love you! Hurry up, you'll be late for school.' I actually jumped up and down in front of her, clapping my hands. I called the nurses into the room; we were all so excited. I hoped it was a sign that she would come back. It seemed obvious that she knew what was going on around her, that she understood I'd be leaving for college soon. But she actually died in her sleep the very same night. Just five years earlier, we were the happiest family in town without a fucking pot to piss in, like Mom used to say. But *man*, we was happy!" Rita looked about the room sadly, not wanting to look either Carolyn or Franco in the face. "I never really got too close to anyone in those five years, cuz I thought if I did, they would die, too. The drinking age had been lowered to eighteen in Connecticut the year before, so I was free to drink and boy, did I! Huh! Not quite twenty and could drink most guys my age under the table. But ya know? I deserved to. I was in Hell and sure I would be lying next to all of them in very short order."

Her voice fell hard and flat. Rita was being thrown back and forth from happy memories to horrific ones that afternoon in Carolyn and Franco's living room. The couple could feel the little girl lost sadness in Rita's voice. Then,

ironically, a faint smile crept across her lips. She continued,
her face brightening. "It was the second day of class. I chose
a film and literature class for my English credits that semester.
I love film and jumped at the chance to study its history and
genres!"

It was a pretty long walk from her last class to her next
one, so Gina hustled along the walkways of the busy campus.
She hated being late for anything, and checked her watch to
reassure herself. Elaine was always the last one in her family
to be ready for any event; she was so meticulous in every way.
It had always been a thorn in the Biancos' sides!

The New England campus buildings were very old;
many had cut stone exteriors. Because she had walked through
her class schedules a couple of days earlier, Gina arrived at her
class with a few minutes to spare. There were only a couple
of vacant seats in the room, so she hurriedly occupied the first
one she saw. Oblivious to everyone around her, she was lost in
her thoughts about which bus to take later that day. She could
walk, but knew she needed to get this part of her schedule
down pat before snow flew. The classroom was noisy around
her, but Gina intently studied a bus schedule. To her right, a
young man had taken the last vacant seat. Glancing up, she
saw him fumbling with books, searching for something. The
professor entered the room, and she focused her attention
forward.

"Hey, do you have a pen or pencil that I can borrow?
Hey!" Gina realized that the person who had seated himself to
her right was whispering to her.

Rude, Gina thought to herself. *Unprepared on the first*

day of class. "Are you talking to me? Hey. Is that what you said?"

"Okay, okay. Sorry, *Miss*. Now do you have a pencil or not?"

"Not!"

"Okay, then." The young man turned and began asking other students around them for a pen or pencil. Amused, Gina watched from the corner of her eye.

Surrounded by people her age, she felt great that day. She would always miss her family, and wished she could share her new adventure with them. So that she could give her grandfather a full report the next time she visited, Gina concentrated on her surroundings. The film and literature class was her last for the day, and she left the building at an unhurried pace. The afternoon sun felt great on her face, so she pulled her long hair back from her face as she walked. The beauty of the autumn day pushed her recall to the day of the homecoming game five years earlier. For once, she forced the thoughts away, knowing that Joey would not want her to grieve forever. The stillness was interrupted by "Hey!" *Oh, no! The boy from class.* Gina turned on her heels to find that Pencil Boy was following her down the sidewalk.

"Is that how you greet everyone? *Hey?*"

"Sorry, just wanted to say sorry is all."

Her classmate stopped a few steps behind her, and Gina felt a tinge of guilt. Turning again, she replied, "No, *I'm* sorry. That was rude of me. It's okay. I understand, being the first day of class and all." She extended her hand, and the young man quickly met it with his. Because they were seated when they met in class, Gina hadn't noticed how tall he was. His green eyes seemed to pop out at her, framed by dark brows. His hair was sandy brown, thick and wavy. He pretended to have a beard, but instead had randomly strewn dark brown hairs on his chin. His infectious grin put Gina at ease and she sensed his apology was genuine.

"I'm Motty, er Mar-ty! How are ya? By the way, you were the only one in class that asked intelligent questions." Marty's expressions and speech were animated, and Gina felt herself smiling broadly as he spoke. He was definitely a New Yorker, she mused to herself. She embarrassingly noticed that he was wearing Converse high-tops, and she, low-tops.

"Oh, thanks, Marty."

"And *you* are?"

"You can call me Hey!" The two laughed. "Just kidding, of course! I'm Gina." They walked along together and talked about their intended majors and the other classes each was taking. Gina had forgotten that she planned a test ride on the bus that day. She and Marty stopped to eat a hamburger on the way. At the junction of Ocean Avenue, Gina said goodbye and explained her apartment building was just a block away. Marty in turn, pointed to a large brick house across the intersection, in which he shared an apartment with another student.

"Well, see ya in class, Gina."

"Sure, Marty."

As they lived in close proximity, Marty and Gina saw each other most days, either on the bus, walking to class and even at the local grocery store. For Gina, it was a comfort to see a familiar, friendly face on such a regular basis. As the semester progressed, they often socialized in the same circles and went to dances and local clubs together. They paired to do an assignment for their film and literature class. Although not at the same time, they had another class in common and coached each other during exam weeks. By November, the two were fast friends. Thanksgiving was approaching, and Marty looked forward to going home to Queens to visit with his parents and friends.

"You go-win home for Turkey Day, Gee?" Marty asked one afternoon at the grocery store.

"Oh yeah, Mart. Yeah."

"Your folks there? You got brothers and sisters? Bet you got lots, huh? Being Italian, and all."

Gina lowered her head and was quiet.

"What? Did I say somethin' bad? What's the matter, Gina?"

"I have grandparents, an uncle and his wife."

"Aahh," Marty uttered. "Sorry, Babe. Didn't mean to pry."

"You didn't pry, Mart. It's okay. I had a *great* brother. Joey. My parents were the best, too. They're d…, uh, they're gone now."

Right there in the supermarket aisle, Marty pulled Gina close. Dwarfed by his size, she felt herself beginning to laugh. "Thanks for caring, Marty."

"And how could I not!" boasted Marty, putting a hand to his chest. Looking down at a blushing Gina, he said, "I'll call my Ma. She would love some girl company. You can come to my place for Thanksgiving."

"Oh, no. My grandparents' feelings might be hurt."

"Come on now, ask 'em. Tell them a girl friend, Ruth, invited ya. You can go at Christmastime, cuz you'll be off for a full month. Huh? *Huh?*" Holding Gina's hands and bending his knees to look her in the face, Gina girlishly giggled. "Ruth?"

"Yeah, Ruth! My ma!"

"Okay, maybe. I'll talk with them. You're right. I can spend a whole month with them later. We'll see."

"We'll see, she says!" Marty seemed to get Gina to laugh at just about anything. They finished up their shopping and walked to Gina's apartment to cook.

"I used to think when I was with Marty, I smiled so much that my face hurt. It was a pain I loved!" It warmed Carolyn and Franco to see their friend smile when she spoke of her college friend.

What does this kid have to do with anything? thought Franco.

Chapter 11

*A*s the weeks passed and the two friends grew closer
weekly, it became easier for Gina to share some of the
Bianco family history. No longer difficult to discuss, Gina
reminisced about her family to Marty, and it had become
happily therapeutic for Gina. Remembrances of the holidays
became a comfort for her again. She held a vision in which her
mother met up with Joey and Dad somewhere, and that Elaine
was a happy mom again. Picturing the three of them together
gave Gina some peace and comfort. The past five years had
made her stronger, but their passing failed to fill the gap of not
being about to see them again. She still had her grandparents
and uncle, and now she was away from her little town and
meeting lots of people. Gina felt grateful that her family
nudged her to go away to school.

To avoid putting his parents in an uncomfortable situation, she asked Marty to let his parents know that hers were deceased, but spare the details. Thanksgiving week arrived and on Wednesday afternoon Gina and Marty took a bus to the train station, duffle bags in tow. They chattered about everything from difficult professors to The Patriots. The train ride to Grand Central was a pretty quick one, less than an hour, and Marty's dad would be waiting. Hurriedly, they ambled up the incline to the station above. As they neared a central ticket kiosk, Marty paused to look around for his dad. Gina was sure they could easily spot a tall, handsome man amongst the thick swarms of holiday travelers arriving and departing Grand Central Station.

"There he is! Hey, Pop!" Marty jumped forward, catching the embrace of a rather average-looking balding man with sandy brown hair and rosy cheeks. *So, where does Marty get the height from? Must be somewhere in his family.* Gina was instantly taken by Dan's warm aura. She could see Marty in Dan's eyes and smile, but Dan was pretty fair skinned compared to his son. *He really **is** a handsome man, too.* Just not what Gina had pictured. They shook hands while exchanging hellos, and Dan took Gina's duffle bag and directed the kids toward a side door. Like a country girl overwhelmed, Gina panned the interior of Grand Central, now dressed in holiday splendor. She had only been to New York once previously and was anxious to visit as many of the museums there as she could, a wish she had shared with Marty. Marty reached out and tugged at Gina's forearm. "Come on, Lady! Ma's cookin supper! We'll look at the terminal again!"

They walked a couple of blocks in the biting cold, the

skyscrapers blocking what little winter daylight was left. Gina felt as though she was walking in the bottom of the Grand Canyon, and she held Marty's hand tight. The street sounds were loud and foreign to her: honking horns, and weaving, fast traffic. They crossed to a parking garage and Gina gleefully answered some polite questions that Dan asked: "what are you studying, a junior or a senior, how do you know Marty," and the like. "Gina sits in the front seat, Motty you sit in the back!" Without skipping a beat, Dan continued, "Mom's cookin a nice pot roast for ya! We can have an early supper and you two can go out or watch TV with us. If you want, that is."

"We'll figure it out, Pop. Maybe we'll just hang out with you and Ma. We got plenty of time to do stuff. On Friday, Gina and I will go to Manhattan."

"We will?" squealed Gina, forgetting for a moment that Dan was present.

"Sure, I just thought we might spend the entire day in the Metropolitan Museum. That is, only if you want."

"Yippee!"

The three laughed heartily, and Marty spoofed: "Not very excited about that, are ya? Do you think there's enough inside that place to look at all day?"

"You know there is, Smart Ass! I think I could spend three days in there!"

"We'll save Saturday for going out and having some *real* fun!"

"Going to a museum is real fun!"

"Yeah, of course it is! Pop, you and Ma should come with us."

"We'll see, Son. I could use a couple of days just

staying put, though," sighed Dan. "Maybe your mother will go, though. Motty, Son: when ya gonna shave that hair off ya chin?"

"Ah, Pop!"

"Ya pick a may-jah yet, Son?"

"Maybe," Marty replied nonchalantly.

"Maybe, nuttin! Ya should be thinkin of ya future!"

"Well, ya know what, Pop? *Maybe,* I'm studying business right now. *And maybe*, I plan to go fa real estate law. But just maybe, mind ya! Fifty-ninth Street, please, driver."

"Now, don't be a smott ass, young man!" Dan shot over his shoulder to Marty. Being privy to this personal exchange was unexpected and Gina felt a little embarrassed. Dan seemed to brood for a long time. Finally, he sighed and said, "Ahm proud of you, Mottin. *Really* proud!"

"Thanks, Pop! When I get the sheepskins, you can tell me how proud you are of me then. Okay?"

"Okay. You're a *great* kid. Isn't he a great kid, Gina?" Gina smiled her approval and the three laughed.

Over the bridge to Queens, the happy travelers sailed, until they reached a quaint brick house. Modestly sized, it looked meticulous in the light of dusk, with an ample front porch. Houses everywhere in New York looked squished together to Gina, but this one actually had some breathing room, as did many in the neighborhood. The street was wide and sparsely lined with oak trees. Dan pulled his old Chevy into a narrow driveway and up to a one-car garage that was separate from the house. The three made their way to the back door, from which light and music streamed when Dan opened it. He ceremoniously stepped aside and gestured to Gina to step in. Gina immediately recognized Perry Como's voice crooning "White Christmas" from another room. Across the room to their right, a woman was stooped and looking inside an oven. She spun and jerked erect. *Wow! She's tall. So, that's where he gets it!*

"Well, I just put the rolls in when I heard you's pull up!" The woman wiped her hands on the apron she was wearing and extended her hand to Gina, "I'm Motty's mom, Ruth. Pleased to meet ya, Gina."

"Likewise," sputtered Gina in awe of the beautiful woman before her. Ruth's deep azure eyes seemed to pop from her face. Gina thought of Elizabeth Taylor, whose riveting blue eyes were also framed by dark brows. But her hair! Her hair was thick, dark and wavy. It was pulled away from her face with combs, and it looked wonderfully 1940-ish to Gina. Ruth had a small, straight nose and a perfect smile. She stood there for a moment, wondering to herself how Dan captured this ravishing creature. The chemistry was instantly obvious, as Dan moved forward to smooch Ruth hello unabashedly in Gina's presence. Gina smiled at Marty, who shrugged his shoulders in mock disbelief.

"Okay, Motty, take Gina upstairs and show her the guest room. Dinner's almost ready."

Gina volunteered, "I can set the table for you, Ruth."

"No, Honey. Dan took care of it before he went to pick you up. You're our guest. Go on, now. Go Motty, you too!"

Gina and Marty looked at each other whimsically. "Okay, Ma. Come on, Gee! Better do what she says!"

Marty led Gina through a small, but lovely dining room. The table was set with cloth napkins and candle tapers ready to light. He marched through a hall leading to a staircase

near the house's front door. The home was built in the 1950s,
and had rich, dark wood throughout. *Aahh! So here is where
Perry Como is performing.* Gina glanced left to see the dimly
lit living room with inviting overstuffed chairs and a sofa.
There were doilies on the arms of the furniture, something
Gina thought only her grandmothers did! Next to one chair
stood a floor lamp, but with a round table wrapped around
it. It held an ashtray and pipe. Once upstairs, Marty flicked
the light to the guest room on. It was furnished much the
same way as the rest of the house that Gina had seen so far. It
looked spotlessly clean. The bed was covered with a cream-
colored chenille bedspread, the same type that Elaine and
Nonna had favored.

Marty promptly sat on the bed, testing the bedspring
by bouncing up and down. "I used to jump on this bed all the
time!" he reflected. "Dad used-ta try to catch me and spank
my butt. Funny, he never did catch me, not once!"

"Joey and I used to do the same thing!" blurted Gina
excitedly, but then stood quietly, a little embarrassed that she
had said it so loudly. She picked up her duffle bag that Marty
had deposited on a chair nearby.

Marty reached his long arm out to Gina and took her
hand. "Come mere," he beckoned, patting the bed. "You
should think about Joey. That's how we keep the people that
we love most alive, right? You shouldn't be afraid to." They
sat side-by-side, Marty's arm around Gina's shoulders.

"I'm not afraid, Mart," smiled Gina.

From the foot of the staircase, Ruth bellowed, "Kids,
wash ya hands. Dinner in a coupla minutes!"

"Sheesh! She still thinks I'm twelve!" gushed Marty.
"I'm a distinguished man of twenty-one! There's a little

bathroom right there," Marty pointed toward a door that Gina figured was a closet. "You get a bathroom of your own, your majesty! I don't get that!" The two friends laughed and shared the little bathroom sink like the two children they still really were, and bounded down the stairs to dinner.

The dining room smelled heavenly. Ruth and Dan were lively and talkative throughout. Gina noticed how considerate the couple seemed to be toward each other, and wondered if this was the norm or just some polite display for her.

Marty asked, "Mom and Dad, is it okay if Gina and I get up early and go out for coffee tomor-rah? We can be back pretty quick to help with the food."

"Your mother and I pretty much got everything ready today. We figured while we were getting a pot roast cooking, that we should keep going. So we worked on Thanksgiving stuff until it was time to pick you up. Take your time getting coffee. Maybe you can help clean up after dinner." Ruth elbowed Dan hard. Dan shrugged his shoulders. "What? What did I say?"

"Of course, we'll do the dishes? Right, Marty?" Gina asked.

"Yeah, yeah," grumbled Marty. "But then we get to sit down and watch TV or some-tin, right Pop?"

Ruth jumped in. "Oh! *It's a Wonderful Life* is on the TV tomorrah night. We can watch that! Is that okay, Gina?"

"But we've seen that a million times!" protested Marty.

"Son, if Mom and Gina want to see it, then we'll watch it again," Dan firmly said. "Gina we can watch whatever you'd like tomorrow."

"I'd love to watch it with you. *Really*. I, I love that movie," stammered Gina.

"Girls win!" squealed Ruth. "Nice to not be outnumbered for a change. Thanks, Honey!" and she touched Gina's hand softly. Gina suddenly felt a pang of guilt, conscious that she hadn't thought of her own family at all that day. It also felt great to be with Marty, Ruth and Dan, eating at a dining room table: music played, tapers burned, and lively conversation flowed. Lit up inside, she was happily aware that her face hurt from all the smiles it was producing.

When everyone was finished eating, the four worked together to clean everything up. "No dessert tonight," said Ruth. "We'll save our stomachs for tomorrah!" She disappeared up the stairs and the remaining three walked to the living room.

Dan turned on the TV to the local news and watched for a few minutes. Picking up his pipe and bag of tobacco, he exclaimed, "Well, before Mother comes back down, I'm gonna sit on the back stoop and have me a smoke!" He was wearing a cable knit vest over a wool Pendleton shirt, so didn't stop to put a jacket on. "See ya in five," and he ambled toward the back door.

When the back door slammed shut, Gina turned to Marty. "I saw the ashtray there and thought maybe he smoked in the house. Why is there an ashtray?"

Marty inhaled dramatically. "Smell that?"

"Smell *what*?"

"Exactly that! Nothin! Ma don't allow smoking in the house. Plus, she's been reading how bad smoking is, and telling the old man all about it. It keeps him from smoking too much. He use ta smoke cigarettes, too. She asted him to stop.

He did, but that's when he started the pipe. The ashtray is just there to rest his pipe in." Gina smiled as she thought about her grandfather's pipe smoking, and also about how Sal Bianco frequently broke Elaine's house rules by smoking indoors.

Ruth reappeared in a bathrobe and slippers, her face freshly scrubbed. "I see your fatha is havin a smoke?" She headed for the kitchen.

"Yeah, Ma," and Marty rolled his eyes at Gina, but out of Ruth's sight. Red and rosy from the frigid night, Dan jogged into the living room spouting his complaints about the cold. "It's startin to smell like snow! Getting close."

In a few minutes, Ruth shuffled back bearing a tray with four cups of cocoa. "Dan, Mystery Movie time! Columbo tonight! I just love that Pete-ah Falk!" Dan winked at Gina, and she smiled broadly. Gina looked around at her hosts. They were just average people, but they were also a well-oiled machine: looking after each other while sharing their positive energies. She felt very comfortable. Easing the cocoa tray to the coffee table, Ruth hustled to the hallway closet. Tossing two pillows to Gina and Marty, she ordered, "Get comfortable. I know I will!" She squeezed into Dan's easy chair with him, and tapped the palm of her hand to her shoulder. Dan rested his head there and they laughed quietly. Gina and Marty exchanged amused glances. Marty put one of the pillows on his lap and tapped it, beckoning Gina to put her head there. "Really? Is that okay?"

"Sure, come on. Get some rest, cuz I'm gonna get you up kinda early for coffee."

"Why?"

"Well, some places might be closed. We might have to walk a little bit."

"So why don't we just make coffee here early?"

"Boy, you ask a lot of questions! Just thought you might want to see my neighborhood, walk past my high school, get a little exercise."

"Sure, Marty. Didn't think of that."

Gina dozed off on Marty's lap toward the end of the movie, but awoke to his gentle touch. They both looked over at Dan's big recliner to see that Ruth and Dan were snuggled together, sleeping like babies. Gina and Marty smiled lovingly at the two. Marty whispered, "Get washed up and get some sleep. I'll knock on your door around six." Marty gently pulled Gina from the couch and the two tip-toed up the stairs. He kissed Gina on the forehead and left the room, quietly closing the guest room door.

Gina obediently stumbled around the room and bath, and readied herself for bed. Delighted, she slipped into the cool, fresh sheets and hunkered down under the covers. Was she in bed at the Bianco home? It sure felt that way: warm, safe and familiar. Content, she knew that she would fall right back to sleep, and did.

True to his word, Marty began knocking on the guest room door shortly after six the next morning. By seven, a semi-comatose Gina followed him down the dark neighborhood street, her face muffled to the late November dawn. "Slow down, Mart. What's the rush?"

"Questions, questions."

They descended to the subway, where there were quite a few people waiting for the train, despite the fact it was Thanksgiving morning. Still sleepy, Gina paid little attention to where Marty was herding her. Resting her head on Marty's shoulder, she yawned, "Your parents are great, Mart. I'm guessing you told them about my family, right? They didn't ask one question."

"Well, they're sensitive people, my folks," Marty bragged. "I mean *really* sensitive to it. Ma's kinda an orphan, too."

"What'd ya mean, kinda an orphan? Did her parents die when she was younger, too?"

"No, actually Ruth's parents were both still alive until recently," replied Marty. He looked down onto Gina's child-curious countenance. "Ruth is Jewish and she married an Irish Catholic man."

"Yeah, so."

"Yeah, so," Marty mimicked, shrugging his shoulders. "She was raised Orthodox. She met Pop at a bank where they both worked when they was young. Pop specialized in home loans, and Ma supervised tellers. They didn't live too far apart in the Bronx. Later, Dad got a job with a mortgage company a block or two from the bank. He and Ma would sometimes see each other in a bakery on their way to work, and have a coffee and pastry. They started meeting for lunch, for dinner. You know: the rest is history." Marty paused. "They wanted to get married, and Ma's parents pitched a fit. Pop's parents wasn't too happy either, but they accepted it. When my Ma married Pop, her parents buried an empty coffin. You know, she was dead to them. Orthodox Jews used to do that in olden times. Her mother passed just last year, without ever making up with my mom. I know she talks to her dad once in a while on the phone. He forgave her, but keeps his distance. I've only seen him a few times."

Gina held close to Marty, and the two fell silent. Gina remembered the smiling Mr. Nathan of her youth. A butcher at one of the small grocery stores in her hometown, Ira Nathan was a Jew who had married a Catholic. Like Marty's parents, the Nathans chose their love over religious differences, hoping their families would grow to understand. In her mind's eye, she could see the radiantly smiling Nathans, walking Main Street together, holding hands like young lovers. Neither of their families ever entirely accepted the Nathan's marriage, as did Marty's grandparents. Ira's parents had also buried an empty coffin. Inside, Gina thought about the deep-level pain Ruth must have experienced in her youth. *An empty coffin! Ouch!* Ruth had been disowned, and her parents were just a few miles away. It had never occurred to Gina much that others experience pain as great as her own. Her parents and brother were permanently unattainable to her, something that the bereaved accept with the passing of time. It must have been horrific for Ruth to know that her love ones lived in a neighboring borough, spurning her because she loved Dan too.

The train slowed and Marty jumped lightly. "This is our stop, Gee!" Gina was still not quite awake; holding Marty's hand, they ascended stairs to a Manhattan sidewalk. Suddenly, there *they* were, looming overhead. Far above floated Wonder Dog, Charlie Brown, Superman, Ronald McDonald. The unexpected surprise jolted Gina to consciousness. Breathless, she put her hand to her chest. They were at Macy's Thanksgiving Day Parade, close to the starting point! Her mouth was gaped open beneath her muffler, her eyes looked as big as saucers. She reached her arms up and gazed skyward, a little girl consumed in the moment. "Oh my Goddess! Marty, help me to remember *every* detail, so that I can report all of this to my grandfather!"

Marty motioned to Gina. "It's early, so if we stand

over there, we can watch them put the whole thing together."
Mindless of the cold and the passage of time, the young friends
crossed the wide avenue and stood amongst the throng of awed
spectators. Afterward, they were swept back to the subway in
a buzzing swarm flying home, anxious for their waiting feasts.

For Gina, that Thanksgiving was like a day at the
amusement park. She gushed the details of the day to Ruth
and Dan upon her return, only to discover they had been in
on the surprise and knew about Marty's plan. Dan solemnly
said grace, followed by a Hebrew prayer from Marty. For the
second evening in a row, music played and candles burned,
this time in a Menorah. Ruth said, "A little early for this, but
so what!" When all felt stuffed to the gills, Ruth suggested
that they all wait for the movie to eat dessert and all cheerily
agreed. When Gina spotted Ruth setting a chocolate cream
pie amongst a myriad of other sweets, Gina remarked that
chocolate cream pie was her favorite Thanksgiving dessert.
Ruth cozied close to Gina and murmured, "Hope it's okay,
Honey, but Motty told me your mom made that special for you
at Thanksgiving."

"It's better than okay," smiled Gina, stretching her
frame to kiss Ruth's cheek. "Thanks, Ruth. Yum, I can't
wait!"

The movie began and it was a colorized version.
"Aahhh, look at that. Amazin what they can do!" howled
Ruth. It was followed by an instantaneous, "but I kinda like it
in the old black and white."

Everyone was quiet while the movie played. Gina
was transported back fifteen years. She had her little head on
Joey's leg, and he was stroking her hair. Gina saw his face
and heard his voice: "You want that moon, Gina? Just say

the word, and I'll lasso it for you." In a half-sleep state, she murmured, "Marty, Joey used to say that to me every time we watched this movie together. See that? I can think of Joey without being sad." She drifted off to sleep. Later on, Marty steered her up the stairs, and through the door of the guest room.

"That weekend was really the beginning for us, and the beginning of a ritual. For the next thirteen-plus years, I would go into New York regularly," Rita intimated slowly to Carolyn and Franco. "Anyway, after the next semester began, I went back to Queens with Marty almost every other weekend. I couldn't go back home every weekend anyway, so my grandparents or uncle didn't question anything. I had assignments to work on, so they must have figured I was doing just that. I was, of course! Some of my fine arts assignments required that I view some pieces that were in New York museums, so it was convenient and just plain fun to go to Marty's. I contributed what I could as to not wear out my welcome. But Ruth and Dan seemed happy to see me and when I missed a visit, Ruth would actually call my apartment to ask if everything was all right. After that first visit and before I left on Christmas break, Marty and I exchanged gifts for the first time."

"How'd ya know, Gee?"

"I see that wallet of yours is pretty spent, Marty."

Marty presented Gina with a small flat box. Inside was a fine-link gold bracelet, its box chain punctuated with perfectly spaced gold beads.

"I was thrilled. I still have that bracelet. We spoke on the phone almost every day until school started again, even if just for a couple of minutes. When I returned, we became lovers," Rita sighed dreamily. "It seemed so natural."

Chapter 12 _____

*A*s time has the unfortunate tendency to do, it flew.
Summer break loomed, and Gina and Marty were faced
with the prospect of a three-month separation. The two would
have to juggle their time spent together. At the end of March,
Gina looked over her yearly budget and determined she could
pay one month's rent for the summer, but if she didn't pay for
the entire summer in advance, the apartment could be rented
to someone else starting in September. To justify her staying
at school, she signed up for two summer classes. She could
attend classes on Tuesdays and Thursdays and head north for
long weekends. Marty signed up for one summer class, and
offered to pay a share of the rent to stay with her two nights
a week. Gina worried about what Ruth and Dan might think
but Marty assured her that they knew and did not judge either

of them. That Dan had sternly advised Marty to "be careful," seemed to be the extent of any judgment passed. Time moved forward and the friends remained close. The summer months at the Connecticut shore were glorious. Gina felt healthy and happy. She enjoyed a light class schedule, free time with Marty and her "second family," visits with her grandparents and ample privacy to study and rest. Everything seemed to balance out very nicely.

The guest room was now referred to as "Gina's room." Summer evenings at Dan and Ruth's were generally spent barbecuing, visiting and watching TV. The four would frequently go for walks, stopping along the way to buy an ice cream cone, or sit at the park close by the house. The neighborhood was rife with children on summer vacation, playing and riding their bikes in the street under the watchful eye of parents on multiple front stoops. From time to time, Marty and Gina walked to Sullivan's bar on the corner to enjoy pizza and beer on their own.

Eventually, Gina became comfortable enough to tell Marty's parents more about her family. They already knew of her brother and parents' fate, but she hadn't shared what each family member was like. During one visit, she showed off Bianco family photographs, and they sat in the dining room to look at them. Dan and Ruth reminisced aloud about the clothing that they had worn in common with Gina's parents, from World War II to the present. They were a little younger than the elder Biancos, but loved the styles.

Ruth offered Gina a couple of pictures to add to her collection. One was of Ruth and her toddler Marty. The other was a headshot of Ruth as a young woman. On the back of the photo was written, *Ruth – age 24.*

"Are you sure you want to give me these, Ruth?"

"Sure, sure Honey. I got at least two of each, three of the one with Marty."

Dan turned to Marty and grumbled, "Did ya notice, Son? Your Ma gives Gina a pitcha of you and her, but not me!"

Ruth shot Dan a corkscrew/shut-up look. An epiphany then lit her face. "I got a *perfect* photograph of you from last year, Dan. Rememba? At Shirley's nephew's Bah Mitzvah. You looked sooo handsome in that navy blue suit. I had a couple more made cuz I gave one to your brother!" Dan pretended not to be at all impressed, but his eyes were twinkling. Gina was entertained by their exchange. Ruth jumped from her chair and almost ran down the hall and up the stairs. In a few minutes she was back in the dining room, photo in hand. Ruth dramatically reached her long, graceful arm out to Gina from behind and over Dan's shoulder. She was giggling like a teenager. "Here, Gina!"

Gina reached her arm to accept Ruth's gift. She eased back onto the dining chair and fondly inspected it. It was a color photograph of a warmly smiling Dan in a tailored navy blue suit, standing on a grassy lawn in the sunshine. From either side of the photo were glimpses of banquet tables adorned with flowers. Men and boys wearing yamakahs peppered the background under an outdoor party tent. Dan also wore a yamakah and held a fluted glass in his hand.

"Dan! I am *so* impressed!" Gina exuded, flirtingly. "You polish up pretty darn nice!"

"Is that *sucha* surprise?" The three laughed heartily.

"Actually, you look the same as you do, *every* day. Handsome as always, just in a suit." Gina walked around the table and bent her arm around Dan's neck from behind. She softly sang the first line of "When Irish eyes are smiling..."

Dan turned his head to kiss Gina squarely on her cheek, each releasing a warm and happy sigh. "Thanks, Honey." After a few seconds of silence, he continued, "Ma here sometimes sings, 'Oh, Danny Boy' ta me! If ya wanna call it singing!" The four roared with glee. She thought, *I have two families now; how lucky is that?*

The summer was passing rapidly, and soon Gina and Marty would be living close to campus again. This time, they were sharing Gina's apartment and living together for the first time. Their fall schedules did not coincide much at all, but both agreed that it was an equitable trade-off. Each would have different class schedules and study times, and would meet when they could. Unable to spend much time together during the week, they looked forward to evening and weekend time. Gina had one evening class scheduled, so Marty planned to go to the library while she was in class, and then they could walk home after dark together.

Ruth and Dan especially fussed over Gina and Marty that first summer spent together as a family. Toward its end, the foursome rode the train to a game at Yankee Stadium, compliments of Marty's parents. Gina and Marty packed as much fun as they could in the final weekends before full-time classes started again. They often went into the city to explore. Gina had never been to Little Italy or Chinatown before that summer. Everything seemed ideal for Gina. Taking two summer classes kept her in a class schedule routine. She traveled "home" after summer classes ended and stayed at her grandparents' for over two weeks. Grandma Sophia teased her about time spent on the phone, and with an un-dentured smile inquired about the person Gina was speaking with.

During those weeks, it became sadly obvious to Gina that her grandfather's ill health had declined further. Federico suffered from gout in one leg, another by-product of stroke and inactivity. A sign of an enlarged heart, his breathing became increasingly labored. Sophia and Gina were sensitive to these warning signs; they appeared regularly now, not just once or twice a year. Yet the old man continued to smile and wanted to know everything Gina learned at school and places she visited.

Today, he asked all the same questions and more, even wanting to know about the Museum of Natural History and how the exhibits were set up. It amazed Gina that they had so much to talk about. Federico, in turn would tell Gina about his youthful travels in Italy before he began working for Sophia's father. He had once spent a month traveling north on the mainland. There were not nearly as many trains as in modern times, so most of the journey was accomplished on foot or by begging a wagon ride. Federico was tall and looked older than his years, so he learned to charm his way onto the backs of trucks or wagons frequently. For his return trip, he ferried along the southwestern coast, visiting as many cities as there were stops. Of all the cities young Federico visited, Rome, Florence and Venice were his three overall favorites.

The idea of a canal city especially intrigued Gina. Her grandfather painted a picture of Venice's Piazza San Marco, St. Mark's Square and the wonderful basilica and bell tower there, many times. As with her grandmother's cake, she never tired of the stories and occasionally, her grandfather would remember a new fact or two! That fall, she inwardly promised herself that she would be around more for next year's early summer to see her grandfather dozing in his rocking chair, inhaling the perfume of the lilac tree above him. Whenever she left her grandparents, she felt renewed strength. Through their example, Gina learned to appreciate life again.

Gina drove back to Fairfield County that first week of September. She would spend a couple of days at the apartment and then head into New York. It felt refreshing to be alone during that time. Still-warm summer breezes drifted through the screened bedroom window at night. In the distance, crickets fiddled their songs. Walking back from the grocery store, Gina caught an infrequent glimpse of a firefly enjoying its last hurrah. No mosquitoes, though. They were gone!

The busy days raced once classes commenced. Marty and Gina managed to keep the pace up well; the schedule differences were definitely to their advantage. Time and temptation to ignore their studies was short. Time for playfulness and fun somehow found its way.

Nervous about her grandfather's fragile health, Gina planned to spend the Thanksgiving holiday with her grandparents. She arrived early the day before to clean their house. There was only the first floor of the modest house to clean, so it was easy to do in short order. Gina was happy to do any work for her grandparents. She dropped in a table leaf and put out the extra chairs. Uncle Jake and his wife offered to make dinner at the Francovilla home. Instead of turkey, prime rib was planned as the main course. Grandma made a wonderful salad and chicken soup with small meatballs and pastina. It was eaten with finely grated Parmesan cheese. Gina baked rolls, set the table, and chose the wine. She planned to wash all the dishes after dinner so that the others could relax. However, the stubborn Sophia was insistent that she dry as Gina washed, because there was little room at the

sink area. Gina convinced Sophia to at least sit down until
the dish drainer was full. They dried the dishes together and
Sophia relaxed in between, while Gina continued washing
a second batch of dishes. Gina looked over her shoulder at
Federico, who sat stiffly at the table, his eyes hollow. Still, he
was clearly having a wonderful time and it warmed Gina to
see him smile so much. Her thoughts flashed to Marty, Ruth
and Dan, and the Thanksgiving spent the year before with
them. She wondered if Marty was thinking about it, too. He
was. Marty phoned later that evening and they spoke for a
few minutes, just to say hello. Both Ruth and Dan insisted on
talking to Gina for a minute, too.

"Tell ya grandma and grandpa hello from us!"
bellowed Ruth.

"She thinks everybody's deaf, but her!" laughed Dan
when it was his turn.

Gina reorganized her duffle bag for the trip back to the
apartment early Saturday afternoon. She toyed with the idea of
just freshening up and going to Queens, but knew it would be
a good idea to stay put and get some rest. Friday night she lied
in her grandmother's guest bed. It was becoming common to
hear her grandfather gasping for air in the night, followed by
the soothing sound of Sophia helping him to sit up.

The cold air outside was now absent of a train's roar;
the station below had closed long ago. Gina would sleep
in the very same bed that she and Joey shared as children
whenever they stayed with their grandparents. *Remember,
Joe? Nonna would tuck us in, kiss us on the head and say,
Buona Riposo. After she went to her room, we'd climb outta
bed and we'd try to guess the constellations from the window.
Remember how we would sneak turns listening in on the party*

*line? It was so much fun stealing tomatoes from the garden
and eating them with a salt shaker, huh Joey? Sophia would
yell at us, big time! We always got away with it, though. And
the thunderstorms! Grandpa said the angels were bowling.
He'd laugh that laugh of his. But the fireflies, that was my
favorite thing in the summer, Joey. Catching lightning bugs
in a jar with you, and looking at them under the covers until
I fell asleep... Soon, we'll be the same age. I sure miss you,
Joey.* Gina drifted off, counting happy memories like someone
contentedly counting sheep.

The remainder of the holiday season came and went
quickly. Unable to spend much time together, Gina and
Marty's relationship remained fresh and fun. Gina carefully
carved out time for both Marty's and her families. They
traveled north so that Marty could meet Sophia and Federico.
Sophia had forced Federico into a sport coat and the elderly
man looked chafed and uncomfortable for the bulk of the visit.
Gina flirted with her grandfather, who still grunted his mirth
in spite of his ill health. She coaxed him out of his jacket
and helped him don a light sweater instead. Sophia protested
loudly to Marty's amusement, and the old couple bickered in
his presence while Gina refereed. "Nonna, he doesn't have to
wear the jacket for us, okay?"

In a blink of an eye it was Ground Hog's Day and
Gina and Marty were well into their final semester. Gina was
doing her student teaching at two schools consecutively to
earn accreditation at both elementary and secondary levels.
This left the couple even less time to spend together, as Gina
was often working on lesson plans in the evening. They tried
their best to remain disciplined in their studies, but carnal
temptation happily interrupted their work. They both were

resigned to a mutual decision that Marty visit the library a few evenings so that each could complete their work. They laughed and lamented at the same time.

Late one Friday afternoon, Gina drove to her grandparents' home to spend the Presidents' Day long-weekend there. Unusual in winter, her grandfather seemed to be enjoying a surge of better health, and she reveled in his company. His spirits were bright and his face seemed rosier and fuller. On Saturday, Grandma Sophia baked her famous breaded chicken, aromatic with a touch of fresh mint. Gina's favorite of Sophia's recipes, the old woman always cooked a giant batch with potatoes, carrots, garlic and onions. Sophia would pack up most of the leftovers for Gina and Marty.

Before leaving the next day, Gina gave her friends big kisses. She rubbed her fingertips on her grandfather's scruffy overgrowth, and he grunted a husky laugh. "I'll be back in two or three weeks! If you need me before then, call me! Cap-eesh?" With a wave, she was off. Cracking the window of her Toyota to enjoy the Berkshires' brittle air, Gina turned the old car south onto Route 8. Before reaching the apartment, she stopped at a convenience store to pick up the bulldog edition of the Sunday paper, so that she wouldn't have to go out in the morning. Within two hours she was carrying bags of leftovers up the wooden stairs to her apartment. Having already laundered her clothing at her grandparents', she stashed them away and headed for a hot shower. Wiped out, she decided to get a good night's sleep before Marty's return the next day. Reading in bed seemed to speed falling asleep. Tonight it was National Geographic Traveler. Gina carried around a weathered copy featuring Venice and re-read the article several times. The copy still held its original pullout map along with lots of sentimental appeal for Gina.

The following morning, Gina lounged around in her pajamas, reading the paper and drinking coffee. Marty probably wouldn't appear until one o'clock or so; she had plenty of time. By noon, she was showered and dressed, and applied some light make-up. She made some big sandwiches on hearty bread and wrapped them up to put in the fridge. There was leftover chicken from Nonna, too. When the hour hand neared two, Gina decided to watch TV until Marty arrived and cuddled up with a blanket on the couch. Her heavy eyelids fought the irresistible temptation to nap, knowing Marty would be there soon.

The sound of the phone ringing woke her, and for a moment Gina wondered if it was in a dream. Groggily chuckling to herself, she realized that it was dusk and she bolted for the phone. "Hullo!"

"Gina. It's Motty."

"Marty, where are you? Everything okay?"

"Not sure. Dad doesn't feel well. He doesn't look well, either. He was sick yesterday, too. Ma and I brought him to the hospital. I can't come back right now, maybe not until tomorrow. It'll be fine. I just want to get him home and stay over."

"Yes. You need to stay there. Tell Ruth and Dan I love them. You better get back."

"Thanks, Gina. I'll see you tomorrow. Good night."

"Good night, Marty." Gina did not sleep much that night. She had napped, but worrying about Dan is what kept her awake.

Gina lingered in bed the next morning, but by three in the afternoon she grew increasingly concerned. She called

Dan and Ruth's repeatedly, but the phone rang unanswered.
She paced her little apartment, and tried to remain calm.
There's a perfectly reasonable explanation, she assured herself.
She needed some fresh air, and took a ten-minute walk to
buy milk. Several unsuccessful calls and two hours later, she
stepped onto the small back porch to take some deep breaths.
She passed the time by organizing her lesson plans and
preparing her clothes for the next day. Since it was getting so
late, she chose clothes for Marty and put them on the bedroom
chair. Gina shivered a bit at having done such a domestic act,
but wanted to be considerate. She knew Marty would be tired
when he finally arrived.

To distract herself, Gina read People magazine on
the couch. She lit a small fire in the fireplace, and pulled
the blanket up around her neck. She couldn't concentrate
enough to read. Seven o'clock came and went. The phone
was positioned close at hand on the coffee table, and Gina
stared at it from time to time. The logs crackled and popped
in the fireplace and she dozed off. She awoke a few hours
later, having forgotten that Marty still wasn't home. Her first
instinct was to put more logs on the fire, which she did. The
phone behind her softly rang as she set the screen back into
place.

"Gee. It's Mart." Gina was perplexed. She looked
across the room at the kitchen stove to see that it was after ten.
His tone of voice seemed normal, but Gina was still in a state
of semi-consciousness.

"Marty! Please tell me everything's okay."

"Everything's not okay, Gina. I'm sorry to tell ya…"

"Oh, Marty. Dan still in the hospital?"

There was a long silence while Marty drew a deep

breath between his teeth. "After I called you from the hospital, he had a heart attack. He was pretty stable, so Ma and I parked in the waiting area chairs. They wouldn't allow us to stay in the room at the ICU all night. We looked at him through the glass door a hundred times. He looked so comfortable." The more he spoke, the more Marty's voice trembled. "At about one-thirty, they came and got us. He had died in his sleep. His heart just stopped, and they couldn't revive him. They said he didn't feel a thing, but I find that hard to believe."

Marty's words reverberated in Gina's head. *He died in his sleep.* She had expected Marty to say that Dan wavered, but was ultimately okay. Gina never imagined that Dan would go this way, or that Marty would experience the same kind of pain she had known.

"Marty, I'll come after school and see if I can take the rest of the week off." Gina whispered.

"Thanks, Gina," Marty replied weakly. "It would be nice to have a friend close by. There'll be a Catholic wake and service. Wake on Wednesday afternoon and night, church on Thursday."

"Okay. I'll be there. Kiss Ruth from me, and try to get some rest."

Marty was breathing through his teeth again. "I'll try. We're both exhausted."

Gina cried softly while washing her face and brushing her teeth. She had to try to sleep in order to survive tomorrow. The following day, she let her cooperating teacher know that a close friend's dad had passed and that she needed a couple of days. The woman ordered Gina to leave school by lunchtime on Wednesday. Gina took the train into the city later that day and Marty met her at the station. Turning around in the

crowd, Gina was shocked to see that Marty had shaved away
his chin hair. It was also the first time she had ever seen
Marty in a suit. She felt a little guilty today for thinking he
looked hot. It was also the first time ever that Gina saw Marty
without a smile on his face, with the exception of sleeping.
She felt broken-hearted at the sight of his deep sadness. They
embraced without speaking and stood still for several seconds.
Marty put his hands and fingers in Gina's long hair and
inhaling, said, "Oh my God, you smell so good. I need that
right now. Thank you, Gina." He looked down into her eyes
and smiled. "Ma went ahead to the funeral home. Shirley
went with her. We'll drop your bag at home and walk over.
Okay?"

   "Of course. Marty, I'm so s...."

   "Gina, nothing we can do about this, so don't say
sorry. Please. He and Ma loved each other a lot. We are so
lucky to have had him. Just sad that it can't go on," and his
voice faded. They held hands and walked to the curb to catch
a bus.

   "Marty, you shaved for Dan."

   "Yeah. Wan-ned ta make the old man happy."

   After reaching Queens and depositing Gina's bag, the
two walked the four blocks to the funeral home in silence. The
parking lot was quite full, but the home had several viewing
rooms. Gina's heart broke at the sight of Dan in his navy blue
suit. She had seen him napping on the couch in the front room
so many times. He truly looked as though he was slumbering
peacefully in that coffin. She stepped forward until she was
standing to Ruth's left. Gina turned to face Ruth, who sniffed,
"See? I told ya! Don't he look great in that suit?" The women
stood there for several minutes, arms wrapped around each

other's waist. Deeply grieved, they still managed to smile for Dan.

Gina did not know many of the people there, with the exception of Ruth and Dan's neighbors. After a time, she looked over her shoulder to see if she could catch a glimpse of Marty. He had been walking around the room, greeting Dan's relatives and coworkers. She spotted him at that moment, deep in a shadowy corner, speaking to a couple of young men. Marty blocked the view of one, but she could see the sleeve of an expensive-looking suit and two gold rings on a man's right hand. The other man was difficult to miss in any crowd: he was very tall, husky with blond hair. His facial structure was definitely Northern European, and he had a blond mustache with a nicely groomed van-dyke. He towered over a tall Marty. The trio shook hands before Gina turned her attention back to Ruth.

When another mourner approached Ruth to her right, Gina stepped forward to kneel at Dan's coffin. This act was creepily familiar. *The Lord is my shepherd, I shall not want...* She said a silent prayer for Dan telling him how happy she was to have known him. She removed a tissue from her purse and wiped her lipstick off, hard. Rising, she leaned toward Dan's body and kissed it on the forehead. "Dan, you look handsome as always, just in a suit." Gina stood and walked to the ladies' room. Running the water, she carefully washed and rinsed both the inside and outside of her mouth.

She powdered her nose and re-applied lipstick. Her movements were mechanical; she had grown accustomed to wakes and funerals. Gina had learned to stay in control of her emotions, but felt disgusted by the number of corpses she had kissed goodbye in her young life, and she knew there would be more.

"It almost tasted like vomit in my mouth," Rita puckered dryly to Carolyn and Franco.

Marty stayed in Queens for a full two weeks, and Gina brooded about whether or not he could catch up on his studies. She visited her grandparents for those weekends to keep a watchful eye on her grandfather's health. When Gina returned to the apartment after the second visit North, Marty was there. Gina was thrilled to see him. They held each other tight, and Marty picked Gina off the floor and twirled around with her in his arms. Neither said a word. Their lovemaking was fierce and sensual. So much emotion and stress, good and bad, had been bottled up for weeks. Breathlessly speechless, they remained locked in each other's arms long after finishing.

"Hi, Gina!"

"Well hi, Marty!" Still embracing, they rolled around on the bed, giggling with the delight of sharing some much-needed release.

The week proceeded as usual, Gina being the first one to embark for the school day. She kissed Marty's head before leaving, and he grumbled a "have a good day." He took the train into the city at every opportunity and usually stayed with Ruth two nights during the week. Gina went into Queens that next weekend. It would be the first time that she saw Ruth since the funeral. Gina marveled at Ruth's strength more than ever. Though weary, Ruth seemed pretty much herself. The house seemed so quiet without the boisterous Dan, and Gina clearly sensed Ruth's melancholy sighs.

Within a short span of time, Gina noticed that Marty did not study, read class notes or go to the library. She was concerned that he was neglecting his schoolwork due to depression. Gently, she broached the subject, but Marty calmly told her everything was under control. *Under control. Hmmm.* Gina had no reason to doubt him, and empathized Marty's losing Dan. As weeks passed, it repeatedly nagged at her. Marty's behavior was normal with the exception of lack of schoolwork. As spring approached and the weather improved, she decided to address the subject again during an evening walk to the grocery store. This time, Gina stood her ground when he gave a mundane answer again.

"Marty, you gonna stop talking to me about stuff? That's no good, you know!" She urged, "Please talk to me about what's going on. *Or*, what's not going on. Okay?"

"You're too smart! Ya know that, Gina? Okay, I didn't go back after Dad died. Ma needs me to help her sort stuff out! I'm takin one semester off, is all. I'll go in the summer to speed it up, too!"

"Your mother is as strong as a bull, Marty! Did she ask you to do this? I doubt it!"

"Right again, Einstein! Okay, okay. She's mad at me, too. I didn't tell her right away, either!"

"Jesus, Mary and Joseph!" blasted Gina. She had never raised her voice to Marty. She stopped short on the sidewalk. "I don't fucking believe this!"

"Come on, Gina. It'll be alright. I already took care of putting up two of Dad's rental houses for sale. Both had option-to-buy leases. One of the tenants is buying one, the other is for sale. Ma will keep the third one for now. Dad didn't leave much insurance because he had the properties. Ruth can pay the mortgage off on her house now." Marty's words trickled away as they continued their walk. "Just one semester, I promise. Early next year after you finish your teaching gig, you might come to Queens to live. I can go back in the fall, and I'll be finished next May."

Gina's hands were thrust deep into her jacket pockets. She stared at the ground as she walked. "I can't move to Queens right away, Marty. I need to live close to my grandparents." Her thoughts trailed off, wandering north. Federico had been battered by various maladies over the years, yet he still somehow managed to make it to age eighty-six. She planned to make her grandparents' remaining years good ones.

"Then you can bring them to Queens. Ruth would love that."

"*What* are you thinking? They can't be uprooted at this stage of the game, Honey." Gina was burning inside. They walked in silence until they reached the store. On the way back, each carried an overstuffed paper grocery bag. Gina continued. "Marty, you could've helped Ruth on the weekends. I know it would have been hard, but I would have helped, too."

"Gina, it's like this. Dan and Ruth paid off most of the mortgage a few years ago. Dad was gonna sell one of the houses anyway, to put some cash in the bank for a new roof and other repairs, another reason why Pop was selling property. He was actually putting that in the works when he passed. So, there's not much in the bank right now for Ruth. The life insurance took care of the funeral and after paying off some small bills, there's not much left for regular expenses."

"So, you blow your tuition and need to be supported to add to Ruth's burden? That doesn't make any sense, Marty!"

"It makes sense if you have a job," Marty replied sullenly.

"A job? You have a job, Marty? Honey, I'm so sorry I got mad. That's really sweet of you to do." Gina felt pangs of guilt for being so hard on Marty. "Where? What kinda job, Mart?"

"It's a pretty easy job. Only takes up about three days a week of my time, too."

"That sounds like a great schedule! What is it? What are you doing?" Gina spouted excitedly, giving Marty her full attention.

Now it was Marty's turn to study the sidewalk. He didn't look at Gina while walking forward, almost ignoring her. His pace quickened, and Gina followed suit. She hissed, "Marty, what the fuck? What's wrong? Slow down, please!" Marty halted as abruptly as a soldier halts from marching. He moved his head from side to side to avoid Gina's stare. She bobbed back and forth to try to meet his eyes. "Marty, do you have another girlfriend, or something?"

"Hell, no! I'll tell ya. You're not going to like it, Gina! Last year, I met this guy over at Sullivan's bar. You know, the one on the corner a couple of blocks from the house. He told me his boss needed some help, so he got me a job."

"You're not answering the question, though!"

"Alls I do is collect money from store owners in some lower east side neighborhoods, mark it in a notebook, bring the money to my friend, and I get a cut. The store owners are all afraid of my friend, but they like me a lot. They have the money ready when I walk through the front door. Piece of cake, Baby."

"And you report the ones that don't pay, too! You think I was born yesterday? You're collecting protection money for the mob! I can't believe this!" Gina was hissing like a rattlesnake. In no way did Gina disguise her anger. "You gotta death wish, or something? I cannot fucking believe this!" she spouted again. Her pace now accelerated and she nearly ran in the direction of the apartment house.

"Gee! Gee, wait! As soon as I get Ruth squared away, I'll quit. My friend's boss has never even met me. I'm not even sure he's knows I'm collecting for Dutch."

"Dutch? Oh, that's fucking beeeeautiful, Marty. A mob guy named Dutch! How original!" Gina shook her head in disgust. She stomped up the stairs to the apartment and unlocked the door, slamming it shut in Marty's face. The rest of the evening was spent in silence. Gina took a long, hot bath while Marty distracted himself watching TV. When Marty reached for Gina during the night, she rolled over as if asleep, groaning. But she was wide-awake, physically and emotionally, embarrassed by her own naïveté. She had practically begged Marty to come clean; he had kept a secret from her. In the days to come, it was difficult to concentrate on just about anything and she sometimes wept in private about the deception.

Turning to Carolyn and Franco, Rita muttered, "With Dan's death, the lock on Pandora's box fell off."

Chapter 13

I told Marty I needed breathing room for a while and he
obliged me. But, every Saturday morning at almost exactly
eight a.m., my phone became an alarm clock. No sleeping til
nine for me! Grinning, Rita reflected on the memory. "No
matter how many times I asked Marty to wait, he always had
a good excuse to call! I was pissed at him for taking that job.
Kept my distance, but was dying to see him, too. I picked up
the phone that morning. I missed him. He always overlooked
people's faults and chose to appreciate their better qualities. I
needed to do the same for him. He never held grudges, either."

"Gee, wake up! Gina?"
"Yeah, yeah, Martin! Jeee-zus! May I please sleep

just one Saturday past eight?"

"This is important, though."

"It's *always* important," said Gina dryly, but what Marty knew but couldn't see was that Gina was smiling that sheepish morning smile that he liked and missed so much.

"Listen, Gina. Go to a party with me, huh? Tonight. A big family party?"

"Family? What family? I never met anybody but your mom and pop. Met your uncle at the wake. Plus Dan hasn't been gone a year, Marty!"

"Come on, Baby! It's holiday time. I'll buy you a new dress and shoes, everything. But you're gonna have to get up now."

"No fair, Marty. You know I'd love a new dress and shoes. I have an assignment to finish. And, besides, you're supposed to be working to help Ruth out, remember?"

"Yeah, yeah, quit complainin! I gotta Christmas bonus. Please? It'll be fun."

"Hmmm. Where is this party, anyway, huh?"

"Does it matter? Meals are brought to the table, free bar, a band! Okay? Come onnnn... Dan would want us to."

Just the thought of going anywhere with Marty delighted Gina, and she never tried to hide that from him. He seemed so eager to go out and have fun. *He needs to go out.* "Of course, Mart. I'll take a quick shower and catch a train in about an hour. Can you meet me at the station?"

"Better than that, I'll pick you up at your place in an hour!"

"Huh?"

"I got a car. It's an old one, of course. I think it's pretty nice, though. I think you'll like it okay."

"What is it, Marty?"

"Nothing that special. All right, already! Are you gonna take your shower or talk on the phone? I thought we'd spend a little time together before we went shopping, *capisce*? Maybe I can persuade you to take a shower with me! You can talk to me then."

Gina shivered a little whenever Marty said even one Italian word, but spending an hour in bed with him overrode any other thoughts at the moment. "Okay, then. You stop talkin too!" The two laughed as each set their phone receivers down and got about their prospective business. Gina leapt out of bed now, glad to have been woken up before nine on this Saturday morning. It would be the first time Marty would shop with her. He bought her nice things in the past, and was a thoughtful shopper. An hour later, she was dressed and ready, and was reading a newspaper when she heard a car's horn repeatedly honking outside her apartment. She looked out of her teeny living room window to see Marty leaning on the passenger side of a blue car. The distance from the window to the curb was at least thirty yards, and with Marty there, Gina didn't recognize the make and model. She grabbed her keys and the door slammed, locking behind her. Gina ran through the apartment house lobby, and down a few steps to the street.

There stood Marty, with his arms crossed at his chest, and his Converse-clad ankles crossed as well. He wore his dad's wool tweed coat that was dwarfed by his large frame and a sly, but proud smile. As Gina approached, he straightened and extended his right arm like a female model at a car show. Gina halted abruptly, wanting to rub her eyes in disbelief. Before her stood a 1966 Chevy Impala, blessed with a perfect navy blue metallic paint job. Shivers again. "Martin," she

whispered, "this is a thing of beauty!" The car was spotless;
Gina felt as though she might cry. "It's perfect. You thought
I'd like it *okay*, did you? Come on, let's go for a ride," she
exclaimed, moving around the exterior of the car, looking in
the windows. "Oh, my God, Marty! I can't believe this. What
a great car!"

"Yeah, like the one your brother had? Right, Gina?"

"Ye-ah, she is! A little younger, but otherwise a lot
like her, Mart!" Having completed a full circle around the car,
she lunged toward Marty, wrapping her arms tightly around
him. They exchanged comical, exaggerated smiles.

Marty then cheerily said, "How about we make *your*
Ferrari engine purr, *then,* I'll take you for a ride in the car?
You can drive if you want, Baby."

"Okay, Mister! The twins miss you," Gina whispered,
opening the neck of her t-shirt with her thumb and looking
downward seductively at her chest.

"Ah, yes. The twins. I've missed them, too," drawled
Marty, licking his lips.

Hands clasped, they swung their arms gently as
they strolled toward Gina's apartment. To reassure herself
of its reality, Gina glanced over her shoulder to drink in the
apparition parked at the curb. Yes, she was sure glad she said
yes to Marty *this* Saturday morning!

Their lovemaking that morning was especially
enthusiastic and highly charged, both physically and
emotionally. Both were still grieving for Dan, but Dan would
be disappointed if his loved ones neglected to celebrate their
own lives. Gina felt some level of sadness, but also recognized
that her journey had taken her to Marty, Ruth and Dan, and the
happiness she shared with them.

After an hour or so of fun, Gina and Marty quickly showered and dressed. The rejuvenated lovers headed toward Manhattan in Marty's "new" blue chariot. Marty parked at a garage near Rockefeller Center, and pulled Gina across Fifth Avenue toward Saks. "Marty, Marty, don't you want to shop at Alexander's or Macy's?"

Extending his arms to his sides like a barreling tenor singing opera, Marty sang, "Naw, today it's Saks for my girl!"

"Wow! That must be some bonus you got! Oh-kay."

They shopped for over three hours. More than an hour was spent just choosing a dress. In the Specialty Petite Dresses department, a gracious older saleswoman with wavy white hair found several appropriate offerings for Gina to try on. Amongst them were a burgundy velvet mini dress and a black gown in which Gina felt totally awkward. At his request, Gina paraded out of the dressing room to show Marty each one. She was beginning to lose her patience when she reached for dress number nine and was struck by her reflection in the mirror. This was *the* dress! Cobalt blue satin, it was strapless with a sweetheart neckline and a fluttering peplum over the tapered skirt. It came with a matching cropped, long-sleeved jacket with a mandarin collar. The moment Gina alighted from the dressing room, Marty's head spun. He definitely agreed.

"It was definitely an eighties dress, but it was sweet!" exclaimed Rita to Carolyn and Franco.

Gina and Marty moved on to buy matching shoes, stockings and a purse. Last, onto jewelry. After leaving

Saks, Marty walked a protesting Gina up Fifth Avenue to a
salon, where he paid to have Gina's hands manicured, and
feet pedicured. He told her to stay put and he walked their
purchases back to the car. Marty appeared again just as Gina
finished, and he paid and tipped the young manicurist. They
lunched in a high-end deli and headed toward Ruth's house.
It would be several hours before the party, and Marty told
Gina that Ruth was looking forward to seeing her. He also
suggested she take a nap before getting ready for the party
and there was certainly plenty of time to do so. Ruth's house
always smelled of home-cooking. After drinking some tea and
raving about the Impala with her, Gina asked, "So, Ruth, what
are you wearing to the party?"

"What, Honey? What party is that?"

Gina shot a look to Marty, who just shrugged his
shoulders and looked down. Gina didn't want to spoil such
a good day by questioning Marty about the party again, so
she excused herself to take the nap. After such a vigorous
shopping marathon, she needed one. She kissed the seated
Ruth on the forehead and did the same to Marty. Gina
ascended the stairs to "her" room, picking her duffle bag up
from near the front door. Marty, you'll wake me in plenty of
time, right?"

"Yes, Babe!"

Gina felt deliriously giddy and drifted off peacefully
with the dusk. A couple hours later, the sound of Ruth running
the bath water in the upstairs bathroom woke Gina. Marty
rapped lightly on the bedroom door, and opened it slowly. He
eased into the room, but Gina was awake and still snuggled
under a light blanket. Marty lowered his face and inhaled
deeply, smelling Gina's hair and skin. She wrapped her arms

around his shoulders and they kissed sweetly, gushing mutual approval.

At the base of the stairs below, Ruth bellowed, "Kids! You have fun at your party! Just be sure to lock up. I'm going to synagogue with Shirley from across the street. Be careful. Marty, you hear me? Gina?"

"Yes, Ma!"

"Yes, Ruth!"

"Gina: I put a nice jacket for you to wear on my bed. It's too cold to wear just your dress and little jacket!"

"Thanks, Ruth!" Ruth bustled away, with her Kelly bag on her arm and an old black velvet cloche on her head. Gina and Marty just looked at each other with expressions of surprise to have suddenly inherited the house to ready themselves in private.

The first order of business was a repeat of their morning reunion. Next, they indulged in a bubble bath gleefully, and took their time grooming and dressing. Marty helped Gina put on her jewelry. She relished playing "dress up" with Marty. Before leaving, they turned on the light in Ruth's bedroom to discover the short mink jacket that Dan had bought for her a few years earlier. The young couple oohed at the richness and softness of the fur, and Marty bragged, "Ma sure loves you, Gina!"

Across the bridge they motored, singing Christmas carols to the strains of a local radio station. "Where we going, Honey?"

"I told you: it's a surprise, Gina."

Gina was somewhat familiar with the territory, but would easily get lost driving in New York. Marty knew the city well. Gina's spotted the Waldorf Astoria ahead on their right, but it hadn't occurred to her that it could be their destination. Marty maneuvered a right toward the hotel's valet parking attendants. "Marty, why are we stopping here?"

"The party is *here*, Baby."

Marty hustled to the car's passenger side to chivalrously extend his hand to Gina, intercepting a parking attendant trying to do the same.

"Easy, Honey!" laughed Gina. "Wow! This is where the party is, huh?"

Marty grabbed Gina's hand and walked her through the lobby and toward the back of the massive ground floor.

Gina was in awe of the richness of the décor all around her. She turned to Marty and exclaimed, "I'm in Oz!" Carefree, they talked and laughed until they reached a large open area, beyond which were several sets of double doors, like in a small theater. Outside those doors were partnered gargantuan males, most with dark eyes and hair. "Holy shit, I'm definitely NOT in Kansas, Toto!" Gina whispered to Marty, after she spotted a not-so-hidden pistol holstered beneath the bearer's topcoat.

"Shhh, Honey. Some of these people are friends of mine."

"Marty, are you sure you wanna go to this party? Is this the right party?"

"Yeah, don't worry so much. It'll be fun."

Gina watched spellbound while Marty was searched at the door by a jovial and courteous ape. The ape knew Marty by name, too. Suddenly the doors were opened before them and they stepped into a room that seemed to have no ceiling above a chandeliered canopy, and filled with close to a hundred tables. At the back of the room onstage, played a full-on orchestra. For a moment, Gina was a doe paralyzed by the light and glamour of the moment. "We're definitely *not* in Kansas!" she mumbled to herself. Holding Gina's hand tight, Marty guided her around the huge banquet room. Waiters seemed to be weaving about the room like bumblebees, their silver trays loaded with culinary delights.

"My friends are saving us seats at their table, I just don't know where they're at." Marty's head bobbed to and fro, until he spotted a figure waving to him from across the room. As the couple approached a table, she spotted the young man that waved to Marty. "Honey, these are some of my coworkers." The four young men at the table laughed gently at what must have been a private joke. Marty introduced them to Gina one at a time. There was Lorenzo, who had a light but muscular build. He was fair with auburn hair and a freckled face, and everyone called him Enzo. Enzo was born in Roma, but his parents emigrated when he was very young. He had a classic Italian nose that reminded Gina of Sal Bianco's beautiful nose. There was Dutch. Dutch was well, Dutch. It took Gina only a split second to recognize him, he was one of the men she saw Marty talking to at Dan's wake. Harry Vandermark was quite tall and very fair, with the chiseled, distinctive bone structure of a Dutch lineage. His relatives were from upstate, which had been largely populated by the Dutch starting in the early 1600s. Dutch had a mustache and van dyke, and short-shorn curly hair. Gina was struck by the contrast of his gentle, child-like demeanor and baritone voice. He was married to a Sicilian girl whose father had mob connections. He always introduced himself as Harry, but as Gina would later learn, he frequently began sentences with: "when you're Dutch." Everyone just started calling him Dutch after a time.

Now, Tony and Carmine looked Italian, and were.
Their dark, brooding good looks stood out from the others.
Carmine was the real deal, born on Sicily. Gina was mildly
rattled by Carmine's resemblance to Frankie, with his big
perfect smile and neatly combed hair. He spoke with a thick
accent. Gina noticed that he wore gold rings, but none on
his marriage ring finger. Tony was boyishly handsome, but
unfortunately boyishly sized compared to his pals. Dutch had
once called him "Tiny Tony," and Tony had put Dutch in his
place somehow. Dutch never used that nickname for Tony
again, and they were the closest of friends.

Within minutes of being seated, covered entrée plates
were being served to the young people. A waiter came by to
put cognac and glasses on the table. There were open bars on
either side of the room. Marty ordered mixed drinks. Gina
surmised the fantastic scene. The mix of people was wildly
diverse. Crystal clear to Gina, they were predominantly
Italian. There were couples on the dance floor, the women
had teased hair and were decked in jewels, their partners,
crisp and nicely groomed. There were elderly ladies in black,
dancing with ringlet-coifed girls in stick-out party dresses.
Later on in the evening, Gina was impressed by the fact that
all the children were corralled up and taken out of the hotel
by ten o'clock. After that, a 70's band with a young baritone
took the place of the orchestra. Marty and Gina danced to
their rendition of Lou Rawls' Lady Love, and flirted on the
dance floor. Amidst the joy of being with Marty, it was still
very difficult to ignore: there were lots of "bouncers" at the
exit doors. She knew that under their sharp looking suit coats,
they were "packing." But everyone seemed relaxed, having

fun; this was most certainly the grandest party she had ever attended. People came and went from the table, and Gina had said hello when introduced. Throughout the evening she and Marty danced several more times, all slow ones. That was more than fine with Gina, because she had her guy all to herself. "Hey, Martin. Why aren't your friends' girlfriends or wives here?"

"Two of them have kids. Enzo and his wife just had a baby, but she wanted to stay home. Carmine has a nice girl, Maria; she's home from college and visiting her folks in Manhattan. Dutch has a wife, a kid and another on its way. I think he chooses not to be home, but is obviously home enough -- if you get my drift. He told me his wife promised each time that she was on birth control. He won't get fixed, though."

Gina stared ahead blankly for a moment. "That's not going to happen to us, is it Marty?"

"No way, Baby," replied Marty as he navigated a light-headed Gina around the massive dance floor. "Hey, wanna go to church, tomorrah, Gina? Huh, my nice Italian Catholic girl? I'll go with ya!"

"Church? *You* go to church with me?" Gina asked teasingly. "Marty," she whispered as she pushed his head closer to her face, "being with *you* is like receiving a sacrament. I don't need to go to church, I can take communion with you." They laughed wickedly but innocently, alone together in a room bursting with over three hundred people.

When the band took a break, Gina and Marty walked toward one of the bars. Marty heard a familiar voice call to him. He yanked Gina's arm gently to signal a stop. The myriad of names and faces was a blur to Gina after several hours, but she was gracious and polite to everyone she met. This time, she shook hands with a chubby older man. The man then introduced a young woman seated next to him. Gina realized that, for whatever reason, this young woman did not like her. She was a homely girl, about Gina and Marty's age, and her long hair looked unnaturally blonde. Her eyebrows were dark and unruly. Gina was poised and quiet while Marty spoke with the man, but her skin crawled as she felt the eyes of the daughter still on her. Gina smiled sweetly, and it was not reciprocated. Finished with his brief courtesy hello, Marty turned Gina once again toward the bar. They ordered drinks and a waiter offered to bring their drinks to their table. Gina started back in the direction from which they came, but Marty playfully tugged her skirt and said, "Let's just walk around the perimeter of the room and take our time."

"Sure, Marty, but our table is right across the dance floor there."

"I know, I know. Just thought it'd be nice."

"Sure, Honey," and they held hands as they worked their way back to their table. "Marty, did you notice that chick back there? You know, the one your friend introduced me to? Boy! Did she hate me, Marty! She wants you!" Gina was being mischievous, but Marty's expression did not change; he clearly wasn't amused for some reason.

"He's not my friend, Gina. He's kinda my boss -- Dutch's boss, really. The chick's his daughter, I think."

Gina let it go. She didn't need to tease Marty about it. The six young people partied until after two, at which time, Marty quietly announced to Gina that he reserved a room for them at the Waldorf. "Mart! I don't have my clothes for morning or anything."

"Oh, yeah, you do. I stashed your duffle bag in the trunk of the Impala when you were doing your make-up at the house. I paid the attendant to have it brought to the room."

"Wow! You thought of everything, Marty."

"Wow is right!" exclaimed Carolyn. "What else, Rita? Keep going."

"Well, the party was fun, but the next day brought reality back. Everybody was nice at that party, but they were mob, or friends of the mob. And, Marty was working with and for them. I started to get nervous about this job Marty had. He suddenly had lots of money. He didn't change otherwise, he was the same Marty, but I was beginning to feel scared…"

Chapter 14

Gina and Marty's second Christmas had come and gone. Gina was finished with her student teaching and had earned her bachelor's degree that May. Her cooperating teacher was about to take maternity leave, and she was invited to stay on at the elementary school. Not a permanent hire, Gina was guaranteed a one-year assignment. She kept her apartment for another summer and took a job waiting tables at a restaurant at the town center's shore. Marty spent as much time with her as he could, and Gina felt safe staying in a now-familiar town.

The first weekend of summer was spent with Ruth, after which Gina returned to her apartment on Sunday night. On Monday morning, she hopped on the highway heading "home" to spend time with her grandparents. The balmy days

of the summer months helped make the commute north easier
and more enjoyable. She hadn't called her grandmother to say
she would visit, but she rarely did. Their guest room was her
room there, and they rarely left their home. Upon her arrival,
her knock remained unanswered. Gina stood at the back
door, franticly rummaging her purse for the house key. Upon
entering, dread filled her heart. On the kitchen table sat plates
with remnants of dry, uneaten food. A glass containing about
an inch of milk in it sat to one side. She raised it slowly to her
nose which crinkled in response to a mildly sour smell. Gina
noticed the flickering of light from the living room and rushed
to find it vacant and the TV on, its volume turned down to an
almost inaudible tone. She jumped to the ancient phone table
and dialed her uncle's number. It seemed to ring endlessly,
until the recognizable voice of her uncle's wife greeted her.

   "Honey, your grandpa took a turn for the worse last
night. Your grandma called and Uncle went there. They're
all at the hospital. Your grandma slept there last night, too."
Gina hastily excused herself and dashed out the door. She
crossed the small expanse of town toward the local hospital.
Berkshire Hospital was an old brick U-shaped building nestled
in the foothills. Gina zipped past a small house on the grounds
known as the Maternity Cottage, the very place where Elaine
had birthed both she and Joey. Breathless by the time she
reached the reception area, she asked for the room number and
ran down a long hall to an elevator. As she zoomed past, she
noticed that most rooms on the floor were empty. Overcome
by panic, the room numbers looked blurred as she raced along
looking for her grandfather's room. She burst into the room,
conscious of the fact that she must be quiet. Her fear melted,
and she felt her face flush. There sat her grandfather in bed,

her grandmother and uncle at his bedside.

"What's going on?" Gina blubbered. Her grandmother
and uncle looked startled and suddenly began to laugh, joined
by her grandfather.

Raising his large, angular hand, her Federico meekly
spoke, "Ciao, Bella!"

Gina's uncle said, "Hi, Honey. We had a scare last
night, but things are a lot better now. I'm trying to convince
your grandmother to take a break and eat a sandwich, maybe
take a bath. I was going to clean up their place a little, but
she won't go! Now that you're here, maybe you can convince
her."

Gina rushed to her grandfather's side. His mouth
widened revealing his punctuated smile. "It's okay, Gee," he
soothed, in a slightly hoarse voice. "I'm-uh better-uh."

Gina dramatically put her hand on her chest and
heaved a sigh. "I got so scared when you weren't home."

"All-uh you go. I'm-uh very tired."

"No!" protested Sophia.

"Oh, yes-uh!" Federico firmly responded.

"But I can stay for a while, Grandpa? Nonna will feel
better if I stay."

"Mah-sure. You stay. You joosta getta here. We
visit."

Gina's uncle turned to Sophia. "Okay, Ma? I'll take
you home and clean up the kitchen. You can take a bath and
a nap. Then Gina will come and get you and bring you back
to the hospital. I have to go rent the hospital bed for Pa." He
turned to Gina, "The doctor says we have to keep his head and
chest elevated at night to keep the heart from enlarging. We
can bring him home tomorrow."

"See?" piped her grandpa. "Go home-uh!" he firmly said to Sophia. Sophia gestured her hand as though she was saluting from her teeth. The old couple smiled fondly at one another and Sophia stepped closer to Federico and touched his hand lovingly with her fingertips. After a few moments, they kissed affectionately. She shot a stern look at Gina, "You come-uh for me, figlia?"

"Yes, Grandma. How long? Two, three hours?"

"Dua."

"Ma," said Uncle Jake, "you'll need more time than that!"

"No! Don't tella me no-ting!"

"Two, two and a half, Gina," announced her uncle, and he winked at her as he guided the old woman out of the door. Sophia shuffled back to steal another kiss from her husband, and everyone laughed merrily, even a nurse who had entered to check Federico's vital signs. Gina made herself comfortable in a chair while the nurse asked her grandfather a few questions. While the nurse patiently took his pulse, her grandfather mischievously rolled his eyes at Gina, making her laugh.

When the nurse left, her grandfather whispered, "They come inna the rooma, middle of the night. Inna, out. Inna out. How I suppose to getta better when they wake-uh you up, all-uh the time?" Gina giggled, relieved that her grandfather was smiling and joking with her. He relaxed back on the many pillows that supported him, and tapped the bed with his big hand, beckoning Gina to sit close. "Gina, bringa me the world. Tella me what you doin. Okay?"

"Okay, Sunshine. I'll tell ya." Gina sat side-saddle on the bed and filled her grandfather in on how excited she was to start teaching on her own for the first time. He wanted to know every mundane detail of her life, even about her waitress job that summer. But the details were not mundane for Federico. He watched Gina's face carefully when she spoke and asked all of the questions she had heard so many times, wanting to know about people she met, what the world outside looked like, how the food tasted. She obliged his every question with a response. After less than an hour, Gina noticed his heavy eyelids and slipped into a chair and lightly napped too. A nurse returned to brutalize her grandfather again, and Gina awoke.

"See-uh? No leave-uh me alone!" Federico spewed. "Gina, you go and I sleep-uh more before Sophia come back. Okay?"

Reluctantly, but obediently, Gina agreed, but she did not rush. She gently touched her grandfather's stubbly cheek with the back of her hand.

"No do that! You hurt-uh you hand!"

He's as feisty as ever! Thank God! She could hear Sophia's voice in her head, too: *Thank you, the God!*

"I'll do whatever I want to my favorite guy!" They laughed as though neither had a care in the world.

"How the boy? The talla one?"

"The tall one is molto bené. You know the lilacs are blooming early this year, don't ya?"

"Si. Warma springa this year. My favorite, the ly-locka."

"Si, Bello. My favorite, too. Well, I suppose I should go get Grandma. By the time I get there, it will be two and a quarter hours. She'll already be mad!"

"She *always* mad-duh!" grunted her grandfather, smirking lovingly. He sighed loudly and the two chuckled when thinking about Sophia's fiery spirit.

"Uncle will set up the hospital bed and I'll see you later."

"Yes, you see me."

"Yeah, you'll see me later."

"You see *me*."

Gina shuddered. She wasn't following her grandfather's cryptic responses. But he was exhausted and was probably not thinking clearly, she justified. "Whatever you say, Baby! It's tutta bené, Papa! It's all good! You're coming home!"

Her grandfather looked thoughtful for a moment before cocking his head to one side. "No, ahm-uh goin home!"

"That's what I said! You're *coming* home. Will you stop that? Geez-Louise!" Gina looked deep into the man's face. There was no mistaking it: he was being totally smug and cocky. He seemed sharp, lucid and fearless. His smile was as warm as the sun, his gaze calm and inviting.

"Ti amo, Gia. You bring me the world."

"Yes, my darling. But right now I have to bring you Nonna, or she will kill us both!"

She was holding his warm hand as she leaned forward to kiss his scruffy cheek.

"You hurt-uh you face!"

"Oh, shut-uppa, you! I love you. See you in a little while."

"You see *me*."

"Stop! Okay, be back soon!" She raised his hand to her lips and kissed the top of it softly. "You know something, Pa? Maybe I bring you the world, but you helped me love it again, not just appreciate it. Everywhere I go, I think about how the air smells, how special the food is, what the land is like. So I can tell *you* all about it, you know? I see how special life is, because of you. I'm going to travel to lottsa places and come home and tell you all about them! Grazie, Papa." They locked eyes, and Gina was gratefully conscious of how strong his grip felt.

"Prego, Bella. Ti amo. But joost-ah for *you*, go to Venezia! Okay? Joost-ah for you."

Gina planted another quick kiss on the old man's face. "Sure, just for me. You know we're going to talk about Venice when I get back! Right, Bello?" Sliding off the bed, Gina glided out the door, refreshed by the visit and nap. As soon as she was out the door, she heard her grandfather still speaking behind her, and knew there was no one else in his room. Pausing, Gina tried to make out what he said.

"Vene. Solo sono," was all that she could make of his words. *Is he saying a prayer? That's all it is, a prayer of some kind.* She pondered the translation, but couldn't quite put her finger on it. She haltingly moved to the elevator, knowing that Sophia was probably already pacing the kitchen floor, waiting.

True to form, Sophia had already donned her coat and had prepared a carry bag with clothing and some sandwiches. The tires of Gina's car crinkled against the gravel of her grandmother's driveway. She was not at all surprised when Nonna appeared around the corner of the house before Gina could even exit her car. She stepped onto the gravel driveway to run around and open the passenger door. She reached across Sophia's teeny frame to lock the seat belt in place.

"Hurry up, you!" Sophia ordered.

"Gee, whiz! Alright, already!"

Gina smelled a light dose of Youth Dew on Sophia.

Her grandmother seemed happier and more relaxed. Gina smiled contentedly as she backed down the driveway and drove toward the hospital. When they arrived at the hospital, they strolled arm in arm in relaxed triumph, for tomorrow Federico could come home. Gina's Uncle Jake would be setting up the hospital bed when Gina returned to the house later on. Stubborn as ever, Sophia planned to sleep in a chair as she did the night before, and Gina hoped that Federico could convince Sophia to go home again.

As they rounded the corner of the doorway of his room, their joy melted into grief. There stood her uncle, tears streaming down his face and dropping from his quivering chin. Federico lay flat and prone, his skin pale. Sophia dropped her purse and put her hands to her head. "Somma-na-bitchem-uh!" she howled and ran to the bed. "Pa. Pa!" She stretched her tiny body until her head was on her husband's unmoving chest, and wept. "No, Pa! No..." Shakily, Gina stepped back to lean against the wall. The room was spinning or maybe she was, she didn't know. Her grandfather had tried to tell her that he knew it was his time. His calm and smiling face entered her mind. *He knew and he wasn't afraid.* She then remembered the words she had heard him murmuring when he hadn't realized that she was still outside of his room. "Vene, solo sono." *Come, I'm alone.* Federico was beckoning death to take him while he was alone. He had kicked everyone out of the room to spare them the pain of watching him die. *But he was supposed to be okay, we could take him home. I'm-uh going home. He knew, and wasn't afraid. Yeah, though I walk through the Valley of the Shadow of Death, I shall fear no evil, for thou art with me. Thy rod and thy staff protect me. How the hell could he have known?*

Sophia stood rigid, and looked from Gina to her son. "You make-uh me go home! Why? You make-uh me." She began talking to Federico lovingly, softly, while touching his face and chin. "Federi, Federi. Ti amo, Federico."

Gina was numb. Too numb to cry. She didn't know how much time had passed, a half hour, maybe an hour before a doctor and nurse reentered the room with a Death Certificate to record the statistics. They respectfully spoke in hushed whispers, and left the room.

"Come on, Ma," coaxed Uncle Jake. "Come on, let's go."

"No!" shot Sophia. Fury raged in her eyes. She had expected to be there when the time came, but no one saw this coming.

Jake said, "I'll take her, Honey. See you there, okay?" Her uncle supported a shaky, weeping Sophia and steered her toward the door.

"Yes, of course." She made sure that they were definitely beyond earshot before approaching her grandfather's body. Gina looked at her grandfather's peaceful face. "Bello, you *tricked* me! You knew." She slowly bent and kissed the stubbly face. Stroking his beard lovingly, she turned and sat in the chair, looking at him. It appeared to Gina that there was almost a trace of a smile, as though he had gotten his way. She stayed until the orderlies came to take the body downstairs. They carefully and respectfully zipped the body into a heavy cloth bag. She walked alongside the gurney until they reached a service elevator. Without asking, she entered with them. It descended, alighting at a loading dock, where she could see the all-too-familiar station wagon belonging to undertaker Jerry Sanderson. Gina stood with her hand resting on the cloth bag atop Federico's chest, until it slid away beneath her palm and into the back of the wagon.

The next morning, Gina rose early and made coffee. She heard her grandmother crying and groaning and entered the bedroom quietly. As Gina reached out to touch her grandmother's head, Sophia snapped, "No, Gia! I be okay. Leave me alone-uh for now! I be okay!" Gina backed out of the room and gently closed the door. It would be another full day before the body would be ready to show. Footsteps could be heard padding on the front porch and a light tap came at the door. Distorted by the glue-chip glass of the door, Gina cringed when she recognized Jerry Sanderson's slight frame. This was his fourth visit in less than a decade. "Hello, Miss Bianco. So sorry for your loss."

"Thank you, Mr. Sanderson," Gina replied blankly, as if reading from an old script.

Offering a plain paper bag to Gina, Jerry stated simply: "Frederick's things."

"Yes, thank you," and Jerry Sanderson was gone as quickly as he appeared. Gina stood in the doorway, watching him go. She looked down at the grocery bag in her hands to see her grandfather's favorite tweed cap sitting smack on top of his neatly folded clothes. Her grandmother most likely folded them at the hospital and put them away in the closet. They were in turn, given to the undertaker once the body was removed, but Gina hadn't noticed at that time. She gently closed the door and picked up the cap. Her knees buckling, she slid into an overstuffed chair. Raising the cap to her nose, she inhaled deeply: the smell of her grandfather alive in his cap. She burst into tears and wept uncontrollably into the hat, now scrunched in her fists. *He's gone. He's really gone. He*

deserved so much better than what he got. The reality was
that Federico *did* die a very happy man, even if he did deserve
more. He knew how to appreciate what he had. Gina knew
that.

Another wake, and funeral. Another goodbye. Marty
and Ruth had driven up from Queens for the funeral, and it
was such a comfort to Gina and Sophia. At the reception that
followed the funeral, Marty and Gina huddled close to each
other. "Marty, when are you going back to school? Will you
do summer session, like you said before?"

Marty avoided Gina's eyes when responding. "It's a
little complicated right now, Gina. I'm not sure I can get back
yet. The money is so good, and we still have one house to
sell."

"But one sold already. You don't have to wait. Why
won't you quit that job? This isn't what you said, Marty!"
Gina felt unsettled like she did the first time Marty lied to her
about quitting school. She feared he was beginning to change,
and it was difficult to ignore that he wore very expensive
jewelry and suits. Her gut feeling screamed that there was
plenty of money being made. Ruth never indicated any fear
in regard to money matters. Gina felt Ruth's eyes from across
the parish hall and turned to look at her. She was too far away
to hear the conversation, but Ruth's face looked anxious. She
smiled meekly at Gina. "This is starting to scare me, Marty."
He didn't respond; his eyes were looking at the floor and not at
Gina.

Gina stayed with her grandmother for over a week,
until the old woman urged her to return to her own life. "You
grandpa say I wear black justa one-uh year! You go back to
your life now, too."

"Well, you better listen to him, Nonna! I don't want to see you in black forever, either."

"I listen," smiled Sophia.

Later that week, her grandfather's doctor called to tell Gina that the autopsy showed death was caused by a blood clot bursting close to Federico's over-burdened heart. At least she had some type of explanation, but it didn't change the fact that he was gone. Still, Federico somehow managed to reach age eighty-six, even with a multitude of physical problems.

Gina packed her things in preparation for the drive back to her apartment. She glanced at the corner where the old man's cane stood propped. Its resting place was the same each night for as long as she could remember. There it would forever remain. Sophia and Gina visited the cemetery together that morning, and the two ladies carried armfuls of lilacs to arrange in a vase. Smiling, they stood holding each other. It was quiet and sweetly warm that spring, and they savored the smell of the flowers.

Gina eased herself to the ground and ran her hand along the grass and the stone marker. "Here, Pa. The lilacs bloomed early this year. Vidi?" *You are always with me -- you will remain in the present for me, I promise.* "You brought *me* the world."

Chapter 15

That summer passed quickly and Gina spent more time at the apartment and not in New York. Marty had not registered for the fall semester and the two increasingly argued on the phone about it. Gina sometimes slipped into Queens to visit Ruth on her own, without telling Marty. By fall, her visits became few and far between. Back at her apartment, she stared at her phone that rang endlessly unanswered. She eventually changed the locks on the apartment door.

In New York, Marty was asked to take on additional collection duties with a promised salary increase. Dutch became lax about meeting Marty to pick up the monies, and often Marty kept the money at Ruth's in a small safe that Dan had purchased. Marty had been pretty much left on his own, as Dutch became more and more addicted to drugs and Asian prostitutes. Marty felt used, but the money was too good to step away from. He was devastated that Gina wouldn't speak with him and figured he may as well continue collecting for the time being. Marty played scenarios in his head about how to approach her. He had an engagement ring made just for her, which he carried in his inside breast pocket on a daily basis. He resolved to get on the train and go to the apartment and simply knock on the door. *Soon, I need to do that soon*, he thought repeatedly.

While on his way back from his rounds, Marty enjoyed the sunny afternoon. A black Cadillac Fleetwood appeared and slowly followed him along the street. Marty recognized the car, and its back window descended. Marty heard a familiar deep voice beckon from the interior. "Marty, Marty!" Looking inside, Marty saw Dutch sitting in the back by himself. "Mart. Get in." Two men that Marty did not recognize were in the front. "Come on, you're going to do a pick-up with me."

"I'm finished for the day. Besides, I don't know these gentlemen, Dutch."

"It's okay, come on. There's a big piece of the pie in this one. We need another guy with us."

Marty opened the door and slipped in. There were a couple of full grocery bags on the seat next to Dutch. "I don't know, Dutch. Why would you need this many guys to go with you? *You*, of all people."

"Cuz this one's a stubborn pain in the ass. He owes a lot and won't pay up. He needs a little fear put in him. The more, the merrier. You know? There's a lot to collect, and you get a cut."

Marty leaned closer to Dutch. "You know that if I

don't leave this soon, I'll lose Gina forever." He reached inside his coat pocket and pulled out the box with the engagement ring. "I'm gonna ask her to marry me."

"Come on, man! You could be a player, like me. Have a wife and fringe benefits on the side, too!"

"Gina *is* the fringe benefits."

"Okay, okay. Gina *is* great and if you want to leave, go. You're missin' out, Pal! One last big score, and you can go. Trust me, Baby!"

Marty sat brooding. He deliberated about asking to be let out at the next corner or continuing on to the "collection." The box still in his hand, he said, "Okay, I'll go this time. Then, I'm done."

"Okay, Marty. Okay. Thanks, Pal. I just gotta drop off some groceries for Josie and the kids. Boy, she's really sick with this one!" referring to the fact that his wife was pregnant a third time and not at all well.

Dutch insisted that Marty come in to say hello, and ever-benevolent, Marty obliged. Marty had not seen Josie in almost a year. Josie was always smiling and Marty was fond of her and the kids. Round like a Ruben's nude, Josie had wavy dark shoulder-length hair. Her skin was fair and her cheeks rosy. So it was in Marty's mind's eye. The Cadillac pulled up in front of Dutch's house which was run-down compared to others in the neighborhood. The front porch was littered with bikes and clutter. Marty and Dutch hustled through the front door, carrying the groceries. A young boy raced toward Dutch, and the father quickly put the grocery bag down so that he could accept his son's welcome. "Dad! Where ya been?"

"I'm here, I'm here!" Dutch kissed the boy on the face

a couple of times. The boy was young but tall. He had thick blond hair, beautiful rosy skin and blue eyes. Marty was so distracted by the child's enthusiasm, that he hadn't noticed the blanket clad woman sitting in a living room chair watching TV. The drapes were partially drawn and the room was dim. "Here Edwin, say hello to your Uncle Marty." The child obliged but skipped away after his father, who moved toward the kitchen through a door straight ahead.

"Hi, Mart!" A weak, but cheerful voice drifted from the blanket. Josie pulled it back from her head. Marty was not at all prepared for what he saw. Josie looked fragile and pale, her hair thin and scraggly. Her once-dazzling dark eyes seemed lost in the recesses of her own skull. Her skin looked slightly blotchy and her lips dry. It was difficult to tell that the skeletal woman was a full five months pregnant. As Marty moved toward her, she held her hand up protectively. "Stay away, Motty! I got some kind of crazy flu or some-tin! Just won't go away. You don't want to catch it." Josie rose from the chair slowly and painfully, putting her weight on one arm. Marty moved a step closer to offer his hand. "No, really, I can get up. I just need to go into the kitchen and talk to Harry. You don't want to catch this flu, Marty." Still wrapped in a blanket, she shuffled around furniture and entered the kitchen. Marty just stood in the living room with his hands in his overcoat pockets. There was a children's program on the TV and Dutch's little girl was propped in a chair watching. Marty realized that the once-chubby, curly-haired toddler was downright skin and bones, and her hair limp and straggly. From the kitchen he could hear a mumbled argument going on. "I need you home, Harry. *Please!* I'm so sick, I can't bathe myself or the kids. Cooking and cleanin is hodd for me right now. Edwin is trying to do everything."

Sadly, Marty heard Dutch reciting his mantra to Josie, "Trust me, Baby, trust me. I'm trying to make some extra money so I can stay home to take care of everybody." Marty knew that this was far from the truth, but Josie wanted to believe anything Dutch told her. So lovable was Dutch, he could "charm the skin off a rattlesnake," Tony used to say. The kitchen door swung open and Dutch headed for the front door, followed by Josie. Exhausted and out of breath, she stopped to put her hand on the wall for balance. Marty shuddered inside; to him, Josie looked like a talking corpse in a shroud. Marty looked over his shoulder at the open door.

"Bye, Marty. Nice to see ya," Josie crowed weakly.

"You, too, Josie. Take care of yourself. Call your sister to come help ya or something, would ya please?" Dutch was already outside, and Marty hastily peeled off five one-hundred-dollar bills and set them down on the coffee table. "Pay her a hundred a week, to come help you out if she can. Spend a couple a hundred on groceries first, though. Tell her that there's more if she keeps helping until you get better. Maybe your brother-in-law could mow the lawn and clean up the front porch and stuff," added Marty as he dropped more bills on the table.

"Thanks, Marty," Josie's sunken orbs widened at the sight of so much cash. "Kids, thank your Uncle Marty." Even though Josie smiled broadly, inside she felt slightly embarrassed that it was Marty who left the money and not her own husband. As Marty passed though the front door, Josie called behind him, "Say hi to Gina for me, would ya?"

While he walked to the car, Marty wondered if he would ever have the opportunity to relay Josie's hello to Gina.

Inside the car, Marty tried to convince Dutch to stay behind
with his family. "Marty, don't you get it? I'm trying to do
some big scores, so I can stay home with them. Come on,
Pal! Trust me!" That wasn't the first lie of the day. Dutch's
drug habit had grown out of control. He frequented whores
in Chinatown on a fairly regular basis. The Chinese mob
strongly suggested he stay away, but Dutch was big, dumb and
cocky. Most of the money Dutch made went to Dutch, not to
his family.

        "A year went by and Marty eventually stopped calling.
It broke my heart when Ruth left me phone messages. She
begged me to call her back. I was torn up inside." Rita
bowed her head as though in shame. "I finally called her
and promised to come down and spend a weekend with her.
When I got to Ruth's, Marty was there. I tried to leave and
he blocked the door. Ruth went out the back door and we
were alone in the house. He grabbed me and I beat him with
my fists, but he held on until I was tired. I wanted to be there
and *not,* at the same time. He pulled me into the living room
and pushed me down til I sat still, all the while telling me
that he needed me." Rita blew hard through her nostrils in
unmistakable rage. Shaking her head she spewed, "That's
when he told me *everything.* He told me about that day with
Dutch. They drove to Brooklyn to collect from a store owner
who quit paying protection money. The guy had a little office
over his store, and the four of them went upstairs. The store
was closed and they surprised the guy who was alone. Dutch
asked him for the money and the guy still refused and moved
around a desk. It was obvious he was trying to get to his gun.

Dutch intercepted and strangled him with his bare hands. Marty tried to leave and one of the other thugs drew his pistol. He watched while the store owner's eyes bulged out of his head and he shit his pants. Marty threw up all over an Oriental rug. Funny, I remembered that... the Oriental rug, not the throwing up part!"

Carolyn put her hand over her mouth, like she might throw up, too. She and Franco looked at each other with disbelief. Rita, however, remained composed when she relayed the story, almost vacant.

"Then, Marty told me Dutch turned to him and said: 'You ain't going nowhere, Marty. You belong to us.' There was an open safe in the room. The dead man was putting his money away, it was loaded with all the payollah he stashed from not paying Dutch. Who knows why he'd be that stupid, leaving it there. Maybe he was too scared to carry it to the street! They stuffed their coats and jackets with the cash while Marty just stood there, dazed. Dutch literally stuffed Marty's pockets too. Dutch dragged Marty out of the room and down the stairs. The three hoods laughed and joked about how surprised and funny the store owner's twisted face looked, all red with broken blood vessels. I just sat and cried when Marty was talking. He was crying, too. Like that wasn't bad enough, he told me that the four of them drove to Dutch's boss's house for dinner with the man and his family. Said he couldn't eat a bite and the boss's daughter stared at him the whole time. I thought I was going to die on Ruth's couch, right then and there. Marty said he took the train to my apartment in the middle of the night, and banged on the door until the landlady downstairs threatened to call the cops. 'Marty! Is that you? Jesus Christ, boy, it's two o'clock. Don't ya know? She moved out weeks ago.'"

"I stood to leave and Marty grabbed my arm and told
me that there was more. I couldn't believe it. I said: 'More?'
He said when I didn't return his or Ruth's calls, he didn't know
what to do. He drank a lot and tried to forget about everything.
Dutch's boss invited him to his house several times and Marty
was eventually ordered to marry the daughter."

Rita gulped hard. Quite matter-of-factly, she stewed,
"And he did. He married her. Just like that. He said they
would have killed him if he didn't." She ran her hands through
her hair. "I stood up and slapped his face, *hard!* Wasn't even
looking at him. Grabbed my sweater and purse and ran to the
subway. From Grand Central, I caught the train to Brewster
where I parked my car. It wasn't until I got to my car that I
realized that I had left my weekend bag behind."

Rita sighed regretfully, "Thinking back to my marriage
to Eric is like watching a bad movie. It lasted less than two
years, but seemed like ten. The shock of Marty marrying a
mob princess was more than I could handle. I met Eric in a
bar during a period of self-medication and married him on the
rebound. Don't really remember loving him, either. He was
an electrician, and was fun at first. I knew he partied a lot, but
after we married and lived together for a while, it was clear he
had a bad drinking problem. Soon, I discovered he came from
a family of functioning alcoholics. I looked the other way,
hoping things would improve. I landed a teaching job near my
hometown, so I could be close to my grandmother. At work,
I smiled and carried on like I was happy, or at least happy
enough. A younger teacher aide named Liz befriended me, and
helped me cope with things sometimes. I would have gone
crazy without her. It was literally days or weeks after returning

from our honeymoon that the shit started hitting the fan! I
could not do anything right for Eric. He hated my cooking,
everything. Everyone else told me I was a good cook, but
not him. You get the picture. *Everything* was like that:
housework, laundry. I couldn't do anything right in his eyes.
Once, he came home from work furious that I had wrapped
up his lunch too well, that's what he said. It had been raining
torrents for days, so I wanted to be sure it stayed nice and
dry. No 'thank you for lunch, Honey.' Instead, I got shoved
and slapped around because his coworkers teased him about
the obstacle course he had to go through to get to his lunch.
He would stay out late and then come home drunk a *lot*. I
cowered under the sheets pretending to be asleep. Sometimes,
Eric forced himself on me. It was gross! I trudged along for
about a year like that. Marty called me once in a while, but
only at work, and in the middle of the day. We only got to
speak for a few minutes at a time and we never actually talked
about our marriages, or about seeing each other again. It was
horrible. Marty always asked if I was happy and being treated
right. I never really answered the questions directly, but didn't
say yes, either."

Gina had a routine before heading off for school each
day. In the very early morning hours, she readied ingredients
for dinner, exercised for a half hour, made her and Eric's
lunches, and then took a shower. This routine gave her some
structure as married life with Eric was often chaotic. Up to
that point in the marriage, Eric had been arrested twice for
drunk driving. He was abusive, both physically and verbally.
A stroke of poetic justice, Eric had been beaten within an

inch of his life on one occasion, as well. On a fall Sunday
afternoon, he argued about a football game call with a biker
type. Unknown to the drunken Eric, behind him sat the
balance of a gang, who jumped him and beat him unmercifully.
One of Eric's friends, a karate master, was in the bar. Due to
the friend's high alcohol consumption, he did not grasp the
seriousness of the attack. Eventually, he protected Eric long
enough to save his life. Police were called and the bikers took
off, disappearing into the fading autumn sunshine, out of sight
and onto a highway.

Gina kept up a front for days. Each day, she returned
home to care for a lump of flesh that looked like a prizefighter
who lost a bad fight. Eric was insistent that he could shower
and allowed the spray to beat his stitched head and face, re-
stimulating blood flow. Each day for a week, Gina found
blood on the carpet and walls. Gina became so physically
weak that she experienced consistent, mild temperatures. In
addition, her weight was dropping. If that wasn't discouraging
enough, she began to occasionally vomit. Her self esteem
low, she had become co-dependent. The security she felt with
Marty was a distant memory.

As spring neared, Gina knew things were not
improving. Inwardly, she casually contemplated suicide. Liz
stopped by to visit, finding Gina either crying or bruised. Gina
greeted Liz at the front door. Liz followed Gina through the
living room where a drunken Eric was smoking a cigar in front
of the TV. *Gina loathes cigar smoke*, she thought. As she
usually did, Liz ignored Eric. The two shared a mutual disdain
for each other.

Tall, green-eyed, blond and pretty, Liz helped Gina
keep a foot in the real world. She visited more often that

spring, as she sensed Gina was becoming increasingly withdrawn and physically weak. That afternoon, she dropped by without calling first. Liz noticed that there was a bag of ice sitting on the counter. "Do you want me to put this away? Why is this out on the counter, Gina?" queried Liz.

Gina looked embarrassed, and didn't answer. Liz realized that Gina was wearing a skirt and not jeans. It was a Saturday, after all. She silently moved toward Gina who was sitting at her kitchen table, and put her hand gently on Gina's knee. Gina jerked slightly, sensitive to Liz's touch. Gina put her index finger to her lips, signaling quiet. In case Eric could hear them, Gina began a contrived dialogue.

"Liz, help yourself to coffee, would you?"

"Sure," replied Liz, as she watched Gina slide her skirt up on her right leg. Liz put her hand to her mouth. Tears welled in her eyes. The front and side of Gina's thigh was blackened. It looked swollen and tender.

"Above the knees," whispered Gina, "always above the knees, so that people won't see. I was icing it when you came in."

Liz was furious. Snarling through her teeth, she seethed, "I'm going to kill him, Gee. You need to get rid of him, soon! You understand me? He's going to accidentally kill you, *on purpose!*"

The words hung in the air. Liz bent to hold a trembling Gina. Suddenly, there was a crashing sound in the living room. The two jumped around the corner to find Eric on the floor, arms outstretched, the cigar still in one hand and close to the carpet. He had probably stood up too fast, and passed out taking a floor lamp down with him. There was broken glass near the wall where the lamp had shattered. Gina

jumped forward and took the cigar from Eric's hand. She
turned the corner to the kitchen and tossed the smoldering
mess into the sink. Arms crossed disgustedly, Liz looked down
at the drunken lump on the floor. "How much longer are you
going to baby-sit this pig, Gina? Look at him." They stood on
either side of Eric. "Gina," whispered Liz, "all we have to do
is bring that cigar in here and set it down on the rug. You and
I should go shopping. The house goes up in flames, and you
become a widow."

"But the few things I have from my mom, my
grandmothers. I would need to put them somewhere. Would
you take them?"

"You wouldn't be able to take anything. Nothing.
No pictures from the walls, nothing. There could be an
investigation. If we were found out, that would be the end of
us."

"Imagine that! Me, being charged with murder!
Arson! Well, we're not going to do it. It was your idea, not
mine!" Gina could feel the hair on her neck and arms bristling,
and she shivered. She shivered because she was tempted, not
because she was appalled by the idea.

Liz took Gina by the arm. "Leave the jerk right there.
I'll pick up the glass for you. Go back to the kitchen and ice
your legs." She led Gina back and sat her down again. Good
friend that she was, Liz fixed Gina a sandwich and urged her
to eat. She cleaned up the broken glass in the living room,
vacuuming around the body on the floor. *Amazing,* Liz
thought. *He's so drunk that a vacuum cleaner a foot away
from his head doesn't wake him!* When she was finished, she
turned the corner to the kitchen to find Gina quietly crying
with her face in her hands.

"What's keeping you from filing for divorce?"

"Money. Don't have enough for the attorney I want. I need about seven-hundred more."

"He must be good."

"He is. Plus, no other way to tell you this, but I'm pregnant."

"What? Not on the pill?"

"I haven't slept with him in ages. I went off to give my body a break. Was only off them for two weeks and he raped me. I had no clue I could be that fertile so quickly. Can you rape your own wife? Today's 'disagreement' was about my becoming pregnant. I told him and he said to get a second opinion. Can you believe it? How stupid is that?" Humored and disgusted, Gina huffed, "Get a second opinion. Ha!" Then, he accused me of sleeping with someone else. He gets so drunk that he doesn't remember what he does. Last week, he kicked me with his steel-toed work boots and the next day wanted to know what happened to me. He is so burnt out that he didn't remember pushing me down the stairs."

"What? You fell down the stairs, too?" gasped Liz.

"Just a few." Gina drew her hair that was draped across her forehead aside. One side of her forehead was bruised and scraped. She buried her face in her hands again.

Liz shouted, "That's it! You're outta here. Let's pack a bag. You're coming to my place." Gina limped down the hall, followed by Liz. They quickly packed a carry bag.

"He's just going to do it again, Gina."

"I know; I'll get out of it. I promise."

In spite of the morning's events, the two friends managed to salvage the rest of the day. Liz stopped to rent some movies, leaving Gina in the car to rest. When they arrived at Liz's apartment, Gina showered and put her pajamas on. It was early evening when Liz ordered delivery pizza. Neither spoke of what had happened earlier. They gossiped about other teachers at school and the problem kids, watched movies and eventually, both fell asleep on the couch. Liz woke around two in the morning, and turned off the lights and TV. She bent to kiss her friend's forehead, but remembered it was bruised. Gina moaned in her sleep and woke to see Liz smiling down at her. "I probably shouldn't have let you fall asleep, considering the bump on your head. Didn't intend to fall asleep my own self!" Liz said. She noticed that Gina looked pale and was perspiring.

Gina pulled herself up to yawn and stretch, but instead doubled over in pain. Shocked, Liz knelt to comfort her. "Liz, bad cramps!" gasped a breathless Gina. "Help!" Gina was wrapped in a comforter, and Liz managed to get Gina into the bathroom. Pulling the comforter away, it was clear what had happened. Gina was miscarrying. The comforter and Gina's pajamas were soaked with blood. Liz sat Gina on the toilet. She wrapped a large towel around Gina's torso to keep her warm until she thought the expulsion was finished.

"I'm right here. You'll be just fine," soothed Liz. "Take a shower and I'll stand right here if you feel faint or anything. Just tell me." Throughout the night, Liz watched while Gina slept, terrified that she might die in her bed. Remarkably, Gina was weakly smiling by noontime and promised Liz she would call her doctor first thing in the morning. Gina needed some clothes and toiletries to stay another night. Going back to Gina and Eric's place for clothes was never discussed. Liz made sure Gina did not exert herself in any way, and this amused and warmed Gina. Liz suggested she take Gina to an emergency room, but Gina protested and promised again that she would call to ask the doctor to examine her at the end of the day.

The next day went as planned. At lunchtime, Liz watched as Gina ate more food than she had witnessed her eat for months. Though tired, Gina appeared animated and happy. At the close of the school day, Liz drove Gina to her home for her car. She followed Gina for a few blocks to be sure she kept her promise to see her doctor. Gina drove directly to the doctor's office. The doctor agreed it appeared she had passed everything while miscarrying. To be sure, he recommended Gina be scheduled for a D&C. One of his associates could do it on Saturday, and Gina wouldn't have to miss any school. After her doctor appointment, Gina slipped into her own home to retrieve more clothes while Eric was working. Gina drove back to Liz's apartment, where she spent the remainder of the week. When she returned home the following Monday evening, Eric grated on her for not being there to cook. Gina quietly told him that there were sandwiches in the fridge and went to the guest bedroom to read before sleeping. Sure he was probably too drunk to remember being informed of the pregnancy, she told him nothing about the miscarriage.

In the days that followed, Liz made it a point to stop at Gina's house almost every morning to be sure that there were no altercations. Gina was relieved to have such a caring friend close by. She enjoyed the company in the morning and often the two carpooled when their schedules matched. Occasionally, one had bus or playground duty. Sometimes, neither was scheduled for any duty, and other times they were scheduled together. One particular morning, Liz arrived at Gina's place just a few minutes after Eric drove off. Liz looked especially radiant that morning, a mischievous smile on her face as she entered Gina's kitchen. Gina was just down the hall, finishing up her make-up and brushing her teeth.

"Gina!" she called. "Hurry up! I need to show ya something!"

"Okay, okay!" Gina gurgled through the sudsy toothpaste in her mouth. She wiped off her mouth and quickly applied lipstick. Down the hall she bolted. "What's happenin', Lady?" she laughed. "Why the fuss?" Gina could see that Liz held her hand on the kitchen table, concealing something under it. As Gina eased closer, Liz moved her hand as though she was fanning out playing cards. At first, Gina laughed loudly at the drama Liz was playing out, but realized that her friend had spread out several one-hundred dollar bills.

"My sister sold her house and I borrowed some money from her. Here's the seven-hundred that you need for the divorce, Gina. Pick it up. You can pay me back a little at a time."

Gina was too astounded to speak. Her mouth wide open, she finally managed to push out the words, "What the? I would have to think it over, Liz!"

"Gina, pick it up now, or I'll take it with me. I won't offer it a second time. Understand?"

Gina did not hesitate. She stepped forward and grabbed the money. Fisted, she held it tight to her chest and jumped up and down like a TV game show winner. Liz hugged Gina at the waist and lifted her off the floor. The two shrieked with delight. That day, Gina made an appointment with the lawyer that had come highly recommended by friends. The following week, she met her new attorney to begin the process of legal separation. Within two weeks, a restraining

order was filed against Eric, and he was required to move
out until the terms of the divorce could be worked out. He
dragged his feet to find legal representation, thinking that
Gina wouldn't have the guts to follow through. But with Liz's
push, Gina gained the confidence to move forward. Her health
began to improve immediately. No longer dreading going
home, she grew calmer. Her doctor referred her to a counselor,
and Gina's feelings of self-worth rose.

"Another couple of weeks passed and Marty called to
say that he and Ruth missed me. I missed them, too. I figured
a trip to New York was a well-deserved treat. I stayed with
Ruth that first visit, but before long, I was with Marty and the
boys again. It was a difficult reality, we were both married to
others. Instead, we chose to create our own reality. There was
really no one else for me. Within four or five months, I was
pregnant again. Not a healthy thing for my body, but I was
ecstatic and nothing was going to stop me from having that
baby. Nothing!"

Gina's doctor warned her to take it easy. She followed
his every instruction to the T. Gina had a ravenous appetite
and quickly became voluptuous. Admiring her roundness in
the mirror, she felt beautiful. Other than Liz, no one knew of
her separation, and Gina happily answered about her growing
tummy. Telling the other teachers at school that she was
divorcing could wait until after the child was born. When it
became apparent to Marty and Ruth that Gina was carrying
a child, she gleefully admitted it. Her visits to New York

became less frequent by the last trimester of her pregnancy. Liz attended birthing classes with Gina and would be the childbirth coach. As she neared the eighth month, Gina was large and uncomfortable. It seemed to be a brutally humid New England summer to her, but it was really about the same as any other year. One day while out shopping with Liz for baby clothes, her water began to slowly break. Just drips, Gina prayed that her water was not going to fully break. There was an additional four weeks to go before she reached full term. Nonetheless, she gave birth the next day after a grueling night of labor, ironically on Labor Day weekend. The baby was small: five pounds, eleven ounces, but not in any immediate danger. Slightly jaundiced, the teeny girl would need to stay in the hospital for a few days. Gina was officially discharged. Due to the fact she had planned to breast feed, this would make life incredibly difficult until the baby was released. A caring maternity ward nurse appealed to Gina's insurance provider, and Gina was granted approval to stay. Gina was now on maternity leave and was scheduled to return to school after the holidays.

The morning following the birth, Gina's grandmother, uncle and her uncle's wife visited. The infant needed to stay in an incubator, therefore a nurse had to bring the baby for the family to see. Everyone talked excitedly, even an exhausted Gina. A small woman in colorful scrubs arrived pushing a tiny bassinet on wheels, containing a precious cargo. She slid the baby into Gina's arms. The preemie had quite a lot of dark hair. Everyone was suddenly still and quiet. Nonna Sophia threw her hands up as though she was about to bow to Mecca. Laughing, everyone rallied around the bed to take a first look. Sophia and Gina looked hard into each other's teary eyes.

"Nonna, look at her! Isn't she gorgeous?" whispered Gina. She grazed her lips along the miniature face. Looking up at her grandmother's glowing face, Gina sighed, "Do you see the resemblance? She looks *just like* Joey!"

Chapter 16

Within a few months, Gina resumed her visits to New York with her newborn. Ruth was always happy to have the child with her, so that Gina and Marty could have some time together. It amazed Gina to see how quickly the child's bright personality and motor skills developed. To everyone's amazement, she even began to walk, however shakily, at ten months.

The holidays came and went and Gina resumed her teaching duties. Gina was daydreaming about her next weekend visit during a lunch break when Marty surprised her with a phone call.

"Baby, if it's okay, I'm going to meet you in Hartford on Friday night instead of you coming into the city on Saturday morning."

"Why, Marty? Everything okay?"

"Yeah, yeah, of course. I thought we'd go to a Sox game in Boston. It would be a nice change, don't cha think? Can you get someone to watch the baby for a couple of days? I'll pay for a sitter."

"That would be fun! I'll ask Liz if she can watch her. Thanks, Marty. If we have time, can we go to the Museum of Fine Arts?"

"We'll see. We'll do as much as we can. So pack a bag and be ready. You don't have to take much. Whatever you don't have, we can buy. Call one of the airport shuttles. Can you be there by seven? I don't need to give you the flight info cuz I'll be waitin' near the Allegheny Airlines door. One of the boys will come with me, okay?"

"I don't care, as long as I'm with you. I can get to Windsor Locks by seven, easy." With only Liz to trust for a sitter, Gina cautiously asked. Liz jumped at the chance. Though embarrassed, she continued by asking for a ride to the airport, too. Gina excitedly raced home that evening to pack a small suitcase. Marty was fun and spontaneous sometimes. Going to a ball game would make a great change of pace weekend. Gina lied to Liz about where she was traveling, saying instead that friends from Boston paid the fare so that Gina wouldn't have to drive up after a long week. Marty knew all about Liz from Gina, but Gina did not tell Liz much about Marty: only that he was a college friend that lived in New York. Liz had her suspicions, but did not push Gina for answers because she felt her friend deserved happiness. *Gina's peelin' away the bitter layers and finding her healthy, inner self,* Liz mystically mused.

Friday couldn't arrive faster for Gina. At dismissal,

she bolted from school, heading straight home for a shower and change of clothes. Liz arrived at five-thirty as promised and they left immediately for the airport. The ride to the airport was almost as long as the short flight to Boston would be. Marty drove up from New York; a flight from Hartford would be more relaxing than continuing the trip by car.

Gina kissed Liz on the cheek and took her wallet out to offer money for gas. "Don't be silly, Girl. Go, and have some fun. I'll be here on Sunday night to pick you up, don't worry!"

"Thanks, Liz!" Gina bounced out of the car and opened the back door of Liz's car to coddle and kiss her daughter goodbye. The child good-naturedly smiled. Liz prompted Gina to get going before the tot realized her mom was leaving her behind, so Gina bounded through the electronic doors of the small airport. She had plenty of time, but she walked swiftly. Every minute spent with Marty was valuable and important. Punctual as always, there stood Marty waiting for her. Tony was there, too. The young couple synchronously draped their arms around each other without saying a word. When the tension of their kiss was severed, each laughed and continued hugging.

"Ready, Lady?"

"You bet!" Just a few minutes passed when the flight was called for boarding, and the cheerful threesome boarded the commuter plane bound for Logan Airport. A limo was waiting when they deplaned, and took them to a Copley Square hotel. Gina loved Boston as much as New York. Quite possibly she loved it even a little more, as it was a smaller city with a vibrant New England look and feel. Gina especially appreciated that skyscrapers were closely interspersed with one and two-story historical landmark buildings. Paul Revere's house, the old North Church, ancient cemeteries: all were untouched in the midst of a bustling city. As always, there was dinner and cocktails. Marty researched jazz clubs and the three walked to one close to the hotel. The weather felt balmy and warm this early June evening. Shortly after midnight, Marty suggested they all go to bed, saying he had a full day planned for them. Gina queried, but Marty was mysteriously smiling. He liked to tease and surprise Gina, so she happily allowed the game to continue. No need to twist her arm, she would go to the hotel whenever Marty said. She couldn't wait to slip into bed with him, anyway. Gina was thrilled to be in Marty's life again, and sad at the same time. He was, after all, legally married to another woman. Gina's brain felt like scrambled eggs when she confronted that demon.

The next morning Gina was awakened by an excitable Marty. Still dressed in pajamas, he stood at the side of the bed. "Come on Gee. If we get up now, we can have some lunch at Quincy Market before the game. I know how long it takes you to get ready."

Gina tugged playfully on Marty's pajama crotch. "Me? Look who's talking! Wouldn't you rather stay here and have some breakfast? You *never* want to get out of bed!"

"Who can blame me?" laughed Marty, bending to bring his face to Gina's neck. Cupping her head in his large hand, Marty leisurely moved his face down the softness of her cheek, her hair and neck, tickling her skin as he exhaled.

Gina draped her arms onto Marty's shoulders. The sheets slipped down her rib cage; she slid sideways on the bed toward Marty. Glancing downward, both laughed. "Your brain all a twitter there, Martin?" They kissed softly, and Marty suddenly jumped to the floor, gently sliding Gina backward onto the bed.

"Okay, lots of time for that later. Let's get going!" Marty ordered, clapping his hands.

Gina blinked in dull surprise. "Huh? Let's get going? Who *are* you, anyway?" Reluctantly, she swung her legs over to the edge of the bed. Totally naked, Gina glided past Marty, sweeping her hands over Marty's face, like a ballet dancer. Marty smacked her butt and they roared and waltzed backward to the bathroom. "Come on, Marty. Hows about a quickie in the shower?" giggled Gina. "Can't we go to the museum instead, Mart? We ate so much last night, I'm not that hungry."

"By the time we get showered and dressed, you might be. We should eat something light before heading to Fenway. That way we won't eat junk at the game."

"Oh-kay," sighed Gina, shrugging her shoulders. She pulled her underwear from her suitcase and headed toward the bathroom to shower.

Outside, the sun was warming the brick sidewalks of Quincy Market. Gina wore a rockabilly-style cotton dress and low heels; she felt feminine and festive on this glorious day. Holding hands, she and Marty walked slowly toward Quincy Market. Tony followed a few steps behind. Before leaving the suite, Marty had tucked a tourist brochure into his coat pocket. Along the way, the trio window-shopped. Gina loved shoes and tried two pairs on in one store, but didn't really like one pair at all. She loved the others but they were uncomfortable, she said. As they approached Quincy Market, Marty turned to Gina and placed his hands on her shoulders. She rose up on her toes to kiss him, but he put two fingertips on her lips and said, "Wait, Gina. I need to talk to you about something." He looked serious, but not distressed, so Gina was not alarmed.

"What, Baby? What do you want to talk about?"

Before replying, Marty produced some bills and handed them off to Tony. "Meet us right here in a couple of hours, Tone?" Tony smiled broadly. "Sure, Marty. See ya, Gee!"

"Tony, wait!" Gina called as Tony strolled away. She turned to Marty and asked, "Why isn't Tony coming to the game with us?"

Marty turned Gina toward the market and standing behind her, put his hands around her waist. "I love the architecture here. Don't you?"

"Is that what you want to talk about? New England architecture? Is everything okay, Marty?"

He turned her around again, smiling. "Everything is fine. I just don't know *how* to tell you, is all."

For a moment, Gina thought Marty might tell her he loved her, but why take her to Quincy Market to do that? She was confident that he indeed loved her, anyway. Her mind raced. Maybe he was going to tell her he was getting a divorce, but she didn't think he would chose this time and place to talk about that, either. Marty took Gina's small face in his hands and looked deep into her eyes. "I remember when we first met and you told me about your family, about Joey's trip to Daytona…." Looking uncomfortable, Marty hesitated before pointedly blurting out: "Gina, your nephew lives in Boston." He drew a long breath like a swimmer who had just reached the surface after a deep water dive. "An American-Italian couple adopted him. I hired someone to find him. He just graduated from high school and works *here* in the summer."

Gina studied Marty's face and shivered while he spoke. Feeling a bit weak, she swayed slightly. She was also smiling like a damned fool. She whispered, "Oh, my God, Marty. Oh, my God! You're the best. I can't believe this. Joey would be so happy. Joey *is* so happy!" She threw her arms around Marty's neck and repeatedly kissed his blushing face. "Thank you, thank you, Martin!"

With his hands on her shoulders, Marty steadied Gina, but realized he needed to keep his own composure in check, as well. He looked from side to side nervously before continuing, "Gina, he waits tables at the restaurant over there. Come on, we'll sit at one of his tables. Now, Honey: take a deep breath. You can't reveal yourself to him, okay? And, *no* crying, understand? We want to come back and see him again, right? We might bump into him the next time we're here. I'm going to tell him we travel through a lot, so that he won't suspect anything if we meet up."

It was difficult to catch her breath. Gina finally forced out a "Sure, Marty, I understand." Marty held her hand tight. They walked to the end of the long Market structure that housed a variety of small shops and restaurants. At the far end of the building, there were several tables surrounded by a wrought-iron fence. Each table had an umbrella on it. The decorative awning at the restaurant entrance matched the table umbrellas. Inside the small restaurant, there was additional seating. Although it was somewhat early for lunch, all the outdoor tables were filled. *They must be eating breakfast or brunch.* There were a few people waiting to be seated as Gina and Marty approached. Marty turned to Gina and said, "I can't guarantee he'll be here, but I asked someone to check and he is scheduled." Gina surveyed the fenced area thoroughly.

Silently, she drew her hand to her mouth. Marty saw tears in her eyes as she slowly turned her back from the diners. "You okay? What's wrong?"

Gina shakily stammered her response. "He, he... he's right over there, Mart. In the corner section talking to the people at the table there." Gina wiggled her smartly-gloved index finger in the direction of the restaurant.

Marty's head bobbed back and forth to find where Gina had pointed. Waiters and waitresses were busily moving about and some customers were rising from their chairs. "You sure, Babe? How do you know?"

The bodies then parted, and at the end of the path stood a smiling young man wearing an apron, speaking to diners. After a few seconds, Gina turned and walked a few steps away, Marty following close behind. When Marty reached her, Gina pushed her face hard against his chest. "I just need a couple of minutes, Marty. See that boy back there? That's him, I know it! He's the spitting image of Joey," she happily gushed. "Just a couple more minutes," she said again. Gina turned in Marty's arms and together they admired the boy from where they stood. Slim and fresh-faced, his skin was radiantly clear, his nose straight, his black hair worn much the way Joey had worn his. The customers must have been asking directions, as the young man turned this way and that, pointing to and fro as he spoke. Even from a distance, his blue eyes jumped out at Gina. *Joey, Joey*, she thought. She smiled through glistening eyes, and Marty produced a handkerchief from his jacket pocket. Marty held Gina tight to his body, looking fondly at her face in profile.

After a few minutes, she turned to Marty and dabbing her eyes said, "Well, what are we doing standing here? I'm *starving*, Martin!" They laughed, and Marty took the hanky and cleaned up some mascara that had traveled down and around Gina's eyes. Her hands shaking, she took a compact out of her purse and applied some face powder and lipstick. Hand in hand again, they walked to the hostess to ask to be seated. Marty asked for one of the corner tables, and said they could wait. The couple seated there had already finished dining, and they now walked past a fidgety Gina and Marty. A busboy hurriedly prepped the table and within a few minutes the two were seated. Marty pulled his chair as close to Gina's as he physically could. Still holding hands, they excitedly looked at each other in silence. Gina jumped in her seat when the server came by and filled their water glasses, her attention broken by the sound of ice cubes clinking.

Marty took one of Gina's hands, and soothed, "Relax, Honey. Take another deep breath. Everything will be okay. Right?"

"Yes, Marty," Gina nodded.

The moment the words left Gina's mouth, a voice said, "Hello, my name is Michael, and I'll be your waiter today."

Too nervous to look, Gina was still riveted on Marty's face. Marty, on the other hand, said: "Sweetie, this nice young man is talking to us."

Gina turned to drink in the specter that stood before her, sunlight behind him. The thought entered her mind that she may have died, gone to Quincy Market Heaven and that Joey was there. Marty elbowed Gina gently, and she nearly toppled over in awe. "Well, hello Michael." Gina's creative imagination kicked in. "My husband and I would like to take our time for lunch today. It's kinda a celebration."

"Yes, Ma'am," replied the beaming angel. Comically,

he bowed slightly and said, "Let me know whatever you need." Gina heard Joey in her head saying, "Just say the word. Anything you want." She wanted to cry, but from complete happiness. However, she promised Marty she would not.

"Ma'am, are you okay?" Gina was suddenly fifteen-years-old again, looking up at Joey's face. *"Remember, Gee. The mission. When I get back,"* she heard Joey say.

"Oh! Of course. I'm sorry, just got distracted. You look a lot like someone I used to know. And, please. This is Marty, and I'm Gina." For the next few moments, all Gina could see was Michael's mouth moving as he recited the day's specials. She could do little more than sit with her elbows on the table, face propped on her hands. Marty ordered a light cocktail for her, and she dreamily watched as Michael went away to order the drinks. When Michael was out of earshot, Gina turned to Marty and gave him a "to die for" look of amazement and surprise. "Isn't he *great*? Isn't he beee-auu-tiful, Mart?" Breathlessly, she kissed Marty again.

They ordered a full lunch, but languished through it, eating less than half of anything that was brought to the table. Michael questioned whether or not they liked the food, but the two reassured him that everything was wonderful. During the course of a full two hours, Gina tried to inconspicuously watch her nephew. The young man was far too busy to notice that he was being watched. Gina began to recognize inflections of Yvonne, too, in the boy's demeanor and face. "The jaw line, especially," she told Marty. A little stronger than Joey's, more like Yvonne's.

Finally, Marty suggested to Gina that they should leave and that Tony would be waiting for them. Gina pouted, but knew that their presence would clearly be too conspicuous if they lingered any longer. "Okay, Honey. I guess we should. Besides, the game must have started, no?"

"No game today, Babe. We're going to the museum. I never had tickets for the game!"

A smile crept across Gina's face. The game story had been designed to bring her nephew into her life. She felt a great sense of joy and relief, and savored the final minutes with Michael while Marty engaged the boy in conversation. Michael wanted to go to medical school, a discovery that warmed Gina with pride. If not for Marty, she might have never realized the dream of finding Joey's child.

Marty apologized to Michael for tying up one of his tables for so long, and tipped the young man with a one hundred dollar bill. Gushing his thanks, Michael glowed. It was difficult for Gina to walk away from Quincy Market that day. Marty literally led her away, and she turned her head to catch any final glimpse of Michael. Tony was waiting and Gina excitedly asked him if he knew about the surprise. Tony looked to a smiling Marty, who nodded. "Yes, Sis," Tony said. "I'm so happy for ya!" Gina and Tony exchanged a quick and tight hug. Everyone was beaming as Tony hailed a cab. "Huntington Av, please. The museum," Tony instructed the driver and they spent the remainder of the day drinking in the visual candy at the Museum of Fine Arts. In the museum gift shop, she chose a lovely brooch for Ruth, and a box of greeting cards for Liz. Gina felt as though all of her bad dreams were turning into good ones. They still had a full day to look forward to together before going back to the real world.

That evening, Gina, Marty and Tony walked around Boston proper, enjoying the subtle promise of the coming summer. They carelessly walked along side streets, so different than those of New York. All three were relaxed and happy. Monday would bring them all back to Earth again. Gina would have only a couple more weeks of school to tie up and then, she could visit Marty and Ruth more often. On Sunday, Gina, Marty and Tony had an early dinner at the restaurant where Michael worked, this time in the indoor dining area. Marty and Gina pretended to be pleasantly surprised to have her nephew as their waiter again. They introduced Tony as a friend from Portland, who had met them there for a visit. They lazily ate and visited with Michael as time allowed. As Gina and Marty lingered behind in the restaurant, Tony left to meet the driver for the ride to Logan. For the second time that weekend, Marty had to almost drag a misty-eyed Gina away from Quincy Market.

The small plane circled the airport until it flew southbound toward Hartford. Gina felt her life also flying full circle. For the first time in many years, words from the Twenty-Third Psalm were welcomed in her mind: *My cup runneth over*. From the window seat, Gina watched the lights of Boston fade from sight. Resting her head on Marty's shoulder, she relished the delight of finally meeting a child she felt sure she would never see. Michael had grown into a perfect, ambitious and handsome man. A multitude of past pain melted away in a single day. Gina believed the Bianco family knew that Marty had found their beloved child. Her love for Marty seemed to burst at the seams, and the weekend proved to be fulfilling days, both emotionally *and* physically.

After deplaning, Marty and Tony walked Gina out into Bradley Airport's front lobby to wait for Liz to pull up. Gina kissed Marty on the sly when she spotted Liz's car approaching. Marty complained about not being able to see his favorite toddler, but respected Gina's privacy, too. Gina could hardly contain herself when she saw her own happy baby in the car seat. She praised Liz for a job well done. Liz stayed the night so they could go to school together after dropping the baby off at day care. Though wildly excited by the unbelievable surprise of the weekend, Gina slept deeply that night, reassured of regained happiness. She drifted throughout that week on a blissful cloud. *Life couldn't be better than when she was with Marty*, she thought, the same innocent way she felt about Joey.

y spring, I began going back into the city at least twice a month on weekends. There was no point in staying home, especially when Eric was practically stalking me. My friend Virginia would often house-sit, or the neighbors watched the place. No pets, so it was easy." Rita drew a long, deep breath. "I brought the baby with me on the train and Marty and I stayed at a hotel. My daughter stayed overnight with her Grandma Ruth. Actually, Ruth insisted that we go off and have fun. I guess she knew if anything happened to us, then my daughter would be okay. The baby was *everything* to her. My mother was long gone before my daughter was born, and I was so happy we had Ruth."

Rita twisted her mouth as she fought to not cry. "Mom and baby both loved Grandma Ruth!" She flashed a broad smile. "Anyway, this went on for over four years. I was a pillar of the community during the week and a gangster's moll every other weekend." Rita flipped her hand up like she was going to laugh and slapped it squarely on her thigh, an expression of combined disgust and humor. "Two nights, twice a month with Marty. I lived for it." Rita's speech was labored, as more hushed memories tumbled out. Her eyes round with wonder, Rita sat in silence.

Carolyn leaned forward. "Rita, ya alright?"

Rita's head turned like an electronic doll's. "Honey, I'll never be alright again. Hannah is going to ki-illll me! Doesn't matter if I'm convicted of murder one, my lovely daughter is going to hang me. That's the only thing I dread: letting her down." Rita shifted in the plush upholstery of the couch and switched the angle of her legs, stretching them out first.

She continued, "It wasn't long until I fell into the club and party scene with Marty and his soldiers, my brothers," Rita said, smiling a rather sarcastic smile. "I was reunited with Tony, Carmine, Enzo, and Dutch. Stereotypical names, huh? I actually fit right in, be-in a Sicilian, and all! Funny, I really loved them, too. I was as loyal to them as they were to me. A typical Cancer trait, loyalty!"

"But your birthday's in April, like mine," remarked Carolyn.

"Sorry, Baby. Rita's birthday is in April. Gina was born in July," speaking as though she was talking about a total stranger. "Part of the alias thing. I'm actually three years older than what I've told you, too," continued Gina, rolling her eyes with a smile.

"No one would ever guess," grinned Carolyn. "Go on,

Rita. Please continue."

"Anyway, being with the boys felt a lot like being with Joey and his friends. They protected me, and were always interested in hearing about my teaching job and my daughter."

"It was difficult for me sometimes, though. We'd be laughing and talking, even holding hands across a table: And, wham! I'd realize that deez guys...." Rita paused. "Deez guys," she said again. The smiled drained from her face. "They eliminated the competition many times in their line of work, with those very same soft, manicured fingers I loved to touch. But if I needed them to change a light bulb or pick up some Rocky Road ice cream, they did in a heartbeat. I always put the bad stuff out of my mind, just pushed it aside. Especially when it came to Marty. He could never hurt a fly." Rita shrugged her shoulders. "One night...."

Marty looked great that night. He was perfectly groomed, and his cheeks were rosy against his freshly scrubbed face. Gina and two of "the boys" went to a Manhattan salon earlier and she had her hair trimmed and her nails done. Before going out, Gina always called Ruth first to ask if her daughter needed her or if she should stop by. The answer was generally the same: they had shopped at Bloomie's, went skating at Rockefeller Center or visited the Museum of Natural History. The baby fell asleep after her bath from the day's workout.

Ruth had no grandchildren by Marty and his wife. Lisa had lost the one baby that she had briefly carried, and never became pregnant again. Ruth sometimes leaned close to Gina's face to say: "Our little girl has Marty's eyes," or "her

mannerisms are just like Marty's when he was that age." Ruth
knew what no one else said out loud. In Gina's Connecticut
life, everyone viewed the child as her ex-husband's, but in
New York, the truth was silently understood. The toddler
called Marty, "Zio Martino," Uncle Martin in Italian. Ruth
often grimaced when the little girl called him that, but never
openly protested.

"Okay then. Let's continue; there's *lots* more. We
didn't go anywhere without the boys...."

It was late March in New York, and still bitter cold.
On Saturday nights, Gina, Marty and the boys usually went
out to a nice restaurant and sometimes on to an out-of-the-way
nightclub. Saturday nights were usually "for the wives," so
Marty was careful to keep Gina out of view of his business
associates, most of whom abided by the Saturday night ritual.
Lisa was generally too drunk to take anywhere, anyway.

New York still held a larger-than-life quality for Gina;
she was still a country girl at heart. Alone in the city, she
would have felt frightened, but her second life with Marty was
a coddled one. The little time they spent together was always
filled to the brim with excitement and romance: the opera,
museums, the best restaurants, horseback riding in Central
Park in the warmer months, sleigh rides in the winter. Even
when they slept, they were never really alone. There was
always one of the guys outside the bedroom door, close at
hand.

Marty bought Gina a new dress, a gown really. It

was delivered to the hotel suite earlier that day. She marveled that he knew her size, and Marty would reply it was easy. "The top of your head is below the bottom of my chin," he'd explain. "Your waist is about yeah-big," he continued, curving his hands apart to mimic a waist circumference. In truth, he had taken her to several smaller dress shops in and around New York. During each shop visit and while Gina was in the dressing room, Marty tipped the saleswomen to note for future reference Gina's size, and what styles and colors were the most flattering. This time, it was cobalt blue satin, a snugly fitted mock-wrap style, cut rather low, and fitted to Gina's feminine curves and small waist. When she opened the garment bag, she gasped at its beauty. To feel so treasured by a man, the only man she'd ever loved as much as Joey, was overwhelming for Gina.

This Saturday night, they planned to dine at deNucci's in Brooklyn, one of Gina's favorite places. The restaurant was old and rich with history: beautiful oak bar, oak tables and chairs, gigantic booths in dimly candlelit corners. An expansive place, it was always full, but somehow Marty got in without a reservation. Gina often questioned why they never made them, but eventually she came to realize that it might be too dangerous to do so. It was worth the risk to be with Marty, yet she always felt totally safe. Prior to leaving the St. Moritz, the friends indulged themselves with the drug cocktail of the day: cocaine. Two of the boys would mix drinks and not imbibe, while two others could take part in the partying with Gina and Marty. The four soldiers shared this duty, toggling back and forth on the weekends that Gina visited. Tonight, Dutch and Carmine were the baby-sitters while the rest partied.

"Even with all the evil spinning around me, there were no other people on the planet. It didn't matter what we were doing. We could be reading the Sunday paper, and I felt connected to Marty. No pretenses. Best friends." Rita's voice fell flat and sad.

"Remember, Gee? The first dress I bought for you was this color. Over ten years ago; the party at the…."

"I can't believe that you remembered the color, Marty! Oh, yes. The *family* party at the Waldorf. You tricked me, Martin." They tumbled down onto the bed, looking over their shoulders to be sure the doors to the outer room were closed and giddily made love in the silky, dimming light of the winter dusk.

Around seven o'clock, they rose and showered together, exuberant and recharged. All the boys wore nice suits and it was fun for Gina to have what she called "five handsome dates." Before leaving the hotel suite, she predictably straightened and tightened their ties. The friends drove to deNucci's in two separate cars. When they were shown to a half-circle booth, Dutch and Carmine sat at each end seat, vigilant of all the comings and goings at deNucci's. The staff knew them well, their memories sharpened by the huge tips left for making sure everything was perfectly timed and never rushed. They were all enjoying tiramisu and coffee, when Dutch nervously ran his finger around the inside of his collar and in his hushed, deep voice said, "Mart." Snapping his head to his left, Dutch was indicating: "look over there."

Marty's face panned the huge room slowly and his

gaze rested on a short, stout, bald man standing at the lobby's hostess stand. He eased back into the dimness of the booth like a turtle retracting into a shell. "Jesus Key-riste!" jeered Marty. Gina was deliriously oblivious to Marty's reaction. She and Tony were talking about the morning spent in the Guggenheim Museum.

"What the fuck we gonna do?" whispered Carmine. Just as the words were leaving Carmine's lips, the little bald man walked out of view and into deNucci's bar, far from their sight. Everyone, with the exception of Gina, heaved a sigh of relief. By this time, Gina realized that no one was listening to her critique of a Lichtenstein painting they had all seen at the museum.

"What's going on, fellas?" Gina queried.

"Nuttin much," soothed Carmine. "We just seen a jerk we know. Bobby the Boob, we call him. An A-hole." The rest of the boys fidgeted with their forks and coffee cups. Carmine's face broke into a wide grin. "Hey, why don't we play a trick on Bobby? You know, the trick we been talkin' about? What'd ya say? I'll bet nobody else knows Bobby came here tonight."

Marty snapped, "But we have *Gee* with us!"

Gina bolted upright in her seat: "I can help with the trick, Marty. Let me help!" The wheels were turning in Marty's head fast; the boys sensed it and remained eerily silent. Again, Gina was ignorant to the body language being displayed at the table. Eventually, each man looked at each other side-to-side, sly smiles creeping onto their lips. They continued to sip their coffee, and thoughtfully ate their tiramisu.

Finally, Marty whispered, tapping his fingers on the

table. "Let's think about this. Yes, looks like he's totally alone tonight, which means he might be waiting for an escort. Bobby likes that, he likes 'em young, too. You wanna help, Gina? Okay. But listen to me carefully. You had a lotta cocktails, so you have to pay attention. Okay, Baby?"

"Sure, Marty. Of course." Gina sobered herself and tried her best to concentrate on the next thing Marty would say. "Go ahead, Honey. But tell me what the trick will be, too."

"Well... Bobby fucked up a business deal of ours, and all five of us lost a lot of money. Three of the guys could just rough him up a little, and then drive him way out in the country in Jersey and leave him there to get home on his own."

"No, Marty, that's *mean!* It's freezin' cold out!"

"No, it's not. The guy's a jerk. We won't really hurt him. We want to scare him is all. That way he'll keep his ugly nose out of our business. Right, fellas?" The four gorillas agreeably murmured, shaking their heads and talking over each other to Gina: "Yeah, Gina, that's right. Bobby did that. Bobby deserves it."

Gina eased back into the softness of the plush booth and said, "You're right. He had no right to fuck with *my* men! Okay, to Jersey with him!" She raised her arm like a queen giving an order, and flicked her hand upward at the wrist. Marty gently took Gina's wrist and eased her back. "Okay, shhhh! Down girl!" All of the men laughed quietly as to not draw attention.

"Okay, then. Everybody listen." Marty began. "Gee, this man is most likely waiting for a whore, so you have to pretend to be the lady he's waiting for."

"Oh, goody! I get to play a whore!" exclaimed Gina giddily, clapping her hands together.

"Dutch. You're going to wait outside to see if any, uh, *ladies* show up alone that look like, well, you know. Pay her to go away." Dutch nodded. "In about thirty minutes or so, Gina will leave the restaurant with Bobby, so make sure he doesn't see you. If you can, meet up with Tony and Enzo in the alley. Gina, me and Carmine will be right behind you. Now, Tony and Enzo, you get your car and park it in the alley behind the building just south of here, you know? Along the side of the flower shop on the corner. Wait there. Gina, are you up for this? Bobby will think you're a whore, so you have to flirt with him. He's an ugly, fat son-of-a-bitch, and stinks of perspiration and cigars. He's probably smoking one right now. He's short, bald and craggy looking. Make sure he drinks, too. He's gotta weak bladder, so he'll probably use the men's room soon. Order a cosmopolitan when you sit down, but when Bobby goes to the john, tell the bartender to mix you a virgin cocktail. You need to stay alert so drink cranberry juice in a martini glass from then on. Tip the bartender a fifty and tell him not to say anything." He reached in his jacket and rolled off a bill from a huge wad, and said, "Here, give him a hundred. He'll definitely stay quiet." Gina nodded her head like an excited child. Marty peeled off more bills and handed them to Dutch.

Gina felt little or no empathy for Bobby the Boob. She *wanted* to be part of this game. She was one of "them" now. "Now, Gina, don't call him by name in case he didn't give the escort service his real name. Just ask him what you should call him. Think of a name for yourself, too. After about thirty minutes, ask him if he's ready to go. He probably planned to eat, so he may protest a little. Tell him you're hungry too, but that you want to take him outside and down the alley for a quick blow job and then have dinner. He'll be so turned on by that and will agree."

"Yuck! You *know* he'll do that? I mean, agree to go outside and come back in for dinner?"

The boys all laughed quietly, and Marty smiled a big smile. "We *know* him. Food and women are the only two things in the world for him. Believe me! He's a pig with both of those. If he can have a little dessert first and then eat, he'll like that even more. Okay, so you'll walk him out of the restaurant and to the left, to the edge of this building, and then left again down the alley. Talk and laugh loud when you're in the alley so that the boys can hear you coming. Remember, there'll be three of us just around the alley corner and two behind you, so don't worry."

"I'm not worried, Martin, Dear," sassed Gina. She crinkled her nose at Marty.

"Everybody but Carmine will take Bobby for the ride to Jersey. Okay, Gina? Oh, and Gina, his name is really Vito. We just *call* him Bobby the Boob. He likes nice boobs."

"Eeeee-oooooooooo," snarled Gina disgustedly. "But, I'm as ready as I'll ever be." Cocking her head to one side and picking up a wine bottle in a mock Oscar-speech pose, she quipped: "I'd like to thank the members of the Academy... nobody fucks with my boys, *this* will be fun." After she kissed Marty on his face, he and Dutch rose to let Gina out of the booth and watched as she crossed the busy room serenely, past the hostess area, and finally disappearing into the bar. Once inside the curved doorway, she stopped to survey the scene. She panned the room with her eyes. *This is quite a large room, too. Wow! Gorgeous! The woodwork. The copper tile ceilings. Why haven't we ever come into deNucci's bar?*

At the booth, Marty paid the tab, Dutch, Enzo and Tony went outside. Marty and Carmine drank coffee and spoke little. Periodically checking their watches, they watched the front door to be absolutely sure they would see Gina and Vito when they passed to exit.

Gina spotted the Boob almost immediately, took a deep breath and slowly walked toward a cloud of cigar smoke at the end of the bar. She approached slowly, and many male eyes watched as she passed. Clearing her throat to get his attention, Gina approached Vito who looked to her like a big frog perched on a bar stool. He was quite stout, quite bald, craggy looking and very smelly, as Marty had described. She felt her stomach twist in a knot. "Is this seat taken?" she cooed demurely.

Turning on his stool, Vito almost looked shocked for a moment. "Wow. You sure are pretty, but I'm waiting for someone." He was surmising her top to bottom and Gina felt creepy about that, especially when his eyes lingered on her breasts. Inside herself, she was now laughing. *They were right, he likes boobs. That's for sure!* "I don't suppose it could be you, doe." *He's dumb, too, and speaks like he has a mouthful of something!*

"I *am* that person." Gina forced her best smile. This pleased Mr. Vito greatly, and he pushed his cigar out in an ashtray close by. *At least he's considerate enough to put the cigar out.*

As Marty instructed, Gina was careful not say his name. She shyly oozed, "What should I call you?"

"Bobby. You can call me Bobby." *This was hilarious. Do the boys call him that to his face? He sure is ugly.* It was very difficult for Gina to not laugh right then, but she took a quick sip of water that the bartender had just set on the bar, and she was able to concentrate again.

"And you, Beautiful? What do I call you?"

"You may call me, uh, Monique." The bartender asked her preference, and she ordered a cosmopolitan. "Made with Chambord, instead of Triple Sec, please. Straight up."

After swigging what remained in his glass, Vito asked for Wild Turkey on the rocks. *What a class act.* As if in a script, he excused himself to use the "little boys room." Gina called the bartender back to hastily deliver her lines about the faux cocktails, and slip the bartender the bill she had produced from her clutch. The young man was delighted to accommodate Gina's request and quickly poured cranberry juice into another iced martini glass, sweeping away her first cocktail. Her eyes darted to the old Gilbert oak-framed clock above the bar. When Vito returned, she chattered flirty small talk for about twenty minutes. He drank the drink he ordered earlier and had yet another. He probably had at least one or two before Gina arrived, as well. Her eyes drifted to the clock again; a total of twenty-five minutes had passed. Sweetly, Gina asked if they were going to have dinner and Vito seemed almost embarrassed.

"Of course, we can do that right now, if you'd like!" Vito spouted merrily.

"Well, hows about this first?" cooed Gina, tugging playfully on Vito's tie while drawing him close. She raised her palm to the side of her mouth and whispered about some dessert in the alley before sitting down to dine. The ugly man shook a finger in her face and replied, "Naughty, naughty girl, Monique!" Their glasses empty, the two slid off their stools, Gina feigning tipsiness. She walked to a coat-check room opening to retrieve the blond mink stole Marty gifted her with last Christmas, and swung it around her shoulders.

Slightly suspicious, Vito suddenly exclaimed, "You must get paid pretty well. The expensive dress. Mink? Are you new to Shirley's joint?"

"Yeah, I'm new. The dress, *I* bought, the mink was my Ma's. What of it?" *Wow, Oscar nomination, here I come!* Gina inwardly smiled. *I can lie with the best of them.*

Gina having said that, Vito seemed to relax a bit. Gina began talking about the weather forecast for snow, and how it "smelt like snow, tonight maybe." Mockingly she thought, *This guy's not really such a bad egg. He can't help it if he's ugly and a pig. He's just an average Joe. Joe.* Joey was in and out of Gina's head often, and she welcomed the bittersweet memory. On the heels of that thought was the sad reality of lives gone awry after Joey's death. Distracted further, her thoughts drifted to Boston, where Gina had visited with Joey's boy, thanks to Marty. The thought comforted her. The beautiful Michael. The combined images of Joey and Yvonne.

Outside of the restaurant, Dutch had long ago paid off the hooker that had been dispatched for Vito. Gifting her with triple her anticipated fee plus cab fare, he sent her away saying, "Go home and get some good rest tonight. Your boss will never know," and the young woman skipped happily away to find a cab. Dutch jogged down the alley to join Enzo and Tony, who were now out of the car and waiting around the corner of a brick building. Dutch drew a cigarette from the pack tucked in his shirt pocket, and Tony reached up fast and grabbed it. "Fucking idiot! Wanna give us away here?"

"Oh, yeah. Sorry, Tone." Dutch murmured in his deep baritone voice. Dutch was really a gentle giant to his friends,

and now looked to the ground, kicking some fluffy snow with
the toe of his shoe.

DeNucci's oak framed doors squeaked loudly when
Vito opened them outward to the chill of that night. Glancing
over her shoulder, Gina looked deep into the dimly lit dining
room. Her gaze immediately met Marty and Carmine's, who
were by now standing and ready to follow. Gina and Vito
complained aloud about the bitter cold night. Gina felt cold
right away, and Vito chivalrously offered his stinky wool
topcoat. "We won't be thaaat long," she teased. Her skin
crawled. *This was harder than I thought!*

They slowly walked up the street, and Gina forced
herself to put her arm underneath his so that they would be
walking close together. *He reeks.* But she knew the entire
walk would only be a matter of three or four minutes, tops. To
the left and down the alley they turned, and Vito slipped his
hand on Gina's waist and tried to turn her to kiss her. *Gross!*
Coyly, she pulled away. "That can wait til later. Come on,
Bobby boy!"

Her steps were choppy in the long, tight dress, but
Vito followed Gina's lead, pretending to give chase. "Naughty
girl, Monique," he bellowed, laughing bawdily. Gina laughed
loudly to be sure the boys definitely could hear them coming.
She zipped quickly around the alley corner to the left. In an
instant, Marty and Carmine appeared. Turning and whisking
Gina away and toward the street, her feet were barely touching
the ground as each man crooked his arm at her elbows. She
turned her head in time to see Dutch trip Vito, and the three
men began to pummel and beat him unmercifully. Vito's head
hit the pavement hard. He moaned from the combined pain of
the fall and the beating. Tony quickly opened the back door

of the Cadillac, all the while continuing to beat and kick Vito. Dutch trudged around to the back door of the driver's side, whipping it open. With his gorilla-like arms, he reached across the back seat and dragged Vito into the car. Gina couldn't seem to catch her breath; no sound left her mouth. Now behind her, the Caddie shot past them and out of the alley, tearing up the street to their right. They maneuvered Gina to the left where Marty's Town Car sat waiting only ten yards away. Marty entered the back seat first and Carmine lifted Gina like a bundled baby, delivering her to Marty's arms. Now at the wheel, Carmine ripped the car from the curb.

Gina could not speak for a full minute. "Marty, what just happened there? You said you wouldn't hurt that guy. Why were the boys beating him? You *lied* to me!"

"I didn't lie. They were just making him a little easier to handle, is all. Then, Bobby has to walk back from Jersey dirtier than he already is, with a nice shiner. Don't worry so much. He'll be alright."

"*Easier to handle?* The guy fell on his head! How much easier to handle could he be?" Confused and shaken, Gina passed out with her head on Marty's shoulder within a few minutes after the Town Car sped away.

The next morning Gina woke to the warmth of Marty, spooned tightly to her back. She felt the subdued sunlight on her face, and Marty's powerful arms woven around her breasts and shoulders. For just one moment, she tried to focus her thoughts to the events of the previous night, but it was far too foggy and more difficult to even bother trying to remember. After making love in their usual long and leisurely Sunday morning fashion, they rose, showered and dressed. No time to sit around and read the newspaper today. Ruth was making a roast with potatoes and they would all have a family dinner together before Gina and her daughter needed to board the northbound train. Gina dreaded Sunday afternoons that way.

"And I simply didn't remember most of that Saturday night. Didn't give a flying fuck about anything or anyone else except where I was at the moment, and *who* I was with. I was exactly where I wanted to be."

Chapter 18

The weeks passed. The snow was melting away and the trees were budding in the Berkshires. Gina especially looked forward to the summer months. As a teacher, it gave her more flexibility to go into the city and stay for several days.

"If Marty was 'working,' I spent quite a bit of time with my daughter and Ruth, at Ruth's house in Queens. It felt as though I reached as normal a life as I could. Maybe I was in denial, but I felt genuinely happy for quite some time. *And*, I loved doing 'girl things' with Ruth and the baby. It was the best time! Just going to the grocery store, baking or making dinner took on a whole life of its own, one I hadn't had in a

long time. A *family* life. I wasn't alone anymore. Ruth was
happy, too. The happiest I had seen her since Dan passed.
By that time, I had been seeing Marty regularly again for five
years – it went by so fast. For so many years I felt as though
I was looking into windows of other people's lives and just
watching. Now, I was living *that* life! I didn't have to *want*
anymore. I had *everything!*"

　　　"On the first weekend that the ground would be
pretty dry and firm, Marty usually took me riding in Central
Park. That spring though, he wanted to take all of us out
to the country somewhere, Long Island, or maybe southern
Connecticut. Marty rented a different house or cottage each
time, usually on a few acres for privacy. A couple of times,
he had three or four horses brought in. It was like Christmas.
Another time, we stayed in a huge beach house on Cape Cod.
That was lots of fun and all the boys came with us. Everybody
had to cook and do their own laundry; the boys were clueless.
The boys wanted to order out for pizza and stuff like that.
They all played hide-and-seek with the baby; everyone had a
good time. On Sunday mornings, we'd go to the closest town
for breakfast. We rarely went into the city like the year before.
I missed it and didn't, but never gave it that much thought.
That last time, we flew to Logan Airport. While everyone else
went shopping, Marty and I went to Quincy Market to see if
Michael was there. We didn't see him. That was okay, Marty
always seemed to know where Michael was, and figured out
when we'd 'bump into him' again. After we had fun in Boston
for a couple of days, we rented cars to drive to the Cape."

　　　While Gina carried her daughter straddled on her hip,

the others moved like hurricanes around her. Having returned from grocery shopping, the boys carried in paper bags bursting with goodies. "Motty, Mottin-Honey! Did ya pack my Victrola, like I asted ya to?" shouted Ruth, bobbing to and fro amidst a sea of male bodies. Everyone laughed out loud.

Dutch would mimic, "Motty, Motty!" and Marty would shoot him a sharp look, which again prompted laughter.

"Ma. It's a stereo, not a Victrola."

"Okay, then! Did you bring my stereo?"

"Yes, Mother!"

After a summer of outings, the troops had the routine down. The house on the Cape was a gorgeous clapboard style, with weathered blue paint and had a wrap-around screened porch that hugged three-quarters of its perimeter. There were no horses this time, as the house was smack dab on the beach. But Marty thought it would be a nice change, and there was a stable right up the road. The evenings were filled with the sounds of Ruth's big band-era 33s. She also was a big Frank Sinatra fan. When putting a Sinatra record on the turntable, Ruth fondly reminisced, "Danny loved the Chairman of the Board."

"Ruth danced with the baby. Marty and I danced sometimes, too, usually a slow one. Once in a while, Ruth would pull the boys out of their chairs, too. Everybody but Dutch. He said he couldn't dance. Who knows? Maybe he couldn't, but he was not looking well that summer. That year, he lost a lot of weight."

When Gina questioned Carmine about this, he explained that after Dutch's wife had miscarried their third child, she never fully recovered. Instead, Josie's health continued to decline, and Dutch was worried. Carmine's last remark was a lie.

"Soon after, I learned that Marty and Carmine paid people to take care of Dutch's family, because Dutch was too fried to do it." Rita reflected sadly. "Marty tried to convince Dutch to stay home, but he insisted everything was fine, and he didn't need to be there."

"The sea air was so nice and we slept so well, at least I did! A couple of times, I'd ask if we could go back to New York for a week, but always got out-voted. That was okay cuz it was great, wherever we were. I had a best friend, a beautiful child, a mom, brothers, friends... a family of my own. I couldn't change what had happened to my own family, and knew they'd be happy for me. Next to having the baby, that was the happiest time. My life in Seattle is good, but I lost more loved ones in exchange for it. Don't know if Ruth is still living, but I think she must be. Marty would have let me know...."

The happy "family" stayed on the Cape for over two weeks. Gina and Marty got to slip away alone so that they could have a few romantic days together on Martha's Vineyard.

"This was the first time in a very long time that we were entirely alone together. Security on ferries was nothing like today," sighed Rita. "Marty packed a .9 mm, I think. No one on the island knew us anyway." Amused by their friend's nonchalance at such a remark, Carolyn and Franco shared sideways smiles. "We needed to do that, you know, go away. Just us. The boys stayed behind with Ruth and my daughter."

It was now late June. *Joey's birthday*, thought Gina, when Marty had suggested an excursion to Martha's Vineyard to celebrate *her* upcoming birthday. Dutch drove Gina and Marty to Wood's Hole to the ferry terminal. Marty insisted that Gina bring a near empty suitcase so that they could buy things on the island, and bring surprises back for Ruth and the baby.

"That was only the second time in my life that I rode on a ferry," laughed Rita. "It was a perfect day, so clear. We stood in the sun on deck the whole time, just talking and laughin'."

After the ferry docked in Oak Bluffs, the couple cabbed to an Edgartown hotel where a reserved room waited. The next several days were content ones for them. Each felt carefree and far from reality.

"We were just like any other couple on vacation. We went to the beach, shopped, ate at nice restaurants, chartered a boat for a day. Well, we even went to a church service to get a better look at an old church. Can ya believe it?" Rita laughed. "It was *so* New England, old, quaint -- inside and out. We joked about being in a church together, and that the roof hadn't caved because we were there!"

Gina and Marty strolled down Edgartown's Main Street that boasted beautiful shops and galleries. They held hands and window-shopped and Gina felt Marty was totally relaxed. That morning, Marty stopped short while looking into a shop window. Peering into the store's interior, he surveyed the variety of goods. Teasingly, he tugged at Gina's sweater, "Let's go in here, Gia," he said. Once inside, Gina slowly walked the perimeter, spotting a small section that featured vintage clothing, and zeroed in to take a closer look. Marty headed toward another area to look at some jewelry in a display case. Gina spotted a black velvet empress-style purse with a Bakelite handle. Upon quick inspection, she looped it onto her arm. She continued through the small shop, paying little attention to the fact that Marty had struck up a conversation with a young man at the counter. Gina spotted some things for the girls, too, adding to the many purchases Marty had already made for his "other ladies," as he called them. When she had finished looking around, she navigated to where Marty was standing.

"Ready, Babe?" asked Marty as he plucked the items from Gina's arms to put them on the counter. "Buying more cranberry soap, I see," Marty teased.

"Just can't help loving cranberry soap! I want plenty on hand to enjoy all winter, Smart Ass."

Marty whipped out the old wallet that Gina had given him during their first holiday as friends. It touched Gina's heart that he had never discarded it. The next day would be their last full day on the island. While discussing what they should do for fun, Marty volunteered to go dancing, something he had never done before. Marty's uncoordinated dance moves were designed for Gina's entertainment. He was being goofy. Gina reveled in the fact that Marty was still a good sport. He wasn't entirely crazy about dancing, but knew Gina was. Marty threw abandon to the wind. In New York, he couldn't play the average American businessman on vacation. Like giddy children, the two were far from every worldly care.

On the morning of their departure, the sky looked ominous and a thunderstorm roared over the island. Marty had arranged to have breakfast brought to their room early so that they would not have to rush for a cab back to Oak Bluffs. The evening before, Gina asked the desk clerk to call the cab for a ten a.m. pick-up.

"The change in the weather was timed perfectly! We were finished with our little honeymoon," giggled Rita, "so we coulda cared less that it was raining."

As planned, they took their time eating and reading New York newspapers. As Gina was thumbing through the Daily News, a photo of a man caught her eye. Gina had turned past page ten, but her eyes darted back to it. Because it hit so close to home, it drew and repelled her at the same time. *Body found identified as local mobster.* Gina slapped the paper shut hard. The thought of Marty meeting such a fate crossed her mind occasionally; she scraped those thoughts away, like food from a plate. Shivering, she looked up at Marty, whose eyes were studying The Times financial section. The article's photo was not well-focused, but Gina could see the victim was an older man, *probably in his late sixties*, she thought. Bald and not at all good-looking, Gina could have passed him on any New York street. Yet, he seemed oddly familiar. Morbidly, she speed-read the article's specifics. Pathologists determined the body might have been submerged for at least three months. It had taken almost two weeks to identify the victim due to a high degree of decomposition. That coupled with the unfortunate fact that what remained of this man no longer included his head or hands. It could not be determined whether the head had been "lost" during or after the person's demise. The article pointed out that police investigators first suspected that the body was one Vittorio Pasqualini, a renowned and feared criminal who dabbled in drugs and prostitutes. *Pasqualini, Pasqualini.* The name seemed familiar as the hundreds of other Italian names Gina heard in her lifetime. Gina quietly folded the newspaper, walked across the room and vacantly stuffed it inside the side suitcase pocket. The remainder of the day went as planned and by the time they arrived back to the Cape beach house, she had forgotten about the article. Her day was now filled with the joy of being with her beautiful child and the others, and lots of conversation about the days on the island.

"But the dream vacation was nearing its end. We planned to drive south in the rental cars, dropping the baby and I off in Hartford to pick up the bus to go home. Marty said it wasn't safe to drive me home in case we were ever followed. This didn't make sense to me, as we hadn't been in New York for the entire spring and much of the summer. I didn't care. Either way, I had to go home. On the night before we were going to head back...."

Marty was reading a magazine in bed while Gina finished bathing. The old beach house bathrooms had tubs only, no showers. The tubs had claw-and-ball feet, like the ones in the Bianco home. During the course of the past three weeks, Gina and Marty shared the tub several times. They drank champagne in the candlelit room late at night. On that last evening, Gina slid onto the bed and put her head on Marty's lap to get his attention. He laughed lightly, putting his magazine aside and turning the bed table lamp off. Candlelight glowed from the bathroom's open door, and Marty stroked Gina's hair gently. Suddenly, Gina realized that Marty was wearing a silver band on the middle finger of his right hand. "Martin. You never wear rings. What's this?" Gina asked pulling his hand close to her face. The ring had something engraved on it. Focusing carefully, Gina read slowly: "Vous et nul autre." She looked up at Marty.

"You and no other. That's what it means. You and no other."

"Yes, it's the ring I showed you at the Boston Museum of Fine Arts gift shop."

"I saw the look on your face when you were lookin'
at it. I've had it for a while, but was waitin' for a good time."
Marty removed his hand from Gina's head and slid it under the
pillow, producing a small jewelry box.

Gina shook her head, a big smile on her face. "Motty!
You bought me the same ring!" They laughed quietly as they
embraced in the bed sheets. Gina flipped open the box, but
inside was the engagement ring that Marty had carried around
with him for years.

"When you showed me that ring, I had the French stuff
engraved on the inside of this one! It was specially designed
for my favorite art teacher." Marty gently removed the ring
from the box and held it close to Gina's face. Look inside,
Baby." Gina carefully inspected the hand-engraving inside
the ring shank. Marty took her shaky hand, and slipped it on
Gina's ring finger. "I've been carrying this around with me
forever, Gina. Hey, look at that! Haven't lost my touch. I
always know your size! You haven't changed an eyelash."
Gina sat up, snuggling close to Marty and they shared a gentle
kiss. "You *know* we're going to be together someday. You
know that, right, Gina? We're gonna have a real life someday,
I promise. Have to clean up some business deals and we'll
have enough money to go away from New York. *Forever*.
We're together now; we always will be." The sheets were cool
and clean, but the air was muggy and warm. Over the sea,
another thunderstorm was creeping closer to the island, and
Gina held Marty tight.

"When you grow up in New England you can fall
asleep to the sound of the summer storms, you get so used to it.

It was the last time. The last time we.…"

Rita sobbed softly into her napkin. Carolyn self-consciously refilled Rita's water glass, at a loss as to how to comfort her friend. "We didn't *really* want to go away from New York, just away from Marty's job in New York. Up to that point, I never doubted his love. Another big storm was coming. Yes, it was."

Chapter 19

*I*t was difficult to go home, but it was good, too. It gave me a chance to have total quiet time with my kid. Didn't want to draw attention by being away too much. My wonderful neighbors watched the house when I was away, and they helped me through a messy divorce. I let them believe I was visiting my old college friends in the city. Not really a lie, right? They knew I really didn't have much of a family. My uncle and his wife were always so nice to me, and I went away without telling them. I still feel bad about that. But I wouldn't have been able to write to them from anywhere, because I had changed my identity."

"What do you mean, Rita?" asked Franco. "You planned to change your name well in advance of doing it?"

"No, Honey. Never planned on changing it. It hadn't

occurred to me at all. Thought my fairy tale would never end, and we would all live happily ever after. A name change seemed small because I had already become two different women, a school teacher and a happy mistress. Some regret, maybe, but overall, little. It was an opportunity to catch the brass ring for a while. I wouldn't have missed that part of my life for the world." Rita's gaze met the floor.

Gina washed up the dinner dishes while her daughter watched TV. After emptying her suitcase, she separated her dirty from clean clothes. Gina set the bag on the floor before helping her precious girl put on light summer jammies. Handing the dark-haired girl a storybook, she asked, "Here Baby, will you read Mommy a story tonight?" Not quite five years of age, the tyke opened the book very matter-of-factly. She paused for a moment, her eyes like two blue jewels on perfect, suntanned skin. *The dark hair, the full lips. Just like Joey.* Gina saw Joey whenever she looked at her; she beamed as the child began her story.

"There was a little girl with a beautiful mom…" the child began. They giggled at this opening line, and Gina eased back onto her daughter's small bed, next to the tiny storyteller. *An angel's voice*, Gina thought, as she drifted off into the twilight of the summer evening.

Gina heard the sound of plates and silverware. The tinkling of piano keys was distant, and a dimly lit room began to come into focus. *Ahhhhh, deNucci's! Oh, I miss deNucci's.* Like a queen with an entourage, Gina stepped through the front doors of deNucci's. She turned from side to side, assured that Marty and the boys stood around her. She floated ahead alone,

turning right into the bar. Deep in the left corner of the dimly
lit room, a woman in a black velvet evening gown was playing
the piano. The gown's neckline draped off the shoulders
and Gina realized that it was the woman from a famous John
Singer Sargent painting. Gina knew the painting's history.
The young socialite was from Seattle; her family owned a
home in Paris. As in the painting, she wore her hair swept
up, her skin was pale and she held her head high. Gina
consciously thought, *Aren't dreams great?* She stood inside
the bar's doorway, looking from side to side, but there was no
one else in the room. *Wait! What is that? To the far right, at
the end of the bar?* A cloud of smoke was suspended there.
Gina turned to the right and began to slowly walk toward the
cloud. As she approached, she saw a disheveled figure on the
last bar stool, its back turned to Gina. Conscious that this was
a dream, Gina comically wondered if it was Norman Bates'
decaying mother from *Psycho*. "Mrs. Bates?" Gina grinned.
A turn of the bar stool revealed a short, fat, bald man instead.
Quite a curious surprise, Gina stopped short, leaving a distance
of several feet between them. The man was wet and dirty.
Bruised badly, too. His clothing was shredded and ragged.
Vito. It was Vito! The man she lured to the alley for a beating.
When Vito opened his mouth, dirty water spewed forth. Gina
grimaced in disgust. *What the fuck?* He sputtered slightly like
he had something stuck in his teeth. Clearing his widely sliced
throat, he winced at Gina and gasped for air. "Hello, Monique.
Is that *you*, Monique? Can you help me? I can't seem to pick
up my cigar," Vito said with an inquisitive look on his battered
face. He extended his arms to welcome a hug. Stunned,
Gina could see that Vito's hands were missing, and his wrists
were like frayed cloth. As if in rewind mode, she was sucked

backward, all the while looking into Vito's face. The face quickly became a blur.

The delicate sound of the piano faded away, Gina's eyelids fluttered. She bolted straight upward, relieved to discover she was sitting on her daughter's bed. Beyond the open window the sky was black and sprinkled with few stars. *At least a couple of hours must have passed*, she thought. The smiling man-in-the-moon night light glowed from across the room. *Wow! What a weird dream!* She rolled over to see her sleeping angel, with the storybook clasped to her tiny chest. Gina carefully stepped off of the bed, put the book away and covered her treasure with the bed sheet. "Buona riposo, my baby," she whispered as she bent to kiss the child's head.

A routine she inherited from her dad, Gina checked the window in the tot's room and walked throughout the house to do the same in each room. Very tired, she express-showered. Still basking in the glow of sharing three weeks with Marty, Gina smiled. She drank a small glass of milk and headed down the hall to her bedroom, turning her face in the doorway of her daughter's room. Gina reveled at the tot's perfect face. Looking down at the ring she now wore, she was already thinking of the next visit with Marty. What surprise destination he would plan? Having forgotten where she set her suitcase, her knee bumped it hard when she entered her dark bedroom. It fell over, and a newspaper slid out from the bag's side pocket. After turning on a lamp Gina moved the suitcase, and the newspaper dropped to the floor. Turning off the light, she slid onto her bed. She thought about the odd dream, but was too tired to ponder it for very long. For the second time that very same evening, she fell asleep within minutes.

Within a short period of time, Gina found herself

sitting up in bed again. Her bedclothes were drenched with sweat and she knew exactly why. *The man in the newspaper is Vito!*

Gina fumbled in the dark for the lamp, nearly knocking it off the bed table. She lunged off the bed and scooped up the folded newspaper. "Fuck!" Gina hissed. Now on her knees, she rapidly flipped through the pages. *Fuck, fuck, fuck! Holy fucking shit!* No doubt about it: there it was. There he *was*, past tense. Vito was dead. Vittorio Pasqualini was Vito from deNucci's! The article said he had gone missing about four months earlier. Right around the time Gina baited him.

"I totally freaked out, of course. Paced around the kitchen for almost an hour. Smoked cigarettes on the back steps, a lot of them. I finally worked up the nerve to call Marty, even though he asked me not to call from my home phone. Calls can be traced and he was afraid it could put me in danger one day."

There was no question in her mind; she had to call him. Gina tried to calm herself and collect her thoughts. Around midnight, she called Marty. On the first try, she reached him at his Ritz Carlton suite. Careful to keep her composure, she was firm and direct. "Marty, I read in the Times that Vito is dead. You need to tell me the truth, Marty. Did you have the boys kill him?"

On the other end, Marty had definitely forgotten that he had been a little cross with Gina for calling him on the phone. Gina's questions had caught him totally off guard.

"Spit it out, Martin! What happened?"

Marty drew a very deep breath. "Gina, it's not what you think. That man was planning to put us all in danger and we had to do something about it."

"How can you say it's not what I'm thinking? You had him killed! You lied to me Marty! You said you wouldn't hurt him. Now, tell me! The boys did him, didn't they?"

"Yes," whispered Marty.

"What the fuck? Was it an accident or something? Is that what happened? They cut his hands off to make it *look* like a hit, right?"

Resigned at where this conversation was heading, Marty quietly answered, "No, Baby. It wasn't an accident. We've been planning to do it a while. And then, that night he just fell into our hands...." Marty stopped rather abruptly.

Gina was blind with rage. At that moment, all she could see was white light around her. She tried to speak, but could do little more than scrunch her face into a snarl. Looking down at the receiver in her hand, she slammed it hard onto the wall cradle. Within seconds, it rang and she picked the receiver up and let it slip back down. After a few seconds, she still heard Marty on the line, begging her not to hang up. She held the receiver down until she was sure the connection was broken.

"In those days, there were no cordless or cell phones. Regular phones made an annoying bleeping sound when you left them off the hook. I closed it in a drawer and walked down the hall to lie down. Sleep was out of the question! I cried, but it wasn't all about me. It was because Marty, *my Marty*, was a murderer. And me, little school teacher Gina Bianco, loved him. He never said he took human life, but everyone knew the unspoken truth. Even Ruth did. In Marty's 'profession,' it is kill or be killed. It goes round and round. Eliminate the competition in two ways: in a business sense, and in a physical sense. You kill, you get to stay alive. On the business side, you move up in the food chain. It's not only *your* mob that you have to deal with, either. You have the Chinese, the Russians. Geez, I was in total denial about everything."

Gina sat with her back propped with pillows. She closed her eyes, but was far too upset to sleep. A little after three a.m., her doorbell rang. Startled, she jumped to her window to look out onto the street. A Lincoln Town Car was parked directly across the mountainous street, under a streetlight, revealing it as Marty's. *Jesus!* Marty had never visited Gina's house. She was always told it was too dangerous to do so. Running down the hall, she reached the front door before he could ring again. She did not want her child to awake to people arguing. She steadied herself and carefully opened the door. In a sharp whisper she said, "Before I unlock this screen door, I'm telling ya, if you raise your voice and wake the baby, I'll be pissed." Marty had Enzo with him. She unlocked the screen door, moving aside to let the two men pass in. "Wipe your feet, please. Enzo, will you stay in the kitchen, just in case the baby wakes up? Marty and I can talk in the basement. I'll set up the coffee maker for you, it takes just a minute." Gina did not turn once to directly acknowledge Marty. At three a.m., the two men both looked as sharp as ever, as if they had bathed and groomed before making the two and a half hour drive to Gina's. Gina marveled to herself about this. Within minutes, she had coffee brewing for Enzo. She pointed here and there toward her cabinets and drawers to Enzo: "Cups there, spoons here. Help yourself to anything in the fridge."

Gina finally looked Marty squarely in the face and said, "Okay, Marty. Let's go downstairs." She opened a door in the hallway next to the kitchen and Marty followed. At the foot of the stairs was a door to the right, leading to the garage. Gina turned left into a large finished-off room. In one corner was a box-type wood stove on a brick platform.

"This is pretty nice, Gina. Do you cut wood for that in the wintertime?"

"Yeah, Marty. Yeah, I do. Now cut the crap. I'm an accessory to murder, an accomplice. Don't feel like talkin' bout the wood right now! *Speak!*"

Marty crossed his arms across his chest and looked at Gina regretfully. His words were sincere, but his voice shaky. "Gina, please, no drama. No one's ever going to look at you for this. This was all my doing, and you didn't know. I'm sorry to have involved you, but you don't have any idea what was going on. The guy fell right into the palm of our hands. He was looking for us."

"Us, who? You mean, you and the boys, right?"

"I mean us, all of us. You and Ruth, too."

"You crazy or somethin, Marty. Back up. What the fuck you talking about? He stuck his nose in your business deal and he was looking for me, too? That doesn't make any sense."

Marty didn't speak. He thrust him hands into his pants pockets and stood looking at the floor. He rolled his eyes up and said quietly, "Gina, I'm so sorry. It wasn't about a business deal."

Gina took three quick paces and pushed Marty squarely in the chest with her palm of her hand. "You're *sorry*? Huh, Marty? I can never trust you again. You used me. You brought me into your dirty business. How dare you do that!"

"How dare *me*? I don't see nobody forcing you on the train to the city, Gina! What the hell? You could walk any time you wanted." Marty immediately added, "I didn't mean it like that. I want you with me, Gina."

"I've been lyin to myself, Marty. We'll never have any kinda life together. It's not your fault, okay?" Gina spouted sarcastically. She took a step toward the staircase, but Marty grabbed her forearm to stop her. "Ow, that hurts. Let go," she snarled.

"Not til you listen to me, Gina."

Gina pounded his shoulder and wiggled to free herself from Marty's grip. He let go, but quickly secured her shoulders instead, shaking her gently.

"Just listen for *one* minute, please! One frigging minute!"

Gina eased, and Marty slid his hands away.

Gina quietly said, "That's fair. You have one minute."

Inhaling deeply, Marty closed his eyes for a few seconds. "Gina, Vito had been planning to find you and kill you. *You*. When he found you, he would have killed the baby, too. I *had* to do something about it. Removing him was the only way."

"What the hell are you talking about, Marty? What did I do to this guy? I never met him before that night."

"I know you don't remember, Gina, but you *did* meet him. It was a long time ago, and probably for not even a full minute. He had more hair then, and he didn't age gracefully since. Gee, Lisa told her father that I had a regular girl. She told him to find that girl and make her disappear, forever. One time when I spent a day at the house she was drunk as always, and told me, 'Wait and see, Marty. Daddy's going to find your lover and that will be the end of her.' Being the doting Sicilian father, he wanted to please his princess. Hypocrites, both of them. Her father slept around on her mother, right from the start, I heard."

"Well, the pot calling the kettle black, Mr. Married Man!" Gina ran her hands through her hair and paced about the room. "So, Lisa's father hired Vito to find me?"

"Not exactly. Gina, you also met Lisa the same time you met Vito that first time. You met them both at that Christmas party at the Waldorf a long time ago, remember?"

"No. How the fuck am I suppose to remember that, Mart? It was a huge party! I got pretty wasted that night. I remember meeting the boys for the first time of course, and a few other colorful characters, but that's about it." She stood still for a moment, her brow furrowed in thought. "I met Dutch's boss for a minute, but I'll be damned if I remember talking to him. But one person I DO remember is the chick that bore holes through me when I was introduced. The bleached blonde with the thick dark eyebrows and funny looking mouth. Oh, God. She hated me just for being there with you, I could tell. But I don't remember meeting Lisa."

Marty took one step toward Gina, and this time gently

put his hands on her shoulders. "Gina, that *was* Lisa."

Shocked, Gina's mouth gaped open. She put her hands over her eyes, and shaking her head said, "Oh my God. Pasqualini. Lisa's maiden name. You killed him before he could send someone after me. You killed your own father-in-law!" Her knees buckled, and Marty caught her before she could fall. Softly, she said, "Marty, I can't do this anymore. What's gonna happen?"

"Nothing is gonna happen. I'm pretty sure Vito hadn't mentioned it to anyone yet, but was about to find the right people for the job. That's why I took everybody out of the city afterward for the summer. Even if no one knew Vito was at deNucci's that night, I couldn't chance anyone making a connection to us." Wearily, Marty sighed and said, "It'll be okay, Gina, and we can go away soon. I want out of this trap, too. You think I want to go on living like this? Ahm an Irish-Jew and will never go anywhere in this business. I can't be 'made' like an Italian. With Vito gone, Carmine and I can continue as partners and make enough money to disappear. Carmine can be promoted and I can move up for now. Me and Carmine have a plan. All those strip malls, we bought: we can unload them now for a small fortune. Everybody wants to build condos now, and we have lots of property to sell. We'll have enough money to disappear soon. You have to trust me on this one, Gina. Please."

"Sure, Marty," sniffled Gina. "You and Enzo should go before it gets light out, though. Come on, I'll fix some sandwiches and coffee for the ride."

Marty chuckled quietly at that comment. Gina, the mother. Marty could buy anything he wanted, and she was offering sandwiches for the ride back. He said nothing except,

"Thank you, Baby," and followed her up the basement stairs.

Franco and Carolyn looked like two dumbstruck kids at a campfire's edge, listening to a story. Their eyes were wide with wonder. For over ten years, they thought they knew the little woman seated before them, and these revelations were overwhelming.

Their friend continued, "I wanted to go back to Marty, but I didn't. I wasn't mad at him, but it was just too much to digest. My grandmother was not very well at the time, so I needed to stay close to home anyway. I took the baby to her place and we stayed often. Nonna loved having us with her. I took care of her and she seemed happy and comfortable.

Early one evening while Nonna was watching the news on TV, her phone rang. Gina leapt to her feet to answer.

"Hello, hello Gina. Why won't you talk to me? Come on, Honey! Please come back. I need to talk to you about something." It was Marty.

"How did you know where I was? I can't come back right now -- say whatever you need to over the phone." Gina's tone was curt, but not rude.

"Well, okay. I want you to think about this. I'm pretty sure I can pull it off now. I have a couple of deals that are about to wrap up, three, maybe four months down the road. We can wait it out in Miami while me and Carmine tie things up. Gina, I'll have enough money for us, the four of us to live in Europe: you, me, Ma and the baby. Your dream, *our* dream, Gina. Put your house up for sale and you can wait for it to sell while you spend time in Miami with Ma. Leave your job, come with me. I'll leave everything else behind. This is our chance to all be together. What'd ya say? Come on, Gee. Remember what you would always say when you were a little mad at me. After a while, you'd say: at the end of the day I still like you, Marty. Remember?"

"This isn't little though, Marty." Gina, tethered to the phone, pulled the phone cord around the doorway to stand inside her grandmother's kitchen. She peeked around the doorjamb to see her daughter sitting on the floor at her great-grandmother's feet, meticulously coloring in a book Gina had bought her earlier in the day. Gina's heart was beating hard and fast in her chest, and she felt light-headed. She wanted to scream, "Yes, yes, yes!" Instead, she bit her tongue and plaintively replied, "I need some time to think about this, Martin. Okay?"

"Sure, Honey. Think about it. Call me in a couple days then?"

"Of course, I'll think about it."

"Gina?"

"Yes, Marty?"

"Nothin, really. Just don't want to hang up, is all. Good night, Gee."

"Good night, Marty." Gina was smiling, and Marty confidently sensed that. Gina felt chills on her arms, too. She had already decided on her answer.

Chapter 20

M arty promised it would be just the four of us and nobody else. He seemed sure he could leave. Carmine would be making the trip to help us get acclimated. Carmine planned to live near his family. We were going to travel throughout Europe for about a year, then decide where we would settle down. Somewhere outside of a city, so that my baby could attend an American school, but not too far out. We talked about buying a small orchard to work, and I'd be free to bring my daughter to and from school each day. Marty said he couldn't wait to ride along, too. We thought we'd grow oranges or olives to generate some revenue and fit in as local merchants. The plan was brilliant in its simplicity," Rita told Carolyn and Franco. "Marty thought the whole thing out. Or maybe *I* just thought it was pure genius. The economy wasn't great in Connecticut at the end of that decade, so I lowered the selling price of my house to make a sale. The most difficult thing was leaving my teaching job. My coworkers were great; I really loved all of them. It was hard to lie and say that I would write and call to share my adventures with them. I told them a made-up story and said I was going to work for a cartoonist in Miami. Couldn't pretend I had another teaching job, cuz no other school system called anyone for references. I hated lying to them, but I was going to have a new life. A life with Marty. Finally." Rita sighed lightly, and turned once again to look out the window. "Hey. It's so beautiful outside. Could we sit on the back deck? I would really enjoy a smoke right now, know what I mean?"

"Not really," answered Carolyn smiling. The three slipped their shoes on, and Carolyn grabbed sweaters for herself and Rita from the hall closet. Franco unplugged the recorder and tucked it under his arm, and they headed toward the back kitchen door. Bathed in sunlight, an outdoor table and chairs stood on the small deck. Although the living room was warm, bright and comfortable, being outdoors was a welcome change. Rita rifled through her purse for her buried pack of cigarettes. There was an empty ashtray on the table, turned upside down. Neither Carolyn nor Franco smoked, but they kept the tray handy for friends who did.

Rita flicked a lighter, and drew a long hit from her cigarette. She hadn't smoked in several hours, and she felt momentarily light-headed. Her eyes looked down slightly to note that Franco had immediately plugged the tape recorder into a covered outlet near the kitchen door. Rita shook her head slightly and quipped, "Well, I guess I should keep talking. There's still quite a bit more...." She rolled her eyes and the three snickered faintly.

Rita then spoke quietly, "After a very bad winter, my grandmother passed."

Franco and Carolyn flinched. They had grown fond of Nonna Sophia through Rita's stories and were startled that she blurted it out so abruptly.

Sensing their discomfort, Rita said, "It was difficult to be sad. She was so tired but still smiled for me. I didn't cry too much. Why would I? She believed she was going to my grandfather and her family. Best of all, I was with her when she left. I was holding her hand. Rita said smugly. "Because I had to get ready for the move, I was close by and spent almost every day until *that* day. The pain was horrible toward the end. They discovered she was ravaged from cancer, far too late to do any real treatment, especially at her age. That last day the pain seemed to melt from her. That night, she saw someone, *something* in the room. She looked up to the corner of the ceiling, and kinda squinted and opened her arms. There was this gigantic smile on her face. Then, her arms dropped and she was dead. Maybe she saw Federico coming down a hillside on his mule, all of nineteen-years-old. So, for once, something worked out just right. I was with my little pal, the only person in my family that I could help set afloat." The three sat quietly for several moments. Not a trace of sadness on Rita's face, she was clearly savoring only the fond memories of her beloved grandmother. "I put yellow roses and spearmint gum in the coffin with her. Sometimes, I smell Youth Dew on the breeze but only after I've been thinking of her."

"Marty sent a UPS package to me. It contained three expandable file folders. Each one contained a set of papers for an alias. You know, birth certificates, family history, driver's license, and resumes with references that would respond if called; Marty had everything arranged. He paid various people to be ready to give references for each alias, telling them he was just trying to help a friend land a better job. It was easy money for the person giving the references. Marty provided scripts, and paid to cover long-distance phone bills. If someone owed Marty something, giving a reference over the phone was an easy way to pay the debt. Some of these people were lawyers, doctors, and politicians. Imagine that! They were ready to give my new name and face a glowing recommendation. The resume references didn't reflect the person's actual career titles, but they were ready to act the part. It just blew me away to know what people did for Marty. He always tried to be fair and not cruel. I looked through each of these packets carefully. It was a funny experience, actually. Marty had my image extracted from photos from a couple of vacations we took and had fake Florida everything made." Rita shrugged her shoulders in exasperation.

"But you were headed for Miami, weren't you? Didn't you go there first, Reet?" quizzed Franco. "I'm not following you here."

"Well, Miami was *the plan*. At that time, I had no idea that I would end up here. I never made it to Florida."

Carolyn and Franco exchanged puzzled expressions.

"I'll get to it, I'll get to it!" interjected Rita. "To cut to the chase, I chose one of the aliases: Rita Napapolus. The sale of my house closed about a week before I was slated to leave. As Marty instructed, I converted my house money to a bank check made out to my chosen alias. I was going to overnight it to Ruth in Miami, but sorta last minute, I decided to just carry it in my purse. In those days, the airlines didn't examine your carry-on and luggage like they do today. It was more like a quick peek in the bag and you were good to go. Especially a young mom with an antsy kid; we got through the lines quick, and went to the boarding areas right away. I put my most precious things in the bottom of a duffle bag: what little jewelry that my mom and grandmas gave me, a *lot* of photographs, my father's gold cufflinks. Stuff like that. Marty gave me quite a bit of cash. He told me how to hide it: in one of those long thin chocolate boxes and wrapped it like a gift. He knew the airline people wouldn't open it if I told them it was a box of candy for my mom, or something like that. I made a false bottom in the bag to hide the jewelry, and covered it with changes of clothes for me and the baby. Over the phone he told me, 'Put your bras and panties kinda on the top, and they won't poke around the bag too much. You and the baby smile pretty, and that will be that.' He was right, he thought of everything. No one ever bothered me when I traveled, the few times I did, anyway."

Rita sighed deeply and paused, suspended for a few, brief seconds. She drew from her cigarette, slowly. The burning rod was almost gone and she had only puffed on it twice. Realizing she had basically ignored it anyway, she crushed it out in the ashtray. "So, the day finally came to take the train into New York. I hadn't seen Marty since that night at my place, but talked to him quite a bit during the planning process. He felt more comfortable about talking on the phone because we would both be gone soon, that's what he said. It was really hard saying goodbye to Liz, though. Eventually, I had told her that I had a boyfriend in New York and that we were moving to Miami. She didn't know *what* Marty

was, though. You know, what he did for a 'job!' I planned
on telling her more once I got to Miami, like my guy got a
transfer to Europe or somethin' like that. That way I could
be in contact with her again using my real name. She could
write to me and even visit someday. I could go back to my real
name in Europe. Marty was pretty sure that no one connected
to Vito ever knew my name, so there wouldn't be anything
to connect me to Marty, either. Liz never questioned any of
it: my meeting someone so fast, moving away. She was one
of few who knew the history of my marriage. It was enough
for her to know that I was excited and happy." Rita paused
thoughtfully. "She was like a sister to me. At least what I
thought a sister could be like. Like Yvonne was for a little
while. Liz helped me pack up and even insisted on taking
me to the train station. I was so sure I would see her again
someday. Ouch. It hurts to think about it." Rita closed her
eyes, recharging in the afternoon sun. "The baby and I stayed
at her place the night before I left. I visited with my uncle
and his wife early that day, too. I think I told you, they had
second-shift jobs. The plan for them was the same. Thought
I would eventually be able to contact them and let them know
where I was after Miami. I went to the cemetery, too. My
uncle promised he'd take good care of 'them' for me."

        "Come on, Gina! Come on! It's time to go. Better get
moving if you're going to catch the eight o'clock train," called
a tearful Liz to Gina. Gina flushed the toilet in Liz's bathroom
and washed and dried her hands. She was sniffling, too. It
would be a long time before she would see her young friend
again. Dismally, the two friends trudged along, put suitcases

in the car, and stopped intermittently to hug each other. Lots of "love yous" were exchanged in the car and remembrances of when they met and fun times they shared. Liz clung to Gina's little girl at the train station in Hartford, looking as heartbroken as Gina felt. Tortured, the two friends tore themselves from each other and Gina and her daughter boarded the train. She hustled to a window seat with child in tow, and Gina and Liz locked eyes while the train slowly pulled away. Within a minute, Liz looked like a mere dot of color on the station platform. Gina's heart sunk, but it would be only a short time before she could share her European plans with Liz.

There was one quick stop in New Haven before continuing on to Grand Central. Wheeling a giant suitcase, carrying a duffle bag and managing a toddler, was no easy feat for Gina. The fledgling was mindful and held Gina's hand tight. Gina piloted through the masses of bodies to reach the street, where she hailed a cab. "JFK, please, driver." It was a little past eleven, and the travelers had plenty of time to make their two-ten flight. Gina felt lit up like a Christmas tree, or a Hanukkah bush! Ruth's smiling face entered her mind; it wouldn't be long before she would be reunited with her, too.

Gina checked her one large suitcase at the Delta airlines counter, and collected their boarding passes. There was plenty of time to eat something and freshen up, and Gina walked her little girl to the ladies' restroom first. "We'll come back in after we eat to brush our tooths. Right, little girl?" teased Gina to her daughter.

"Mommy, that's teeth, not tooths!" said the tyke. The two giggled and headed back out to the terminal, where they lingered over lunch. Afterward, Gina bought herself a magazine and a new coloring book for the child, knowing it would be well exercised during the flight.

"You are just soooo smart, Girl. Let's go brush your *teeth* and make another pee. Then, we're going on the airplane!" The girl clapped her hands delightedly. Gina stopped at a bathroom close to their boarding gate. They freshened up a second time, and left the bathroom. Gina turned left toward her gate, and immediately saw three familiar-looking men crossing ahead of her, heading for a different Delta gate. Her first instinct was to call out to them, but she stopped short. The men were Carmine, Tony and Enzo. *Huh!* Gina tugged her child's arm gently to stop, making the excuse that she needed to re-tie her tennis shoe. She faced the girl on bended knee and looked over the child's shoulder to see that the boys were joining the last few people in line to board a different flight. She clearly heard the flight number being called and the boys were definitely in line to catch a Miami departure. Rising, she guided her daughter in the opposite direction, around a corner and out of sight. *Why are the boys at the airport?* Their flight would reach Miami about forty minutes prior to hers. She suddenly felt panicked and unsure. *Would he lie to me again?* Marty lied about returning to school, and about setting up Vito. *No, no! Marty doesn't lie to me.* Feeling a bit wobbly, she leaned up against a wall for a minute, holding her daughter's hand tight.

"Mommy, when will we get on the plane?"

"In a little while, Honey. We're going to sit down over here first and wait until they call our turn," and she led the child toward a flight gate across the terminal wing. There, they would blend well until their own flight was called, she thought to herself. Feeling jittery after a mere five minutes, Gina turned to her daughter and said, "Baby, what'd ya say we go for a little walk before we get on the airplane. Remember what I told you about the airplane?"

"Yes, Mommy!" chirped the blue-eyed celestial face. "It's like a bus. We have to sit most of the ride. We can only get up when we need to go potty!"

"Right again. We gotcha a new coloring book. We should probably go back and get some new crayons, too!"

"Yeah! Okay, Mom!" exclaimed the little girl and she sprung from the chair.

They walked until they came upon a newsstand-type shop. That first stop yielded no crayons. Gina steered ahead and they found some on a second try. When she was paying for the crayons, Gina checked her watch. Less than twenty minutes to take-off. The passengers must be boarding.

"It was then, when I was putting the change back into my purse that I heard a flight being called. Seattle. Flight something-or-other boarding at gate whatever. I remembered reading about how beautiful Seattle and the state of Washington is. Something clicked in my head. Even if Marty hadn't lied about the boys, I wasn't entirely convinced that he'd be able to break from his career. My mind was reeling and I began to think that I was jinxed and everyone around me expired before their time." Turning to Carolyn and Franco, Rita comically asked, "Tends to give one a complex; know what I mean? I sometimes wondered if I could jinx my own daughter, too." Rita surrendered a reflective sigh. "Plus, I had never really stood on my own and at that moment, I wanted to *fiercely*. We walked to an information booth and inquired about flights to Seattle. There was just one for early the next

morning that had seats available, departing around five a.m. I
walked to the Northwest Airlines ticket counter and actually
waited in line to buy a ticket. The lady who processed the
tickets couldn't hide her expression when I opened my purse
and paid for the tickets with cash. After I produced an ID, she
seemed less suspicious. It took about a half hour to work our
way entirely out of the airport, and I chose a direction and just
started walking. My poor kid was starting to lag, so I needed
to find a hotel. We passed a little beauty shop, and something
clicked again. I went in and had my hair cut *very* short. When
I left the shop I realized that I could very easily become
disoriented, so I hailed a cab and asked him to take us to a nice
hotel close to the airport. By now, our flight had long left,
about an hour, I think. The cabbie asked if The Sheraton near
the airport was okay. The desk clerk gave me the same look
as the lady at the ticket counter. Rita Napapolus had her own
credit card, but I knew if I used it, I would be tracked faster
if anyone were so inclined to look for me. There was a nice
restaurant and a pool. The clerk there directed me to a bargain
store where I bought some cheap swimsuits. We napped for a
couple of hours in the room. Afterward I took the little one for
a swim, showered, and we ate at the hotel restaurant. I called
the desk to ask for a three o'clock wake-up call; the two of us
were out for the count by eight p.m. The next morning seemed
unreal...."

Chapter 21

She was content with her new life and her new name. It wasn't exactly what Rita Napapolus had in mind for her future. For over half of that first year, Rita felt like the last person on Earth. Walking the town's pleasant streets lined with hanging flower baskets was not a comfort when no one's face was familiar. Even though her daughter was her constant companion, Rita was lonely for Marty and Ruth, too. Her hastiness would probably cost her the chance to ever see Michael again, something she hadn't contemplated when leaving JFK.

In that first year in the Seattle area, Rita guardedly made a few friends and socialized with others at the modest complex of town homes where they lived. She called her daughter Hannah, telling the child it was a game. The two slowly ventured out, taking the bus to the town beach, and did a lot of exploring in the area during their first summer there. Rita struck up a friendship with two brothers that ran a small newspaper in town. Eventually, Hannah attended a summer day camp for three days a week while Rita did administrative work, wrote ads, and helped with billing at the newspaper office. Her young boss came in one day to say he had a good friend that needed a gal-Friday at his company. The position would give her a full-time job close to her townhouse. Rita felt confident that she was gaining all the skills of total independence, and was continually delighted to find that she was a natural at it. Naïve for too many years, she needed to stand on her own feet. Her grandfather encouraged her to see more of the world. *Seattle was a start*, she thought.

Hannah was enrolled in a modest Catholic school, and she and her mom attended the adjoined church on Sundays. Rita participated in school and church activities to be close to Hannah. That turned out to be easy for her, as the graphic arts production company she worked at was a short distance from Hannah's school. Her two employers were childhood friends and family men, so they encouraged Rita to arrange her schedule however she needed to be accessible to her daughter. On one occasion when Rita's car was being tuned up, her new boss, Rick insisted that she drive his little Subaru wagon home and that his wife would pick him up from work. He justified it by saying, "You have to have a car to stop at the store, or if our Hannah gets sick." Rita felt so lucky. Rick said *our* Hannah! Work was busy and Rita made more friends.

One rainy Friday night, Rita Napapolus hustled her first grader through the garage and kitchen door. The narrow townhouse was miniscule, at best. But it was Rita and

Hannah's first home, just the two of them. The rooms were sparsely sprinkled with warm accents that Rita had added over the course of their first year there. The Napapolus girls each carried grocery bags. Rita set hers on the counter; Hannah's were set on the floor.

Although Rita was interested in her six-year-old's day, she was often so tired that it was difficult to concentrate on her daughter's endless energetic chatter.

"You're not listening, Mommy!"

"I'm sorry, Hannah. I'm listening. Tell Mom more, please." She smiled thoughtfully and acknowledged the child's enthusiasm. Hannah had pretty much forgotten their hasty move to Washington, and Rita didn't discuss it.

Rita went back into the garage to retrieve the last bag of groceries, and called over her shoulder, "Hannah, wash your hands, okay? Then come back and help Mommy put stuff away?"

"Sure, Mommy!" chirped Hannah. Skipping happily, her braided ponytail whipped to and fro.

While Hannah put some things in the lower cabinets and fridge for her mom, Rita called and ordered a pizza. Hannah was hurraying quietly while Rita was on the phone. "Thanks, Mom!"

"Thanks, nothing! Ahm tarred, Baby! Ah don't wanna cook nothin!" They began tickling each other when the phone rang. Rita stood, closing some cabinets. "Baby, would you answer the phone for Mom?"

"Sure Mom! I bet it's Tiffany!" Rita and Hannah had few callers, but generally it was a classmate of Hannah's or a lady from church asking Rita to serve on a committee. Rita didn't have much of a social life, so she caved when called upon. But she happily caved. Staying involved in her church community helped Rita stay focused on Hannah.

Hannah was not speaking into the receiver, as Rita would have expected. If it were one of her school friends, the little girl would have been immediately animated, talkative. She turned to look from the open kitchen area, to face Hannah, whose face looked dwarfed by the receiver in her delicate hand. She looked doe-eyed and puzzled, but not particularly concerned. Rita moved closer, "Who is it, Honey?"

"I'm not sure, Mommy." Hannah's expression was inquisitive as she extended her arm to Rita. "I don't remember for sure, but it sounds like Uncle Marty."

Aghast, Rita asked, "You remember Uncle Marty?" All the while, the child held the phone receiver extended toward her mother.

"Kinda, Mom. Aren't you gonna talk to him?"

"Oh my gosh! Of course! Sorry, Honey. Here, I'll take it. Why don't you go take a quick shower now, and you put your pajamas on. That way you won't have to do it after pizza. Now hurry! I'll sit at the top of the stairs in case you need me."

The little girl was a little startled, but obeyed without argument. Rita stared at the phone while the child raced up the stairs.

"Hullo?"

"Gina." Rita felt chills up and down her arms.

"This is Rita speaking."

"Okay, sure. Whatever you say, *Gina*." It was definitely Marty.

Rita didn't know whether to feel terrified or relieved. Had Marty become an obsessed nut? Should she fear him?

"Marty," she gasped, "It *is* you." Rita felt a little dizzy so she sat down at the foot of the narrow staircase. She looked over her shoulder, as she knew Hannah was scurrying by the top of the stairs with fresh underwear and nightclothes headed toward the bath. "How did you know where I was?"

"Come on, Gina. I know. I've known for almost as long as you've been there. See, I've been leaving you alone. It's okay. I just want to talk to you and make sure you're alright. Just couldn't bite my tongue anymore. I guess I figured you would contact me, but when you didn't, well... I miss you."

His voice was like satin for Rita. She suddenly felt ashamed that she could ever even consider fearing Marty. As always, whenever they had been apart, their reunions were as if no time had passed. There was comfort in the sound of his voice. Rita did not feel fear or sadness, she felt reassured.

"Marty. You make it so hard. All the time! You have to let me stand on my own feet. Understand?"

"Stop, stop! Have I interfered at all?" Marty teased, lightheartedly. "Why did you go away? Are you mad at me? At the end of the day, you still like me, right? You always told me that."

Rita felt her defenses breaking down, but she gladly let them slip away.

"Please, Gina. Tell me about the baby, and how she likes school and all of that stuff. You don't have to tell me anything else if you don't want to. Honest."

Rita slowly moved up the stairs. She could now hear the bathroom shower running. She had taught Hannah well not to step into a steaming hot shower. The bathroom door was open and she peaked inside. "Marty, hang on for a minute, please! How ya doin, Baby?"

"I got it, Mommy. See? The water is just right now,"
screeched Hannah.

"I'm going to sit on the top step, okay? Brush your
teeth while you're in there!"

"Okay, Mommy!"

When Rita brought her attention back to Marty, she
could hear him breathing on the other end. "Where are you
anyway? You sound like you're down the street!"

"I'm in New York. She sounds so big, so
sophisticated! Like her mom!"

"Her mom is a girl from the country. She's going to
know a lot more than her mom."

"Her mom is a girl from New York, too!" A half
hour disappeared, and the pizza was delivered. Hannah had
finished up her shower and was in fresh pajamas. Rita towel
dried Hannah's hair with one hand and helped comb it out, all
the while talking to Marty. Hannah ate pizza at the foot of the
sofa, transfixed by a children's TV special. Rita was relieved
that Marty did not press her about why she flew to Seattle
instead of Miami. The relief did not last, however.

"Marty, I don't really want to talk about it."

"Come on, Gina."

"No. You know why. At least I think you do. I saw
the boys at the airport and knew it would never end. Plus,
everyone I get close to seems to have the bad habit of dyin' on
me."

"What are you talking about? You saw the boys at the
airport. That was *it*? Enzo and Tony twisted my arm a little.
Threw that Italian guilt on me. 'Come on, Marty, we're not
going to see you, Gina or Carmine again. Can't we spend a

coupla days in the sun with you and Gina?' They didn't have to twist too hard. I didn't think anything of it, figured you'd be happy that we were all there together. Je-zuz, Gina. All this time I been pullin my hair out because of *that*?"

Both of their voices began to escalate. "Don't make fun of me, Marty. Look at where you are. You went right back to it!"

"We were all in Miami going crazy, cuz you didn't get off your flight. We didn't have anyone there to look for you right away because we were in Florida. Ruth was beside herself with worry."

"Wow! Talk about guilt. What is *that,* Marty? Irish guilt? Doesn't work on me, remember? I'm a Sicilian! It's an art form for an Italian!"

After a few breathless seconds, the two erupted with laughter. "We just can't out-do each other, Gina. Jews have the guilt thing down too, you know!"

"You gave me a new name, Martin. It's Rita Napapolus. You should call me that."

"You will always be my Gina."

It felt good to laugh with Marty again, even if over the phone. Rita munched on a slice of pizza as Marty talked. Hours passed, and now Rita inched toward the couch to see Hannah fast asleep on the couch. She pulled a light flannel blanket over the child, loosely draping it around her shoulders.

"So, Marty, I didn't see Dutch at the airport that day. He didn't go to Miami? Too much sun for him?"

"Believe me, he would have gone, but we made him stay behind." Marty paused, drawing a breath through his teeth. Solemnly, Marty stated, "Josie died, Gina. If Dutch had gone to Miami, she would have died with only her sister and kids with her. It's debatable whether he was really there. He said he was."

"What are you talking about, Marty? I didn't realize that she was that sick. The others told me that she came close to full term with the last baby. Their third, right? I knew she lost it, and that she was ill a long time afterward." Like Marty, Rita held the mental image of Josie as robust, rosy and friendly. "What happened to her, Marty?" whispered Rita.

"Sorry to tell you, Gina, but Josie died from complications of AIDS."

"Hmmm. Died from complications of AIDS. You say that like, 'let's go to the movies.' What the hell? How did she get AIDS?"

Rita could hear Marty rustling on the other end of the line. She pressed Marty for an answer. "You gonna tell me or what? Was it from a blood transfusion?" she asked.

"Dutch did not carry his weight at all, and I got the word that he was going to be offed. He was causing trouble in Chinatown, and was shooting up a lot there. He wasn't taking care of his family. I offered to take him under my wing and get him working again. Enzo and Tony pretty much baby-sat him, Gina. They kept him out of trouble, but he would sneak away long enough to go to Chinatown to get laid and high. So, needles and tainted whores. We think the mob planted a tainted whore. *Which* mob? I'm not sure. Could have been ours, but who knows? Several people wanted Dutch to go away. He bullied a lot of people in his day. A whore with AIDS could sell her services to any unknowing client. In exchange for a set-up like that, the working girl gets paid well and earns good money for any kids she might be leaving behind. A few poked holes in a condom will do it. It's like chemical warfare. The John takes it home to his family. Part of the punishment is to kill the seeds if possible. I'm sure it never entered Dutch's burnt brain that it could happen."

"Marty, stop! That's enough. That's disgusting. I can't believe it. He's so gentle, docile. Like a dinosaur. Moves slow, talks slow."

"He *was* gentle, Baby. But he had severe addictions."

"Was. Had. He's dead, Marty?" Rita asked flatly.

"Yes, Baby."

"What about his kids?"

"Edwin is pretty traumatized, I hear. The little girl is sick and confused, her mother had been ill for so long. Josie's sister doesn't really have much of anything, but wanted the kids. So, I've been contributing to the aunt's household. Everyone is living very comfortably, including Josie's sister. Carmine and I kept Dutch insured over the years thinking Josie could easily be widowed: good thing I did. Dutch died from disease, so there were no insurance issues to overcome. Years ago, I arranged for the insurance to be put into a trust for college, starting at age eighteen. Edwin will get it all. His younger sister was infected in utero. He will be the only survivor of the Vandermark family."

"Poor kid," sighed Rita. "I definitely know how it feels to see your family slip away, one by one."

Although she was moved by Marty's generosity, Rita thought: *Marty is the original benevolent mobster. They really do exist. Or, is he a benevolent **monster**?*

Marty continued, "Josie's sister Suzie told me that Josie's mind went downhill, along with her health. As the pain became more intense, she cursed *me* out loud, and in front of the kids. Dutch had actually told her that it was me and Carmine who tricked him into the joining the mob, not the other way around. Carmine had no intention of making the mob his career, either. He was a dumb kid like me, just wanted to make some fast money and got sucked in by Dutch. I could never figure out why all the shopkeepers handed their money over so nicely to me. I found out that when they didn't pay me, Dutch would beat the crap outta them the next day. Next time I'd show, they were happy to see me instead of Dutch, so they paid on time, every time. Carmine just wanted to marry Maria and have some kids. Poor Josie, I highly doubt that she even knew what she was dying from. She wanted to believe everything that Dutch told her."

In the early eighties, AIDS research was still relatively new. Those who contracted HIV generally took a trip to full-blown AIDS quickly. Pregnancy and miscarriage took its toll on Josie. She had become frail and succumbed quickly.

"Did you take care of them afterward, Marty? You know…"

"Baby, Josie had the finest funeral that money could buy. The best coffin, everything. I brought in special equipment and garments for the undertaker, cuz nobody wanted to touch her body. I paid one guy triple to embalm her for the wake. She looked beee-autiful, Gina. I remembered what your grandmother told you, 'No carnations, they look cheap.' There was nothin but roses for Josie, everywhere. Then, I had her cremated and put in a pretty green marble container."

"Oh, Marty, that's so sweet." Rita definitely could appreciate such a nice tribute. "And Dutch, you did the same, right?"

"Baby, I buried that ass-wipe in the plainest wood box

I could buy. I didn't have a wake or service for him. He was supposed to have been embalmed, but I paid the undertaker to lie on the paperwork. He was buried just as quick as they could dig the hole, early the next day, I think. We got the cheapest plot, in the shittiest location, and near a sewage plant. I'm sorry, Honey. I was so pissed at him for what he did to his family. He was gentle and docile because he was brain-dead. First, he was selfish and self-centered, then brain-dead. His son is so devastated, Gina. He wanted to be just like his dad. If that kid only knew."

Rita was saddened by the way Marty bitterly rattled off the details of Dutch's demise, but understood his anger.

"Marty, I had no idea."

"It's done. He's no longer a monkey on *any* of our backs. If we didn't watch him so close, he probably would have sold all of us for a fix."

"He was near my kid at the Cape while we were on The Vineyard, Marty!"

"That was when we first knew, and his thinking was still pretty clear. He knew well enough that he'd better not touch the baby. The boys said he was fine, and felt well while he was there. The sea air was good for him. He passed just a little over a month ago. He held on for a long time."

Rita recognized a great opportunity to change tracks. "Ruth? How is Ruth? And Michael?" Marty assured Rita that he continued to visit with Michael and that "the boy" often asked about her. Tears welled in Rita's eyes.

Another hour slipped into the night. Rita had turned off the TV and sat in the dim light that lit the stairs from the upstairs hall. Her eyelids were heavy and although she wanted to hold the phone in her hand forever, she realized her hand was stiff and numb from doing so. She chuckled softly. "Hey, Marty? Now that you know where I am, and there's no hiding from you, you'll have to call back another time. I have a little girl to put to bed."

"I can call back another time. I'll call tomorrow, okay?"

"No, Marty." Rita said firmly. "You have to give me a little time to digest, please. I don't want you trying to convince me to come back, either. A couple of times a year, maybe three. For now, I mean."

"You crazy or somethin?"

"Bossin me around already, Marty!"

"Okay, okay, your wish is my command, Gina."

"Rita."

"Goodnight, Gina."

"Goodnight, Marty."

Wow! Unbelievable! Almost four hours on the phone, Rita thought as she walked about, checking doors and windows. She carefully lifted the leggy girl from the couch and carried her up the stairs to her bedroom. *Hannah is getting pretty long and heavy for six,* she mused. She took a quick shower and enjoyed a well-deserved sleep. In the morning she awoke to sounds of clattering in the kitchen below. She called, "Hannah?"

"Yes, Ma! It's me, I'm making cereal."

"Can I stay in bed for a while? Will you watch cartoons?"

"Yes, Ma!"

Rita scrunched down in her blankets and hypnotically closed her eyes again. She drifted in and out of sleep for another couple of hours, and finally rose. She eased her way downstairs to make coffee. When she reached the bottom stair, Hannah was straight ahead speaking on the phone. She had eaten and dressed herself for Saturday fun. Turning to Rita the child asked, "Can Tiffany come up and play if her mom walks her up the back path?"

"Sure, Honey!"

"Can we walk her down the path later?"

"Of course. We'll make sure she gets home. She can stay all day. Ask her Mom if it's okay if she goes to the store with us, too. We'll probably go down to the park near the water, first."

Hannah excitedly relayed Rita's comments to Tiffany and finished the call. "Thanks, Mom."

"Oh, you're welcome, Baby."

While Rita waited for coffee to brew, she put away dishes and utensils she washed the night before. Hannah approached. "Mom, were you talking to Uncle Marty last night? I woke up a couple of times and you were on the phone for a long time!" huffed the youngster.

"Well yes, I was."

"Why didn't he just come over?"

"He can't, Honey. He's far away."

The child looked bewildered. "Yesterday, I remembered what he looked like. Then, he called."

"You mean, hearing his voice yesterday helped you remember what he looked like," Rita said nonchalantly.

"Not exactly. Yesterday, I saw a man that looked familiar. But I couldn't remember who he was."

Rita froze. "Who did you see yesterday? Where? What was he doing, Sweetheart?" Rita now had her hands on Hannah's shoulders. Hannah looked a little scared and Rita brought her intensity down a few notches. "Sorry, Honey. Just curious."

"He was walking near the playground with the sisters. They walked to the spot where the church wants to build a new learning center and day care. He stopped and waved, but I thought he was waving to everybody. The sun was in my eyes, but now I remember that's what Uncle Marty looked like. And then, Uncle Marty called. Funny, huh?"

Shaken, Rita felt a little weak and she eased herself onto a living room chair. "Yes, Honey. That's pretty funny."

Rita and Hannah greeted Tiffany as she scurried up a wooded path behind their townhouse. From a seawall on the beach, Rita watched as the kids played on the sand. She spent the afternoon nervously looking over her shoulder, but did not see or sense anyone watching.

The weeks to come would bring a donation from a private benefactor so large that construction began within a month on the new day care center. The month after that saw the framework of the learning center building. Years ahead brought occasional anonymous tuition payments to help Hannah remain in Catholic school. Rita wondered if it were at all possible her wonderful friend and pastor, Father John could lie about where the donation came from. *Perhaps Father John really doesn't know,* Rita rationalized, and kept her concerns to herself.

"That's really all there was to it. I ran away from home is what it amounts to. As for Brandon Perry, I have no idea why he was murdered or by whom."

"Is there a possibility that your friend Marty could

have anything to do with this?" Franco asked cautiously.

"Absolutely not, I don't see how," flipped Rita. "He was merely one more reason I moved so far away. Talked to him maybe once or twice a year after that."

Carolyn looked up at Franco. Rita's last remark just didn't ring true for either of them, but they said nothing.

It was late afternoon and the three were all weary and drained of energy. Rita called her police contact to advise that she would be returning home. For the second time in a week, she kissed her young friends goodbye. Carolyn and Franco walked Rita down the few concrete steps to her car and watched as she drove away followed by an unmarked police Crown Victoria.

"What do you think, Franco?"

"Not sure what to think at this point Babe. I doubt she killed him, but she's holding *something* back...."

Chapter 22

*R*ita looked out the living room window for a long time. Her arms crossed, she surveyed the scene. The police took care of everything. They moved people along, mostly reporters and nosy people who wandered into the cul-de-sac. An officer occasionally walked around the entire house. Two nights ago someone had scaled Rita's back fence, probably on a dare. In an awkward twist of fate, the teenaged perpetrator's clothes snagged on the fence, delaying his escape. Police found him a block away.

Gratefully, the throngs trickled down to a few curiousity-seekers, anxious to catch a glimpse of a middle-class murderess whose million-dollar bail mysteriously materialized. Rita had little freedom to go out, but she was afraid to, anyway. Gail made a trip to the grocery store for

Rita right after the arrest and release. On clear days, Rita sat outside her back door to breathe some fresh air. The rainy season would be finished soon, about the same time the trial commenced. Diligently, she cleaned the house in preparation of Hannah's return from Europe, and burnt off additional nervous energy by working out in the garage and cleaning closets. Explaining the current goings-on to Hannah would be uncomfortable, and Rita wasn't looking forward to it. Rita had always felt that she was an embarrassment in Hannah's eyes. As a rebellious teen, Hannah once asked Rita if she was a lesbian, in an attempt to understand why her mother's relationships with men never materialized into anything. Rita responded with questions: *Does it really matter, Hannah? Am I hurting anyone by keeping to myself?* Now, she wished for the opportunity to talk to Hannah before information about her past leaked out. She'd need to explain who she *had been,* not who she was. Hannah might never forgive her, and the fact she might go to prison seemed insignificant in comparison to embarrassing her daughter. There were only a few more days until Hannah's return. Feeling isolated and nervous, Rita smoked much more than she usually did.

Rita wanted be at the airport when Hannah's flight arrived. House arrest meant only a walk within the cul-de-sac was permitted: anything else would require a police escort. Rita remembered that she had Brent Parker's business card in her purse, and decided to call him to ask his advice. Backing away from the window, she walked to her bedroom to find the card. Expecting to get a busy detective's recorded message, she was greeted with a serious-sounding, "Detective Parker speaking." Rita cheerfully advised Brent that Hannah would be arriving in Seattle in a mere ten days, and asked if she could pick her daughter up. Rita explained that Hannah would expect to see her mother waiting at the airport. Even though she dreaded it, Rita knew Hannah should be informed of the arrest right away and she wanted it to come from her.

"Ms. Napapolus, I can arrange a police escort for you. That way you could go, no problem."

"Could a plain clothed officer accompany me, Detective Parker?"

"I'll have to check to see who might be available, so I can't guarantee. Well, wait -- I'm actually not working that day. I would be happy to do it. It would eliminate any scheduling problems, and would still be 'official.' Would that be acceptable, Ms. Napapolus?"

"Acceptable? Yes, but only if you cut the Ms. Napapolus and call me Rita."

"Okay, then, Rita. I'll call early the day before. Since I'm off-duty that day, I just need to clear it with my superiors, but I don't expect any problems. I live just northwest of your place, so I can drive to you and we can take either car."

Rita though to herself, *Such a kind young man.* In truth, Rita didn't trust any of the police at this point. She needed their help and was exceptionally polite and friendly when she dealt with them. But so far, she had noticed that Brent Parker's demeanor seemed neutral compared to most other officers she had come in contact with. In the presence of most of the police she had recently dealt with, she felt as though conviction and sentencing had already taken place. Rita was trying hard to remain optimistic, but the situation had been totally out of her control from the start. She didn't feel the same way when dealing with this young detective, however. He always offered a genuine smile and a "yes,

Ma'am" to Rita.

Brent Parker was not alone in his office as he sat the phone back on its cradle. Detective Chandler occupied Brent's guest chair.

"The Napapolus broad?" snapped Chandler. "What did she want?"

"She asked for an escort to pick her daughter up at the airport is all."

"Is *all*? This is a perfect opportunity to pick her brain, Kid. See if you can break down her defenses and get her to slip up somehow." Detective Chandler rose and abruptly left the room. Brent wrestled with how he might satisfy his boss's request.

In the days to come, "the Napapolus broad" continued to keep herself very busy. Like a woman on the verge of giving birth, she was in preparation. She cleaned the house, organized paperwork and started to paint a canvas, something she had planned to do for a very long time but couldn't ever get to. She cleaned her daughter's room with ultimate precision and paid special attention to the small details. *I'll put fresh flowers in here on the morning of Hannah's return.* Planning a grocery store trip, she listed ingredients to make Hannah's favorite dishes. It felt great to have the time to do so, but those feeling were sharply punctuated by the uncertainty of her future. She lived minute by minute, day by day. As ironic as it was, she felt content to be home and was reminded that the smallest acts brought maximum joy: sitting on the couch with Bella on her lap, painting, restoring a vintage dress. These were things she so enjoyed, but rarely had time to do. It was like being on an extended vacation. Unfortunately, this vacation could end in Hell. She pushed the thoughts out of her head and replaced them with those of Hannah coming home, even if it inevitably meant facing more stress.

Rita needed to grocery shop if she wanted to get some cooking done. A practical woman, she planned to spend three or four days cooking then freezing several meals to free time for Hannah. For trial preparation, she would meet with her new attorney, John Sciandra, next week. Prepared food in the house was necessary to avoid repeated trips to the store while working on her case.

The tracking device prohibited her from walking farther than her mailbox. During Rita's first week of house arrest, cop cars were stationed at each side of the cul-de-sac, round the clock. Rita retrieved mail daily and waved to the officers, at first to their dull surprise. Their schedule adhered to a predictable pattern: she was called on the phone just a few minutes before they orchestrated a shift change. They parked in the same place. One car pulled up, the other drove away. As weeks passed, she noticed that the changing of the guard became sloppy. She could dart to the store, but if she failed to pick up the phone the next time they called, a bench warrant *would* be issued for her arrest. Rita did not want to ask her neighbors to shop for her, as they were searched when they entered her home to get money and a shopping list. Gail devised an easy plan: an officer would go to Rita's door for her list. When Gail returned with groceries she brought them to the front door and Rita wrote Gail a check, in plain sight of the officers sitting close by. But Gail had a life, and Rita did not want to burden her friend any longer. She was very apprehensive about leaving the house, but had heavy-duty cabin fever, too. Rita's adventurous side nudged her. If she pulled out and police saw her, she could circle the cul-de-sac

and re-enter her garage. When questioned, she would say
she just wanted to drive her car for a minute. She would be
reprimanded, possibly arrested and say "Yes, Sir, I won't do
that again." By the time her absence was tracked, she could be
finished with her shopping and be back home. It would appear
totally contrived, but so what? Yes, she would be reprimanded,
but she was already under house arrest for *murder*. The cops
would be totally embarrassed by their mistake and have some
of their own explaining to do.

　　　　The housecleaning was a productive but thinly-veiled
procrastination tactic for Rita. If she was to make progress
cooking and baking for Hannah's return, she needed to become
more proactive. With only five days left, Rita summoned the
courage to go to the store. Her house now impeccably clean
and organized, she had run out of manufactured excuses not
to. Rita took exceptional care dressing and getting ready, even
though it was just to shop for groceries. Pride always a factor
of Rita's grooming ritual, this time she especially wanted to
look her best and project an air of calm in the midst of this
controlled chaos.

　　　　She had plenty of gas in the Volvo, so there was no
need to stop at the gas station. The phone call came from
the police. They always asked the same questions. Today's
was: about what time did she plan to shower? She watched
the police car drive off and dashed to the garage to "make
her escape." The Fred Meyer store was just a few minutes
away, as was the Mail Mart where Rita rented a mailbox. She
wondered just how much mail had backed up, and did not
look forward to sorting it all out. The weather was cold, but
very clear and sunny that day. Rita cracked the sunroof a bit
to air out the car. The Grey Ghost had been in the garage for

over two weeks. *Good thing the store is only a few minutes away*. The garage door rose: No police. Rita turned toward the opposite direction of where they usually arrived. Her hands shook on the wheel, and she concentrated hard. *Don't want to get a ticket for anything*, she sarcastically laughed. A mass amount of mail was at the Mail Mart, the bulk of which was junk. Her next and only other destination was the store. Rita parked her car in a spot quite a distance from a side entrance, and sat for a few moments to organize some coupons. Positioning its brim low, she pulled on a newsboy cap. Her hands continued to shake and she reminded herself, *You're procrastinating. Come on; you won't get any shopping done sitting in the parking lot. You got to get back quick. You're making too big of a deal of it. No one will even recognize you.* Within ten minutes, Rita moved quickly throughout the store. She thought she heard hushed whispers, but halted herself, *Don't be paranoid, stay focused, keep moving.* To avoid standing in a cashiered line, Rita opted for the self-checkout. Doing so kept her eyes down and unable to meet anyone's gaze. Her concentration was dissolved by the sound of her own name.

"Rita! Wow!" It was Tyler, a young man who managed the produce department, and who Rita had befriended. He opened his arms to her and she hugged him, relieved to see his welcome face. He radiated a bright smile, as he always did whenever they met. Tyler's boyish face and curly blond hair had instantly endeared him to Rita when she first moved to the neighborhood. "Where ya been? Oh, that was a dumb question!" he gushed, suddenly blushing and looking embarrassed. "We're all thinking about you." They held hands, facing each other. Tyler bent closer and quietly whispered, "We all know you didn't do it." Touched, Rita wanted to cry on the spot. Other employees drew close, surrounding her, offering words of comfort and encouragement. After a few minutes, they excused themselves one by one to get back to their work. Tyler said, "I can take a break and walk out, if you'd like!"

"Oh, Honey. You have no idea how much I'd like that! Thank you so much!" The two finished packing up Rita's purchases and put them into her cart. Tyler aimed the cart in the direction Rita entered to avoid the central store aisle.

"You look great considering what's going on."

"I worked on my face and hair for an hour before leaving the house! Takes longer every year," moaned Rita.

"Oh, stop!" It felt so good to laugh out loud that Rita wondered why she had been afraid to leave the house. This was almost worth getting arrested for. Rita and Tyler strolled through the parking lot, where they deposited groceries in her car's trunk. Tyler invited her to call him to talk or vent, then hugged her tightly. "Well, I need to get back to work," lamented Tyler.

Rita watched him walk toward the store, savoring the few moments of reassurance that she had been gifted. Tyler turned to wave. He blew Rita a kiss. Inhaling deeply, she unlocked the door of the old Volvo and slid in. Placing her purse on the passenger seat, she was startled to see a cell phone there. Knowing full well it was not her cell phone, she panned the parking area quickly, but saw nothing suspicious. Looking up, she realized that she had forgotten to close the sunroof entirely, leaving just enough space to slide a mobile phone through. Not daring to touch it, she recognized it as a mobile for which you purchase blocks of minutes, without needing a carrier account. Immobilized by fear, her mind raced to grasp why someone would drop a cell phone into her car. In the same instant, the device shouted an obnoxious, tinny ring tone. Rita just stared at it until the ringing stopped. Again, she looked around her for activity in the parking lot. None. Rita shuddered. Should she touch it? Toss it out the window? Start her car? She jumped at the sound of the ring tone a second time. She chose to pick up the phone and flipped it open. "Hull-o," Rita choked. "Hello?"

"Gina. Gina it's me." The hairs on Rita's neck bristled. Stymied, she was speechless. "Hello? Gina, are you there?" It was Marty.

Hoarse, Rita whispered: "Marty! Jesus, Marty! Is that really you?"

"It's me, Babe." It *was* Marty; Rita felt instantly reassured. As if no time had passed, his voice sounded the same as in Rita's memory and dreams.

"Marty, I'm in trouble, BIG trouble. I don't know how this happened, but I've been arrested and will be tried for murder." Dead silence. Rita thought the call dropped. "Martin, Martin?"

"I know, Honey. I know."

"Whad'ya mean? How could you know that?" Again, Marty did not respond. "Hello?"

"I seen it on the news. Gina, I love you." Catching her totally off guard, the hairs on the back of Rita's neck bristled sharply again. Marty had never actually spoken those words to her.

"I love you too, Marty. Please talk to me. *Please.* I'm so scared, Marty. Can you help me? This time, I'm *asking* for your help."

"Yes, Gina. I'm trying to. I sent John to you. It was me that put up the bail money."

"In the back of my mind, I wondered if you knew!" Silence again. "Marty, Marty! Are you there? What is going on?"

"I'm risking your hating me forever, Gina. There's no easy way to say it. On and off for years, I had someone look in on you. Around the time that you were dating Mr. Perry, I asked an associate to visit Seattle for me. I just needed to know that my girls were okay, and to put my mind at ease. Selfish of me, I know." Marty's words fell hard. "This man has an inside person at Seattle PD. Tough bunch, those Seattle cops. On a whole, pretty honest..." Marty was clearly dragging his feet for some reason, so Rita did not push. His voice wavered as he continued, "He asked the cop to check any local records for Rita Napapolus. It was then he discovered you were being investigated for your association with that Perry scum bag. The cop also said you had reported some mail was stolen and that credit card checks had been written to various individuals, all male. I asked my contact to check the guy out on his own, and he did. He called to tell me that he found some of your credit card checks at Brandon Perry's house. There's more to it, though."

"What are you talking about, Marty? You sent a hood to Brandon's place? Why? Why, Marty?" Eerily, Rita felt like she did the night Marty came to her house in Connecticut to explain Vito's death. Disgustedly she deliberated, *Men think women have drama. Men have more!*

"I wanted to be sure that there wasn't anything of yours at Perry's." The words hung heavily in Rita's ear. *Too late*, she thought to herself, *my fingerprints were already there*

anyway. "He was only supposed to do that. The police and
FBI were getting very close to pulling in enough evidence to
arrest Perry on several counts. I had Perry followed for a few
days. You know: to learn his routine, go into his house when
he wasn't there." Marty's tone was dryly sarcastic. "But the
plan went bad the day my person visited." Rita could hear
Marty sigh deeply before continuing. "Because he worked for
a car dealership, Perry drove a loaner car home one day while
his was being serviced. My associate saw Perry's car parked at
his work, and of course assumed he was there. You know how
heavily wooded the area is. It was after dark, and he had a
black car and broke in through a back door. No alarm system."

Marty stopped speaking. Rita urged, "Please Marty,
go on."

Rita heard Marty talk but it was like a bad dream. In
her mind, she saw the interior of Brandon's house as Marty
painted the unsettling picture. "He told me that when he
entered, it was quiet. He walked around and saw a bedroom
to his right. Straight in front of him was a huge bed with a
holster slung over the bedpost, and thinking how odd it was,
went in to take a look." Rita had slept in that room a few
times; the bed frame was wrought iron and the holster hanging
there was a fixture on Brandon's bedpost.

Rita heard Brandon's voice now, distant and ghostly,
as he often bragged about his firearms collection. She saw his
mouth moving, the space between his front teeth, and heard
his slight Australian accent as his words ebbed. "This one's
my baby. No one dares come near me with this as my bed-
partner," Brandon crowed. "Ain't she a beauty? An H&K
Mark 23, she is. .45 caliber, see that? One of the finest semi-
automatic weapons made. Probably, *the* finest." Rita felt

dizzy, even though she was seated in her comfy old car. She
remembered the handgun well, a Socom. It *was* rather pretty,
if you considered guns pretty. At Brandon's request, she
held the weighty pistol in her hand. It was matte black, with
a seven-inch barrel. Recalling the size was easy. Brandon
had bragged that his "barrel" was longer than the Socom's.
"Threaded barrel, with a fitted suppressor, ambidextrous safety
and a tri-com sight. Takes a thirteen-round clip -- twelve in the
clip, one in the chamber. Black talons, they're called. Hollow
point. It spools when airborne. When it hits the victim's face,
it makes a nice clean hole in the front, but an explosion out the
rear! When the suppressor is on, all one hears is a dull click,
nothing more. The *last* sound one hears."

A look of dull surprise on Brandon's face was the
next image that flooded Rita's mind. Brandon's forehead
bore a crisp, red hole. His dark brown eyes were round with
wonder. His neatly-shorn hair was peppered brown and grey,
but the back of his head was missing between his protruding
ears. Behind him, his bathroom mirror shattered and sprayed
with brain matter. His slim frame crumbled to the floor, arms
and legs buckling like an abruptly dropped marionette. Rita
shivered hard and pulled her wool coat close to her neck.
Brandon was killed by the very same weapon he called "my
baby." Rita thought he may have appreciated the irony.

"So if this guy went in to look around, why did he kill
Brandon? Did Brandon draw on him?"

"Apparently, Brandon didn't hear a thing. He was
taking a shower. My associate was sure no one was home; he
was fascinated by the collection of guns he saw on the table
and then took the .45 from the holster. He saw it was loaded
and released the safety. The next thing he knew someone was

behind him in a bathroom doorway, saying something like, 'who the fuck are you?' Instinct kicked in, I guess. He turned and shot."

"You guess. *You guess?* This is my fucking life on the line here! Why did you do that, Marty? And you had me watched over the years? And this asshole you sent. Dropped the gun, instead of taking it. Even *I* would have known to take the gun and lose it somewhere."

Rita's questions were not answered. Marty had drifted to another train of thought. "I never stopped thinking about you. Hoped you might come back to me someday, you and the baby. I thought I was protecting you, Gina. I never meant to hurt you." Rita's eyes filled with tears and her anger dissolved. Marty still referred to Hannah as "the baby" after all these years. He haltingly continued, "When Eric was wailin on you, I had the bar hit set up, hoping to get him out of your life."

Rita sat wide-eyed in her car, listening, but not fully grasping the scope of Marty's words.

"Gee, I got you into this, and I'll get you out. One way or another."

"Who is the guy who did it, Marty?"

"A guy from Portland." Neither spoke for several seconds. What Marty failed to mention was that the man from Portland no longer walked the earth. Ever-benevolent, Marty avoided violence at almost all cost. Blinded by rage, however, he flew Tony to Portland to address the gunman's moronic mistake.

"At the questioning, my attorney friend Franco asked if there were any other prints on the gun. We were told that there were just mine and Brandon's. I don't get it."

"Sweetie. The guy from Portland wore surgical

gloves."

Rita responded with a dull, "Huh. Okay." Both were placid for the next few moments.

"Marty?"

"Yes, Gina?"

"Promise me somethin', huh?"

"Anything. Anything you want, Gina. Just say the word."

"Yeah. It's a BIG favor, Marty. If I'm convicted, if I'm convicted, I'm askin' you to off me, Honey. I can't go to prison and let my daughter see me rot there. I can't let her be embarrassed for life. I could sit for years waiting for an appeal if I'm convicted. If I died, she could move away and start over, like I did. Marty?" But Marty was silent. "You said *anything* I want, Marty. I want this. I *need* this."

Even though twenty-seven hundred miles separated them, Rita felt Marty close to her. On the verge of tears, he whispered, "How can I do that, Gina? How? I couldn't kill you. I would die, too."

"No, Marty, you wouldn't. See? We've survived all these years without each other. You'll be fine. Nothing will really change. We still love each other after all this time. Nothing can change that, not even death."

"Yes, we've *survived*. That's very different from being alive, Gina."

Rita's voice was gentle, but firm. "Now, say yes. *You said*: just say the word. *This* is what I'm asking. Say yes. Promise me. It will be better for my daughter. She'll need to wipe the slate clean, and start over. You'll be giving her a gift."

Marty was quietly sobbing, gritting his teeth to try to

hide the fact from Rita. He was shaking as he spoke, "Yes, Gina. Anything you want. I promise."

Rita heaved an audible sigh, and smiled in relief. Forcing a blasé tone, she said, "Whew! Thanks, Marty. I won't be convicted, though. Then you won't have to worry about it at all. Right? You sent John to me, he's the best there is, at least *he* says so." The two laughed half-heartedly. "I don't want to hang up, Marty. I want to talk to you forever."

"Me too. I can take you away right now, Gina. I can be there in a matter of hours and have the tracking device removed. We could fly to South America. They'd never find you."

"Marty, listen to yourself. My daughter will be home in a few days. I can't just disappear. The Feds would be all over her. I have to stay and face the music. I don't need Interpol after me, too. When it's over and my innocence is proved, I'll move away. You can go with me, but only if you divorce, Honey." Gina expected a laugh, but there was only silence at the other end. This time for sure, she thought she had lost the connection.

Marty gingerly spoke, "I'm widowed."

"Oh, my. I don't know what to say, I didn't know. What happened?" Rita replied respectively.

"Ovarian cancer. Four years ago. The doctor said she must have had pain for some time. She wanted to die, didn't go to the doctor until it was too late. Lisa wasn't a bad person, just a spoiled one. She deserved to be loved." Marty drew air through his teeth, and Rita knew he was still there. "Anyway, I'm a respectable widower, and I've waited a long time. I think it's okay to ask my best friend out on a date. Don't you agree? We can't change the past, but we can plot a future.

How's that? Corny enough for ya? Happens to be the truth."

Rita was cautious, yet intrigued. Marty was right.
If she wasn't found guilty, they would both be free. "Okay.
When the trial is over?"

"It's a date! When the trial is over!"

They were both trembling in anguish of having to say
goodbye again. "I have ice cream melting in the trunk of my
car, not to mention I'm not at home and can be arrested at any
moment."

"You and your ice cream! You better get a move on,
then. Honey, destroy that phone after we hang up. Don't take
it with you. Everything will be okay, Gina. I promise you. "

"I believe you, Marty. This time I'm gonna trust you.
I made everything a big mess the last time I doubted you. Bye,
Marty. See you later, right?"

"See you later, Gina."

Each stared at the cell phones they were holding and
reluctantly broke the connection. Rita dropped back in the
seat of her car, almost doubting the conversation she just had.
Popping the glove compartment open, she grabbed a tissue
to blow her nose and dab her eyes. A police cruiser slowly
moved through the store parking lot and she panicked thinking
they were looking for her. The car continued on, oblivious
to her presence. She opened the car door and stretched
her left arm forward, underhandedly tossing the cell phone
behind the front tire. She dreaded explaining her absence
if she were found out. She knew she could shame the new
change of guards into keeping her secret by pointing out that
all the attention would focus on their missing her absence.
Straightening her torso, Rita buckled her seat belt and inserted
the key in the ignition. Backing over the cell phone, she turned

the Grey Ghost toward the city street. "Home, Baby," she spoke aloud. "That was quite the trip to the store."

Chapter 23

*H*annah's return loomed in Rita's mind, day and night. Her house, wardrobe and food were ready. The yard was cleaned up, yet Rita was a nervous wreck. She wasn't ready to explain the arrest to Hannah. Rita did her best to relax by drinking cocoa while watching TV. Tomorrow, Brent Parker would accompany her to the airport. While she couldn't wait for the day to arrive, she dreaded it for obvious reasons. *Gotta take the good with the bad.* Brent Parker called while Rita was relaxing to confirm she checked flight times, and asked what time she would be ready. "You're doing me a big favor, so tell me when *you* would like to leave, Brent."

"How about you check the flight again at two tomorrow, and I'll call you at about two-thirty? We can decide then. Not a whole lot happening in town, being a Tuesday, so traffic will be okay. But if the flight is on time, we might leave by five, just to be sure we don't cut it too close."

"That works for me! I will talk with you tomorrow, then."

Rita anticipated that she wouldn't, but instead slept well that night. Especially during the last few days, she had worked hard, and needed to rest. Tomorrow's flight was not expected until after seven, so she had most of the day to get ready. The following day brought a lot of stress, even though everything was physically ready. A full day to prepare to drop a bomb no longer seemed like a gift, as it gave her more time to ponder her daughter's reaction. In the past, Rita was historically successful in figuring out solutions. Her decisions did not always result exactly as planned, but she learned from mistakes. Today, there was no right way or simple solution to what she faced.

Brent Parker's cheery, youthful voice lifted Rita's spirits. "So, Rita Napapolus -- did you check the flight times?"

"Yes. So far, it shows that her first flight departed on time. The second is scheduled to take off on time, ideal weather conditions were noted." Rita felt suddenly self-conscious, like she was pretending to be a weather reporter, or something.

"That's great!"

"Mr. Parker?"

"Brent."

"Oh, yes, Brent. Maybe you could get here a little before five?"

"Of course."

"Is it permissible for me to have a cocktail before my daughter's plane comes in?"

"Why, yes. It is."

"Good! I'm probably going to need one! See you around four-forty-five?"

"Yes. Four-forty-five," and Brent disconnected the call with a bewildered smile.

Rita felt a little calmer. A car ride had become a luxurious treat, and she looked forward to going beyond the Fred Meyer store. Best of all, she would see Hannah. By four, she had darted in and out of the garage several times to smoke. Intermittently, she brushed her teeth until she heard a car in the driveway at four-forty. For the trip to the airport, she chose a business pants suit. Pants concealed the hideous tracking device on her ankle. Before Brent could ring the doorbell, Rita excitedly swung the front open. The young man looked surprised and said, "Well, hello Rita. How are you?"

"I'm excited. Very excited. Very nervous. Well, I'm a little nervous. Can you tell? You might have an idea why."

"Yes, I understand."

"Oh, please come in. I'm being rude."

Brent Parker looked around at the modest home. The walls were painted in muted pastel colors, few of which were the same. Many were painted contrast colors. The ceiling was painted in a lighter color, too. The living room walls were aqua, others soft coral.

Rita watched his face as he looked around the room. "Kinda Florida colors, huh? And pink flamingos on the lawn, you must think I'm a nut! Hannah hates those flamingos, so I keep 'em there partly to yank her chain!"

"I don't think you're a nut. I like it, Rita. Most people don't paint like this, but it works. Makes my place seem bland."

"Well, *this* is boring for me! I'm trapped here, day after day."

Brent shook his head after Rita turned to get her coat and purse. *She is a character*, he thought to himself. "Rita, I'm sorry, but you'll have to be searched before we leave. The female officer outside needs to come in."

"Sure, sure. My house was searched. I have no weapons."

"Yes, but you also took an unscheduled trip to the grocery store recently, too."

Rita scratched her head in mock surprise. Graciously extending her arm and hand, she smiled, "Of course, invite her in."

Motioning his arm out the front door, Brent summoned a tall, serious-looking officer. The woman appeared within a minute and knocked lightly. "Will you search me in the kitchen?" Rita requested. The office nodded obligingly. Although he was accustomed to seeing people searched, Brent felt a little uncomfortable, but only because Rita did. In a few moments, the women reappeared.

"She's totally clean," spoke the serious lady officer. "Nothing in her purse, either."

"Great. Thanks for your help."

The officer exited and Rita realized that she wanted to brush her teeth again. She told Brent so. He said he needed to summon the officer again.

"Geez, Kid. You can stand in the door of the bathroom. I'm not gonna pee, just brush my teeth. Come on, Brent. Take a look."

Rita flicked the light switch of the hall bathroom. Brent stepped in and looked around the room, and behind the shower curtain of the tub. "Okay?" asked Rita. Dancing around each other, they traded places and Rita set about to brush her teeth and rinse with mouthwash. She powdered her face and applied lipstick. "Guess I'm ready." she sighed loudly. "Please, may I drive my car? I miss driving. I love to drive."

"That would be fine. Would you like to drive my car? It might be a nice change for you. It's my personal vehicle. It's old, but I think you'd enjoy it. Can you drive a stick?"

"I can do a stick. Actually, the Volvo is the first automatic that I've owned in my life."

Rita donned her suit jacket and grabbed her purse. Distracted by the journey at hand, her eyes were cast down as she turned to see a red 1972 Volvo P-1800 there. "Well, well, well!" she exclaimed. "An *old* car? You meant, a very *vintage* car. Almost bought one of these when I moved to Seattle, but got a '79 364GL instead. Nice car, the 364. But always regretted passin on buyin a P-1800. You're on, Pal. I'm drivin."

Expertly, Rita backed the car down the driveway, and exited the cul-de-sac. She cheerily waved to the officers on watch. They could have a few hours break while she was on her field trip. They nodded in their usual bewilderment of Rita's seemingly upbeat demeanor.

Driving relaxed Rita almost immediately. Brent Parker sensed that offering her the chance to drive would. He preferred that focus, rather than trying to distract Rita into talking to him about Brandon Perry's murder. "What do you think, Rita?"

"This is great, Brent. I miss driving a stick. Clutch pedal feels stiff, though."

"The clutch was replaced somewhat recently."

"I know. I didn't say it was the clutch. Master cylinder is starting to go. Just watch it. Depending on how much you drive this, you probably should do it within a couple of months."

"Huh? You're a car mechanic?"

"No, Smart Ass! Oops. Excuse me, Detective Parker. With all due respect, I know about cars I love! Forget it. I'm probably wrong, anyway." She flashed a "so, there" look and stopped talking.

Brent felt his defenses dropping. His gut struggled: the woman driving his car was quite possibly a murderess. She could crash his prized possession and escape into Seattle. It was too late to change his mind, and pondered that he let his imagination wander like that. He carried a weapon, so needn't fear, but struggled with *that* thought. Brent had doubts that Rita was capable of murder. She was funny and playful, smart and unusual, even child-like. *Don't be fooled, most murderers are psychopaths.* He reminded himself of "normal" people that had been shockingly revealed as murderers or serial killers. This little lady could be one of them. Detective Brent Parker was finding it difficult not to smile, but maintained a serene façade.

"This is fun, Brent!" glowed Rita. Once again, Brent looked to the middle-aged lady whose dark hair whipped around a very broad smile.

As always, the traffic slowed just north of the Ship Canal Bridge, and Rita and Brent bantered on. Rush hour was all around them. Suddenly, Rita blurted: "We, I, I totally forgot that Hannah might have a lot of luggage! How will we fit it in this car?"

"It'll fit. There's nothing in the back seat or the trunk."

Southward they crept until traffic loosened up. There was still plenty of time before Hannah's flight arrival. Brent was impressed that Rita respectfully pulled the P-1800 into an end space, so that only one car could park next to it. They leisurely crossed the skybridge to the main terminal and as they passed a lounge, Rita fluttered her hands and tweeted, "Cocktails!" She veered toward the bar.

There were small booths, which Rita preferred to straight back chairs or stools. She ordered a chocolate martini, with the excitement of a child ordering a milk shake. "I can get you into a lot of trouble! Right?"

"Not really. I'm not going to drink, just watch. Besides, it's my day off."

"Oh well. Cheers!" Rita kissed the rim of the martini glass. "Mmm. That's yummy! Women and chocolate: the perfect love affair." She looked around the bar and gazed out its giant glass windows. The sun was beginning to set, and she grew quiet. "What am I going to tell my daughter?" she sighed aloud. Shaking her head, she asked, "Did I say that out loud?"

"Well yes. You did, Rita. I wouldn't know what to tell you on that one. Tell her the truth. Tell her what really happened."

"You know, you look a little like John Cusack. Anyone ever told you that?"

"No." Brent smiled.

And with that Rita went back to her thoughts. She savored the martini and relaxed into the booth. The two sat in silence for several minutes. Rita turned and quietly spoke, "The truth is: the truth. I didn't kill anyone, Detective Parker."

"Detective Parker? What about Brent?"

"Well, right now you're being Detective Parker, *Brent,*" she chimed cockily. Rita slid a sideways look at the embarrassed detective. "Not going to talk about that with you. Come on, now. You know better, and so do *I.*"

Changing the subject, Brent quietly said, "Rita we should check the arrival times soon. Okay?"

"We have plenty of time!" Rita pretended to ignore him, and sipped the drink in a tortoise-like fashion. "Okay, *Brent.* I'll finish up."

Side by side, they stiffly strolled through the concourse. With time to spare, there was no need to rush. Brent wondered to himself what secrets drove this woman to a different coast. He felt impartial, but she was the ONLY suspect. He reminded himself that he was there to guard her, not socialize with her. Still, he could not fight the feeling that she was unjustly charged.

They found Hannah's flight arrival on a monitor. It showed only about eight minutes behind schedule. Rita visibly fidgeted from the anticipation. They continued on toward the arrival area. With over forty minutes before the flight's touch down and deplaning, Rita blurted, "We're going to be here for a while. Can I go outside for a smoke?"

"Huh? Rita, once we go out, we have to walk all the way around to get back in and through the detectors. We don't want to miss Hannah."

"Come on, Mr. Parker. That'll take five minutes. We have tons of time! Please don't make me pace here for an hour. Can't you badge them or something?" She wrung her hands in a comical begging motion, and quizzically studied his face.

"Okay, but stay right next to me and walk slowly.

Understand?"

"See? You said *slowly*. We have lots of time." Rita turned and the two walked toward an exit. Once outside, Rita opened her purse to pull out cigarettes. Displaying a book of matches, she said, "I was careful not to throw a lighter in my purse. Didn't want it seized!" she spouted mockingly. "When Hannah's around, I hear about the smoking," she grumbled. "A prisoner in my own home. Ha! How crazy is that? I am a prisoner in my own home!"

You like to yank more chains than Hannah's, Brent thought. He was amused that this could be entertaining to Rita, but figured she needed to joke to keep smiling. He carefully scrutinized their surroundings to become acclimated to the direction they would re-enter the building after Rita was finished. Rita leaned against the inside corner of the building and closed her eyes for a moment. "Funny, I couldn't wait to get out of the house, but I wish I was home, too!" she sighed. She smoked the remainder of the cigarette in silence, then carefully crushed it out with her shoe. Reaching into her purse again, she produced a pack of gum and promptly offered some to Brent. He slid a piece from the pack. Rita quickly stuffed two pieces into her mouth. "Sure was a nice day today. Wasn't it?"

"Yeah. Still pretty nice out, just a little chilly."

"Chilly, but not raining! Okay, I guess we should mosey."

"Thanks, Rita."

"Thank *you*, Kiddo! It's nice to get out, drive a sweet car, stand outside like this and smoke a cig. I didn't mean what I said about wishing I was home instead. I'm just scared to talk to Hannah." Rita reached down to retrieve the crushed butt and held it in her fingertips until they reached a trash receptacle, where she dropped it in.

Inertly, they walked through the terminal a second time. Rita's nervousness was peaked. Lingering at the gate where Hannah would appear, she paced the floor. An eternity passed until passengers began streaming through the cordoned security section. Rita stood on tiptoes in an effort to spot her daughter. "Oh my God, Brent. There she is!" Rita exclaimed excitedly. "Hannah! Hannah!" Rita called.

"Mother!" Smiling ear to ear, the two women locked eyes. Hannah looked very weary to Rita, but Brent was dumbstruck. Tall and beautiful, Hannah made her way through the swarms to reach Rita. Her long, straight dark brown hair was rumpled from sleeping on the plane, yet her blue eyes twinkled. "Mother! You little thing! How are ya?" she asked, wrapping her long arms around her Mom. Hannah abruptly scolded, "You're smoking again! I can smell it!"

While in Hannah's embrace, Rita flashed Brent a "see what I mean?" look. "Still have a bloodhound's nose, Daughter-Dear. Sorry, yes. Life's been a little stressful without you here."

"Well, that's new! It's usually stressful when I *am* here."

Brent stepped forward and cleared his throat awkwardly. Mother and daughter had been lost in the moment. Rita turned to him and smiled at the glazed look on Brent's face. *The lightning bolt!* she thought. *Like in* The Godfather, *the look of love at first sight.* Looking back at Hannah, Rita hesitantly pushed out the words, "Honey, this is Brent Parker."

"Brent Parker," Hannah repeated, clearly unimpressed. "Well, he's an improvement over the last one, Mother!"

Hannah leaned in close and whispered, "What was that last guy's name again? This one's a little young, don't ya think?"

Rita could feel her face warming and knew she must be beet red. "He's not my boyfriend! Please don't be rude."

"Just who is he, then?"

"Let's head down to baggage claim and he and I will explain."

"Explain what?"

"Just come on." Rita took Hannah's hand and pulled her gently. "I made all of your favorite foods, Hannah. Are you hungry?"

"Not terribly, but I'm exhausted and will probably sleep for a week!"

Over her shoulder, Rita shot Brent a look of exaggerated terror. He followed the ladies down an escalator to the baggage claim area, but his eyes were following the delicate shape of Hannah's face as she spoke. He rigidly stood by while Hannah told her mother about the great things she had bought and people she had met. Rita and Hannah were holding hands, and Brent melted. When Hannah caught Brent staring, he nervously cleared his throat and looked the other way.

"Who is this guy, Mother?" Hannah persisted.

Brent was well within earshot, and quickly stepped forward. "Would you ladies like to have a late dinner or snack? Maybe a drink?"

"Maybe a *drink*?" asked Rita, sarcastically.

"Sure, I don't have to have one, but you two can."

"Let's see how quickly we get the luggage," retorted Hannah suspiciously.

Distracted, Brent stuttered, "Yes, of course." As

Hannah turned back to the luggage conveyer, Brent shrugged his shoulders at a very amused Rita.

Hannah had just two suitcases in addition to her carry-on bag, and it took only a few minutes to find Hannah's pieces after luggage was spit out onto the conveyer belt. Hannah always tied red satin ribbons to her suitcase handles, making them easier to spot. Brent grabbed the two larger pieces, and Rita took the duffle bag. Hannah didn't have to carry anything but her purse. He directed them to an elevator near the parking garage sky bridge. Rita paid for the parking at a ticket kiosk while Hannah grumbled about the long hike to the car. When they reached the P-1800 Hannah sarcastically spewed, "*This* car? Whose old car is this?"

"It's Brent's, Darling! Isn't it lovely?"

"Oh, Mother. You and old cars! I'll never figure you out!"

The three carefully put the luggage into the small trunk and into the back seat, where Rita quickly claimed occupancy. "I'll ride in the back. More leg room in the front for you, Hannah." Within minutes, they were northbound on I-5.

"Okay, Mother. Spit it out. What's the big mystery here? Who is this mystery man driving?" It was as if Brent wasn't sitting right there.

This girl is like her mother, thought Brent as he watched the road ahead. *Sassy.*

"Come on, Mom."

"It's like this, Hannah. Remember you asked me about Brandon Perry?"

"You mean, like twenty minutes ago? Geez, Louise. I'm not *that* tired. Of course, I remember."

"Well... well, he's dead."

Turned in her seat, Hannah shook her head. "That's very unfortunate. How'd he die and what's that got to do with anything?"

Rita picked her words as carefully as she could, considering the levity of the situation. "He was murdered, Hannah."

"Wow! I've never known anyone who's been murdered before." Hannah's tone was flip and disrespectful. "I didn't like that guy much anyway, Mother. You're way too classy for him. Sad way to go, though. Now stop changing the subject and get to the point."

"I'm actually working my way up to it. Brandon's murder is why Detective Parker is here at the airport with me."

"*Detective* Parker? I'm not following any of this, Mother. Could you kindly speak English? Tell me what this is all about."

"Hannah, there's no easy way to say this. I've been arrested for the murder of Brandon Perry. I'm under house arrest and a trial is scheduled to start next month."

Hannah's jaw dropped. Shaking her head as if sobering up, Hannah's shouted, "Jesus, Mother! Do you think you're funny? Come on, get real. Tell me what's going on!"

Rita dropped back into her seat. Neither she nor Brent spoke. Hannah looked back and forth at each of them, waiting for a response. Covering her face with her hands, she whimpered, "Oh, my Jesus! Unbelievable. This *can't* be true."

"Hannah, Honey," soothed Rita. "I'm sorry. It's very complicated. In a couple of days, my attorney will come to the house and you can sit in on the meeting. Franco and Carolyn are going to assist him. I haven't even met him yet. His name is John Sciandra. He's from San Francisco."

"Attorneys. Oh, goody."

Without warning, Brent politely intervened. "Hannah, I'm a member of the investigative team. May I suggest you sit in on your mother's meetings with her attorneys? I'm sure this will have a positive conclusion."

Both women were taken by surprise. Hannah thought, *May I suggest...? What a chicken-shit,* a pronoun her mother sometimes used to describe limp personalities. Rita quietly stated, "You shouldn't be volunteering stuff like that, Brent."

"Rita, I've had severe doubts of your guilt since the first time we met and have been considering withdrawing from the case. The truth is, there are no other suspects. Tag, you're it. Just like in the movies. I don't feel good about it, never have."

"You really should keep your mouth shut. You'll be sorry you said that tomorrow, Kid!" replied Rita.

"I highly doubt it," snapped Brent, as he exited the highway toward Rita's house.

"I'll have that drink now, Mr. Parker," moaned Hannah, shakily. "I would say that I'm quite a bit more alert than I was an hour ago. Mom? How about you?"

"You don't have to twist my arm," sighed Rita.

"Point me in the right direction, ladies!"

There were several restaurants close to Rita's neighborhood, and Hannah directed Brent to a local steakhouse. Mother and daughter shared a meal and Brent ordered a huge steak. They talked for over an hour and then left so that Hannah could get some rest. Hannah was upset, but understood that the evidence against her mother appeared to be mostly circumstantial. Rita had been careful not to trust Brent totally, however, and spoke mostly in vague terms. She knew that defendants are found guilty on circumstantial evidence much more than people realize, even when reasonable doubt has been clearly planted in the jury's mind. The days to come would prove the truth about Brent's beliefs.

After the bags were deposited in the living room, Hannah thanked Brent and said goodnight. Rita walked him to the front door, and took a turn thanking him a second time. He knew full well that Rita was not convinced he believed in her innocence, as she shook his hand stiffly.

"Goodnight, Rita."

"Goodnight, Brent."

Chapter 24

*T*wo days later, Rita was scheduled to meet with John Sciandra. John's practice was in San Francisco, so Rita was intrigued as to how *exactly* he was retained. She wondered if she would have the opportunity to ask him point-blank how well he knew the person who hired him. *Does John know about my past? Does he know about Marty?*

On each of those two days, Detective Parker called on the Napapolus girls. Hannah complained to Rita about this. Rita bustled about the kitchen setting up the coffee pot. So everyone would stay focused on the trial preparation, she prepared two different types of sandwiches. "I'm listening, Hannah, Darling. Just want to have some stuff ready so I don't have to do it later."

"Does this man stalk you like this all the time? Is this

how the police monitor you, by dropping in unannounced?"

"Well, yes they can do that, Hannah. I'm under house arrest." Of course, Rita was not volunteering that young Mr. Parker was not assigned to check on her. Rita knew that he was no doubt dropping by to cast his fond gaze upon the oblivious Hannah.

"Bummer! I can make myself scarce all the time, or I can get searched each time I come home. Let's think about this one." She placed her index finger to her chin and tilted her head, eyes looking skyward. "Hmm. Kinda tough to choose," she lamented morosely. "Maybe I'll ask Heidi's parents if I can live at their place. It's close by in an emergency." Hannah must have read the disappointed expression on Rita's face. "Sorry, Mother. I didn't mean it like that. If you need me to be here, I will be."

Rita drew a slow breath. "I *do* need you here, but it might be a good idea to stay at Heidi's for a few days at a time. Just to be safe. You need to go out with your friends and share your new European adventures with them. Right? But I hope you'll stay for one or two meetings with my attorney John Sciandra, so you know what's going on."

Hannah cheerily replied, "Of course, Dah-link! I still have a twinge of jet lag, anyway. I'll stick around."

John, Carolyn and Franco would converge at Rita's house at eleven, and planned to meet at least twice a week to discuss the case. The first half-hour or so was spent explaining to Hannah what had happened to date and why evidence pointed to her mother. They gave her a quick run-down on circumstantial evidence as compared to physical and forensic evidence. One key fact was the most difficult one to explain, so the attention then turned solely to Rita.

"Carolyn, Franco and John can't explain this part, Hannah. It has to come from me. I can't tell you why, but I changed my identity to take you away and start our lives over," she hesitated, "on our own."

"I'm not getting what the big deal here is, Mom. I'm sure other people have done that before."

"There's lots more that the prosecution can taint the jury with, Babe. Brandon Perry had his hands in lots of people's pies. Because I dated him, and used an alias, we think the prosecution will try to show I was linked with his scams in some way. We're pretty sure that's how they'll play it. Brandon stole blank credit card checks from me and cashed them using aliases. They'll push that as the main motive for the crime. They'll insinuate that I possibly had a business deal gone bad or something. Even if statements are stricken from the record and the jury is advised to disregard it as evidence, it still sticks in the jurors' heads. The prosecution is known for pushing the envelope to drive a point, whether it's true or not. I've always known that there's a wide divide between law and justice, but now I'm the one falling into it." Rita was not feeling sorry for herself; she was simply stating facts about the frightening challenge that lay ahead. Both she and Hannah would need to summon up their strength to face this.

Hannah sat dumfounded; her stare was glassy as she spoke. "All these aliases, Mother."

In the weeks that followed, John, Carolyn and Franco faithfully met with Rita twice a week. There was no conclusive evidence to show that someone else might have killed Brandon Perry and Rita told no one about her phone call with Marty. Religiously, they reviewed all the information, hoping to find a flaw in the prosecution's shared discovery.

John said he felt certain that the jury would recognize that reasonable doubt clearly existed and that a verdict of Not Guilty was attainable. The hair found in Brandon's hand was indeed Rita's, but forensic tests proved that it was old and brittle, suggesting that Rita had left her hairbrush at his place and Brandon must have been trying to clean it for use his own use when he was killed.

Whenever they met, John repeatedly asked Rita if she knew anyone else who might have killed Brandon Perry. At first, Rita thought he asked these questions for the benefit of Carolyn and Franco, but as time passed she wondered if that was really the case. Shortly before the trial date, she took the opportunity to ask John some questions privately. Arriving a half-hour earlier than the time she had given Carolyn and Franco, she had ensured she would be alone with John.

John arrived meticulously dressed, as always. Of average height, his bald head looked polished, and his graying hair and beard were perfectly trimmed. He wore wire-rimmed glasses, and had soulful hazel eyes. He reminded Rita of Sigmund Freud images. John readily accepted freshly-brewed coffee. "John, Dear, I'm going to ask you point blank: who hired you to represent me?"

John looked at Rita with mild surprise. "You mean, you don't know?"

"No, I don't. Why would I be asking?"

Almost challengingly, John looked Rita squarely in the face. "Garson Doyle of San Francisco called me advising he had been called by a client on the East Coast. Garson said he was retained to find the right person to defend you. From that point, all I need to know lies with you, Rita."

"Garson Doyle, who is that?" whispered Rita,

breathlessly.

"We go way back, and are currently partners at rival firms. But Garson knew that your case had my name on it. To ensure success, you sometimes need to swallow your pride and pass the case along to someone with the right experience and perfect record. I knew nothing about you until he called."

Acting somewhat befuddled, Rita responded, "Thanks, John. I just don't know who could have posted bail and sent you. I thought you could tell me." *Whew! John really doesn't know much about my past other than what Carolyn and Franco shared with him*, she thought. Even though John was a well-known criminal lawyer and commanded a presence everywhere he went, Rita's case did not look hopeful. He was perfectly composed as he took his coffee to the living room and set it down on the table. He pulled some papers from a small zippered leather case.

"What's that, John?"

"Don't want to disappoint you, but nothing new. Just reviewing what we already have. I was hoping that something would jump out at us, that something else would click."

I'll tell you what would click, Honey. My former lover is a mobster from New York. He got me into this predicament. A long time ago, we were going to run away, but I got cold feet at the last minute. Now, I'm accused of murder because a hood from Portland fucked up. All to protect helpless me. If I had been left alone, I would be free to come and go from this house right now. But I'm not free. God, or whatever energy is out there, please help me to be free again!

She watched John as he puzzled over the papers on the coffee table. He was oblivious to the importance of Marty's existence. She *could* tell John about Marty, but it occurred to her that putting that information forth to a jury could land her in the psychiatric prison for a long time. Her concentration was broken by the sound of the doorbell. "The kids, no doubt." Mulling over her lack of conversation with John, Rita carelessly opened the door. It was Brent Parker.

"Hello, young man! Now is not a good time to visit. Your being here is totally a conflict of interest. My attorney is here and Carolyn and Franco will be arriving soon. You remember them, correct?"

Brent definitely picked up on Rita's pissy vibe, but before he could respond, Hannah appeared from the hallway. "It's okay, Mother. He's here for *me,* we're going to the movies."

Crooking Brent's arm with her bent elbow, Hannah turned him toward the front door. Looking over her shoulder at Rita she said, "Mother, Brent withdrew from the investigation weeks ago!" Hannah closed the front door quickly as to avoid a response from her mother. Turning to Brent, she said, "See? That was easy! I knew you could do it. She's in there right now smiling her ass off!" Hannah pecked him hard on the cheek. A car other than either of Brent's two sat in the driveway. "Hey, I thought you were taking the P-1800 today."

"Oh," mumbled Brent. "It's at the mechanic's. The master cylinder needed to be replaced."

Hannah knew Rita better than she could have imagined. Inside the house, Rita smiled. The fact that Hannah was dating Brent pleased her. Brent just never fit the detective-cop persona in Rita's mind. She laughed inside when she compared Brent to Detective Chandler, imagining Chandler shining a light into a suspect's eyes, like in a B-Movie. In a dumpy coat and hat, Big Bob Chandler's haggard bulldog face seemed like a cartoon stereotype compared to the darling Brent.

Rita's mind speculated about how Marty was going to get her out of this mess. *There is no way.* She wanted to think more positively. The start of the trial was fast approaching, and she hid at the front window blinds as Brent and Hannah drove away.

Secretly, Brent and Hannah discussed possible leads that led nowhere. They were desperate to find a link to anyone else who may have killed Brandon Perry. Repeatedly discouraged, Brent kept Hannah's spirits up. "They don't have a confession or anything close. Rita kept cool during questioning. I truly believe she's innocent, and the jury will, too, Hannah," he cheered.

After the movie, the couple stopped off at the store to get some Rocky Road ice cream for Rita, as it was her favorite flavor. While in the check-out line, Hannah felt slightly nauseous. "Brent! Look at the upper-right hand corner of People Magazine!"

Brent's eyes swept over the tabloids and magazines near the register. There it was: a small photo of Rita. She looked angelic in a pretty blouse and skirt, but an angel in handcuffs, nonetheless. The tagline read, *Seattle's Madame X. Who is she? Did she kill her lover? Where did she come from?* "This is horrible, Brent!" trembled Hannah. "What's a Madame X?"

"I don't know, but it can't be good," lamented Brent.

Oddly enough, Madame X was one of Hannah's grandma Elaine's favorite movies. It starred Lana Turner as a woman who cooperates in staging her own death, after her heartless mother-in-law convinces her that she is not good enough for her rising politician son. Lana Turner must leave behind her angelic blond toddler, who grows up to be the dreamy Kier Dullea, an attorney who unknowingly defends his own mother who is accused of murder. The main character will not and cannot reveal her true identity, especially after she realizes the attorney representing her is her very own son. In the movie, the press dubs her Madame X. Rita had watched that movie more than once with Elaine on TV.

Hannah stomped out of the store and into the parking lot, Brent on her heels. He caught Hannah's arm at the elbow, but she pounded his chest with her fist. Crying hysterically, she screamed, "She's ruining my life, I *hate* her!"

Brent finally wrestled Hannah to a stop, wrapping his arms around her. She sobbed uncontrollably onto his chest as staring shoppers walked by. "Honey, you don't mean that. It will all work out." Brent pulled Hannah away at arm's length, and looked hard into Hannah's red face. "Let's put this into prospective here, Hannah. She may go to jail for the rest of *her* life! We both know she's innocent." He pulled Hannah close again and she calmed.

"Brent, I didn't tell you. The TV station retracted their offer. Felt that it could be bad publicity for them. Even *when* Mom is proven innocent, I have no dream job waiting for me! Maybe it's best that I don't stay in Seattle anyway, when this is over. You're right, Honey. I don't hate Mom, but Goddamn, this is hard."

"I know, I know, Baby," and he stroked her hair soothingly. "What'd ya say we go back in and pay for that ice cream, huh?"

Hannah sniffled and wiped her face on her jacket

sleeve. Wearily, she replied, "Thanks, Brent. Yes, let's get Mom her Rocky Road!"

Rita, Hannah, Brent, John, Carolyn and Franco, tried hard to remain upbeat and positive going into the trial. They shielded Rita against the swarms of people waiting on the steps of the courthouse each morning when they arrived. On one occasion, a reporter accidentally shoved her microphone into the side of Rita's face. A horrified Hannah grabbed the mike and threw it to the pavement. Days seemed murky and blended for Rita and she wondered if she could be having a nervous breakdown. Carolyn's bright and beautiful face helped bring Rita back to reality. She was seated next to Rita at the defense table, and often held Rita's hand. After days of deliberations, voices became distant, disjointed echo-chamber sounds. Trying to focus, Rita grew sleepy being indoors for long periods of time. At home, she could at least step outside for air when she needed to. So in control of her expressions, Rita was dubbed a cold-blooded killer by the press. Sadly, if she had smiled or laughed during the trial, they would have described her the very same way.

After a few days of proceedings, Rita's back hurt deeply. She had always found it difficult to sit still for long periods of time. Sitting in a chair with her hands in front of her on the table hour after hour, day after day was becoming painful. Rita shifted in her seat. Not wanting to appear uneasy, the discomfort was almost too much to bear. She was thoughtful in her moves; hoping the jury wouldn't misinterpret her discomfort as one of guilty squirming. Screaming inside, Rita had long grown immune to any pain relief that acetaminophen might offer her. John brought pressure-peel "relief patches" infused with deep heating lotion, and the courtroom matron helped Rita put one or two on her back before court started. Sleep was elusive for Rita; she got little. Nothing held her attention much during the first two weeks of the trial, but that was about to change.

"The state calls Gail Brown to the stand."

Gail came forward, stepping up to the witness chair daintily. The court clerk held a Bible while she was sworn in, her voice trembling as she took the oath on the stand. Gail Annette Brown was Rita's neighbor and good friend. Her agitated gaze darted back and forth from the court clerk to Sean Duggan, the prosecuting attorney. Duggan was a slightly built older man. His suit looked quite expensive, but also looked a little baggy on him. He had grey hair and angular features, but was handsome.

Gail's nervous gaze met Rita's, who nodded a soft, reassuring smile to her friend on the stand. *It's okay, Babe. Tell the truth, no matter what,* Rita channeled a warm and wistful look to Gail, who tried to relax. Gail then took a very deep and audible breath. From a seat behind Rita, Gail's husband Robert, nodded and smiled to his wife.

Gail was a few years younger than Rita, a couple of inches taller. She wore her brown hair short, highlighted. Layered, it framed her freckled face in cherub's curls. With an ample bottom and hips, Gail's physique was pear-shaped. Her soulful brown eyes reminded Rita of her own father's eyes. *Brown, brown and brown,* Rita used to think. Gail and Robert were loyal neighbors and friends. Both sometimes helped Rita with heavier chores that homeowners perform: like hauling debris to the dump after a home project or picking materials up in Robert's pick-up truck at the local Lowe's store. Gail and Rita enjoyed walking Gail's two dogs when they could do so during the drier months of the year. Rita occasionally was a spectator at the couple's co-ed softball games and was included in their circle of friends. They were great neighbors in a great neighborhood.

Attorney Duggan approached the witness stand slowly. He began his questioning with the usual, mundane opening questions: "How are you acquainted with the defendant, Rita Napapolus?"

"Rita is my neighbor."

"How many years ago did you first meet?"

"Shortly after she bought the house next door, about nine years ago."

"What kind of relationship did you share?"

"We are pretty close." Gail paused. "Neither of us has a lot of leisure time, so we get together when we can, usually at one of our homes. Sometimes, we hang out in Rita's garage. She fixed it up nice, with chairs and a table in one of the bays. She calls it The Grotto," Gail said with a wide remembering grin. "Rita lit candles. We opened the garage door sometime. Mostly we sat around, drank wine, smoked, talked, laughed. You know, girl stuff."

"Well, very nice, Mrs. Brown. Did she confide in you about her relationship with Brandon Perry?"

"Sure."

"Did she share any details of her relationship with Mr. Perry?"

"Sometimes, we talked about other stuff too: our jobs, relationships, our kids."

"Okay, but let's stick to the question, Mrs. Brown. Did she speak of Brandon Perry?"

"Yeah, we talked about it a little."

"Mrs. Brown, where and when were you and the defendant when she confided those details to you?"

"The Grotto. I mean Rita's garage. Don't know exactly when. About four or five months ago, I guess. We talked about it a couple of times."

"Go on, Mrs. Brown. May I call you Gail?"

"Sure." Gail paused again and shot a helpless look toward Rita. Rita smiled again and nodded. "Well, a few months ago, Rita told me that she decided to go online to try to meet guys. She was lonely, you know. She's a nice lady. She wanted to meet someone. She's active and hoped to meet someone the same. She corresponded with several guys and sometimes met them for coffee, or dinner, stuff like that. I've been married for a long time, so it was fun to hear about her dating experiences."

"And then she met Mr. Perry?" Sean Duggan urged.

"Yeah, I mean yes."

"And was Mr. Perry what Rita thought was a good match for her?"

"Well, yes and no. At first, she said he had some redeeming qualities and that no one is perfect. He was non-athletic, a heavy smoker, too. But she thought he was funny and charming. He was born in Australia, he told her."

"Over the course of the months following Ms. Napapolus' meeting Mr. Perry, how would you describe the course their relationship went?"

Gail was cautious. "It wasn't going well."

"Why do you think that was, Mrs. Brown? Did Ms. Napapolus share why it wasn't going well?"

"Yeah, yes, she did. She said that Mr. Perry constantly talked about making money, and wanted Rita to invest in his business deals. Rita got sick of it. She said she didn't think he was interested in her, that all he was interested in was money. He became cross when she wouldn't contribute to a real estate flip-deal and she told me he said she was missing out on making some easy money."

"Anything else?"

"Then, Brandon asked her to meet him on one of the San Juan Islands where he had to travel for business. She thought it might be fun, took the ferry and drove to the motel where he said he was staying. He wasn't there. It was very embarrassing for her. He never called to explain or apologize, either." Gail cast her eyes down to her hands clasped on her lap and drew another deep breath. "Rita is a trusting person. She was appalled that people treat each other that badly. She hadn't done anything to deserve that kind of rudeness."

Sean Duggan then turned to Judge O'Connor and requested, "Your Honor, I ask that the last few statements be stricken from the record. They are strictly conjecture and are the personal opinion of the witness."

Judge O'Connor considered the request for a moment, but then stated: "No, Mr. Duggan. The witness knows the defendant well. The defendant has good qualities, too, so it's important to get a full picture of her character. The remarks will remain."

"Yes, Your Honor." Turning to Gail, Sean pressed on. "Did Rita ever mention if she went to his home? Were there any other details that were mentioned about Brandon Perry?"

Gail took a few moments to pondered Mr. Duggan's questions. "Rita told me that Mr. Perry said he had been a member of the Australian Special Forces, something like that. He kept a handgun in a holster slung across his bedpost. Rita said she was scared and amused at the same time. She said it was her impression that people who have been in that line of work don't talk about it all the time and apparently Brandon babbled about it. Rita used to say Brandon was such a unique storyteller." Gail looked dismayed and abruptly stopped.

"Mrs. Brown, something else?" Gail was definitely hesitant to answer. "Mrs. Brown?"

Again, Gail looked toward Rita, this time with a panicked look.

"A couple of weeks after his last visit, Rita realized that an old pair of cufflinks were missing from her place. Her father's cufflinks. She told me that she only kept them in her bed table drawer, in a box. One day she opened the box just to take a look at them, they were gone. She never wore them or put them anywhere else. She cried a lot about that. She said that was all she had from her father."

"Did Ms. Napapolus say if Mr. Perry had access to that drawer, Mrs. Brown?

Gail looked rattled. "Yeah, well. They were lovers for a short time."

"And what did Rita say after she admitted she thought Mr. Perry took her father's cufflinks?"

Gail looked down at her hands again, her eyes welling with tears. Her mouth open, she did not speak.

"Gail: what did Rita say about the loss of the cufflinks?"

Gail stammered her response. "She, she said that she called Brandon Perry and confronted him point blank over the phone about the missing cufflinks. She said he laughed at her and called her a stupid bitch, and said something like 'prove it; what ya gonna do about it?' He laughed about standing her up at the San Juans, too. She was mortified."

"Did Rita Napapolus say anything else about Mr. Perry at that point?"

As she shook, tears streamed down Gail's freckled cheeks. "Yes," she whispered.

John broke the silence by standing and saying: "Your Honor. I'm not understanding where this line of questioning is going, plus the prosecution seems to be leading this witness. But to what point?"

Judge O'Connor turned to Sean Duggan and said: "I tend to agree with Mr. Sciandra here, Mr. Duggan. I was about to ask, as well. Is there a point?"

"Yes, Your Honor. I ask the Court to endure just a few more questions and then the point will be crystal clear."

"All right then," Judge O'Connor nodded. He looked toward John, back to Sean and said, "Proceed."

Judge O'Connor then turned his gaze toward Gail, nodding to the clerk long enough to say: "Please give this witness a tissue." In a gentle, low tone he said, "Gail, you'll need to answer the question now."

"Yes, Your Honor," Gail sniffled and dabbed her eyes and nose. "Well, we had been drinking wine; I'm sure Rita didn't mean what she said. She was upset. I would be pretty upset, too."

"Mrs. Brown," Judge O'Connor interjected before Sean Duggan could. "What did the defendant actually say?"

Gail looked at Rita again, her forehead furrowed. "She said that she knew someone in the mob back East, that all she had to do was say the word and Brandon would be 'offed.' And she said something like, 'maybe I should write a book someday about a woman who runs away from her past, but gets screwed over by a bastard, and has him whacked!' It was a *joke*, Your Honor." Gail's voice cracked as she turned to Judge O'Connor and continued: "She didn't mean it. We laughed after she said that. Rita couldn't hurt anyone, *ever*."

At first there were a few muffled hints of nervous laughter, but in a split second the courtroom exploded like a marketplace full of loud voices and bustling activity. Judge O'Connor hit his gavel hard against the sound block. "Order, order! Everyone: quiet, *please*."

Rita felt numb. How could she have said such stupid things, however innocent? *I'm fucked*, she thought to herself, *totally fucked*. She looked over her shoulder at the madness, but it looked like a spinning blur of color and lights. She thought she might faint, but realized no such luck! Judge O'Connor was banging his gavel hard. It took a full minute for the chaos to return to just a few light whispers.

Attorney Duggan firmly continued. "Did you ever see the cufflinks, Mrs. Brown?"

"Yes. Rita showed me once. We shared stories about both our dads once in a while."

From the evidence table, Sean Duggan picked up a small zip-lock bag. He turned to the witness box and placed the bag in front of Gail. "Look at these cufflinks carefully, please. Are these the same ones Rita showed you?"

Gail picked up the plastic bag, turning it over several times. Biting one side of her lip slightly, she said: "Yes, these look like the same ones."

"Look at them again, Mrs. Brown. Are you sure they're the same cufflinks and why?"

In a bewildered whisper, Gail replied: "Yes, I believe they are the same ones. The engraving, the style."

While gesturing with the plastic baggie in his left hand, Sean Duggan stated: "Let it be noted that the witness has identified the cufflinks found at Mr. Perry's house, as the property of Rita Napapolus." He turned to Gail once again and asked, "Is Napapolus Rita's maiden name or married name, Gail?" Duggan placed the cufflink bag down gently on the beautifully crafted ledge in front of Gail, and took a step back. Holding his elbow with one hand and his chin in the other, he waited for Gail's response.

"Her maiden name. She returned to her maiden name because her family had a good reputation and her ex-husband didn't. And she just liked her name better."

"Yes, that's nice. And did Rita tell you what her father's first name was?"

"Well, yes. His name was George, George Napapolus."

"Would you pick up the bag and take another look at those cufflinks, please?"

Gail turned the plastic bag carefully over and over in her hands, examining the cufflinks closely. Her wide eyes blinked hard. It appeared she had a slight epiphany.

"Mrs. Brown: do you notice anything different about these?"

"Well, not exactly different. But I noticed something I hadn't before."

"And what hadn't you noticed before, Gail?"

Sorrow and confusion were evident on Gail's face as she quietly said, "The initials on these cufflinks are S.A.B. and not G.N."

The room became a beehive again, and Judge O'Connor's gavel was getting a heavy workout.

"No more questions of this witness at this time, Your Honor," bellowed Sean Duggan.

And I thought I was totally fucked before! Rita thought to herself.

Chapter 25

G ail's testimony had brought the inevitable truth about
Rita's real identity to light. During pre-trial preparation,
Rita and her defense team had discussed its high probability.
Duggan was out to destroy her character and place doubt in the
juror's minds. Doing his job, Attorney Duggan stressed more
details of Rita's negative past: her association with Brandon
Perry, her fingerprints on the weapon, and a motive for murder.
His words echoed in Rita's head like far-off whispering, and
his closing remarks stung. *Is that me he's talking about me
or Lizzie Borden? Jesus, I'm a good person. I just changed
my name!* Tired, she zoned out beyond the courtroom's
gargantuan windows and into the sky.

      John's closing remarks revived some hope for Rita.
He exhibited a valiant self-confidence that Rita coveted. None

of the State's evidence was conclusive, he said. Although
there was physical evidence, Rita could not conclusively be
placed at the scene of Perry's demise. She readily admitted to
police that she held Perry's Socom during a visit. She did not
confess. Rita simply set out for Seattle to get a fresh start. She
said things in anger but did not act on it. She lived a quiet life
with her daughter.

Afterward John, Rita, Brent and Hannah tried to relax
in a comfortable room in the courthouse chambers, sure that
they would be sent home while jurors convened for the night.
They were dismissed to spend the night at Rita's. Brent took
the couch, and John, the guest room. Carolyn and Franco
headed home. Hannah shared Rita's bed.

When Rita bent to kiss Hannah goodnight, her
daughter responded, "That felt so good, Mom. It's been ages
since anyone has tucked me in and kissed me goodnight!"

Not believing her own statement, Rita replied, "We'll
have lots of opportunities to do it again, Lovey." She stroked
Hannah's cheek for a moment, feeling as though the clock had
turned back twenty years.

The four were preparing for the courthouse, just in
case, when Brent got a call at nine the next morning. He
solemnly announced: "The jury is in." Everyone was silent.
The ladies finished their last-minute grooming and everyone
piled into John's car. Outside, two police cruisers waited,
ready to escort the foursome South.

John and Brent looked at each other gravely. Both
knew when a jury reaches a verdict quickly, it usually results
in a guilty one.

Rita felt ill as everyone took their seats. The
ceremonious rituals of rising and sitting had long ago become

robotic. She was asked to stand to hear the verdict, and did so. The forewoman's lips moved but Rita did not hear a thing until the woman said, "Guilty on the count of first-degree murder." The room erupted in mass hysteria. Rita stood frozen, expressionless. Judge O'Connor banged the gavel repeatedly for order, but it fell on deaf ears for several minutes. Outside the doors of the room, a press agent shared the verdict with the swarm of waiting reporters. Brent held Hannah close to his chest. Rita turned to Hannah. She felt relieved in a way; the trial was over. She would need to gather all of her strength now, to move forward toward the next step that was discussed earlier: an appeal.

"Order, order!" shouted the weary Judge. "Order!" After several minutes, the room was ironically reticent. "Ms. Napapolus, do you have any words for the court at this time?'

Dreamily Rita answered, "No. Thank you, Your Honor."

Judge O'Connor continued. "Ms. Napapolus will await sentencing at an undisclosed location. Remove the prisoner, please."

The prisoner. The prisoner. The words rung in Rita's head like a tolling church bell. She wanted to die. Shakespeare's Romeo and Juliet pierced Rita's thoughts: *Come death and welcome, Juliet wills it so.* The matron gently helped Rita from her seat and shackled her wrist and ankles. Hannah sobbed hard against Brent's chest while her mother meekly smiled over one shoulder. As she was led away, Rita turned at the waist and held her arms out toward Hannah, Hannah doing the same.

Brent's position as a Seattle Police investigator made it less difficult to gain access to the entourage that would escort

Rita out, and so Hannah and Brent were allowed to follow her
through the courtroom's side exit door. It was predetermined
that if the verdict were a guilty one, that Rita would be spirited
out of the Seattle area to quaff the media circus that had
prevailed for the past several months. Brent had arranged a
room at a hotel close by for the night in the event reporters
or curiousity-seekers showed up at Rita and Hannah's. Local
police had been asked to patrol the neighborhood, and the
neighbors all agreed to watch the home best they could that
evening. All had Brent's cell phone number and were ready
to help. Rita asked to freshen up and was escorted to a ladies'
room close by. Afterward, Hannah was allowed to sit with her
mother in a holding area while paperwork was processed for
Rita's ride to an Oregon prison. The two held hands tightly,
each looking down at the joined fists, then deep into each
other's faces. They were distraught by the prospect of their
long and possibly permanent separation.

"I love you, Mom."

"I know, Babe. I love you, too."

Shaking, they were asked to separate so that Rita's
journey could begin. Brent stepped forward and hugged Rita.
Quietly, he comforted Rita by saying that he would arrange
for their visitors' passes within a few days. He added that he
would drive Hannah there once a week as soon as they would
be allowed to visit. He reminded her that John and Franco
would be busy working on her appeal and that he, personally
would be sure that Hannah was okay. Rita asked the guard and
Hannah if she could talk to Brent for one minute in private.
Rita and Brent huddled tightly in an inside corner of the foyer.

"You can skip the pep talk, Sweetie. Move in with her,
okay?" queried Rita to Brent.

Brent blushed a deep red. "Geesh, Rita. Only if Hannah wants me to!"

"She wants you to," sighed Rita with a demure smile. "That would make *me* happy, anyway. Not that it matters much!" They laughed out loud, forgetting for a split second where they were. Afraid to waste too much time chatting, Rita burst forth information that she wanted to share with Brent. She told him where to find some things in the house that would help Hannah heal from discovering her mother's secret past in the manner in which she did. "You and my daughter should look at these things, maybe in a month or so. It will give her some idea of where she came from and who my family was. And, you'll do the other research I asked you to do?"

"Yes, Rita," soothed Brent, kissing her on the forehead. "I'll take care of it, *and* her. Try not to worry about that too much. Hannah is tough stuff, like her mom."

Rita closed her eyes for a moment. "Thanks. You're a good son." Looking up at Brent, they silently turned and walked the few steps to where the others stood.

Hannah was straining to smile. Rita was re-cuffed at the wrists only, and the heavy glass doors to the outside slid open. Rita and the guards stepped forward, and the doors slid shut. Looking over her shoulder, her loved one's faces were just a few feet away behind thick glass.

Within minutes, the Ford van pulled up, and the true heartache began. Mother and daughter locked eyes until Rita was led to the back of the van, disappearing behind its open door. Hannah, looked down to see Rita's thin ankles nestled in white cotton socks clad in Converse, sans the laces. One foot disappeared into the van, then the second. Doors closed and locked, the van pulled away curving its way down to a city street gate. Hannah's eyes never left the van. It pulled out slowly past the crowd control officers, who managed on-lookers. There were a few reporters on the sidewalk as well. She wondered to herself if, as a TV reporter, she would one day be required to report the guilty verdict of an innocent person. She shuddered as the van turned left and out of sight.

"Come on, Honey. Let's get some rest. Let's go." They meandered back through the maze, and Brent steered Hannah toward the parking garage using an interior route. "Let's get to the hotel so you can rest. We'll get room service; we shouldn't go out anywhere."

"You have my vote on that," wept Hannah, sinking into the passenger seat of Brent's car. She closed her eyes. "Poor Mom. Hope she gets some rest."

As he had promised Rita, Brent took very good care of Hannah that evening: drawing a bath, ordering room service, tucking her into bed. Hannah was too exhausted to protest; she fell asleep when her head hit the pillow. Brent looked at her for a few moments, and thought about Rita on her way to prison. It had been a very long day, so he extended his arm over the head of his sleeping angel and flicked off the light. The two slept deeply the entire night, not waking once.

It was almost eight when the phone rang. Brent groaned and Hannah rolled over, but didn't wake. Brent leapt to answer. He whispered, "Hello." On the other end of the line was a familiar voice, a detective sergeant friend from work, Brian O'Malley. Brian was a likeable middle-aged cop with rosy cheeks and a ready smile. Brent hadn't seen much of Brian in the past couple of months due to the challenging trial schedule. "Brian, what's going on?"

"Hey, Pal. I need to speak to you right away. I'm right

downstairs in the lobby. They gave me your room number, of course. I'm calling from a phone across from the concierge area. I'll wait here until you get dressed." He abruptly hung up, robbing Brent the opportunity to get in a dazed "huh?" Brent washed up quickly and donned sweats and tennies. He tiptoed to Hannah's bedside and lightly whispered that he was going downstairs for a paper, confident that Hannah would not question it. She grumbled a response and turned over again. Brent pulled the covers up close to Hannah's neck and headed out the door toward the elevators. He found Brian in the lobby below, his hands thrust into his pants pockets, his heavy tweed coat falling to his sides. He paced the marble tile floor. Around one of his wrists he carried a plastic bag, the contents of which might have come from the Rite-Aid store. Absent from O'Malley's face was the wide grin, in its place a wistful and serious look. Brian invited Brent to sit on a sofa nearby.

Brent listened patiently while Brian explained that the van containing Rita had never arrived at the women's prison. Brent was dumbstruck by Brian's statement. The news went from bad to worse when Brian described the scene of a vehicle explosion on the Oregon coast, about two hours north of the women's correctional facility -- Rita's destination. Brian spoke in low tones, his eyes cast down. "A driver reported an explosion and pulled over cuz of all the smoke. Investigators have been at the scene since dawn. The cliffs are hundreds of feet high in spots, and the bay, very deep. If it is the van that Ms. Napapolus was in, then it had to have left I-5 at least ten minutes prior to the crash and headed directly west to the cliffs. It was so windy and rainy last night that there are no discernible tread marks. Mostly gravel on those roadsides, anyway. So far, Oregon Staties found charred bits and pieces of clothing. I convinced them to drive one item up that they found intact, so that we could have a look at it." Uncomfortably stressed, Brian shifted his weight from one foot to another. "Sorry, Pal, I need you to tell me if you recognize who this might belong to. Police sent rock climbers down to pick up any debris they could find. It must have flown out when the vehicle was falling."

Brent swallowed hard as Brian O'Malley slid his hand into the plastic bag. Brian hesitated, and the two men looked at each other before looking back at the bag. Brian pulled out a small, navy blue Chuck Taylor Converse sneaker, no laces in it. Brent drew a long, shaky breath, and felt weak.

"It belongs to Rita Napapolus," Brent whispered, swallowing hard.

"You're absolutely sure, Brent?" Brian asked sympathetically.

"Oh, I'm sure. *Absolutely* sure." Brent buried his face in his hands and thought about his slumbering friend in the suite above.

Chapter 26

*B*rent Parker's freshly scrubbed face was a welcome sight for Hannah when she opened the front door. It was early afternoon and true to form, drizzling in the Seattle area. He carried what looked like a black leather laptop case, which Brent used as a briefcase. He passed it to her while he removed his navy blue raincoat. They exchanged the usual polite amenities, but then slipped their arms around each other to share a long and lingering kiss. Brent had been so supportive throughout the past months' ordeal, and she was grateful for his friendship. Rita's memorial service was now over two months behind her; Hannah managed a genuinely warm smile as she took Brent's coat. "Let's sit in the family room." Hannah led the way through a small kitchen and family room area. There was a fire in the fireplace, but on closer inspection, Brent saw that it was a gas insert-type.

"I don't remember seeing that before," he said, nodding to the fireplace. "A fire in the cold months feels so good. That looks new. Is it?"

"Yes, that was one of Mom's last projects. You probably don't remember seeing it, because this is the first time it's been used. She was always doing something to the house. She wanted it for years and finally did it last October. It's a shame she never got to enjoy it." Wistfully, Hannah sighed. "Anyway, I feel like she's here, and I'm happy to be able to keep this little house for now. She worried about stuff like that, but I thought we were talkin' forty years from now," she guffawed, shrugging her shoulders. "She was such a worrier, my mom." She smiled fondly and put up a good front, but looked melancholy. "It's funny, sometimes Mom almost cried during Hallmark card commercials; she was so sentimental. I used to make fun of her. Then she'd say, 'Sicilians don't cry.' It never made sense to me. I asked her about the Sicilian-thing, and she'd explain it by saying 'the mainland Italians used to say that Sicilians were Greek, so it's all the same.' *Now*, of course I get it! She slipped and talked her way out of it. One time, she muttered that Sicilians don't cry; they implode. I wish she were here so that I could tell her how much I love her. Didn't do that enough."

Brent stepped forward and Hannah leaned her head on his chest for a few moments. "No doubt in my mind that Rita loved you, Hannah, and that she *knows* how much you loved *her*, too. She did what she felt she had to, to protect you and give you as good a life as she could. The last time I visited with Rita, she asked a favor of me, but I wanted to wait a while to follow through on it. Wanted to give everything a rest for a while first."

"Sure, Honey," sniffled Hannah. Hannah extended her arm and Brent sat on the sofa where he set the brief case to his right. Hannah sat on her knees a couple of feet from him. It was very quiet, and the rain was beating on the kitchen skylight in a soothing rhythm.

"Well, first I have a gift for you, but I hope *you* think it's a gift. I figured you might want to do research on Gina Bianco, but I know that your mom's death will hurt for a long time. Your mom asked me to do the research for you. It might help to make you feel better, faster." He spoke with a very cautious tone: "So, I went ahead and dug my hands in, I have so many resources available to me. Know what I mean? But please don't be mad about this, and tell me if I've crossed the line by doing it."

Hannah swiped the side of Brent's knee with her hand and grinned. "Give it up, Pal! I want to see what you found!" Clearly happy at the prospect of discovering her true family history for the first time, she leaned forward on her knees. Craning her neck, Hannah peered wide-eyed at the briefcase. Brent slowly unzipped the case an inch or so to pique Hannah's curiosity, but she was clearly not amused. "Cut it out, Shithead! Open up!" she shouted. They both laughed hysterically, as Brent grabbed Hannah's hand when she slipped it into the briefcase.

"Alright, already!" Brent comically moved his eyebrows up and down a couple of times. His fingertips languished on the zipper tab, and he slowly pulled it around the case's curved corners. He moved the case away teasingly, and put his hand inside gently. Brent presented a crisply printed stack of papers, bound with a large binder clip. He held it out to Hannah, who suddenly halted, her eyes transfixed on the thick stack. Sheets were paper-clipped within that stack, creating various sections. She eased back on her legs beneath her, as if she were steadying herself.

Brent quietly said, "It's all good, Hannah. I traced Gina Bianco's lineage back to her great-grandparents in Sicily. It's all here. You had a Grandpa Sal, an Uncle Joey, a Grandma Elaine. There's information about their parents and grandparents, too. Was able to trace your grandfather's brother and his wife. Sorry, but they're deceased. Elaine has one brother still living, and I tracked his address. He's getting up there, but apparently living in an apartment complex for the elderly in the Berkshires. If you're so inclined, we might fly there to meet him."

Hannah was overtaken with delight and began to howl. She breathlessly gasped: "An uncle, I have a regular uncle, though, right? That's my mom's brother, Joey, right? She told me I looked like him, but that's all. Where is he?" Hannah read Brent's obvious expression. She knew it was a disappointing one. Drawing her lower jaw outward and baring her teeth, she then murmured: "No more uncle, huh?"

Brent gently picked up one of Hannah's hands, cupping it in both of his. "Sorry, Babe. Vietnam. As you know, your grandparents are gone, but at least you'll know who they were and where they came from. There are *some* silver linings here."

"I could use a silver lining right now! At least I know. Hard to feel sad for losing loved ones that I never met, but I suppose I'll cry later. But you know as well as I," Hannah said sarcastically, propping one hand on a hip, "Sicilians don't cry!" She sighed a happy sigh. She folded her arms across

her chest and pushed her lip forward. Brent was absolutely
melting inside; he adored her so much. *You're more like
your Mom than you think,* he thought, *only younger, taller*,
and guiltily: *prettier, too*. In Hannah, Brent saw the image of
a wise-cracking Gina. "Okay, then tell me about the silver
linings, please!"

"Yeah. Let's start with this stack of paper. It contains
copies of your mother's birth certificate, and those of your
uncle and grandparents. I printed out information on the
cities and provinces where your great-grandparents were born,
too. Catania and Siracusa. Gina hid close to two hundred old
photographs in this house for you. That's the favor she asked
of me before she got into the van. When she boarded that
flight to Seattle from JFK, all Gina was carrying was you and
one duffle bag. She checked everything else and off it went to
Miami. She told me that when the two of you left New York,
she packed the duffle bag with a change of clothes for each of
you, toothbrushes, the few pieces of her mom's jewelry that
she had, the pictures, money, stuff like that. She didn't want to
chance checking the things closest to her heart."

At this point, Hannah jumped to her feet and shook
Brent by the shoulders. "Spit it out! Where are they? Come
on, come on."

"In the bottom of the hamper in her bedroom."
Hannah leaped to her feet and raced through down the hall
toward her mother's bedroom, the door of which had been
closed for several months. Flicking a light switch, she darted
to the tall half-moon shaped hamper that stood just outside of
Gina's little bath, and threw open its lid. Brent was several
paces behind and watched as Hannah pulled an assortment of
things out of the hamper that included a box containing a new

pair of shoes, some decorative patio lights: things other than dirty laundry or towels. Amused, he leaned against the door jam of the bedroom and watched Hannah. At that moment she looked like a cartoon character, strewing the items about the room over her shoulders, some landing on the floor and bed behind her. Finally, she stopped. Hannah bent to reach the bottom of the hamper. She rose slowly, and held a clear plastic bag containing three bulging manila envelopes. Hannah closed her eyes and, held the plastic bag to her chest. Turning her head toward Brent, she smiled broadly and said: "Let's take a look, shall we?" Holding the bundle in front on her palms, she marched past Brent and walked the hall to the family room. Hannah tossed couch pillows to the floor, and eased herself down. Handing the valuable find to Brent, she solemnly asked, "Will you open the first one, please?"

"Of course," replied Brent, and he carefully opened the plastic bag and placed them on the floor in front of Hannah. The friends grinned from ear-to-ear. Picking up the top envelope, Brent began, "Gina says all of them are marked with each person's name and are dated. Some were already dated, and some she had to figure out for. She said she was spot-on for most."

The next few hours were spent carefully inspecting each photograph and marveling at the images. Hannah identified Sal and Elaine right away, as Gina shared features that resembled each of them. She smiled, laughed and cried simultaneously. She remarked to Brent that this was more overwhelming than seeing the Coliseum in Roma, and being surrounded by momentous, ancient architecture. Hannah never imagined that she would match that sense of awe by looking at old photos, many of which were yellowed, tattered and photographed with black-and-white film.

It was almost five-thirty when Brent suggested that they take a break to get a bite to eat. There were lots of small restaurants in town, and several near the shopping mall, close to Hannah's place. "Let's go out, Hannah. There's more to talk about and it's a lot to absorb. You need to get out of the house for a while."

"Yes, please!" The sky was quite clear when they stepped out into the coolness of the March evening. A few clouds seemed to glide through the sky at breakneck speed, skimming over a three-quarter moon. Hannah directed Brent to a spotless mom-and-pop place pretty close to the house where they ordered locally brewed ales and burgers on toasted kaiser rolls. Hannah ate voraciously, and it made Brent happy to see her smiling and talkative again. In turn, it had been a long time since Hannah had felt so relaxed and happy.

As soon as they took their last bites, Hannah waved the waitress over for the check. Brent asked what the hurry was and Hannah burst: "Silver linings *is* the hurry."

"Well, Hannah, the first silver lining has an addendum, so we'll save it for the very end of the evening."

"The plot thickens. I thought nothing could top Mom's story," Hannah said cockily, the beer having loosened her tongue. "Let's go back."

When they returned, they carefully put already-viewed photos in a large, sturdy hatbox that once housed one of Gina's many vintage hats.

There were only about twenty-five or thirty photos on the floor, when Hannah and Brent sat down. They quietly took turns reading the names and dates on the back of each photo, marveling at their age. Hannah picked up what looked like a torn piece of paper, seven inches long. After turning it over, she realized that it was a torn photo. "Look at this, Brent. It's a picture of Mom. I know the picture; it's right on her little vanity. She's with a college friend in the photo." She leaned toward Brent, who looked at the image of Gina at nineteen years.

"Wow! Your mom was hot!"

"Don't be creepy, okay?"

"Will you go get that picture? I want to see what the man looks like. Let's try to figure out who it is."

Hannah agreed, and disappeared down the hall to retrieve the picture. "It's just a guy friend, Mom told me," she said, after cozying next to Brent on a floor pillow.

Brent looked a little too serious, making Hannah slightly uncomfortable. She shifted her body a couple of times while waiting for Brent to speak again. "Do you have any idea who the man in the photo might be?"

Hannah's lower lip moved up and down like a ventriloquist's doll, but no sound came out. "Uh, supposedly, my biological father is tall. Maybe it's him."

"But you're not sure? The photo was probably taken before she met her ex-husband."

"Of course, I'm *not* sure." Defensively, she continued, "Mom never talked much about old friends or family. Never realized it much til now."

A highly trained observer, Brent saw how rattled Hannah became. "You're right, Babe. Nobody really knows, but by the looks of it, the man in the photo must have been tall, about six-three. Look at it again, Hannah."

"*No*, Brent. I don't *have* to look at it again. Think we're lookin at mug shots or something? That's Mom, but I don't know who the man is!" Hannah seemed almost angry.

"Okay, okay. Will you look at another one? There's no name or date on the back of this one, though."

Hannah looked as though she had catapulted her mind through the sliding glass door of the family room and deep into the darkness of the misty night.

"Hannah. Hannah?"

"Yes, Brent. The other photo, sure. Let's take a look," Hannah said, batting her eyelids as though she was coming to.

"This one is an older photograph: a woman and kid. The dress she's wearing looks like late fifties, early sixties." Brent passed the photo from his hand to Hannah's. The photo showed a smiling woman in a well-pressed and starched day dress. A wavy-haired male toddler sat against her hip, one hand around her neck, his hair shiny in the bright sun of that day. He held his other hand over his eyes like a visor to shade the bright light. He seemed long-legged. "Hannah, do you see what I do in that woman's face?"

"No, Brent," replied Hannah softly. "What are you talking about?"

"Remember the picture of you on Ruth's hip? This one's not as well focused," gestured Brent with the photo in his fingers. "It's obviously Ruth as a young woman with her child. She's either very slim or very tall, and so is her boy."

"So, my mom was given a picture of Ruth when she was young. Big deal, Mr. Detective!"

Brent's eyes were riveted to the side of Hannah's face. He passed the photograph to Hannah. "The shape of the face, full mouth, dark hair, eyes could be blue. They look light. You look like this woman, Hannah."

"Coincidence," snapped Hannah, in a husky whisper.

"I look like Uncle Joey and he had dark hair and blue eyes. That's all, merely a coincidence." In her head, she heard Gina say: *there are no coincidences in life.*

Brent dared not say another word. Hannah slowly offered the photo back to Brent, but he put his hand up and said, "Maybe you'll remember something later."

They didn't say anything for what seemed to be ten minutes, but it was really just two or three.

"Brent, there's still silver linings in that little briefcase, right? Let's see one!"

Brent steered Hannah by the shoulders and sat her down on the couch. "Think you're ready?"

"I just lived The Twilight Zone. I think I can handle just about anything. Mom always said 'whatever doesn't kill you, makes you stronger.' Go for it."

Brent paced for a few seconds, but really there was not a lot of space to pace around in for very long. He sat down next to Hannah and took both of her hands in his. "Deep breath, Hannah." Hannah looked perplexed. "Your Uncle Joey had a son." Brent looked away for a moment to give Hannah time to digest this new revelation. "He was born out of wedlock. Joey wanted to marry his girlfriend, but the girlfriend was from a rich family and the mom talked her into giving the baby up. Your Uncle Joey was devastated. About a year later, he signed up for, and was deployed to 'Nam. He was within a few days of completing his tour duty when he was killed."

"Is this one of the things my mom asked you to tell me the last time you spoke with her?"

"Yes, Honey."

"So, this is the big, devastating news? I'm not

following you here, Brent. There's not a whole lot we can do about that, is there?"

"Han-nah," he drew her name out slowly. "I know who and where your cousin is. He grew up outside of Boston, and has always known he was adopted. You have a cousin, Hannah. The two of you look alike; you look a lot like your Uncle Joey, according to Gina. By chance, he has an Italian last name, too. A friend of Gina's had found your cousin's whereabouts a long time ago, she said. Again, maybe I've overstepped my bounds but I called him to let him know about you."

Hannah's mouth dropped. She sat there, numb for a few seconds. A smile slowly warmed her face. "My cousin. My cousin?" Her palms extended, Hannah searched Brent's face with an expression of expectation.

"Michael. His name is Michael, but his friends and family call him Mickey. We'll save the details for tomorrow, though. Maybe I should leave now. This must be a little too much right now to grasp."

"After all that has happened? Nothing surprises me much any more. I'll never be able to sleep if you leave now! Is there more?"

"Michael remembered seeing your mom and a man over the years in Boston. He believed that he just bumped into them from time to time. But he remembered Gina especially. Said he remembered that she smiled all the time. Michael said Gina and the man were affectionate and always looked happy. He even met them for dinner a couple of times. Michael was pretty sad to hear about the trial and what happened to Gina. Shocked to learn that Gina was his aunt, too. But he said he kinda understood why she didn't tell him. And...."

"And, *what?* Come on, Brent!"

"Annnnd... he wants to meet you!"

"Woo-hoo!" howled Hannah, waving fisted arms. After hugging Brent again, Hannah thought the surprises would never end. Then she remember that Brent had mentioned an addendum earlier. "Is the addendum related to meeting my cousin?"

"Not related. Then there's one final thing after that."

Drawing a long breath, she said, "Okay, I'm ready."

At this point, Brent just nodded. This was a lot for anyone to deal with in a day. He reached into his jacket pocket and produced a zip-locked sandwich bag. He offered the bag to Hannah, who now looked up with a demure smile. Both her hands pounced onto the open palm like a cougar jumping prey. She shrieked: "Oh, my Jesus! How did you do this?" she gasped. It was the baggie containing Sal Bianco's cufflinks.

"I was able to twist my boss's arm a bit. We were able to write this out as personal effects of a loved one. After all, they *did* belong to Gina, so now they are yours."

"Brent, thank you, thank you, thank you!" Hannah jumped on the sofa like Tom Cruise on Oprah.

Brent watched, but knew that the final silver lining presentation might not be as well received. Maybe he was being pessimistic, he thought. "Okay, Hannah. That's just about wraps things up, except for one more thing."

"Wow. This has been *the* day for me!" exclaimed Hannah. "I don't think anything else will surprise me *ever* again!"

She clapped her hands together, and put them out before her, beckoning Brent to bring on more. "You promised an addendum!" Brent wanted to go home; he felt uncertain about delivering this last piece of information.

"Okay," said Brent with a sigh. Again, he slipped his hand into the unzipped brief case. He produced one single white nine-by-twelve envelope. "Inside this envelope is your birth certificate, Hannah."

Because Brent seemed so serious at this moment, Hannah was a little frightened. Whispering, Brent said, "Your birth name is Sophia. I was also able to locate the man Gina was married to when you were born. He's in jail, killed someone driving drunk. Your mom returned to her maiden name, so your birth surname is different from hers."

"No, it's not, Brent," Hannah said soothingly. "My last name is, and always was, Bianco. Like Mom." She inhaled blissfully, relieved to know *all* of the truth. Brent drank in the peace he saw on Hannah's face. Hannah said: "Well, Mom said my birth father had a drinking problem. I'm not surprised. I don't care about him. I won't ever try to find him anyway, Brent. Funny, Gina always used the word birth and not biological when referring to her ex-husband." An awkward silence followed.

"One more thing, Hannah. He's not unusually tall, he's average height. Gina always told you that your father was pretty tall, right?"

"Oh well. Everyone was tall compared to Mom, Brent. What are you saying?"

Inside, Brent thought, *Gina's and his blood-type didn't produce you, Sweetness. But we'll leave that one alone forever.* Instead, Brent grinned, "Nothing else to say, except goodnight. You need to get some rest. Whenever you're ready, we can talk about stuff." He put the envelope in Hannah's hands.

Hannah moved hypnotically behind Brent while he

donned his coat and moved toward the front door. "Get some sleep now, Hannah." Brent put his arms around her.

"Sophia, the name's Sophia," she whispered. She stepped backward and said, "I always disliked my first name. Always thought Mom was crazy for naming me Hannah! Got called Hannah-Banana in school a lot! Besides, when I finally find a news reporter gig, Sophia Bianco is the name of choice." She seemed relieved, happier, and Brent felt much better, too. "Don't worry, Brent, I'm okay."

"You're sure?"

"Absolutely fine, really. It's a lot, but now I know. Can't wait to meet my cousin, too!"

They exchanged one more hug and a lingering, affectionate goodnight kiss. From the front doorway, Sophia waved to Brent as he backed his car into the street. She languished with her back against the door for a moment, trying to grasp the scope of the day's events. She walked back to the kitchen and family room. There were still a few photos on the floor, the rest were in the hatbox. Sophia slid her hand under one of the pillows she had tossed to the floor earlier, her fingers seeking a treasure she hid there earlier that day. *Here it is*, she thought to herself. The back of the photo revealed the scrawled words: *Ruth with Sophia – 17 months*. She recognized the toddler as herself. Who was Ruth? A family friend? There were a few photos of Ruth in the hatbox. Sophia reached out to the picture she had dropped to the floor when Brent questioned her about it. She compared the two pictures, side by side. Ruth held baby Sophia to her hip, much as she had in the photo with the boy toddler. Even though it was obviously the same woman, she was at least twenty years older in the photo with Sophia. Sophia shivered. Ruth and

Sophia did look a bit alike at young adulthood. She set the photos on the kitchen counter. She walked about the room turning off the fireplace and a table lamp. Bending, she picked up the torn half of a photo and its complete framed version. She carried them down the hall to Gina's bedroom, and lovingly sat the framed photo on her mother's small antique dresser. The vanity was draped with Gina's scarves and hats, and its center was cluttered with purses, sunglass cases, gloves and a vase. She adjusted the photo a bit to reflect its original spot, recorded by dust. Lovingly, she placed the torn photo over the identical image of Gina and stepped back to look at the smiling couple one more time before turning off the light. *Who was this man?* She knew that there was more to this than what was on the surface. Sophia suddenly felt exhausted. She methodically washed her face and brushed her teeth and went to bed, falling into a deep sleep.

Chapter 27

Sophia was awakened by a knock on the front door, followed by the doorbell. Annoyed, she jumped up and out of the bed and trudged down the hall to the living room. *What the hell? Who would be ringing the doorbell so early in the morning?* She peered out the window to see a FedEx truck outside. Opening the door just a couple of inches, she heard a woman say, "Oh good. You're home. This one needs a signature." Dazed, Sophia signed the electronic signature board, and quietly closed the door. She carried the envelope to the kitchen, where she was surprised to see that the stove clock read almost eleven a.m. *Wow! I slept for at least ten hours! Guess I needed to do that.* Still groggy, she turned her attention back to what got her out of bed. She mindlessly opened the envelope thinking that it might be from Franco, who handled all of her mom's estate issues. Expecting to find documents inside, Sophia drew out another envelope, but a very small one. It seemed rather odd, but she had received so much mail in the past few months, certainly not FedEx envelopes with mysterious greeting cards though. She raked her eyes over the FedEx airbill and noticed it had been sent from New York. *It must be a sympathy card. After all, Mom knew people in New York. The **wrong** people! Some rich lady FedEx'd her sympathies!* Sophia tossed the unopened card onto the counter and continued with her morning routine.

As she did every morning of the past month, she fixed chai tea, sat on the couch, and watched the news and weather. It was a gym day, so she took a shower just long enough to refresh and waken herself further, and dressed in gym gear. Sophia grabbed her keys from the counter and headed for the garage. As she reached for those keys, she caught sight of the little card on the counter. She tore open the flap, and pulled out a card that featured a beautiful photograph of a rose. *See? That's all it is, a sympathy card.* Within a split second, a small key dropped from the inside of the card, hitting the tile counter with metallic clinking sound. The top part of the key was stamped with the words: Property of Greyhound - Seattle WA. She drew the card close to her surprised eyes. *Huh?* The print inside the card looked to be typewritten. *Are there still such things as typewriters?* she snickered. *Greyhound. Denny Way. Locker 102. Leave key there. Do not look at contents until home. Discuss with no one.* She plucked the key from the counter and looked closer.

This felt totally creepy and too dangerous to do by herself. She scanned the shipper information on the envelope again: a Manhattan address. Her friend Mia now lived in

Manhattan, but neither her name nor address appeared on the
bill. Sophia studied it more carefully. There was a phone
number. Definitely a Manhattan number, area code 212.
She grabbed the kitchen phone and hurriedly punched in
the number. *I'll get to the bottom of this!* Sophia felt pretty
smug and was ready to discuss the mysterious package with
its sender. After three rings, her answer came in the form of a
recorded voice that advised: "You have reached a number that
has been disconnected or is no longer in service." Shaken, she
dropped the small key on the counter in favor of car keys and
out the door she went. But the trip to the gym was in vain; she
could not concentrate and left after a mere twenty-five minutes
of cardio. She did not park her car in the garage, but instead
left it in the driveway. She ran to the bathroom, washed her
face with cool water and brushed her teeth. Next, she rifled
through her bed table drawer and withdrew a small container
of pepper spray. Grabbing the locker key and the card, she
drove toward I-5 South.

It took less than fifteen minutes to reach the
Greyhound station, and Sophia parked a couple of blocks
away in an open lot. It was a lovely spring day: clear and
comfortable. She sat in her car for several minutes, debating
whether or not she should walk to the station. She read the
instructions in the card a second time. *Could it be a reporter's
trick?* Several reporters had hounded her the first month
after her mother's death to give her side of Mom's story.
Sophia had even been asked by a local true-crime writer
to be interviewed about her mother's life and murder trial.
Though flattered, she was keenly aware that the story might
be misperceived as a story of a murderess that lived a life of
deceit and then dies in a fiery crash on the way to prison. She

couldn't risk that. Sophia now better understood why her
mother hid her past, and knew that Gina had not murdered
Brandon Perry.

As it was broad daylight, Sophia decided to at least
walk the street and take a look. After all, if it *were* a trick, how
would the package sender even know that she might bite? She
stuffed her purse under the driver's seat, taking only her car
keys, pepper spray and the locker key with her. Sunglasses
on, Sophia strolled to the corner of Stewart Street at Eighth
Avenue.

She had forgotten that the Greyhound station was on
the corner perpendicular to a courthouse. Even though it was
not where her mother was tried, she still felt a wave of dread.
She hadn't been downtown since the day her mother was put
into the back of a van, to be taken away from her forever.
Memories of past chaotic scenes on courthouse steps flooded
Sophia's memory. The courthouse near the Greyhound station
was a Federal one, and the trees outside were beginning to bud.
Sophia inhaled deeply, reminding herself that no one could
change what happened. Gathering her composure, she walked
up the street and past the doors of the old building that housed
the bus station. Nothing looked unusual to her. She felt silly
for being so dramatic, but wanted to be safe. She walked a few
more blocks to relax, and turned around to try again. There
was a young couple standing outside, suitcases at their sides,
smoking cigarettes. Probably in their 20's, they each sported
jewelry in their pierced faces and multi-colored hair. Sophia
and the couple exchanged hellos as she passed.

When she reached the station doors, Sophia entered
cautiously. To her relief, she immediately saw a sign
indicating where the lockers were. The dingy waiting room

was much fuller than she might have expected, but then
again, she had never been in a bus station before. To the rear
of the room were double doors where travelers found their
departing buses. On that rear wall to the doors' left, ticket
vendors were researching and producing bus tickets for a few
waiting travelers. No one seemed to notice her, and Sophia
felt a second wave of relief. The slight smell of urine and
disinfectant burned her nostrils. Oddly enough, there was
an open access door that led to a Vietnamese restaurant that
shared a space in the building, but whose front door was
situated around the corner. As discreetly as possible, she
walked up a short ramp that led to the locker room. The room
was small and also had doors leading to the boarding area. The
lockers varied in size, and she found Locker 102 within a few
seconds. It was mid-sized, compared to others. She quickly
unlocked it, not out of anxiety, but to see if there was anything
at all worth seeing. She reminded herself that the note had
said: *Do not look at contents until home.* She thought *bomb*,
but chuckled to herself after thinking, *Drama Queen*. Hesitant,
she opened the locker door. Totally mystified by what she saw,
she extended her arm toward a large leather carry bag. It was
black caviar leather with a saddlebag flap and a decorative
close latch. Sophia knew her designer bags and immediately
recognized the brand. *This may not be a trick, after all*,
she thought. *This bag easily goes for over fifteen hundred.*
Guardedly, she slipped her fingers around its handles and slid
to toward her. *Wow!* Not knowing what to expect, Sophia
nearly lost her grip on the handles, as the bag was quite heavy.
Steadying herself, she bent her knees slightly to look inside the
locker. There was nothing else in there, so she tiptoed out of
the station and crossed the street to begin her drive home. She

set the bag in front of the passenger seat, and eyed it several times during the drive North. Her thoughts flirted with other possible scenarios, one of which was that the contents of the bag might be from Brent, who made up a fictitious name and address. But she knew that Brent would never play a scary joke on her, especially after a day like yesterday.

       Upon her arrival at home, Sophia entered the house without the bag. While showering, she pondered when and if she should investigate the bag's contents alone. She retrieved it from the garage and it sat in the middle of the living room for almost an hour before her curiosity could wait no longer. She picked the bag up and warily placed it on the coffee table. Inching her right hand toward the bag's latch, she turned her head slightly and gritted her teeth. Click. She unsnapped the latch and tugged the bag's flap upward. *Ooh! No explosion!* She peered downward to look inside. A twist-tied white trash bag. With shaky hands, Sophia untwisted the wire tie and prudently pulled the bag open. "This is a joke! What the fuck!" she shouted aloud, laughing. In the bag was what looked like packets of money: one-hundred dollar bills. She clapped her hands together, and laughing, plopped backward into the couch. "Phew!" *What a relief! It can't be the real thing. It's a joke, but from who?* She stretched her arms upward, and put her hands behind her head to relax. Propping her feet up onto the coffee table, she accidentally pushed the designer bag over. Toppling over, it exploded its contents onto the floor. She laughed out loud, but within seconds sobered. Both top and bottom of the packets looked like front and backs of one-hundred dollar bills. She lunged forward to pluck a stack from the floor. She fanned the packet, revealing that each piece of paper looked and felt like crisp, new bills, front and back. Another stack, then another. She fanned through ten stacks or more. *They're all the same.* Mindful of any further surprises, she held a packet at arm's length, turned her face away, and popped apart the packet's band. *Not a dye pack* and the bills floated to the floor. *All one-hundred dollar bills! All of them! This is insane!* She picked one up and held it up to the light in the room's bay window. It was water-marked perfectly correct. Sophia plucked the trash bag up by its bottom, spilling the remaining contents onto the floor. An envelope then dreamily dropped, landing on the stack of packets. *This day was turning out to be almost as flush with surprise as yesterday,* thought Sophia, her heart racing like a frantic rabbit's.

She stepped back and crossed her arms for a moment while eyeing the envelope that glaringly sat on top of a pile of money. Humorously, she thought she might run down the hall to get her camera. However, Sophia was too transfixed by the image that lay before her on the floor. Larger than the one received earlier that day, the envelope looked like a greeting card style.

"Well, are you going to open it or not?" she asked aloud, looking from side to side as if there was someone close by. The only other bodies present were Sydney and Bella, who had been attracted by the rankling of a plastic trash bag and items being dumped onto the floor. Bella stepped forward and began sniffing around the piles of bills. Sydney just rolled over and lied down, stretching and yawning. "Okay, here goes!" exclaimed Sophia as she gently picked the envelope up. It was ivory in color, and closed with a wax seal. "This is very cloak and dagger!" Inside was another card that looked much like the card in the FedEx package. The cover featured

a rose, photographed. She hesitated, and carefully opened it.
A torn piece of paper fell from the card and rested amongst
the bills on the floor. Sophia saw the paper fall, but her eyes
sought the message scrawled inside the card: Love, from your
father. "What the Hell? From my *father?*"

She stretched to reach the paper that had fallen from
the card. Turning it over, she gasped, realizing that it was half
of the torn photograph that now sat on her mother's vanity.
She ran to her mother's bedroom. Sophia placed the two
tattered and torn pieces together, proving what she already
knew. They were an *exact* fit!

Chapter 28

*T*he year that followed was a very busy one for Sophia and Brent. Brent moved into the little house so that the couple could plan their future together. Gina had paid a premium for mortgage insurance, so Sophia inherited the house free and clear. This stroke of good planning on her mother's part gave Sophia the time and freedom to tie up loose ends. Sophia kept the secret of the Greyhound locker to herself, weighing the pros and cons of doing so. Brent assumed she was managing on the proceeds of Gina's life insurance policy. In reality, Sophia purchased money orders to pay all of the household bills with cash taken from the well-hidden designer bag. Brent considerately paid half of the expenses, which Sophia simply deposited into a savings account to fund their honeymoon.

As soon as they could arrange it, the couple took a trip to the Boston area to meet Sophia's cousin Michael. When Sophia first spoke with Michael on the phone, she asked if they could meet at Quincy Market, and he obligingly agreed. Sophia wanted to meet Mickey where her mother had first met him. She had decided a long time ago to request they meet there. It was late April and the young couple stayed in Boston for five days, taking a trip to Cape Cod and back. They met with Mick for lunch twice, once for dinner out with his wife, and once for dinner at his place in Framingham. Sophia glowed for the entire week. She brought some of the old photos with her, especially those of young Joey and Gina. She had also snatched the photo of young Gina that had been displayed on her vanity for as long as Sophia could remember. They sat at Mickey and Jenna's dining table and looked them over after supper dishes had been cleared.

"Look, look, Mickey. This is my mom before she even turned twenty!"

"Yeah, Cuz. She still looked a lot like that when I saw her in Boston," crowed Mickey. "Wow! And she stayed with that guy all those years, too. Is that you Dad?"

Sophia was momentarily stunned. "You recognize this man?"

"Sure. Of course. His name was Marty. He didn't have a goatee like in the picture. He was quite a bit younger there, but that's *definitely* the same guy."

Sophia and Brent looked up at each other from opposite sides of the dining table.

"Yeah," continued Mickey. "He asked a lot about what scholarships I was applying for. Don't know why. Just being polite, I guess. Once, he asked me to send him any change of addresses in case he came across some I might qualify for. I followed *every* lead. Over the years, I got several scholarships and grants and they got me through Med School pretty nicely. I would say that almost every tuition payment was covered for about six years straight. The tuition was paid directly to the university, but I also received monies for living expenses that came directly to me. Funny, I had a shit-load of luck back then."

Sophia looked up at Brent again to try to read his thoughts a second time, but he was already staring at her face.

On their last day in Boston, Michael had an emergency appendectomy to perform, so could not see the couple off. He called their hotel room on his way to the hospital to let them know, but promised that he and his wife would be in Seattle for the July wedding. Throughout their visit, Brent took almost a hundred pictures of Sophia, Michael and Jenna. Sophia often asked, "What's your problem?" Brent always good-naturedly replied, "Just recording the memories, Baby!"

The modest wedding was to be held in one of Seattle's gorgeous parks rather than a church, and a banquet room was reserved at the couple's favorite downtown hotel. They focused attentively on making the timeline work, and it was falling into place nicely. Brent planned on starting a private investigation agency wherever Sophia found a new position. Sophia targeted southern Oregon and northern California in her job search, with Brent's total support. She loved the San Francisco area, but did not want to take Brent too far away from his family, who lived in eastern Washington. During that year, she had netted three good offers and began to weigh each one carefully. She requested three weeks to a month to consider offers from the three stations, each unaware that she was considering multiple ones. She and Brent traveled to each city to look around, spoke to real estate agents about the local housing markets and spent a few days in each to get an overall sense of the quality of life there. Brent did online research on crime rates, too. The happy couple both had strong gut feelings about their visit to the San Jose area, and Sophia accepted a position as a junior reporter at a station there. During each interview process, she had been assured she could take as much times as needed before relocating and assuming her new job. The station manager stated that waiting for the right person was an inevitable part of their own hiring process, with candidates applying from anywhere in the world.

Sophia and Brent spent almost a month plotting out a honeymoon route. It felt liberating to have the money to take a long vacation, and both knew that once they got back to work, it might be some time before they could break away again. Sophia no longer felt a burning need to tell Brent about the designer bag filled with money. She was taking care of all the wedding and honeymoon arrangements while Brent worked. Other than discussing the wedding menus and honeymoon travel plans, money was not discussed. Whenever Brent asked what she needed toward the expenses, Sophia simply threw out a fictitious figure and banked it for their future.

Sophia and Brent planned a first stop in London to stay for a few days in and around the city. Then, onward to France and Spain. Then a flight to Catania, Sicily so that they could visit Great-Grandma Sophia's village, which was now a booming metropolis. A ferry would take them to the southeastern mainland, where they would take trains northward to Rome. They planned detours for a day or two along the way to visit various places, among them Tuscany. From

Rome, they would visit Florence and some smaller towns and villages. Then on to the grand finale: Venice. Venice, which Gina dreamt and talked about. Carolyn and Franco had visited Venice on their honeymoon, too. Yes, a dream, but one with a tart aftertaste. Even Brent was brought to Sophia by her mother's misfortunes. Gina had often said to her daughter, "there are no coincidences," meaning that people come into our lives for a reason. It may be an insignificant reason, but nonetheless they impact our lives in varying degrees. Sophia took comfort in that thought, as everything else in her life was otherwise perfect. She worked hard to accept the one glaring disparity, her mother's absence. Sophia now strongly related to Gina's pain: being orphaned, starting a new life, and hungering for a family. Her life had now become like her mother's! Unlike Gina's, Sophia's future promised security and happiness. *I treated her like an asshole,* Sophia sometimes thought. *She gambled the odds to give me a good life. Wish I could tell her how sorry I am that I judged her, too. That was the last thing she needed to bear.*

Gina's house went up for sale, and as Sophia had time to do so, she packed up what things she wanted to move and dispersed the things she didn't. The wedding was just a little over two weeks away now, but the young couple was too busy to think about being nervous. When Sophia had officially accepted her new job, Brent put in his notice at work. As planned, he would take the month off for a honeymoon, and return to work for another week to clean up and archive files, and say his goodbyes. Those last weeks before the wedding were spent having lots of fun with friends, and preparing the house for realtors to show in their absence. Gail Brown would take Bella and Sydney, a remembrance of the friend she knew

as Rita. To keep the wedding festivities more traditional, Brent
would stay with his friend and best man the night before the
wedding and meet up with Sophia at the park. Sophia would
stay at home that same evening with her maid of honor and
best friend, Heidi. Just three days before the wedding, a young
family made an offer on the house, and Sophia accepted it.
The buyers still had a lease on the house they were renting
and asked for a delayed closing date; they needed to satisfy a
little over a month before their lease expired. There couldn't
be better circumstances to meet everyone's needs. It would
give Sophia and Brent plenty of time to get back from their
honeymoon, gather what little they had in the house and head
for San Jose.

Finally, the day arrived! Naturally, both Sophia and
Brent were nervous. Confirming vows was not the source
of their jitters, however. Instead, it had everything to do
with the beginning of a satisfying life together. A happy life.
Everything went smoothly for the couple in the year behind
them and it brought well-deserved tranquility. It was early
July, and the weather was warm but not hot. The Puget Sound
breeze kept the air fresh. The park was across the street above
Elliott Bay and was a lush, green and romantic venue for a
small wedding. It was Gina's birthday and the date had been
chosen for that reason. Sophia made sure that Carolyn and
Franco, Gail, Scott, and others from Gina's life were present
to help celebrate both occasions. And there was cousin
Michael, smiling broadly. Even more handsome in a dress
suit, he and Jenna had flown in from Boston the day before.
Inwardly, Sophia felt she knew how Gina did when she met
Michael for the first time. Michael was a puzzle piece in the
lives of both mother and daughter. When the minister asked,

"Who gives this bride in marriage?" a shaky-voiced Mickey stepped forward to state, "The mother of the bride, myself and all present, happily give Sophia in marriage today." Gina's friends and acquaintances smiled through tears. Everyone applauded. There was little sadness, and so much joy. Joy for the promising couple and for time spent knowing Rita Napapolus. The day was a happy, fun one for the wedding party and guests.

So embarked Sophia and Brent on their journey. The first few honeymoon days proved to be relaxing ones. The couple took their time in London, going to clubs and pubs, and enjoying sightseeing and shopping in and around the city. Having made arrangements with Gail, they planned to ship any larger finds to her to avoid lugging anything but personal items with them. Time in France and Spain were filled with museum trips, drinking in lush landscapes, and eating gourmet food. Having traveled in Europe before, Sophia was now able to share some of her favorite places with Brent, and experience new ones, too. On Sicily, Sophia found some of her great-grandmother's relatives, but had hardly mastered the Sicilian dialect before seeking them out. She carried along a hard-copy family-tree chart, outlining her genealogy dating back from her great-great-grandmother. The simple chart came in handy when trying to explain who she was to her distant relatives. The very first family she visited invited them to come back later for dinner, and Sophia and Brent did so. Even though there was a language barrier, it was clear that the newlyweds were feted as the guests of honor. They were toasted with fine wine, and were fed until they couldn't move. Sophia and Brent made sure they brought their hosts a gift before leaving the city. They ferried to the mainland and continued

on. Veering westward, they fit in a side trip to the breathtaking
Amalfi coast. As honeymoons should be, it was romantic and
fun. Each day of their vacation seemed more blissful than the
days before.

As with all good things, honeymoons must come to an
end. The couple traveled to their final destination, Venice, to
spend almost a full week.   They hoped to wind down before
the long flight back to The States. The first full day was spent
wandering throughout the city, enjoying the sights, taking a
gondola ride, and visiting the Museo del Vetro Murano to drink
in as much Murano glass as they could feast their eyes on.
Sophia especially liked St. Marco's Square as she had seen it
while watching old movies with her mother. "Mother would
have just loved this, wouldn't she have, Brent?"

"Yes, Honey. That she would. But don't you feel her
here?"

"You're right," sighed Sophia, smiling warmly. They
laughed carelessly, and walked through the square on their
way back to their hotel after dinner. Their hotel suite had a
small terrace with a table and chairs. The left-hand side of the
terrace afforded a partial view of the Rialto Bridge. There was
a balmy and light breeze. The couple wriggled onto a chaise
lounge chair and continued their fun by drinking champagne.
"Maybe a week is a bit long to stay in one place, Brent. We
should explore the countryside, too," remarked Sophia.

"Well, we can play it by ear and decide tomorrow. For
now, let's get to bed early," said Brent. "The concierge told
me that on very clear mornings the Campanile looks glorious
when the sun first hits it. Maybe we should take a look."
Brent was referring to one of Venice's most recognizable
symbols of the city: a bell tower that stands alone in a corner

of St. Mark's square, near the front of the basilica.

"We've walked past that thing ten times already," pouted Sophia, but then quickly stopped short. *This is Brent's honeymoon, too*, she reminded herself. "Whatever makes you happy, Baby," Sophia smiled. *He's the sweetest.* "How will we know what time, though?"

"Oh, I asked the desk clerk to ring our phone about a half-hour before. We can pull sweats on and quickly walk over and then come back for breakfast."

"Honey, please call him and tell him an hour, okay? You know it takes me a little time to wake up in the morning. I can take a quick shower, while you stay in bed."

And with that, Brent gently pulled Sophia down onto the bed and cooed, "Or I can shower with you tonight and tomorrow, too!"

"Absolutely!" While Sophia prepared to shower, Brent excused himself to run to the lobby to speak with the desk clerk. He returned in just a few minutes, in plenty of time to join Sophia.

They slept fitfully that night, worn out by the miles and hours of walking during the previous weeks. Three weeks of consistent activity was beginning to wear them down. In a little over a week they would be back in the good old U.S. of A., and the dream honeymoon would be a pleasant, life-long memory.

The phone on the bed table blasted obnoxiously. Sophia groaned and rolled over. Vaguely, she heard Brent's cheerful and affirmative tone of voice. Sophia complained, "Can't we do this tomorrow, Sweetie?"

"Sophie, the weather is just right this morning!"

"Okay, okay..." yawned Sophia. "Ahm gettin' up!"

With that, she rose and shuffled toward the bathroom. Brent excitedly straightened up the bed and took the clothes Sophia had chosen the night before and laid them out. He did the same thing for himself, and listened for the sound of the shower running before heading to the bathroom. When the couple had finished, Sophia returned to see her clothes on the bed. "Well, I'm going to get pretty spoiled there, Pal. Now you're laying clothes out for me?"

"This morning only, ma lady," replied Brent, bowing at the waist. "Just wanted to help." Brent thoughtfully watched the time and prompted a slow-moving Sophia, who was fussing with her hair in the bathroom mirror. "Let's go, Baby!"

"Okay! There, I'm ready."

They tiptoed silently through the hallway to the stairwell of the little hotel. Slyly looking at each other, they gushed their amusement at sneaking out so early in the morning. Only the occasional citizen walking or biking to work was on the street, along with a few tourists returning after a long evening of fun. The air was cool and misty. Sophia turned to Brent as they strolled toward the square. "It's not a very clear morning. What's all the fuss about seeing the tower in the morning, anyway?"

"Oh, by the time we get there the sun will be coming up. I just wanted to get an early start, so that we wouldn't have to rush!"

What a darling boy! mused Sophia.

Not quite dawn, the square was still beautiful, nonetheless. The silence of the morning was a refreshing change. A light fog graced the air, and softened the lines of the architecture like images in an Impressionist painting. Several pigeons had already begun to congregate in the center of the square, the first rays of sunlight having warmed their wings. The Piazza San Marco looked different devoid of crowds. Free of pedestrian traffic, Sophia re-discovered the brick pavement there, set in a distinctive geometric pattern. The couple stopped in the square's center to savor the peace of the moment and the history that surrounded them. Standing behind Sophia, Brent wrapped an arm around her neck and shoulders. She hung her hands on those arms. "Tell me again what we're going to see, exactly?"

"Well, we're going to see just how gorgeous the Campanile looks when the sun hits the top of it, and the rest of the square is still dark and quiet," Brent said dramatically. They rocked back and forth and giggled quietly.

Sophia wistfully rolled her gaze up to the bell tower of the Campanile. Turning her head to look into Brent's face, she whispered, "It *is* really beautiful. Thanks for getting me out of bed in time, Brent."

"Oh, Baby! You ain't seen nothin yet! Look!" Brent pointed to the bell tower's pyramidal steeple. The sun kissed the top of the Archangel Gabriel weathervane, and it glistened in the golden light.

"Sweet," cooed Sophia as the light slowly cascaded down the tower's spire. A bicyclist zipped by with baguettes sticking out of the bike's basket and Sophia was happily distracted. Her eyes panned the corner of the square at the tower's base to see that others had also ventured out early in the morning. They had quietly appeared from the Basilica doorway. Sophia's eyes drifted downward from the tower to see three people walking in her direction. Their gait was very slow, and they paused to thoughtfully look up at the tower.

It was still a bit shadowy in the square, but Sophia easily discerned that there was a couple and a singular woman in the group. As a law enforcement officer, Brent had coached Sophie to be a "trained observer," and be aware of everything and everyone around her. She forced her concentration back to the tower, but soon was distracted again. "Brent, look at that woman over there. Mother would have just loved how she is dressed. So Audrey! The scarf over a French twist, the little dress fitted at the waist, the kitten heels. Wow! Guess I learned a little bit more about fashion history from Mom than I thought," Sophia laughed.

Brent moved his hands so that they were now resting lightly on Sophia's shoulders. *It's barely light out, and she has sunglasses on. Europeans are so sexy!* Sophia thought. With a smirk, Sophia cockily thought, *Yes, we are!*

The trio continued to advance in Brent and Sophia's direction, even though they could move about anywhere in the square. This now captured Sophia's full attention. Brent took a step backward, but she didn't notice because her eyes were riveted on the small woman who now seemed to lead her companions closer to the spellbound Sophia. The mist parted around the woman like sheer curtains moving in a summer breeze. For a split second, Sophia nearly burst out laughing. *Am I at the hotel suite dreaming? This looks like a fabric softener commercial being filmed in Venice!*

The woman drew closer. Suddenly, chills raced from Sophie's wrists to her shoulders like wind ripping upward from a deep canyon. The feeling took her breath away, and she shuddered hard. Rather than walking past, the woman stopped short about fifteen feet in front of Sophia. She wore a three-quarter length sleeve cardigan over a crisp dress.

Methodically, she raised a gloved hand to her sunglasses and removed them, looking deep into Sophia's face.

Shocked, Sophia felt faint. Her knees buckled and Brent quickly stepped up to catch her. He held her tight. Sophia's head was spinning and the Piazza seemed to whirl around her. Choking her sobs, Sophia cried in Brent's arms for a few long minutes. Drawing a long breath, Sophia turned to the woman, who stood by helplessly. "Hello, Mother. I didn't recognize you right away. You look great. I mean, *really* great for a dead woman." Behind Gina, a man and woman stood in a huddled embrace, looking deeply concerned. Sophia sighed, "I see your hair is long enough for a French twist again! Even with a sweater on, you look pretty fit. How'd ya do it, Mom?" Everyone laughed in relief. Mother and daughter threw themselves into each other's arms.

Trying to catch her breath between sobs, Gina said, "Honey, we have an orchard and lots of animals to take care of. It keeps *all* of us in great shape!"

"Let me guess. You have some horses, do you, Mother?"

"Yes!" squealed the little girl in Gina. "Three. Some goats, chickens, a pony! Even a dog and a cat! Guess what the cat's name is?"

"Oh, Mother! Is it *Bella*?" Sophia held her hand to her ribs, to help contain her laughter.

Gina touched her fingertips to Sophia's face. "Oh, you're *real*! We're together; can you believe it? I want to stand here and hug you all day! What a sight for my old eyes. You too, Brent." Gina fondly studied Sophia's face for several moments. Silently, she stepped past her daughter and slipped her arm into Brent's, so that they faced Gina's companions.

Gina reached her arm out toward the waiting woman, taking her hand. This woman was at least twenty years older than Gina, but she stood erect and tall. Her thick white hair was fashionably bobbed. She wore a tasteful navy blue day dress and sweater. Her blue eyes bore into Sophia's. For each, it was a little like seeing a reverse reflection in a pool of time.

"Ruth?" Sophia gently asked.

"Yes, Sophie-darling. I'm Ruth." They embraced, mutually thrilled to do so. Ruth turned to the male companion. Both he and Sophia were transfixed for a few moments. He was tall and good-looking, with deep-set eyes. His hair was also wavy, mostly grey, but with a touch of golden brown streaked throughout. Smartly dressed, he wore a sport coat and pants. His shirt was casually unbuttoned at the neck. His lips parted, but he didn't speak right away. "Hello, Sophia. I'm your --."

"Marty! Oh my God!" blurted Sophia loudly. This was followed by a long and uncomfortable silence. Sophia teasingly stepped closer to Marty and rested her hand on his chest. "This is a *lot* to digest so early in the morning. Let's start with Marty, okay? Give me just a little time to get used to this. Deal?"

Marty gently took Sophia's hand, kissed it, and agreed, "Deal."

At that moment, Sophia realized Brent must have known that her mother was alive and waiting in Venice. Her hand still held in Marty's, Sophia turned to Brent and scowled. Gina quickly stepped forward. "Sophia, Brent has only known about this for about a month. Don't be mad at him. We'll explain everything to you. Brent had nothing to do with what happened after the trial. We'd like you to come to the farm, our house. You can either come today or tomorrow, but we hope you'll spend your last week here with us. That is, if you'd like."

"Well, I think we might be able to check out right now and rent a car, if the three of you are willing to wait for us." Brent nodded eagerly.

"We have a car large enough for all of us, Babe! Oh, this is going to be *so* fun! I can teach you to ride horses!"

"Mother, you know I don't care to."

"You can ride my horse, Sophie," chirped Ruth. "She's like me: old and slow. Just right for Ruth."

"And, just like Ruth! Lots of spunk!" snapped Gina. Walking arm in arm with Sophia in the middle, the three women walked happily toward the hotel. Exchanging smiles and handshakes, the two men cheerfully followed.

Chapter 29

The drive to the farm took almost an hour and a half. After some casual conversation, Brent asked Gina to explain the van crash and escape to Europe with Marty. Gina was sitting in the back seat of the car between Sophia and Brent. "Are you sure you want to hear it now? Carlo and Maria will be making lunch and we can talk about that after dinner. I want to show the farm off to you first. Besides, the countryside here is so gorgeous; you should enjoy it!"

"Who are Carlo and Maria, Mom?"

"They're our business partners, and friends. Carlo is Italian. It's a great help to have someone here that speaks the language. Marty and I are learning slowly."

The countryside was indeed stunning. Brent had his arm around Gina for the entire ride to the farm, but tickled

Sophia's face with his outstretched fingertip. There were
only a sparse few houses and barns sprinkled throughout the
landscape. The sky was so blue, it looked violet to Sophia.
The cypress and poplars were tall, ancient; the hills were
deep emerald green. Gina and Marty waved to the occasional
pedestrian along the road. One man wore a tattered fedora
and walked alongside a mule-drawn cart. A little girl on
a bare-backed pony raced along a fenced pasture calling,
"Signora Giovanna! Ciao!" Sophia flashed a stretched smile
at Brent. "How darling! Isn't she beautiful!" Turning to
Gina, she asked, "Whose child is that? A neighbor's? Who is
Giovanna?"

Ruth, Gina and Marty chuckled lightly. "Giovanna,
that's me, Darling!" sighed Gina. "My new alias! Do you
know the translation?"

"No, *Signora*. You *know* I don't," Sophia simpered
sarcastically.

"The locals know me as Giovanna, JoAnna. Just
thought it'd be fun, you know, to have a new name? We
haven't come up with anything for Marty yet. Our workers
just call him Boss! The girl is Maria and Carlo's daughter,
Pitrina. She's my pal. At six, she's already an expert horse-
woman and speaks both English *and* Italian pretty well."

"Here's our little ranch!" announced Marty.

"Little?" piped Sophia. She craned her neck to see
what looked like a small stucco villa cradled in the hillside.
The road to the farm was about a quarter of a mile long and
lined with poplars. Brent and Sophia saw rows of orange trees
that appeared to have no end. The surrounding hills were lush
with a variety of hardwood trees and wildflowers. Marty drove
under and through an old carriage porch, to the back of the

house. A large, stucco rambler sat about fifty yards beyond the main house. The roof was tiled in the same way the villa was, but scaled for its size. Definitely a newer structure, it was freshly painted and twinkling in the sunlight. Sophia could see that it was strategically built amongst several trees to give it just the right amount of shade from the hot summer sun. It boasted a large, screened front porch.

Everywhere Sophia looked was rife with flower gardens, "This is paradise, Mother!"

"That, it is." Gina gushed.

"Signora! Signora!" Breathlessly, a miniature goddess appeared on a flying pony. Kicking one leg upward, she leapt off the animal's back like a gymnast. Delighted, all applauded as Pitrina rushed to Gina's open arms. Gina caught the girl's embrace and lifted her to her bosom. "Cia, you did not kiss me goodnight last night!" Pitrina sputtered breathlessly.

"Well, Uncle and I went into a city to pick up our friends, vidi?"

Sophia was transfixed by the opulent jewel Gina held in her arms. Pitrina was wiry and fair, with rosy cheeks and a sunburnt nose. Her long, thick auburn hair was wavy and cascaded almost to her waist.

Eyeing Sophia and Brent shyly, Pitrina asked, "Who are these peoples, Signora?"

"People. Remember?"

"Si, si!" the child agreed eagerly. "Pee-pull."

"This is my daughter Sophia, and her husband, Brent." The child looked at Gina in exaggerated surprise and shaped her mouth into a gigantic O! She slid from Gina's arms, smearing soil down the front of Gina's pristine dress.

"Oh, no! Momma's gonna kill me!"

"Not if I have anything to say about it, Bella," smiled Gina. "It's just a cotton dress and it'll wash right out. Now, go say hello. Pronto!"

The child hesitated. Sensing Pitrina's cautiousness, Sophia lowered herself to the ground on bent knee. The child raced to Sophia. "I'm Sophie. How are you?"

"Very well, Signorina Sophie! I'm Trina."

"I'm very pleased to meet you, Trina. You know, we're kinda cousins!"

The girl repeated the same surprised expression, and looked over her shoulder at Gina. "Oh, Signora Giovanna! You didn't tell me you were bringing me a *cousin!*" Everyone laughed at the innocence of the moment. Brent bent to extend his hand to the child, and was tickled when Trina kissed his face instead.

Within a few seconds, a man and woman appeared from the back of the villa. "Trina! Come in and wash that pony off! Andiamo!" The couple was suntanned and smiling. They extended their welcoming hands to Sophia and Brent. "Benvenuto! We've been waiting for you!" sparkled the woman. She had short-shorn, dark reddish-brown hair and twinkling green eyes. It was immediately clear to Brent and Sophia that the slim woman was Trina's mother. An American, she spoke with a New York accent. A dark handsome man followed Maria. "Hello! I'm-uh Carlo." Carlo bore a striking resemblance to Carmine.

Sophia surmised that Pitrina may have been a "last chance" baby, as Maria seemed close to middle age, and Carlo, slightly older. After the travelers relaxed for a while, the rest of the day was spent touring the grounds and house.

Pitrina held Gina's hand while mother and daughter walked. A huge stone mantle displayed a number of photographs of Gina and Marty. Some were obviously wedding photos, Gina resplendent in a 1950's-style knee-length dress.

Sophia squealed. "Mother! You're married?" She lifted Gina from the floor, and they giggled like schoolgirls.

Sophia continued to inspect the photos on the mantle. The wedding dress seemed familiar to her. The fabric looked like a soft taffeta, with a white Chantilly lace form-fitting overlay. The taffeta lining was shaped in a strapless sweetheart neckline beneath the lace, which fell snugly scooped around Gina's shoulders. The princess waist showed off Gina's still-small shape, and the skirt was gathered. Carlo and Maria, in formal garb, stood on either side of the beaming couple. Pitrina stood in front of Gina in a pale pink satin dress, a crown of pink baby roses and baby's breath gracing her gorgeous hair. She held her head high and proud, playing the camera like a model. Gina's cascading pink rose bouquet grazed the child's shoulder to one side.

"Mother! This dress is in the closet at home! How can this be?"

"I *hated* leaving those things behind, especially that dress. Marty bought it for me in New York, oh, over twenty-five years ago. We had a dressmaker in Rome duplicate it for the wedding."

"Well, the next time I visit, I'll bring it back with me. Maybe one day Trina will wear it when she marries."

"Oh yes, please! May I?" asked the child, jumping up and down.

"Of course, my darling," cooed Gina.

"So many pictures, Mom! Florence, Rome, Venice."

"Marty and I had a *lot* of catching up to do, Babe. Like you and I do!"

"Oh, almost forgot to ask! When did you marry?"

Gina stood silent, savoring the moment. Slowly she spoke, "On my birthday, Love."

Laughing, tears once again teased their eyes.

"Well, what a coincidence."

"Sweetness, in life there are rarely coincidences!"

Maria appeared and coaxed Trina into the kitchen. Gina and Sophia spent the afternoon walking and talking through the meadows and orchards, holding hands.

In a moment of revelation, Sophia gushed, "Oh, Mother! I forgot!" Her young daughter extended her right hand to Gina, displaying the engagement ring Marty had given her twenty-five years before. Gina wept softly at the sight. "Please don't cry, Mom," said Sophia as she removed the ring and slipped it on Gina's finger. "It was in the hamper, of course!"

The two hugged rhythmically rocking from side to side in the warmth of the sun. In a hushed whisper, Gina replied, "Thank you so much daughter."

The happy family shared a reunion feast on a stone veranda early that evening. Gina drank in every word that Sophia spoke, most especially when her daughter relayed the details of her meeting and visiting with her cousin Michael. Brent magically produced a manila envelope filled with photos of Michael, Sophia and Jenna. Her eyes misty, Gina turned her gaze toward Marty.

Feeling Gina's eyes studying the side of his face, Marty quietly said, "After Sophia has spent more time with Michael, maybe we can let him in on our secret and he and his wife can come here. We'll let Sophie decide, but let's give it at least another year. Okay?" Gina leaned her face close to Marty's and they nuzzled affectionately.

A little embarrassed at seeing her mother flirt with her father in everyone's presence, Sophia purposely changed courses. "Mother, I notice that you haven't smoked a cigarette yet since we arrived. Is that just for my benefit or have you quit?"

"Quit for good, I think! I need my breath more with all the work and animals, and I don't remember feeling so good for *such* a long time," Gina gushed while glancing at Marty. "Sophie, *you* of all people know that almost everywhere you go in Europe, people are openly smoking. I miss the cigarette with the morning coffee, though," sighed Gina.

Sophie then bulleted, "Now, Mother! It's *your* turn. You said you'd tell us what happened on that ride to you-know-where."

Maria quickly intervened. "Trina, andiamo. Bath time! Pronto, pronto!"

"No, no!" protested the child, tightening her grip on Gina's hand.

Gina wrapped her arms around Trina and gently said, "You listen to Momma. I promise to kiss you goodnight later. Maybe Sophie will walk there with me, if you'd like."

"Yes, please Giovanna." Hanging monkey-like onto Gina, the child leaned back to kiss Marty's face, too. To Sophie's surprise, the child jumped from Gina's lap and ran around the table to do the same to her. "Buona sera, Cousin."

"And what about Papa!" Carlo exclaimed. The child leapt into Carlo's arms. He kissed both of the child's cheeks and passed Pitrina to Maria. Looking over her shoulder, Trina was led across the yard, all the while smiling and waving.

"Okay, Mother. Tell us about your infamous ride to prison. *Shoot!*"

Gina propped her elbows on the table, resting her face on closed fists. Deeply inhaling, she spoke. She gulped hard as everyone silently waited. "I had no idea it would happen the way it did. I believed that if I visualized my freedom, I would keep it. It was a nightmare being torn from the two of you. I'm sure you remember the pandemonium after the verdict was read better than I do. I felt like I was sleep-walking. I was so sure that the jury forewoman would recite an innocent verdict and I would go home. When the judge said the *prisoner* would be removed to a facility to await sentencing, it seemed so foreign."

After Rita Napapolus was escorted out of the courtroom, she was led to a holding area to await transport to a women's correctional facility. John Sciandra advised her she would be taken out of state to allow things to die down a bit. John walked with Rita and talked about an appeal, but this fell on deaf ears. Rita stared at the door until Hannah, Brent, Carolyn and Franco appeared and jumped to her feet to embrace her shaken daughter.

"Honey, everything will be all right. This is just a temporary setback. John and I are already talking about my appeal. Right, John?" Rita flashed Brent a helpless look while he reached his arm around Hannah's waist. The three nestled together, knowing it wouldn't be long before Rita was put into a police van. "It'll take a few days to learn the schedule and see what privileges I'll have, but I'll call as soon as I can,

Babies." They sat in the room making small talk about the weather. Another twenty minutes passed and an officer arrived to say, "We're ready, Ms. Napapolus." Rita drew air through her gritted teeth. The officer gently advised, "We have to cuff you, Ma'am."

Hannah was full-blown furious. "This is ree-diculous. You don't have to cuff my mother! She weighs all of a hundred pounds now!"

"This is very standard procedure, Miss. I have no choice."

"Hannah, Honey, it's okay. Stop yelling!" Ironically, Rita and Hannah laughed and pulled each other close. "You okay now?"

"Yes, Mother," Hannah replied contentiously. She rolled her eyes in an ironic change of mood.

"Okay then, young man. May I put my sneakers on first?" The guard smiled and nodded his approval. "Hannah, did you bring my Converse like I asked?"

Brent produced a small canvas carry bag and handed it off to Hannah. "We had to take the laces out, Ma. They don't allow laced shoes." She produced the navy blue shoes and white cotton socks and handed them to Rita, who sat down to swap her low heels for the comfy tennies. Rita rose, and trying to make light of the matter said, "Okay, *now* I'm ready!" In an all-too-familiar ritual, she put her arms out, wrists close together. The young guard gently cuffed them.

"Is that comfortable for you, Ma'am?"

"I suppose. I'm pretty used to these *bracelets* now."

Officers walked in front and back of Rita, Hannah, and Brent. John, Carolyn and Franco followed the solemn parade as it maneuvered through a maze of sterile, fluorescently lit halls until they reached a pleasant-looking glass foyer, sprinkled with tropical foliage. There were two sets of doors, the first of which were electronic sliding doors, but they didn't open when the party approached. They were operated by electronic key access only. Rita asked the guard if she could speak with Brent privately for a moment and the two were allowed some space in a corner. The conversation was brief, all of two to three minutes. The officer who had cuffed Rita turned to Brent and Hannah. "Ma'am, I'm afraid you'll have to say your goodbyes here."

Both Rita and Hannah looked pale, their combined energy and fight drained by the arduous ordeal of the past months. "Not goodbye, see you soon, Mother," Hannah brooded. "Take care of yourself and call as soon as you can, understand?"

"Yes, *Mother*!" retorted Rita, who beamed with maternal pride. Crying, they kissed.

The guards navigated Rita through the glass doors leading to the outer foyer. Two officers went outside, one walking to the right and out of everyone's sight. Rita looked over her shoulder at Hannah and Brent until the doors parted again, and Rita and the other officers stepped outside. She looked to her right and realized that she was standing on a sidewalk next to the rear of the courthouse-parking garage.

The next few minutes were spent savoring the biting crispness of the day, and rays of the afternoon's sunlight slipping over the tall buildings. Rita knew that it would be some time before she would stand outdoors *anywhere* for a while. She looked around toward the surrounding structures, hoping that Marty had planted someone nearby to make good on his promise. She stood very still and waited. *Please,*

Marty. Did you send someone for me today? A helicopter's chatter graduated in volume and Rita looked skyward, praying for her turn with an Angel of Death. Her heart sank when she clearly recognized the logo of a local TV station on the aircraft's belly. As quickly as the chopper appeared, it was gone.

Before long, the absent guard reappeared, driving up to collect his cargo. Jumping out of a white Ford E350, he jogged to the back of the van and opened up the doors. It was a plain van, no logos or designations painted anywhere on it. Rita turned to see a weeping Hannah being held close to Brent's side. She smiled broadly, craning her neck slightly in a vain attempt to look composed. Keys were passed, and a guard climbed into the cab of the van, while the other, the same young man who had cuffed Rita, guided her to the back of the vehicle. Rita languished in a long look into Hannah's face, the two forcing smiles. She waved a double-handed, handcuffed wave to her sobbing daughter. The Converse were loose and flip-flopped as Rita walked to the van's rear. The young guard leaned forward to chivalrously offer his hand to help Rita keep her balance while stepping up.

Blowing another kiss to Hannah, Rita looked straight ahead into the van and stepped up. There were plastic benches on both sides of the interior. A twelve-by-twelve window between the cab and the back had a metal grill over it. The inside was devoid of anything, including seat belts and windows. There was an acrylic-covered light on the ceiling only. Rita stepped in and sat, followed by the young guard, who also sat and faced her. The guard advised Rita that if she felt cold, she should ask for the heat to be turned on; she could let him know by speaking through the small window.

He nervously produced the key to the handcuffs and unlocked them, removing and shoving them into his jacket pocket. "I had to cuff you until you were in the van, Ms. Napapolus, but it's not necessary to ride all that way in cuffs. It's too long of a drive."

John had once mentioned to Rita not every prisoner is cuffed while in transport. There was nothing in the van that could harm her. "Bless your heart, young man. I don't think you and I have met, have we?"

"No, Ma'am. But I feel like I know you. My wife told me to be nice when I was assigned to transport you. She's a big fan of yours, and followed the trial every day. I'm sure she's probably gonna be pretty pissed when I get home tomorrow after bringing you to prison." He shook his head and his voice drifted off as he sighed at the thought. "She says she knows you're innocent."

"Well, please tell your wife thank you for me."

"Yes Ma'am," the young guard said respectfully, and he stepped out of the van. "We'll be leaving now, Ma'am." He politely tugged the visor of his official guard hat.

"Yes -- what's your name, anyway?"

"Phillip, Ma'am."

"Okay, Phillip, let's get going then," Rita said solemnly.

"Yes, Ma'am," and with that, Phillip closed and locked the back doors of the van. He took his place in the cab and fastened his seat belt.

Rita tried to relax into the corner of the cab wall. The van rumbled away from the courthouse, and she thought about Hannah, turning to leave, the trial finally over. Optimism and hope had slipped away, now that Rita knew she was on her way to jail. The light inside the van was purposely dim. After a few minutes, she looked up at the small window and could see that it was dusk. The silhouette of Phillip's hat contrasted against the dancing succession of lights on the highway. Knowing that the correctional facility's admittance process could take a couple of hours, Rita tried to nap. The van rocketed southward on I-5 toward Oregon. The rhythmic sounds of traffic and the vehicle's wheels became white noise that lulled Rita to sleep.

After what seemed to be just a few minutes, the quaking of the van's abrupt stop woke Rita. She was groggy and thought perhaps they were at a rest area. She heard one of the cab doors open and shut. A moment later, she heard the second open and close. An eerie silence prevailed for what seemed to be an eternity, sobering Rita. She sat very still in the dull light of the van, until she heard distant, muffled voices. She stooped to look through the window to the cab, but the guards were gone. There were no lights or buildings that she could see. They were definitely not on the highway nor at their destination. Far in the distance, she saw a few strewn roadway lights, and figured the front of the van was pitched away from the road. "Phillip? Phillip?" she called through the window. No response. Puzzled and frightened, she eased back onto the bench. Suddenly, she felt silly and stupid. *They're just peeing, probably. That's all. Oh my God! That's what they're doing.* She could use to do the same. But when a few more minutes passed and the guards didn't return, Rita became anxious again.

Outside, she heard the crunchy sound of wheels on gravel, and a car's engine running. After the engine idled, the sound of footsteps followed, but no conversation. Both doors

of the van violently swung open and Rita felt like a small
animal in a trap. There was a car only about ten feet behind
the van, and she was blinded by its high beams. She knew
that there had to be a person at each van door and dared not
move or breathe. *This is it! This is IT! Oh, Marty! He sent
someone after all!*

As though she was being propelled through time
and space, effigies of Rita's life whipped through her mind,
her daughter and brother in the forefront. *Okay, take a deep
breath.* She closed her eyes, and the fear melted away. This is
what she had begged for, this is the way she wanted it. As she
had always sought comfort from reading it, Rita began to recite
the Twenty-Third Psalm in her head. *The Lord is my shepherd,
I shall not want.* Wind was whipping her hair around her face
and she could hear what she thought were waves breaking
on a beach. She felt a rainy mist as she sat rigid against the
back wall of the van. *He maketh me to lie down in green
pastures, He leadeth me beside the still waters.* She hoped that
it wouldn't hurt, but knew that it wouldn't last long anyway.
A car door opened and closed, much the same way the doors
of the van had. Shivering from the cold, she pulled her coat
tight around her and waited. Oddly, it sounded as though two
sets of footsteps were moving closer, the sound of the gravel
under their shoes taunting Rita. *There's two of them. They're
moving in close to get clean shots, it'll be fast!* But when the
footsteps stopped and no shots were fired, Rita opened her
eyes sheepishly. Now the vehicle's lights were positioned
to a lower intensity, and she could see what looked like two
male silhouettes in topcoats. For the last time in her life as
Rita Napapolus, she scrunched her eyes closed tight again.
She thought about her grandfather's absence of fear moments

before she left his bedside, and she calmly smiled. *Yea, though I walk through the valley of the shadow of death, I shall fear no evil, for thou art with me: thy rod and thy staff they comfort me.* Impatient, she shouted, "Thank Marty for me, huh?"

But there was no sound of gunfire; instead, the sound of a gentle voice fondly offered, "You can thank me yourself."

She blinked in absolute disbelief, thinking that she was dead already, and tickled that she didn't feel a thing. And the angel's voice, it sounded like Marty himself! One of the silhouettes moved forward into the subdued light of the van. "Well, I'm here to pick you up for our date. You said see you after the trial. So, here I am!"

"Oh, Marty!" the newly reborn Gina Bianco bellowed as she lunged into Marty's arms. He looked almost exactly the same to Gina, his hair now streaked with white, but his warm smile was the same, his eyes, twinkling and inviting. Marty moved in to kiss her, but all at once Gina felt self-conscious. "I haven't brushed my teeth in hours, Marty! My hair! I'm a mess!"

"Will you shut up, please?" And they kissed hard and long, breaking the momentum again with breathless laughter. "Okay now, we gotta hurry. Gina, here." Marty extended an arm and Carmine appeared from the mist.

"Carmine! Give me a hug!"

"Hi, Gina. Nice to see ya."

Marty piped, "Gee, take off your coat and throw it into the back of the van. *Hurry.*" He motioned to Carmine, who produced a large shopping bag. He drew out a small pea coat and held it open. Gina whipped off her own wool coat and tossed it. Carmine pulled out a shoebox while Marty buttoned up the coat for Gina. Carmine extended his arms to reveal a new pair of Converse, sized six. Gina looked at Marty with a cocked eyebrow and said slyly, "You're unbelievable, Pal. You still know my sizes!"

"Well, you haven't changed an eyelash, Baby. Give me the old ones; put these on." Gina sat on the edge of the van's floor and put on the new shoes.

While they bustled about, Gina asked: "How is Ruth?"

"She can't wait to see you. We'll talk about Ruth later, we have to keep moving. We don't have a lot of time. Ready?" Carmine slammed the back doors of the van closed.

"Ready!"

Marty took the old shoes and jogged away into the darkness. Gina realized that they were all standing at a small, rural roadside turn-off. The crashing waves were far below, at the bottom of a rocky cliff. Along the side of the road about twenty yards ahead, the two guards where rummaging in the trunk of another car. They were in plain clothes now: jeans, bomber jackets and ball caps. Gina saw Phillip's tall, lean frame contrasting against the trunk's low light, while he pulled out a box. He turned and tugged on the visor of his cap the same way he had earlier that day and nodded his head, smiling. Gina blew Phillip a kiss, and turned back toward Marty in time to see him nonchalantly toss one of the old shoes onto the rockery below. He turned to his left and pulled his arm back like a quarterback and pitched the other shoe hard. "Where are we, Mart?"

"We're on the Oregon coast, a couple hours or so north of the prison. Come on, let's go. We have two hours to disappear." He reached for her upper arm and directed her back to an older Nissan Pathfinder, followed by Carmine.

Carmine drove and Gina and Marty sat close together

in the back seat. Masterfully doing a 180, Carmine drove what Gina guessed to be a rental car north again and up a mountainous incline. "Not too-too fast Carmine. There might be Staties around this stretch, and we don't need to get caught in a borrowed car," Marty warned.

Carmine was driving north, but it was of no consequence where they were going. This was a dream for Gina, like a spectacular movie escape. The three began hooting, hollering and laughing. Consumed by the complete surprise and glee of this twist of fate, Gina abruptly realized that her daughter would be scrutinized due to her mother's flight. "Marty. Tomorrow, the cops will be all over my baby." She studied the side of Marty's face, which had instantly changed from elated to serious.

"They may talk to her a little bit, Gina. But it won't last. You have to trust me on this one. It'll hurt everyone for a while. You'll have to wait to let her know where you are." Totally baffled by this cryptic response, Gina asked: "You mean, I'll be able to tell her where I am? The cops and the feds won't be all over her?"

"You're not listening. They may…"

"I know, I know. They may talk to her a little, but it won't last. What's that suppose to mean?"

"Carmine, you know where to pull over, right?"

"Yeah, Marty."

"You gonna throw me over a cliff, Marty?" Gina asked mockingly.

"Wait, Gina. Carmine, would you pull the car around to face in that direction?"

"Sure, Marty."

"What is going on?" pressed Gina.

"Genius. Genius is going on, Gina. Now *watch*."

Carmine reached the crest of a high hill. He carefully turned the car around to face the direction where they had just been. He then turned off the lights and engine.

Marty turned to Gina. "Slide up and look out the front window. What do you see along the road?"

Baffled again, Gina did as Marty asked. There were a few lights along the rural road, just enough light to make out the curve of the coastline, sculpted by millions of years of wear. "Uh, I don't know. We're at a higher elevation. I see a few lights, the road a little, but that's all."

Marty smiled. "That's *exactly* what you're supposed to be seeing. See the part of the road that's farthest west? Where it sticks out into the bay?"

"Yeah, I can see it."

"That's where we *were*. That's where the van is now."

"Well, that's all very nice. But how does this solve the dilemma for my daughter? If I disappear, they'll question her first."

"Okay. The third time's the charm here. Keep your eyes on that cliff while I'm talkin'." Gina humorously pouted and turned her eyes back to the coastline below. "They *will* talk to her, Gina. But it will die down within a couple of months, and be dead within a year. Please trust me. This one's gonna take a little time to work out. You can make contact after about a year. Now, no more questions. Look down there. And Jesus, Gina! Isn't it about time you said *our* daughter?" Marty shushed Gina's laughter and pointed to the cliff below. They sat silently in the car, intently gazing down into the darkness. Within a couple of minutes, the cliff's side birthed a tumultuous fireball that exploded a second time as it fell to the rocks below. Gina screamed, having been totally caught off guard. Marty put his arms around her to calm her.

"Holy fucking shit! What the fuck was that?"

"I just threw you over the cliff. That's what the lady asked for. Isn't it? You wanted to spare the kid, so now you're conveniently dead. The upside to all of this is that it *will* be possible to see her again someday, and often. We just have to lay low for a while. Thanks, Carmine. Let's get outta here."

Gina felt totally alive. Her second birth, unlike her first, was one that she would remember throughout her lifetime. The trio drove through the darkness for less than an hour, stopping for just a few minutes in a wooded area to stretch their legs and pee. The pre-dawn air was cool and refreshing. They drove on, while Gina dozed lightly on Marty's shoulder. No one spoke.

Intense orange light began to appear on the horizon when Carmine pulled the Pathfinder up to the edge of a huge field. He pulled off the road about thirty feet onto a gravel drive. Up ahead was a large wooden swing gate, behind which stood a tall, muscular man. The denim-clad man approached and quietly said, "Good morning, Miss, Sirs." It was difficult to discern if he was young or middle-aged in the low light. He politely opened the door of the vehicle, extending his hand for Gina. Carmine walked ahead to the gate and held it open for Gina and Marty. Behind her, Gina heard the Nissan backing away on the gravel, the tall man now behind the wheel. She and Marty followed Carmine through the gate and into the open field. Straight ahead sat a single small jet, waiting for them. The plane suddenly took on a life of its own: interior lights came on, the engines began firing up, and stairs descended from the fuselage. Now the three were jolted with a surge of electric energy. Even though the craft was large enough to accommodate at least fifteen passengers, the only additional persons onboard were the pilot, copilot and a male attendant who greeted them as they stepped through the door. The attendant was average in size and looks, and wore a henley top and jeans. "Good morning," he smiled warmly. There were changes of clothing on the plane for all of them. Gina zeroed in on some comfy workout pants and a loose T-shirt. After takeoff, she carried the clothes to the plane's teeny bathroom. The attendant was brewing coffee and fixing bacon and eggs nearby. When she came out, breakfast was being served and she ate like a horse! She had been awake almost entirely twenty-four hours, having had only a short nap during the ride to the Oregon coast.

"Okay, Honey. Please tell me about the crash." Gina was already comfortable being her mischievous self again around Marty.

"Oh, of course now that *you're* ready." Drained, but deliriously happy, they laughed quietly as not to wake Carmine, who had eaten and fallen asleep on some seats closer to the cockpit. "Well, it was pretty simple. That cliff peak was probably the highest one along that stretch of the road, and just a short detour from the highway." Rather coyly, Marty continued, "A van, for instance, would break apart falling off that cliff, especially if it was rigged to explode. It would break up into a million pieces. Burnt clothing could become airborne, so some might be found. But the current there: the current is so strong that any vestige of a body part would get washed away. If it didn't, who would know? The tide was just about to come in when the van went down. No one could ever dive there. They'll repel down and pick up a few things.

They'll look, but won't count on finding bodies there. They'll look again when the tide goes out, but won't find anything else. The guards' clothes were in the front cab, but again: at best, only a crumb of burnt debris *might* be found."

"But, Marty. Won't there be trace explosives on what they find? They'll know it was staged."

"No, Baby, plastic explosives leave little or no debris. Besides, all the explosives were attached under the chassis, and not near any clothing. Are you listening? It'll be too difficult to find much of anything at the base of that cliff. By the time Forensics gets there, the tide will have taken the debris away. The two drivers are plants that we bribed months ago to be assigned to run you to your new digs. They rigged the van and took off in a car that Carmine used to tail them. I followed Carmine to that spot in the borrowed Pathfinder."

"Wow!"

"Wow, nothing. Now try to get some rest." Marty put the armrest down and pulled Gina down on top of him. He had the attendant bring a blanket earlier, and he pulled it up and over Gina. For the first time in twenty years, the two snuggled and fell asleep.

Marty and Carmine thought of everything. The plane to freedom flew to Montreal, below the radar and without registering a flight plan. It landed in a remote farm field, very much like the one it departed from, but this time on the other side of the continent. When they woke up, Marty gave Gina new IDs and a passport. Each contained a photo of her, computer-enhanced to make it appear that she had short, curly hair. Staying on top of new technologies, the passports included microchips that recorded past foreign travel. Gina's new passport's chip recorded many destinations, even though she had not personally been to any of them!

Whimsically, Marty produced a wig from a duffle bag. Accepting the wig in her hands Gina asked, "What is this? I can't pull this off, Mart!" Standing at the bathroom mirror, she fashioned her hair into a short pony tail. She pulled on the wig. "Oh, my Jesus! This is definitely *not* my style. Now I know what it feels like to be the oldest Bond Girl on the planet!" Laughing loudly, all three secretly felt as though they were standing in a St. Moritz suite, decades earlier.

Marty and Carmine did some mundane changes with phony facial hair. A goatee for Carmine, a mustache for Marty. Marty slicked his hair flat against his head. Holding a passport up in front of Gina, he looked like the image in the book. "See? Carmine and I practiced. Just like Halloween!" He donned a felt fedora.

Within two hours, they boarded another chartered plane bound for Italy. The trio stayed on the southern mainland for two days to rest, and then took northbound trains to where Ruth was waiting. The couple was happy in the coming months, but Gina missed her beautiful daughter and longed for the time when she would see her again. Back in New York, Marty's former soldiers did his bidding long enough to keep an eye on Brent and Sophia. They learned of their marriage plans and reported this to Marty. Gina recorded a message on a CD that was sent to Tony in New York. In turn, Tony called Brent's cell phone number several times, but played the CD only after Brent personally answered. This way, the call could not be recorded and saved to the network's voicemail.

Gina knew that Brent would immediately recognize her voice. The recorded message was short and sweet: "Brent

Darling, listen carefully. Don't try to interrupt, as this is a recording. You *know* who this is. I did *not* die in that crash. I can't tell you where I am right now, and you *cannot* tell my daughter that you heard from me." The tone of Gina's voice then lightened. "Good show, Pal. You're gonna marry my kid; I couldn't be happier. I'm praying that you'll visit Venice on your honeymoon. While you're there, the desk clerk will tell you about a wonderful sight that you shouldn't miss, and will ring you up the next morning. It's important that you get your bride out of bed early. I will be where the clerk tells you to go. Don't worry; we'll know where and when you're in Venice. I'm counting on you to be there! I love you, Son! Take care of my baby. Until Venice, then. Bye, Sugar!"

Elated to hear that Gina was alive, Brent was also mystified. Who did Gina mean by "we'll?" He smiled and pressed the disconnect button on his phone. On the other end of the line, Tony waited to be sure that Brent broke the connection first. On the Lower East Side that evening, Tony threw the CD into a burning barrel where homeless folks were warming themselves. He tossed them some loose bills and walked away smiling, knowing that Gina and Marty were a half a world away, finally together.